REPARATIONS

L. A. BURCH

BOOK THREE OF THE MASTERMINDS SERIES

L. A. BURCH

Reparations: 1) Something that is done or given as a way of correcting a mistake that you have made or a bad situation that you have caused.

2) The act of making amends, offering expiation, or giving satisfaction for a wrong or injury.

3) Money that a country or group that loses a war pays because of the damage, injury, or deaths it has caused.

L. A. BURCH

Amazon Digital Services-KDP

Cover Design: Michelle D. Josey

ISBN: 9798990247239

Dedication

I want to dedicate this book to all the Brothers and Sisters who are incarcerated but keep pushing. The cliché, "Do the time, don't let the time do you!" is a real thing. I just want to acknowledge the people who, when they encounter an obstacle, they go over it, through it, around it, or under it. They never let anything stop their grind!

L. A. BURCH

Reparations

BOOK THREE OF THE MASTERMINDS SERIES

L. A. BURCH

Prologue

At only five years old, Daniel found himself terrified, running for his life. He had just returned from his Uncle Kenneth's funeral where everyone had been sad and crying and Daniel didn't understand it one bit. Since he could remember, everyone said you went to this amazing place in the sky when you died. So, it confused him to see everyone so sad.

They had reconvened for the reception at his last remaining uncle's house. His Uncle Glen had a huge house right in the middle of Philadelphia, with grass and swings and even a swimming pool. He had asked several times if he could go swimming and his crying mother told him no.

His siblings, Delmas, Reggie, and Kashonda, were eating and watching TV in the family room. Daniel said, "Delmas, let's go out back and swim for a while."

Delmas shook his head and said, "You can't even swim. Just find somewhere to sit down and be quiet."

Daniel frowned. "All you had to say was you're scared. Don't worry about it, I'll go by myself."

He ran off to the room his uncle kept for him and Delmas and grabbed a pair of swimming trunks. After hiding them under his suit jacket, he made a mad dash through his family and friends. When he finally made it outside, he ran over and hunkered down behind the tool shed. He watched the path behind him to make sure no one had followed. About ten minutes passed before he felt safe enough to change into the swim wear.

Daniel knew he was a genius. He could figure out complex equations faster than his teachers could write them down. So, if mean ass Delmas could swim, it shouldn't take him more than a few seconds to figure it out.

The young Daniel peeped around the tool shed and quickly pulled his head back. Speak of the devil, his older brother was standing next to the pool, fully dressed, looking around, no doubt trying to catch sight of him.

It was the end of May, so the sun was shining bright with not a cloud in the sky. No breeze to cool the skin or set the trees in motion that separated the yard from the street. Delmas was walking around the pool area squinting, trying to see better with the sun shining in his eyes. Daniel giggled as a new plan formulated in his mind.

The timing had to be perfect, but a full-clothed dunking sounded about right for his bossy brother. As soon as Delmas turned his back, Daniel launched himself from behind the shed at full speed. Just before contact, Delmas spun and tried to avoid his outstretched hands. Everything moved in slow motion after that.

The church shoes were not made to have any grip on the slick tile and, with arms and legs akimbo, Delmas went airborne and came down in the water. But not before his head hit the edge with a sickening crack. Daniel tried to grab him, but he sank under the water at an alarming rate. Blood was bubbling to the surface when Reggie ran out of the house, shedding clothes as he ran. The rest of the family was hot on his heels to attempt the rescue.

Daniel was in a state of shock. There must have been ten people diving in to save his brother while all he could do was stand there and watch. When he looked up, he felt a terror that kicked his fight or flight instinct into high gear. His Uncle Glen was looking at him from the other side of the pool with tears rolling down his face and a baseball bat in his hands. All Daniel could think was escape.

He took off running in the only direction available to him, towards the street. He heard the screams and shouts for him to stop, but the terror had him in its grip. Right before he reached the trees, he looked back and saw his uncle with an ugly grimace covering his face. He was in full stretch mode in his effort to reach his prey.

All Daniel could do was scream and scream as he felt cold fingers wrap around his arm, and steel himself for the feel of the bat crashing into his fragile, young body.

Chapter 1

Daniel jerked up from the bed with sweat drenching his body and darkness surrounding him. He tried to get his breathing under control as he banished the terror of his 5-year-old self, and regain the poise and discipline of the 38-year-old man.

Without looking, the 6-foot 1-inch, 200-pound, muscular man knew he was alone in the California King bed. He never had the nightmare when his woman was by his side. His shaved head and light brown skin glistened as he swung his legs around and settled his feet on the carpeted floor. From experience, he knew he wouldn't get anymore sleep after the nightmare, so he decided to get an early start on another long day.

He turned his head and looked at the other side of the bed. His beautiful fiancé, Alisha Harden, had been up for a while. He only knew this because her side of the bed was made up to perfection. She always spent 30 minutes to an hour getting ready in the morning and the bed was the last thing she did.

One look at the phone on the nightstand had him jumping up, realizing it was not as early as he thought. The winter nights were long and cold and what he thought was darkness was the heavy curtains pulled across a view of an overcast day.

He rushed over to the luxurious bathroom and gave the voice command for the shower to turn on. He relieved himself and took care of his oral hygiene as he let the steam billow up in the shower area. He removed his boxers and entered the enclosure, letting the steam wash over him for a minute before he stepped under the hot spray.

Daniel had grown up around wealth and had gotten accustomed to a certain level of class. His Charlotte, N.C. compound took luxury to a whole new level. He had bought the house for $150 million about four years ago. After a couple years and a bunch more millions poured into it in renovations and upgrades, the house was now worth north of $400 million.

Daniel had actually bought the properties bordering this one and he used all the extra land to add the security needed to keep the main property protected. With a huge 18-foot wall, and sensors to detect everything a human, animal, or machine could do, this gigantic mansion is probably the most protected place on Earth. With the treasures he had, and the enemies stacked up against him, Daniel needed every bit of the security to keep his mind at ease.

He finished up in the bathroom and made his way over to his 1,500 square foot closet and clothed himself in some workout gear. Leaving the bedroom, he decided to look in on his adopted daughter before heading down to the training complex. All was quiet as he approached her door, but he knew she had been up for hours. Reading or studying or taking one of her advanced on-line classes, enticed his daughter to beat the sun up on most days. He glanced around the doorframe and today was no exception.

Gabriella Burke had lived a very hard and tortured life. When she was two years old, a mad man by the name of Patrick Young, AKA Black Ops, had broken into her home and murdered her parents. Her sister Emily had saved her younger sibling, but only to be adopted by Gregory and Nicolas Black, a married couple who abused and raped both girls.

Daniel, in turn, murdered everyone responsible for his angel's pain, including her sister Emily. Daniel had legally adopted the astonishing girl six months ago and had vowed she would live a charmed existence for the rest of her days.

The now 11-year-old Gabby did everything in her power to please him, like getting up at the crack of dawn to show she was serious about her studies.

He watched her, bent. over one of her laptops, trying to do a quadratic equation without the help of a calculator or pen and paper. His stomach did a little flip as he felt the love surge for his magnificent little girl. She was so sweet and smart and so talented at so many things, he couldn't imagine how anyone could do her harm. She typed in the correct answer and gave a little fist pump. He smiled as tears flooded his eyes.

With her back turned to him, she said, "You're making me nervous, Dad. Come back in an hour and I'll be done with this lesson." Although he hadn't made a sound, he wasn't surprised that she knew he was there. He'd been training her to feel the small atmospheric shifts a person makes by moving and breathing. She was gonna make quite the warrior when she was old enough for him to really start her training.

"So, you're too old now to give me a hug and kiss?" he asked her. "All I get is a go away, Dad?" He was teasing her, but he knew she wouldn't skip the chance to express her love for him.

She turned and the breath left his lungs. Every time he saw her face, that looked so much like Alisha's everyone thought she was her real mother, his heart filled with joy. She saw his face and couldn't miss the tears in his eyes. Jumping to her feet, she hurried over and wrapped her arms around his midsection. She asked, "Is something wrong? Did something happen?"

"No, Princess, I'm just happy to see you." She had been a shell of a girl when he'd taken her in. To think what those bastards did to her made him wish he could revive them and kill them all over again.

"Did you have the nightmare again?" she asked.

"Yeah, but don't worry about me, sweetie. One of these days my subconscious will catch up with my knowledge and I'll be alright." He'd told both of his girls about his recurring nightmare. He had explained why it didn't make sense because the ending had been anything but scary.

His Uncle Glen had grabbed him and what Daniel had first thought was a bat was really a pool floaty. His uncle had wrapped him in his arms and held him until the terror had abated. Uncle Glen had still been crying, but he explained to Daniel that he was crying because, as the oldest Burke, it was his job to keep all of them safe. He felt that he had failed in his duties.

Delmas had been taken to the hospital with a nasty gash on his head, but he recovered after a couple of days. So, the nightmare made no sense, but nothing besides Alisha next to him could keep it all at bay.

"I love you Daddy, and I wish I could baby you all day, but I need to get back before my time runs out."

"Go ahead," he said with a laugh. "I love you too, and I have to go find your mother".

"She's in the training complex, hopefully beating the pants off Det. Ann. Now go before you get me in trouble." He watched her focus in and do one more problem before he walked off to find his soon to be wife.

Even though the original mansion was three stories, he kept his family on the second. The third floor was pretty much closed off and reinforced with everything needed to keep them safe from any air attacks. All the exterior walls were made of semi-transparent metal that most people thought was glass, but would stop anything short of a nuclear blast.

He'd had images super imposed on the metal so, when light shined on it, you would see an image that falsely led you to believe you were looking inside the house. Some would think it overkill, but with the enemies he had, he upgraded his security on a daily basis.

He hopped on the elevator and took it to the second underground level where the training facility was located. With every piece of workout equipment known to man, the training complex boasted something for everyone. It had multiple obstacle courses, boxing rings, octagons, saunas, swimming pools. Basically, anything you'd need to get in shape or stay in shape. With his three new semi-permanent house guests, this part of the compound had become the most popular. Well, other than the kitchen.

He exited the elevator and walked pass the empty treadmills, bikes, and ellipticals until he could hear the battle going on in the next section. He entered and his eyes zeroed in on the two women engaged in combat inside one of the official sized MMA Octagons.

From the demeanor of both women, he could tell this was a real match. No pulling of punches or shows of mercy. One of these women would probably need medical attention after this was over. No matter how much he wanted to jump in and protect the love of his life, he stayed back and watched from the doorway.

Both women were about the same size with only five pounds separating them. Detective Ann Grace was a very attractive woman at 5-foot 8-inches and 140 pounds. She had her waist length black hair tied in a tight braid running down her back. Her light skin and high cheekbones hinted at her mixed European and Cherokee Indian heritage. At 36 years old, with almost 15 years of law enforcement under her belt, she was smart, strong, well trained, and alluring all condensed into one determined and competitive package.

Now maybe he was a little biased, but none of that appealing package registered with him because his heart and soul belonged to the other woman in the enclosure. Alisha Saffiyah Harden was the most intriguing woman in the world to him. She was 5-foot 8-inches also and outweighed Ann by five pounds that added a plushness to her curves that made his mouth go dry.

She had glowing, soft, dark chocolate skin, perfect coffee-colored eyes, long natural hair, and juicy pink lips that made all kinds of sinful thoughts enter his head. Her body was the perfect slim\thick mix that made people think of Megan Good when they saw her. She had been part of a gang when he met her two years ago, now she was the Queen to his King. The heat that melted his once cold heart.

The fight looked to be about even, but they weren't stopping in between rounds for a rest. Alisha would pick up an advantage from that as she was 11 years younger than the detective. Daniel had been training Alisha for almost two years now and Ann for only one. Both had previous training, but Ann's had been a bit more serious, geared towards self defense and not offense. It would be a good fight that could go either way, but Ann had more wins over Alisha since they started training together.

His eyes tracked to the model like woman standing outside the octagon with the med kit ready to help if need be. Denise McCarthy was a dime and a half when stacked up against normal attractive women. With her voluptuous curves packed into a 5-foot 5-inches, 130-pound, nut brown body, she was born to be an entertainer of people.

When you factored in that she had gone to Duke University on a full ride for Journalism and Criminal Justice, it was no wonder she became one of the top reporters in the country. Well, he had a little to do with that with all the exclusive material he'd given her on the PGK. When you put the whole package together, the 41-year-old could put to shame women 20 years her junior.

All three women were dressed in the black spandex sets he'd bought by the hundreds because they were easy to clean and maintain. Not to mention, they fit all three of them to perfection. He smiled as he remembered Alisha accusing him of just wanting to perv out seeing three gorgeous women in tight clothes. He admitted that the other two women were sights to behold, but neither of them did a thing for him. He only had eyes for his Queen.

Daniel looked up just in time to see Ann land a three-piece flush to Alisha's face. The fourth punch was on its way to finish her off when Alisha grabbed the outstretched arm and went airborne. She turned her body sideways and locked the offending arm between her legs. This move forced Ann to fall to the mat in order to keep her arm from being pulled from its socket. Once on the floor, Alisha kept the pressure on Ann's shoulder, trying to force her to tap out.

Daniel walked into the room with a frown marring his handsome face. "Tap out Ann!" he ordered in a loud, commanding voice. Denise joined the chorus as they both tried to get Ann to tap out before permanent damage was done to her arm and shoulder. "Dammit Ann, fights over. Alisha, release her."

Alisha let go and swung to her feet as Ann surged up towards her, hands raised, still ready to do battle. Daniel took off at a run and vaulted over the octagon's wall. He launched himself at the attacking Ann, grabbed her by the waist, and slung her to the other side of the enclosure.

He glanced back at Alisha with fury on his face. "Good match. Now step out so I can teach the detective some fight etiquette." When she hesitated, he narrowed his eyes and said, "Go!"

Not thinking for a moment, she would continue to defy him, he turned his attention to the hard-headed woman in front of him. He bent low, stalking her, cutting off any escape she thought she had.

"You're a sore fucking loser, Ann. And for some reason, you think you don't have to listen to me anymore." He was close enough now that she started getting nervous and he saw real fear in her eyes.

"So, you must think you're better than me now. You want to try that with me," he said as he tauntingly swiped at her.

"Daniel, stop! You're bullying her!" shouted Alisha.

Hearing her say that dashed cold water all over his fire. He looked at Ann and saw blood and bruises all over her body. The warrior in him acknowledged her need to not give up after going through so much. He felt shame melt away the last of his anger.

"I'm sorry, Ann. I'm a dick for coming at you like that. I have no excuse and I beg your pardon."

Ann understood that she had crossed the line also, so she put her fist out and he bumped it, both letting the other know that it was peace. He swung his arm around her shoulder and said, "Good fight, but you have to remember we're a team. You're making her better and it's the mark of a good teacher when your student can beat you."

She nodded and said, "You're right, and I'll be better from now on."

Alisha said, "Hey! I won the fight. Why does she get the hug from the hunk?" They had just exited the octagon and the comment caused everyone to laugh and start ribbing each other. He smiled as once again the togetherness of his family was returned.

After a while, Daniel told Denise to take Ann into the medical wing and clean her up a little bit. He grabbed Alisha's hand and pulled her in the same direction the other women were going. Denise and Ann traded a look and Denise said, "If the loser got a hug, imagine what the winner is about to get." Alisha blushed and the two older women turned into one of the medical rooms laughing and making lewd comments.

Daniel led them into another of the rooms and, once they both entered, he closed and locked the door and said, "Strip." Alisha glanced at him and he was sure love and admiration was shining clear in his eyes, along with a healthy dose of lust. She actually shivered when their eyes met.

He walked over and turned the shower on. He started to strip out of his own clothes, his eyes hungrily devouring every glistening inch of her skin as she peeled out of the spandex.

Once he touched her, he wasn't going to be able to wait, so he started talking to her to get her ready. "Damn you look delicious. I wouldn't mind turning this into a delectable make out session where I wash you and caress you. Then I'd make slow love to you, but I can't because you're too damn alluring. Whatever man said this is a man's world obviously never had a woman like you."

Her bottom was already bare to his greedy gaze, but when she lifted the stretchy top over her head and revealed her succulent C-cup breast with her hard, jutting nipples standing proud, all restraint went out the window. He marched over and lifted her in his arms, fusing their mouths together as his body sought her entrance of its own accord.

He turned and walked them into the shower where he said, "Congratulations on your win, but for some reason, I think I'm the one getting the prize." He put her back against the tiled wall and penetrated her, luxuriating in her tightness and her cry of passion. She was sweaty and bruised, but he'd never smelled or seen a more ravishing woman than Alisha when he was giving her pleasure.

Two hours later, they were snuggled up on the hospital bed, naked, and half asleep, when a knock sounded on the door. Denise said, "Sorry to bother you, but Walt just entered the gate."

He gave Alisha one more kiss and told her to chill and relax a few more minutes as he got up to handle the other part of their lives. Sergeant Detective Walter Rogers had just returned from a very important mission, hopefully with some good news.

Chapter 2

Detective Walter Rogers parked the satin black Dodge Challenger SRT Demon in front of the museum masquerading as a house, with a sigh of relief. The 50-year-old ex-football player, ex-Army MP, and hopefully still SBI agent, was exhausted. For the past two days he'd been torturing a man, trying to get him to cough up information regarding a drug ring at a prison in Craven County North Carolina. The man had been steadfast in his innocence all the way up until the end. But eventually, the pain and damage caught up to him and he bared his soul.

With 28 years of law enforcement under his belt, Walt never thought he could do the things he was now doing. Physically, at 5-foot 10-inches, and 230 pounds of solid muscle, he could do lots of things. It was the mental part that took a lot of getting used to. Even now he couldn't fully leave behind what he'd just done.

It all started two days ago with an early morning text from Daniel. It read: 'Task 8 today. Don't want to hear your shit and don't come back until it's done.' Walt already knew what he had to do, so he'd jumped out of bed, went and told Ann and Denise what he was doing, and took off for Craven after gathering supplies.

The drive had been long and boring, but it gave him time to reflect over the previous 14 months. Before the massacre at the prison, the phone call to Cpt. William Graham, his boss at the NC SBI, had been brutal.

When Will answered, Walt had tried to be upbeat. "Hey Cap! What's going on?"

William Graham was the same age as Walt. They had actually started at the SBI in the same year. But Will's political savvy, charm, and All-American good looks had taken him higher than Walt. With his ex-jock, ex-frat boy, and superior attitude, Will was a pain in the ass most days. But every day, he was loyal and honest and Walt knew he could trust him.

"I've been trying to reach you for hours! Where the hell are you? I think your killer just tortured another officer and his wife, then killed two cops."

"Listen Will, I don't have a lot of time, but I need you to trust me."

Will was silent for a while and then said, "I hope this conversation is gonna end with you telling me you've caught this son of a bitch or he's really dead this time."

"Even better," said Walt. "I have Ann and Denise with me, but in order to get away clean, we're gonna have to disappear for a while."

"How long is a while? And what do you have to do to get away clean?"

"As far as the time frame, maybe a year to 18 months. What I have to do is something best left unsaid. Just know that everything is for a reason. And if I don't do it, then we all die."

Will was very smart and picked up on things fast. "So, this goes beyond the killer and the CIA." He paused for a minute. "What do you want from me?"

"I need you to cover for my and Ann's absence. When all this is over, I'd like to resume my job and so would Ann. As far as Denise goes, she'll be hidden, so leave her status as is."

"So, you're the accomplice? No, no, don't answer that. I don't need or want to know. I'll do what I can, but I'm warning you Walt, if you leave a shred of evidence that links you to any of this, I'll be the one snapping the cuffs on your wrist."

"I understand, Will, and thank you so much. I'll stay in touch with you as much as I can. Trust me, I'm only doing this to free all of us from this situation." They had said their goodbyes and Walt had talked to him at least once a month since he'd gone off the grid.

After the massacre at the prison, Daniel had begun training the three new arrivals and sending Walt out to complete his task. Mostly, they had been murders of people funneling cash to the WRA, the Agency Daniel's family founded that was now out to kill them all. But some had also been training exercises to see how far Walt's training had progressed. Task 4-7 had been mild if not downright easy. But task 8 had taken a toll on him.

Michael Smith was a case manager at Craven CI, as well as a drug dealer who was sending money to the governor. Daniel had known for years now that the governor was a World Redemption Agency asset. Walt had been tasked with getting the info on how and when the money transfers were made. Then he had to force the man to set up a meeting with the governor, asap.

Walt had ambushed the man when he had entered his home by hiding behind the door and injecting him with Daniel's paralysis drug. Mr. Smith had crumpled to the floor and, still fully aware but unable to move, Walt had staked him to his living room floor by driving nails into his widespread hands.

With mask firmly in place, Walt had expressed his need for total silence when the man could speak again. He explained that there would be consequences if the man decided to disobey. Predictably, as soon as he could, the man yelled for help. Walt hit him with a small dose of the drug and then used an ice pick to take out the man's right eye.

He reiterated his need for silence, which should only be broken to answer some very specific, very detailed, questions. Before he would fess up to even being part of the drug ring, Walt had had to pull out over half the man's teeth. By the time Walt got the info on how to reach the governor for a meet, he'd had to take two fingers and the thumb from each hand.

After a day and a half of continuous torture, he had gotten everything needed from the man. As far as Walt knew, the man was still alive, staked to his floor, stewing in his own waste.

Feeling a level of disgust, mixed with a little pride, he knew Daniel would love the fact that he'd managed to set up a clandestine meeting with the governor later tonight. Walt would need to get some much-needed rest before the meet as all of them would need to be at their best to pull off task 9.

Walt exhaled loudly and then opened his door so he could find Daniel and tell him the good news. Everyone needed to start the preparations now so everything could go smoothly tonight. He stepped out of the car and came face to face with the business end of a 9mm Beretta.

He froze and studied the man holding him at gun point. At best, the man was volatile. At worst, well, no one wanted to meet Daniel Burke at his worst. A few times Walt thought he had, but every time the other man proved just how much worse he could get.

Walt stayed still and tried to gauge the man's mood by studying his face. As usual, his expression was blank, but Walt could still sense the anger coming off of the man. Their shared history was long and complicated, so Walt said nothing, just waited to see where Daniel wanted to take this.

Years ago, Walt and Ann had been assigned a case involving a serial killer. Someone was traveling all over North Carolina killing guards and former inmates. On a few occasions, the inmates had been serving time when they were either murdered or seriously injured.

The Killer, as Walt had thought of Daniel then, had reached out and started taunting him and Ann to prove they were no match for him. He then gave them the impossible task of freeing an innocent man from prison in under a week or he would start killing a guard every day. In the process of their one-upsmanship, Ann was kidnapped and taken to an underground prison.

A series of events led to a lot of death, but also a lot of understanding as to what was really motivating Daniel. Walt ended up killing a man he thought was the killer, which resulted in Walt becoming a slave to Daniel. And while Walt thought he was getting the better of Daniel, Denise was also taken.

What followed all that was the revelation of an undercover war being waged where Daniel ended up being the good guy after all. And all the horrible things he made Walt do was really a bid to save his life. Now, Walt, Ann, and Denise were on his side in the war against the World Redemption Agency, who seemed to be trying to rule the world by profiting off every vice known to man.

So, to have this unpredictable, trained killer holding a gun to his head, had Walt a little nervous. Finally, after a couple minutes, Daniel said, "How many times do I have to tell you, you're not safe no matter where you are? What if while you were gone, we had all been killed and the WRA had set a trap for you? You sitting out here daydreaming in the fucking car, and let me walk right up on you." Daniel shook his head and put the gun away, clearly disappointed in Walt.

Walt said contritely, "You're right. It won't happen again." He didn't offer any excuse of being distracted. None of that would have saved his life. Plus, Daniel would see any excuse as a weakness.

"Good," said Daniel. "Denise is getting everyone into the War Room now. Go and get washed up, grab a snack, and then meet us there for your report." He walked away, never doubting for a second that Walt had a report to give. Daniel knew that if he didn't have the information, Walt would still be torturing the man to get it.

Walt felt the ebb of the latest adrenaline rush as he made his way over to the side door that was the closest entrance to his suite of rooms. As much as he wanted to, he couldn't fall out yet. He would take his shower, eat about five energy bars, drink a gallon of coffee, and then go through the plan with his team. Then, he would sleep for as long as possible before he had to be up to complete his part in the next mission.

15 minutes later, Walt was on the elevator headed towards the first underground level which contained the War Room and Daniel's arsenal. As Walt walked down the clinical hallways, he pictured what was behind each deceptively innocent door he passed.

The doors looked to be regular institutional doors, but these literally had hearts of steel. And wrapped like they were, with titanium infused Kevlar, each door protected the entrance to its very own safe room.

Daniel was a certified weapons freak. He had whole rooms of specific handguns. Different rooms for rifles, mines, pipe bombs, machine guns, drones, grenades and grenade launchers. Walt had even been shown a room of regular household items that blew up at the press of a button. There was literally something on this floor to deliver death to anyone at any time.

Walt passed by all these rooms until he reached the vault door at the center of the maze-like corridors. To gain entry, he looked in three different cameras head on, swiped a key card, entered his personal code, and finally said his name for the voice print match. The vault door seemed to disengage 50 different locks before it swung open exactly two feet, where it would remain for five seconds before closing back.

He slipped his bulky form inside where he then encountered another obstacle, which could only be opened once the heavy door to his back closed. When the time came, he entered a separate code for this door and entered the War Room.

This space couldn't go by a more fitting name. It didn't matter how many times he entered it, he still had to look around in wonder. The 50-yard by 50-yard box had screens completely covering three walls. Since the walls were 16 feet high, it was hard not to be impressed with the view. On the final wall was a huge monitor that Daniel used to teach them everything they needed to know about surveillance.

Four other people were in the room and they all watched him as he made his way over to the first of four conference tables. Daniel eyed him with no expression, but Ann and Denise looked him over to make sure he was okay. Alisha just smiled and nodded, but he knew from experience that her eyes missed nothing.

Ever since they had arrived at this compound, Walt had kept Daniel's advice close and treated both Ann and Denise the same. He knew Denise had been hurt and confused at first, but after a while, he was sure she understood the real reason he fell back. With that in mind, he kissed both of them on the cheek before taking his own seat.

He had kept everyone waiting long enough, so he filled them in on what he had learned the last two days. It was strange that it had taken him two days to collect it all, but only four minutes to deliver it. After he was done, Daniel said, "Good work. Everyone already knows what their role is gonna be. Just plug this new info in and prepare for the worst-case scenario. Any questions?"

Denise said, "I know the stage is already set, but what do I do if we've missed something? I mean, I won't see any of you until everything is done."

"Denise," Daniel said, drawing her eyes to him. "You're ready. I would say you were born to play this role, but I fear I'd have to fight all of you." Everyone laughed just like Walt was sure he'd hoped. "I told you I got you. If at any time I feel you are not safe, I'll get you out of there. Okay?"

"Okay," she said. "I'm sorry. Just a little nervous. As much as I hate to admit it, I'm really more nervous of being separated from all of you. I'll miss you guys," she said with tears in her eyes.

Of everyone who could have comforted her, the least likely one stepped up. Daniel said, "You've surpassed my expectations by leaps and bounds. You are truly one of us. One of mine. I am proud to work by your side and I would give my life to protect you. This is just a brief separation and then we'll all be able to live our lives in the open." He paused and looked each of them in the eyes.

"Each and every one of you are my family. Those people I share blood with, only a few of them ever have a chance of falling under that title again. I love you guys and I respect you all. But more importantly, I trust you. I trust you with the lives of the two young ladies that hold my heart," he said glancing at Alisha.

Every eye, even Daniel's, was a little misty when he clapped once loudly and cleared his throat. "Alright with all the mushy stuff. Let's get to work."

Chapter 3

"Sir, you do know every time we allow this, we're all putting our jobs on the line."

Governor Garvin Johnson looked at the man as if he had lost his mind. "Allow? Allow?" Gov. Johnson yelled. "Just who in the fuck do you think you're talking to. You don't allow me to do shit!"

Garvin was in the process of leaving the mansion, but the head of his assigned security detail had decided to grow a pair. The state assigned protection was very good, but for Garvin, that was the problem. They always hired these gun-ho motherfuckers who were more loyal to the station than to the man.

"Sir, with all due respect, I just think one car following at a discrete distance would suit both our purposes well."

Garvin was sitting in the driver's seat of his silver BMW M850i wondering why he was even indulging the simple-minded man. "You think? Boy, before you could ever have an intelligent thought, I'd be the king of the whole fucking world. Now, open this fucking gate before I have to get out and do it myself."

The man swallowed audibly and motioned for the gate to be opened. Garvin put the vehicle in gear and said, "And if I see one car that even looks like it's following me, I'll personally hire a hitman to kill you and your whole family. Got it?" The guard nodded and Garvin pulled off with a little chuckle.

It was one o'clock in the morning, but the governor didn't have far to go to get to either of his planned stops. If all went well, he would be back at the mansion this afternoon having gained some wealth and shed some stress.

Garvin looked at himself in his rearview mirror and smiled at the image reflected back at him. His deep brown eyes and salt and pepper hair had gotten him a lot of trim in his life. His 6-foot 3-inch, 240-pound muscular body also added to his body count. At 55 years of age, he was still in excellent shape, which could trace all the way back to his days in the Army.

He had a personal chef and nutritionist. A personal trainer, as well as a life coach. Pretty much, the only bad thing he indulged in was some of the women he'd picked up over the years. It was just something about those smart mouth, neck snapping, freaky, hood rat, black girls that did it for him. Before his position with the WRA, he could only afford one every now and then. Now, he had them stashed all over the country. And his main one, Asiah, he was going to see in an hour or two.

But business first. This guy Michael Smith, who worked at the prison in Craven County, was a real go-getter. Michael had no idea the money he made was funneled to the WRA, and he didn't need to know. But he made so much money, Garvin decided to start dealing with the man in person. Make the man feel important so he would keep up the good work.

The latest text he sent was in code, but said he had $200,000 for pick up. One thing Garvin learned was that you never let people hold life changing money because it had a way of talking to people. That kind of money could make the most loyal soldier change up and become your worst enemy. So, Garvin had sent a text for the man to meet him, asap.

All the other guys he collected from, even the officials at the bigger prisons, couldn't keep up with Michael. When Garvin asked what his secret was, he'd shrugged and said, "Most inmates will buy anything they can't get on a daily basis. And since they're spending money they didn't work for, it's almost like they can't wait to give it away."

After that conversation a couple years ago, Garvin had given him the direct number to the WRA supplier and all he did now was pick up the money.

Garvin turned to go down the driveway of the old farmhouse, but paused at the entrance to make sure no one followed him. After sitting in the darkness for five minutes, he was satisfied no one else was coming along, so he started the car back up and drove on.

He smiled when he saw the black Dodge Challenger parked beside the structure. Michael had been driving a rust bucket for years and Garvin had told him he needed to buy a new one. He'd explained to the man how important it was to have a reliable vehicle. Michael had told him the car provided all the misdirection needed for him to stay low key, but Garvin guessed the man had finally taken his advice.

The governor exited the car and walked over to the barn door, head on a swivel, always looking for trouble. He pulled the heavy door open and stepped inside, closing it behind him. Might be his paranoia, but he always locked the door so no one could sneak up on the meeting.

This was the only part of the operation that left him vulnerable, but he felt it a necessary risk to keep the money flow coming. And business being business, he never took money without counting it first.

He walked into the small office area and paused. There was a black bag sitting on the desk with money stacked beside it, but no sign of Michael. Garvin shook his head, thinking the man was probably using the bathroom. But then he frowned. The barn had no bathroom and no way would Michael have left the money out with the door unlocked. Before he could turn around or react in anyway, he felt a small sting on the back of his neck. Then he crumpled to the floor, unconscious before his hand could even reach the stung area.

. . . .

Boom! Boom! Boom! "Open this door right now!" *Boom! Boom! Boom!*

Garvin was swimming back to consciousness, or at least he thought he was. His hands flew to his aching head as his naked body lay sprawled on the couch. Wait, naked body? Couch? He looked around and wondered how the hell he'd managed to get himself to Asiah's house. It was still dark out, so he hadn't been out for that long.

"Fuck it! Take the door down!" Garvin's head whipped in the direction of the door. He'd thought the noise was a carryover from some kind of nightmare. Then the door crashed open and what seemed like hundreds of armed men stormed into the house.

Before he could begin to make sense of it, he, Garvin Johnson, the governor of the great state of North Carolina, was slammed to the ground and his hands were cuffed behind his back.

"Hey! Hey!" he yelled. "What's the meaning of this? Get your fucking hands off of me. Do you know who I am?"

The officers in SWAT gear ignored his rant and continued to read him his rights. Garvin was confused on so many levels, he didn't know where to start. How the hell had he gotten to the house? Where was the $200,000? Where was Michael? Where were his clothes? How had the police found out about his illegal activities? Oh, that motherfucker! If Michael had set him up, then the fucker would be dead by the end of the day.

Another SWAT guy came over and helped the other one pick him up. They threw a blanket around his body, placed the ends in his hands and ordered him to hold it tight.

This was a high-end neighborhood in Raleigh, so when they perp walked him outside, plenty of neighbors were out with their cell phones held high. He dropped his head and prayed none of the vultures would recognize him. As he was led to the police vehicle, he saw his BMW parked in the driveway with the trunk open. A young female officer was holding a black bag and he heard her tell one of the SWAT guys, "Looks like it's full of money."

There was no doubt in his mind now that Michael Smith had set him up. The ungrateful bastard had probably gotten caught with something and promised a big fish if they offered him a deal. Well, the snitch wouldn't live long enough to get the deal anyway.

They put him in the back of a black SUV and then left him alone with his thoughts. He watched all the activity as his thoughts turned to the WRA. He had to get word to them that he wouldn't talk. Whatever was going on would lead to him pleading guilty to some small charge years from now with no jail time. He definitely didn't want them to think he'd talk to anyone about them.

A month after he'd moved into the Governor's mansion, he'd awakened with an icepick at his jugular. The man introduced himself as The Author and said he was the WRA's problem solver. He was a dark-skinned black man, medium height, and probably weighed 220 pounds. He'd had this dead look in his eyes that said he hoped to one day have a reason to label the governor as a problem.

The Author had said, "I don't do sneak kills. I like to look into my victims' eyes as they die. So, you can take some comfort in that. If they ever have reason to send me, you'll at least see it coming." Then he'd faded into the shadows and was gone.

Even for a military man like him, The Author scared the living shit out of him. And the worst part was, they could send someone else who he would never see coming. But he could nip all that in the bud with one message for his lawyer to deliver.

He was getting restless just sitting in the vehicle with nothing but a blanket to cover his nudity. And, even though the windows on the SUV were blacked out, it wouldn't take people long to figure out it was his car the crime scene people were combing through. Wait! Why the hell were crime scene people here? Because of the money?

A flurry of activity started up as an ambulance screamed up and two paramedics rushed inside the house. Damn, he hadn't even thought of Asiah. What if the people who set him up had hurt her? She had to still be alive or it would have been a coroner van instead of an ambulance.

Then they walked a woman out with a similar blanket to the one he'd been given. She was walking with the help of the paramedics, but she grimaced in pain with every step. "What the hell?" he muttered as they led her to the emergency vehicle and pulled off.

The two officers who'd walked him out exited the house and made their way to the SUV. When they entered, he immediately launched his verbal assault. "What the hell is going on here? Why am I being arrested? I'm the victim here! Earlier tonight, I was assaulted and dumped at that house over there."

The officer in the passenger seat turned around with fury all over his face. "Why don't you exercise your right to silence and shut the fuck up you kidnapping, raping, piece of shit!"

"Hey, fuck you," replied Garvin without thought. Then the man's words registered. "Hold up, kidnapping? Raping? Hell no! You motherfuckers aren't gonna put that shit on me. I demand to see my lawyer, right now!" Garvin kept up the tirade, but it was purely out of desperation. If the WRA found out he was facing charges like that, whether right or wrong, they wouldn't take any chances that he might shoot for a deal.

"I need to talk to my lawyer, right now!" he yelled as the tears started falling down his face.

Chapter 4

"Yes," said Reginald Burke. "I appreciate the info, but how sure are you that it's accurate?" After the answer came through on the other end of the phone, he said, "Okay, thanks. I got something coming your way in a little bit. Watch for it."

Reggie calmly ended the call, put the phone in his side holster, sat still for about 30 seconds, and then went ballistic. "Fuck!" he roared, swiping everything off of his orderly desk. He punctuated every repeated, "Fuck!" with fists slamming down on his desk.

After about two minutes of unleashed fury, he sat calmly for about three minutes and then cleaned up his mess. It only took him a few minutes because the only files left on his desk were pertaining to his little brother, Daniel Burke.

Reggie was the oldest son of Lucille Drake, the head of the WRA. At 43 years old, he was the Head of Operations for the World Redemption Agency, second only to his mother. At least on paper. As far as the Agency went, he was the top dog, because his mother got all the praise, but he got all the blame. In his book, that meant he was in charge.

At 6-foot 3-inches, and 240 pounds, Reggie was a physically imposing man. His dark skin, low cut salt and pepper hair, and rippling muscles have made him a hit with the ladies since he hit puberty. Although he indulged himself from time to time, he took his role of oldest male Burke to heart and did his best to protect the family.

Daniel was far from the only genius in the family. All of the Burke children had IQs in the genius level, but Daniel's and Reggie's couldn't even be tested. Reggie had graduated from Harvard with four different degrees. To keep everything balanced, he also had black belts in four different

Martial Arts disciplines. When the Burke family went after a target, the target didn't stand a chance. Unless that target happened to be a Burke himself.

Delmas Burke and Lucille Drake rushed into his office with guns drawn. "You alright? What the hell happened in here? We got an alert for seismic activity down here." Even though it was clear nothing was going on, Delmas still swung his gun from side to side.

"Put the guns away," said Reggie. "Just got some pretty bad news and went a little crazy. Have a seat. Might as well fill you both in now."

Delmas was the middle brother and was the spitting image of Daniel, or since he was older, Daniel was the spitting image of him. He was the Head of Mission Development for the WRA, which placed him third in command. He is one of the most acclaimed field agents the WRA has ever had, but he now only goes in the field to solve major problems. He and their mother took seats and looked at Reggie with trepidation.

"So, I just got a call from one of our Raleigh PD assets. He says the governor has been arrested and is sitting in interrogation right now."

"What!" Delmas and Lucille shouted as one.

Delmas asked, "Is it Daniel?"

"Yeah, D. I'd have to say it's him."

"Well, how do you know that? You sure it wasn't just a sting on his operation?" asked Lucille.

"Well Mom, if Paul was still alive, we would already have all the answers. But, as of right now, I just know the charges and the victim."

Silence ruled for a minute after Reggie's subtle admonishment. A little over a year ago, Paul Stevens, an area CIA agent and WRA agent, was executed by Lucille for being a traitor. The only proof she'd offered anyone was her word that he was helping Daniel defeat them. With no interrogation or real evidence, a lot of people questioned what her real motives were. But these were the situations where they needed his connections with local police to fill in the blanks.

Delmas was the one to break the silence. "So, what are the charges? They have to be drugs or some kind of white collar, money bullshit."

"You would think so, but Daniel would know we could get him off on those," said Reggie. "So, he kicked it up to something we're gonna have to gather some intel before we can move on it."

"He didn't plant a body at the mansion, did he?" asked Lucille seriously. There was no telling how far Daniel would go to take them down.

"Let me just tell you what the asset said. A woman by the name of Asiah Winecoff called the police and said she had been carrying on a paid relationship with the governor. At the house where they would meet, he had a room he always kept locked. That is until he fell asleep and forgot to lock it after coming out of the room tonight. She snuck into the room and found a woman locked in a cage and it looked like she'd been there for a while. When she couldn't get her out, she ran from the house and called the police."

Delmas shook his head. "So, he's a freak. What's wrong with that?"

"The woman was Denise McCarthy and she's saying the governor has been holding her since she went missing last year."

Delmas glanced from one to the other. "That's a major hit right there. With us still being locked out of our system, this could really shut us down. Not to mention the governor has a hell of a get out of jail free card."

"Yeah," Reggie sighed. "We've lost all our major legitimate contracts and are now solely dependent on our illegal activities. The governor and the prison operation made up 45% of that money. So, with this one move, Daniel has fucked us from both sides. He's killed our money flow and set us up to be exposed by the governor."

Lucille stood up and quietly began to pace as her sons watched her. At five feet tall, and 66 years of age, she was thinly built, but had the bearings of a military commander. She had a head full of gray curls and wore very thick glasses. But, anyone who looked at her and didn't see the deadly threat lurking under her light brown skin, had to be blind. As the leader of the WRA, she had to be smart and cunning. As the oldest person alive with Burke blood running through her veins, she had to be ruthless and merciless.

Finally, she stopped and addressed Reggie. "So, we're down to desperate measures now. Let's get in contact with Daniel and try to broker a truce."

Reggie was already shaking his head. "That ship has sailed. When we tried that last attack at the prison, that made any talking with him a dead end. Any truce talk has to be initiated by him."

Delmas said, "That's why we need to stop trying to talk and play the game how he's playing it."

Reggie looked at him snidely. "He didn't kick your ass hard enough last time? Brute force won't work against him, and the only people he cares about are locked in that fortress with him. And don't forget, he still has all our money. If he dies, then it's gone forever."

"But we still have billions in assets," said Lucille. "If he would just stop sabotaging everything we do, we can build our reserves back up."

"Okay, geniuses," said Reggie. "Obviously you've been talking about it. Tell me what ya'll think we should do. And tell me the whole plan so maybe this time it can work."

Delmas and Lucille glanced at each other and then Lucille took her seat again. They talked for 15 minutes without Reggie interrupting. When they went silent, he said, "Alright, I have to admit, it could work. But doing that might be something he's expecting us to do."

Delmas shrugged and said, "It's all we got left. It's a way to force a confrontation and, if everything goes to plan, we get our money back and we take him out for good. If we fail, we're right where we are now, so we have nothing to lose."

Reggie nodded, agreeing with the logic of his younger brother. That still left one more decision. "And the governor? Do we trust him to stay quiet?"

Lucille laughed. "The biggest fear of the newly rich is that they'll end up poor again. He'll do anything and say everything to get back to his ivory tower. Remember, a potential threat is already a threat. This has to be handled now."

"I have a couple of assets I can use. One of them, we won't have to spend anymore money, but it'll be messy." After a pause in thought, Reggie continued. "Fuck it. Don't worry about the governor. I got it handled."

Lucille and Delmas got up to go start the plan they all hoped would finally get them back on track. Reggie shook his head as he watched them leave. Their plan was foolhardy at best, but they might get lucky. Delmas would once again be out in the field, but this time, he'd have a huge score to settle after Daniel embarrassed him the last time.

Reggie dismissed what he couldn't control and pulled out his phone to take care of what he could. It was a long shot, but the payoff would be huge if he could pull it off. The phone was answered on the first ring like always, but the man remained silent. Reggie said, "Ghost, I have a very difficult job for you. It has the potential of making your name legendary again. You want to give it a shot?"

The line was silent for a full minute until the man said one word. "Speak."

. . . .

When Ghost hung up the phone, he had a huge smile on his face. The legendary WRA agent was finally gonna have the chance to reclaim his top spot. After Daniel made a fool out of him at the failed prison assault, he'd pretty much become persona non-grata in the intelligence community. The fact that he still didn't know why he'd been left alone in that field while all the other soldiers were sent back to the WRA bothered him. But that was in the past, and this job would solidify his future.

The Ghost, AKA Jamar Gorden, was the most prolific killer the Agency has ever had. Well, other than Daniel. But Ghost only killed for the WRA whereas Daniel only killed for himself or Military Intelligence. So, technically Daniel's kills didn't register in the WRA catalog.

Ghost was a 5-foot 10-inch black man with albino skin and long dreadlocks. At 240 pounds, it was hard to figure how he was the best stealth killer in the game. But he undoubtably was. His methodical movements, paired with his deceptive speed, made him impossible to spot if he didn't want to be. And his non-threatening demeanor made it possible for him to walk right up on his victim before they even knew they were in danger.

But this job coming up was all about stealth and speed. He had to sacrifice planning, but he already had a workable plan in his mind. He never got credit for being smart, but he was about to prove just how intelligent he was. The art of murder without killing anyone was an art indeed. Tonight, he would prove he was the best at it.

He swung his legs out of bed and heard, "Babe? Where are you going? Is everything alright?"

Damn! The stealth king, busted by his wife. "I just got a call about an emergency at work. Go back to sleep and I'll take you and the girls out to dinner tonight."

"Okay, sweetie. Be careful and I love you."

"I love you too," he said, bending down to kiss her cheek. His wife and two daughters were the reason he was so good at his job. He would never allow some second-rate agent to take him away from his family. What happened with Daniel could never be allowed to happen again.

After he did this quick WRA hit, he could go back to working on his plan to get even. Daniel damn sure wasn't a second-rate agent, but Ghost couldn't afford for an agent to be walking free when that agent scared him to death.

Chapter 5

The detectives looked at each other and laughed uproariously, causing Governor Johnson to slam his cuffed hands into the table. "I'm telling you the truth. I'm being set up and everyone is part of this conspiracy to take me down. I was assaulted, drugged, and no one seems to care that I'm the fucking governor of this state!"

The older detective in the grey suit got himself together and just stared at Garvin. The black man flashed startlingly white teeth before asking, "And that's the story you're sticking to? You're not doing yourself any favors like that. You're gonna be in a cage for a very long time unless you tell us what we want to know."

Garvin had at first asked for a lawyer, but when he saw the duo they sent in to question him, he knew he could outsmart them. Now, he wasn't so sure. Both detectives just seemed to take him for a joke, and he found himself talking a lot more than he should have.

The young detective in the black suit said, "Just tell us the truth, man. We'll take you to Burger King, get you something to eat, and you'll be sent to a nice warm single cell to get a full night's sleep."

They had introduced themselves earlier, but Garvin hadn't even taken the time to memorize their names. It was either old or young, grey suit or black suit. That's all these two assholes got from him. And after all this mess was cleared up, he'd have the jobs of everyone involved in making him look like a criminal.

Through gritted teeth, Garvin said, "I'm telling you the truth. I'm not married, so I have to find my pleasure somewhere. I pay all the bills, but Asiah lives there. I come around once or twice a week, take my pleasure, then leave."

The young white detective said, "And you never asked what was in the locked room?"

"I didn't go there to take a fucking tour. I showed up, took care of my business, and left. Why is that so hard for you idiots to understand?"

They didn't seem to like the insult very much, but there was no time to respond before the door was pushed open. A middle-aged white guy, about 5-foot 10-inches tall, and with the body of a serious runner, entered the room and just stared at Garvin.

Now, this wasn't a guy he wanted to tangle with. He had dark hair and was seriously handsome, but intelligence and cunning flowed out of the man's eyes. He glanced at the two detectives and said, "I got it from here fellas. I'll catch up with you guys later."

The older detective snickered and said to Garvin, "Should have talked to us. You're fucked now." The detectives exited, leaving Garvin alone with the newcomer.

The governor was intimidated by the man and he didn't even know who he was. The two detectives hadn't even questioned his dismissal, so he had to be someone pretty high up. Garvin said, "I don't want to talk to you. I want a lawyer."

The man didn't respond, he just walked over to the chair across from Garvin, smoothed his $1,000 suit, and took a seat.

"Did you hear me?" he yelled. "I want my lawyer right now!"

Calmly, the man looked around the room and said softly, "I heard you, but the problem is, no one else can. You see, this is a Special Cases Interrogations Room. No two-way glass. No cameras. And the only person who gives a fuck about your rights is you. But I'll take it easy on you and remove some of the mystery." He squared himself towards

Garvin and said, "My name is Captain William Graham and I work for the SBI. And like my colleague told you before he left, you're fucked."

Garvin could sense a knowledge in the Captain that told him to shut up and listen. So, that's what he did.

After a few seconds, the captain went on. "Now, I won't lie to you. Most of our evidence is at the lab being tested as we speak. But, because of your time in the military, and your job as governor, we already have your prints and DNA on record. If the story being told by the women are true, you will be in prison for the rest of your life. Unless you have something, you can barter with. If that's the case, we might can help each other."

Garvin indeed had a lot to barter with, but he needed to know the totality of the evidence before he would risk talking. He asked, "What evidence and what are the women saying?"

The SBI agent shook his head and said, "Sperm, hair, skin cells, saliva, pretty much everything a human can leave behind that contains DNA. But even without that, the story being told by these two women match up to where one's story fills in the blanks of the other. Together they paint you as a monster of epic proportions. Do you really want to hear what they said?"

Even though he knew it would all be lies, he nodded his head because he needed to know how far he had to go to save himself.

The agent started. "Asiah Winecoff said that she was pretty much a prostitute that you paid a monthly amount to so she is always on call. She said that the house is yours and she only comes over when you call her to come. After you finish your business with her, she would clean and do laundry while you go into the locked room for one to three hours. Afterwards, you would come out, get dressed, give her a tip, and leave. Until tonight, the door had always been locked while she was in residence. Tonight, you came out of the room exhausted, forgot to lock it, and fell asleep on the couch. She snuck in, saw the woman, attempted to free her, and when she couldn't, she ran from the house and called the police."

After the dialogue, both men sat silently staring at each other for five minutes. Cpt. Graham asked, "Do you need to hear the rest, or do you understand now why you're fucked?"

Garvin had thought this whole situation was tied to Michael Smith and the WRA somehow. But that would mean Asiah and the other woman were involved with the WRA, and he just couldn't see that. He said, "Since all of this is a complete fabrication, the only way I'll know is if you tell me."

Agent Graham didn't smile or laugh or show any emotion at all. He just picked up the tale where he left off. "So, the other woman, Denise McCarthy…."

"What!" shouted the governor. "Oh, hell no! I didn't have anything to do with her. Is that who the woman was? I swear I've never seen her before other than on T.V."

"Now you see, I'm trying to help you. Lying to my face will get you a very short ride to a long stay in prison."

"I swear man, I've never seen her other than the news. I didn't even recognize her."

"So, Denise and Sgt. Det. Walter Rogers didn't come to your office trying to get you to free Timothy Washington?"

Fuck! thought Garvin, he had forgotten all about that. It was hard to relate the beautiful and elegant Denise McCarthy with the downtrodden woman he'd seen carried from Asiah's house.

"You're right," he confessed, shaking his head. "I had completely forgotten about that. I was under a lot of stress then just like now. I'm sorry, it completely slipped my mind."

"That's okay," the captain said. "But Denise says you became infatuated with her after that. You would call and email and bother her at work. Anyway, she says the Prison Guard Killer kidnapped her because she refused to give him anymore coverage. She also played a role in trying to capture him, an operation I was on with her.

"Denise said that the killer took her to that house and told her he had a good friend who would take care of her. Then the PGK introduced you and she's been in that cage ever since."

"That's a Goddamn lie!" roared Garvin.

Cpt. Graham went on like he hadn't heard the man. "She said that you would have her use toys on herself while you stood at the bars naked and watched. You wouldn't feed her for days and then you'd force her to put on a show for her food and water. According to her, you would sit in the recliner outside her cage and masturbate during her shows. Sometimes you would make her come to the bars so you could sexually assault her."

"I'm not a fucking rapist! Bring in your lie detector equipment and you give both of us the test and see who's lying. I've never been in that room and I've never touched that woman."

The captain sat impassively during his rant, then leaned forward, counting off on his fingers. "One, both women took lie detector test and passed them. Two, we have calls and emails from your phone and computer hounding Ms. McCarthy for days leading up to her disappearance. Three, we have DNA and hair samples at the lab that we have taken from the shower connected to the room, the recliner, the floor, and her leg where she said you ejaculated earlier tonight."

Garvin Johnson dropped his head into his shackled hands and started to weep. The frame up had been perfect. The WRA had to have set all this up, there was no one else capable of doing it. He knew all the evidence would match him perfectly and both women would testify if need be.

"She also has bruises all over her body which she says she got from you because she refused to come to the bars at first. So, that's just another couple of years you can add onto the 100 you'll already have."

Garvin cried and thought. Thought and cried. He would never last 100 years. Hell, he wouldn't last two years in prison. With that realization came an epiphany: The fuckers wanted to take him down, why not return the favor. "You said I could help myself. What did you mean by that?"

Cpt. Graham stared at him for a moment, then said, "I want the Prison Guard Killer. Just his real name. You give me that and I'll..." The door was pushed open and a young, red-headed, uniformed cop entered the room.

He said, "I know you didn't want to be disturbed, but the woman. Asiah Winecoff was taken to the hospital. The Chief needs to see you now." Cpt. Graham jumped up, but paused at the door. The young uniform said, "Don't worry sir. I'll stay with him until you get back." With that assurance, he dashed off to find out what the Chief wanted.

The young officer closed the door, but stood facing it for a while. When he turned, he had tears streaming down his face and a gun in his hand.

"No!" said Garvin, jerking back as far as the restraints would allow. "Please! Whatever they're paying you, I'll double, no, triple it. Just don't kill me."

"I'm sorry sir, but it's not money," the young man said. "The monster has my family."

"Listen, I can help you. I know these people. Either your family is already dead, or they're just playing with your mind."

Sniffling, the officer said, "It's already too late. He's killed my little boy and he's holding my daughter and wife. I'm really sorry, but I don't have a choice."

The officer raised the gun and walked closer to the cowering governor. The door opened again, but it was far too late. William Graham yelled, "NO!" just as the officer's gun exploded, peppering the institutional green wall with blood and brains.

The governor didn't get to see the officer get the drop on Will, who was scrambling for his own gun. The governor also didn't hear the officer say, "I'm sorry, they have my family," then turn the gun on himself.

No, the governor didn't get to see or hear any of that, but Will Graham did. As more officers flooded the room, taking in the carnage, William heard a phone ringing. He hushed everyone and figured out it was the fallen officer's phone.

He pulled it from the officer's pocket and answered it. A woman said, "Baby, we're safe, and Mark is still alive. The man had only shot him with some kind of knock out bullet. He left about 30 seconds ago and now we're safe. Are you okay Matt? Matt?"

Will didn't have the heart to tell her what had just transpired. He just hung the phone up as a new thought entered his head. With no cameras, how did the mystery man know exactly when to leave the officer's family. And if one officer could be used, why not another.

Chapter 6

Daniel, Walt, and Ann arrived back at the compound after a night of hard work and a perfect plan executed. It was late morning with the sun shining brightly and Daniel could admit to feeling good about the operation and his new team. Everyone listened, everyone did their part, and there was no hesitation in the field. Even when Denise had to end the life of Asiah Winecoff.

Walt and Ann were now experts at flying his death delivering drones, but both of them had balked at killing the young black prostitute.

"We're already paying her," said Ann. "She has no reason to betray us."

"And won't her death cause more questions to pop up instead of less?" asked Walt.

Daniel had studied both of them in the War Room weeks ago. "You guys think like cops and that's a good thing. But, you're looking at it from the point of having the answers already. The WRA is gonna kill Garvin Johnson and Denise will mention the PGK. If neither of you knew we were the ones killing her, anyone would assume the PGK killed both of them. Not one person has reason to believe a cover up on our part, or even that we exist."

"I'll do it," said Denise, shocking everyone. "Hey, I learn quickly. A potential threat is already a threat. A prostitute sells her body for money. Anyone who will do that won't flinch at bribery, blackmail, or all out betrayal. And when it comes down to it, I'm the only one she could betray. So, I should be the one to kill her."

Daniel had seen it in her eyes that she was serious, so he had revised the plan to include a slow acting toxin that

43

Denise would rub on the woman's arm when she tried to free her from the cage. Denise had simply told Asiah that she would need to put her fresh fingerprints on the bars for the crime scene techs. Soon as the woman was close, Denise scratched her and that was the beginning of the end for Asiah Winecoff.

They were all extremely tired, but Daniel guessed none more than Walt. When they entered the kitchen area together, Alisha already had breakfast made and coffee brewing. Gabby was at the table in her workout clothes and she asked Ann if she wanted to play some basketball after they ate.

Daniel started to object, but Ann shook her head at him. "Of course, I'll whip you on the court. Your Momma kicked my butt yesterday, so I have to take my wins where I can."

It was something so small, but Daniel almost teared up at the love he felt for his family. Just minutes ago, Ann had been stumbling on her feet, but just to make his little girl happy, she would sacrifice and push on. Ann gave him a soft smile to let him know that she acknowledged his gratitude.

"All of you really need some sleep. Don't forget, we still have one of our own out there." Alisha didn't ever go out on any of the missions, but she was in on all the planning. And she swore Daniel was spoiling Gabby, so she ended up being the voice of reason most of the time. "Gabby, Ann, one game and then sleep for Ann."

Gabby knew exactly who Daniel was as she had been present when he killed her foster parents and sister. He had never expressly told her so, but he assumed she thought Walt, Ann, and Denise helped him get rid of the bad guys. She never judged them or asked questions. She just loved them all because they all loved her.

Daniel ate a few slices of bacon, drank some orange juice, and he was good to go. He said, "We'll reconvene in the War Room at 18:00. Everybody, get some sleep. Denise will have police protection because she's the last one alive from that house. I had a service keeping up with all of your homes, so she should be okay. Babe," he said turning to Alisha. "Keep an eye on our girl until she makes it home and then you sleep too. I know you've been up watching those screens all night."

A series of satellites and drones covered them whenever they left the compound. They all could watch the feeds on their phones or in the War Room. One of the things Alisha had started doing was watching the action live since Daniel refused to let her participate. He really wanted her as far from that life as possible, but he would take what he could get.

Daniel kissed both Alisha and Gabby but stopped to address Walt before he left. "She's got this, brother. She'll be okay. I know it'll be hard, but she needs you to rest up because this is far from over. We just made them kill their last big source of income. They'll try something major and we will be ready for them. Because, not being ready," he said, glancing at Gabby and Alisha, "is definitely not an option."

He patted Walt's shoulder, smiled at the women, and walked off so he could recharge his batteries. A war was coming, and it would be all-hands-on-deck.

. . . .

It was noon and Denise was just being released from the police station. Technically, she could have left at any time, but that would have made her look suspicious. A man kidnaps you for 14 months and you don't do everything in your power to bring justice; people might start to question why.

And then the other two people associated with the crime dies; one murdered, and the other under mysterious circumstances. If she had made a fuss about leaving, it would have made all the focus fall on her.

As soon as Denise got outside, the flashes started. The media was out in force to welcome back one of their own. She wasn't looking her best but, with clothes from the lost and found, she wasn't supposed to.

She really hated not talking to the media, but again, that would have been suspicious. So, she had already told her police escort to expedite the situation by making a path through the crowd. When she made it through all the shouted questions to the back seat of the SUV, she leaned back and breathed a huge sigh of relief. It would have been nothing for the WRA to have tried something in the chaos.

"Are you sure you don't have a friend or relative you could stay with for a few days?" asked the female driver. "It's gonna be pretty hard on you for the foreseeable future."

Denise smiled at the officer and said, "No, I don't want to impose on anyone. Hopefully my house isn't too bad, but cleaning would give me something to keep my mind occupied."

She turned towards the window, hoping the lady would get the message that she wanted to be left with her thoughts. I mean, she had just killed someone who believed her to be a friend.

When Denise had first approached the woman, Asiah had only one question: "How much?"

Denise had paused for effect and said, "$1 Million cash." Asiah had shaken her hand and the start of a yearlong operation was underway.

The governor had refused to wear condoms with Asiah. That made it easy for her to go to the bathroom after they finished and store his semen for later use. Daniel worked on the locked room whenever no one was around. As soon as it was ready, Denise started sending her hair and waste to the woman to spread around the room. Denise gave her a crash course on how to do it without compromising the evidence. After a few checks by Daniel, it was confirmed Asiah was doing her part very well.

When Daniel said the young black woman would have to die, it only confirmed what Denise had already figured out. With the least bit of pressure, Asiah would have broken. And depending on when, it could be catastrophic for Denise. So, she volunteered and she'd followed through. It just gave her a new insight into some of the decisions Daniel made on a daily basis. Who could live and who had to die? How far could you trust people? And what could you trust them with?

Denise wasn't sure she could make those decisions on the fly, but with enough thought, she would do whatever had to be done to live a normal life again. Speaking of normal, the officer turned onto her street, and she saw her home for the first time in over a year.

She was thinking of her welcome home soak in her huge tub when she spied a vehicle parked in her driveway. Her first thought was the WRA was waiting for her. After a calming breath, she realized how ridicules that thought was. They were more likely to blow up the car than to be sitting in the driveway patiently waiting for her to come home.

Her next thought was the media. As they got closer, she realized that her second thought was exactly right, but not in the way she assumed. She squealed as she recognized the red Toyota Supra with black trim that belonged to one of her best friends in the world.

When they turned in, Denise was scrambling for her door handle as a short, gorgeous, brown skinned woman climbed out of her car. They both paused as Denise heard the officer yell, "Hey! Who are you and what business do you have here?"

Denise and her friend ignored the officer as they rushed into each other's arms with tears flowing down their faces. They stood holding each other and crying for five minutes before they pulled apart.

Her hands stroking her friends long, silky, black hair, Denise said, "You're still as glamorous as ever."

Ashley Kirt said, "Well, I'm sorry girl, but you look like shit!"

They wrapped their arms around each other and made their way to the house. The officer said, "Hold on, Ms. McCarthy. I need to do a walk through before you can go in."

The wait was short as the one story, two-bedroom home was big and airy with not many spots to hide. After the officer gave the all clear, she went back to her SUV to guard the house. Denise and Ashley went inside to catch up.

True to his word, her house was immaculate. Whoever Daniel had keeping up with their homes deserved an award. No dust, no dirt, and, although the fridge was empty, the cabinets were full with non-perishables. Ashley was in the master bath running Denise her bath water, so she used the time to eat a couple of snacks.

The hot water felt divine when she finally sunk her tired body in up to her neck. Ashley had lit scented candles to go along with the scented water. After a while, all this caused Denise to drift off to sleep.

The next morning, Denise was awakened by her doorbell ringing. She had no memory of getting out of the tub, but she guessed Ashley had accomplished that feat. She was still naked, so she grabbed the robe hanging on her bathroom door. She made her way to the front door to see who had come to visit.

Ashley must have had to get to work because the house was empty. This made Denise wish she had a gun to keep her company. Daniel had given her extensive training in all types of firearms, to the point where she felt bereft without one.

She glanced out the front door's window and saw she didn't need a gun after all. It was the female cop from last night and Denise wondered how long the woman had been on shift.

Denise opened the door and the officer said, "Good morning, Ms. McCarthy. I'm sorry for bothering you, but they asked me to bring you back to the station. I guess with the deaths yesterday, they have a few more questions."

"Okay," said Denise. "I'll be ready in a few minutes." 20 minutes later, they were back at the Police Station. Except this time, Denise was escorted to one of the higher up floors.

Denise was led to an office with windows overlooking downtown Raleigh. A nice female detective stood up from behind her desk and offered Denise a seat. The detective apologized, but asked her to once again give a detailed account on what she went through over the past year. She took a fortifying breath, and launched into her story.

She was about halfway through the tale when the detective stood up and walked to the floor to ceiling windows. With her back turned, she said, "How about let's cut the bullshit and you tell me who you're working for?"

"Excuse me?" a crying Denise asked her.

The detective spun around and screamed, "You're a lying bitch! Tell me who you're working for or so help me God!" The woman pulled her sidearm and cocked back the slide.

"I don't work for anyone," Denise calmly explained. "I'm the victim here, remember?"

"Victim my ass." Then a nasty grin split her face. "Oh! I see. You thought you could outsmart the WRA? You thought you and your band of idiots could best the world's premier Intelligence Agency?"

Denise could do nothing except play dumb. "I don't know what you're talking about, Ma'am. That man has had me in a cage, using me for his personal pleasure for over a year. I'm not trying to outsmart anyone!"

The detective tapped the barrel of her gun on the desktop. She laughed and said, "Daniel is good. Really good. Whenever you can convince a pawn she's really part of the team, you're a mastermind. A supreme manipulator."

The woman obviously knew what was going on, so Denise prepared her mind and body to take the woman down. All she needed was one opening and the detective would be dead. With the other cop being the one who killed the governor, it would be easy to convince everyone that the woman had tried to kill her.

The detective went on. "Sacrifice is one of the mainstays of the intelligence community. You, my beautiful pawn, have been set up to be sacrificed to protect the king. You, Asiah, the governor, all of you are pawns in this deadly game we call life. And just like pawns, after you are no longer useful, you die."

The jig was up. There was no more use trying to continue playing ignorant. "So, what is it that you want?" asked Denise.

The woman laughed again and said, "Nothing, Denise. I don't want anything from you. But I do need one thing." After a pause, Denise gestured for her to continue. "I need you to fulfill your destiny as a pawn."

When the woman raised the gun, Denise threw her hand up and yelled, "Wait!" But it was already too late. Two bullets penetrated her upper torso, damaging her heart and lungs beyond repair. Denise toppled out of the chair and was already dying as the detective walked over to her.

She said, "Don't worry, sweetie. Walt, Ann, Alisha, and Gabby, will soon join you. After all, they're pawns just like you." The woman pointed the gun at her head, but Denise never heard or felt the bullet that ended her. She just drifted away to nothingness.

Chapter 7

Reggie hung up the phone and shouted, "Yes!" as he finally had something to cheer about. One of the other Raleigh PD assets had just told him the good news about the governor's untimely death.

Ghost had always been one of their best for wet work, but people held it against him that he'd lost to Daniel. Seeing as Daniel continued to best all of them, Reggie wouldn't hold it against the stealth operative.

On a tight schedule, Ghost had put together a marvelous plan. To find a cop who had mental health issues already, and then push him over the edge. It was genius and damn near foolproof. Too bad the Agency didn't have the extra money. Reggie would love to give the man a bonus for such good work.

Feeling like they all could use some good news, he reached for his phone to call his mother. The phone rang as soon as he touched it, showing the number of the compounds head of security.

"No bad news, Mike. I am in too good of a mood."

"Only you could celebrate the killing of your most profitable asset," said the voice on the other end of the call.

Reggie jerked out of the chair and looked at the display again to make sure he had seen the number right. "Who the fuck is this, and where is Mike?" Reggie was about to press the panic button to lockdown the facility when something about the voice caused him to stop.

"Mike is probably still in his office eating doughnuts, like always. But, who I am is a whole nother matter."

"Well, this is gonna be a quick conversation if you don't tell me something," said Reggie. Now that his heart was calming down, he eased his muscular, suit clad body back down in his chair. He couldn't quite put his finger on it, but since all the calls were recorded, he would analyze the voice later.

"All of my research on you tells me you're a very intelligent man, Reggie. So, I'm trying to figure out how you've let the WRA be run into the ground?"

"What concern of it is yours?" Reggie asked the man. "I don't know you, so why do you care about my Agency?" Something about the man's voice was familiar, but he couldn't catch why he felt that way.

"Let's just say I have a vested interest in whether or not the WRA succeeds," said the man. "Anyway, as long as the traitor is in your midst, failure will continue to plague you. Get rid of the cancer and you might be able to solve your problems."

"Traitor? Cancer?" asked Reggie in confusion. "Listen man, I don't know who you are, or why you're fucking with me. I don't play these types of games. So, either tell me what you're talking about, in plain English, or you can kiss my ass!"

A few seconds of silence, and then, "Reggie, this is something you have to figure out on your own. Do your research. Talk to your family. Figure out why you keep being left out of important decisions."

"I run this company!" shouted Reggie. "No decisions are made without my approval!"

"If that's true, all hope is lost for the WRA," he said softly. "The one who could give you all the answers was executed. Branded as a traitor and shot down like a dog. Do your due diligence and maybe we'll talk again."

"Wait! You mean Paul? Hello? Hey!" but the voice was gone. Reggie laid down his phone and stared at the wall opposite him. No one had been told about Paul's execution.

Everyone had been told he was somewhere deep undercover. In a business where agents went missing for years, no one questioned the explanation.

He snatched his phone up and called Mike who said nothing was going on and the compound was locked up tight. To hack into one of the WRA phones was difficult to say the least. But the man had also known about Mike always eating doughnuts.

No one but WRA personnel knew the make up of their headquarters. So, either the man had been inside before, or someone had fed him that information. Maybe that's why the man had brought up Paul's death. Paul had been the traitor after all.

Reggie picked up his phone again to call his mother, but stopped to consider the possibilities. He wasn't stupid. He knew exactly who the caller was implying was the real traitor. It was just hard for him to see it as truth.

Finally, he dialed the number of someone who had to know more about the situation than he did. Maybe this person would be willing to talk if he made sure to express his interest in hearing the truth. After about 10 rings, the call was answered and Reggie got the reception he had expected to get all along.

• •

"Boy, if you don't answer that phone, I swear I will kill you in your sleep," Alisha snapped.

Daniel counted the first 10 rings and knew the caller wasn't gonna give up. He glanced at the display and noticed the time, 5:05pm, and the number, which caused him to groan in dismay.

"Daniel! I'm not playing with you. I'm trying to sleep." She swung a backhand, connecting hard with his stomach.

"Damn Alisha! Alright," he said, picking up the phone. "What the hell do you want? You can't tell when someone doesn't want to speak to you?"

Reggie chuckled and said, "If you weren't in your lab cooking up your next evil plot all night, you wouldn't be so tired."

"Fuck you," Daniel muttered to his oldest brother. "And if you're calling about me releasing the money, I gave ya'll the opportunity before and you blew it."

"Don't bullshit me, Turtle boy. You knew what we were planning, so you never intended to give us anything."

Daniel actually barked a laugh at Reggie's joke about him using the name Manny, which had been the name of their pet turtle growing up. "Man, you're just jealous you never thought to use the name. Anyway, I'm keeping Alisha up right now. What do you want?"

"Listen little bro, I really need to speak with you. I got a call from some mysterious guy a little bit ago. He was making some wild accusations against the family that I don't like."

"What kind of accusations?" asked Daniel. "I have to tell you, you guys are so corrupt, whatever he accused is probably dead on." Alisha swung at him again, so he got up and walked into the bathroom, shutting the door so she could sleep.

"Normally, I'd agree with you. But I need to see you face to face so I can ask you some serious questions."

Daniel greeted this request with silence, so Reggie continued. "I swear on the Burke name that I'll come alone. You can bring whoever you want, but this is serious. The man knew about our HQ, and he knew about Mom executing Paul."

The caller and the information revealed were nothing new to Daniel, it was all part of his plan. But Reggie calling him for answers was actually a surprise. Fuck it, thought Daniel. He would take his team out and use this as a training exercise.

He opened the bathroom door and pressed the mute button. "Alisha! Go get everyone into the War Room. Something important just came up."

His Queen jumped out the bed and grabbed her phone without complaint. Daniel watched her naked body moving across the room before he sighed and shut the bathroom door again.

He unmuted the phone and said, "Okay, I'll meet you. But I won't tell you the place until the last minute. That's more to keep the idiot soldiers you like to use alive. I'll tell you now; If anyone but you show up, I'm shooting first and damn the questions."

"You know my word is good, but I wouldn't expect anything less. What do you want me to do?" asked Reggie.

"Just drive this way and, by the time you're close, I'll give you the meeting spot. I'll have a satellite on you the whole way, so don't try anything."

Reggie hung up and Daniel entered his bedroom. Alisha had to have used the bathroom down the hall, because she was already gone. He took a quick shower, dressed, and headed for the elevator. When he got to the War Room, the first thing he asked is, "How is Denise?"

Alisha said, "I was waiting for you so I can tell everyone at the same time." Walt, Ann, and Alisha were all sitting in front of the big monitor with a live feed of Denise's house front and center.

"So, she arrived home at 12:20pm to a woman sitting in her driveway. I ran facial recognition and it came back to a 36-year-old news anchor named Ashley Kirt."

Walt interrupted. "Yeah, we all know her. That's the woman who owns the house we set the trap for old Manny here. But he turned the tables on us like the amateurs we were. Anyway, that's Denise's best friend."

"Alright," continued Alisha. "So, the cop has been sitting outside since doing her initial walk-through. But, before I went to sleep, it looked like she was doing a round every 20 minutes or so. Heat signatures right now show one person in the tub, more than likely Denise, and the other person laying on the master bed, which I assume is Ashley waiting on her."

"Good," said Daniel. "For the time being, she should be safe. But now, I have another OP we need to prepare for." He gave them a quick rundown on the call with his brother. Then he explained what each of them would do to make this meeting a success.

"Everybody understand?" When everyone said yes, Daniel excused Walt and Ann to go get their gear and get to their assigned positions.

Alisha said after they were gone, "If this is a set up, they won't be enough. Are you gonna call him in to watch your back?"

Daniel walked over and pulled her out of her chair and spent a few minutes luxuriating in her warmth. He kissed her soft, pink lips and ran his hands all over her beautiful body. He pulled back and continued to stare into her eyes.

Then he said, "Look behind you." She did and gasped when she saw the man standing 10 feet behind her.

The older man smiled and said, "You got good taste boy. If I was a little younger, I'd fight you for her."

Alisha laughed and greeted him with a fond hug and kiss. "You know I'm learning fast. You keep sneaking up on me like that, you can't hold me accountable for my reflexes." They playfully squared up and traded a few light blows.

Daniel shook his head at their antics and then said, "Children, we do have an OP going on right now." They both turned and gave him mock salutes, causing him to laugh. He sobered up and said, "I don't think he'll try anything, but if he does, we'll need to take him down fast. He really is a beast. Best hand to hand combat artist I've ever seen."

The old man nodded and said, "Alisha, don't worry. I'll be this boys shadow until the day I die."

Daniel gave the man a more serious salute and then turned to Alisha. "I'll need you to keep your eyes on us and Denise. Just make sure our six is clear. We'll have the earpieces in, so you'll hear everything going on. If you see anything, just say it and we're out of there. Got it?"

She nodded and he kissed her one more time before addressing the old man. "You take all your medications and vitamins? I'll need you at your best."

"My best is the only level I operate at. You just make sure you can keep up. Just know, if you go down, I'm taking your house and your girl for my own."

Chapter 8

About 30 minutes after Daniel received the phone call from Reggie, Denise was yanked from her nightmare just as the detective's last shot would have killed her. The dream had felt so real. Her chest actually ached where the two bullets had entered. She'd felt like she was alright with the outcome of the past 12 hours. Obviously, her subconscious felt differently.

She was thrashing and sputtering, trying to dispel the swallowed water while warm arms held her out of the water. "It's okay, Denise. It was just a nightmare. Breathe for me, baby girl, just breathe." Ashley was patting her back and murmuring softly, trying to coax Denise back into real life.

"I'm okay, Ashley. I'm okay," said Denise after all the water was gone from her lungs. It was only then she turned to her friend and saw the tears pouring out of her eyes. "Hey! Sweetie, I'm good. It was just a nightmare."

"I know, but knowing you've been living a real-life nightmare for the past 14 months, breaks my heart. I prayed for you every night." Ashley wrapped her in her arms once again and they just held each other until Ashley noticed her shivering.

"Oh, God!" moaned Ashley. "I'm in here crying like a baby while you're freezing." She grabbed a heated towel from the shelf and wrapped Denise's naked body when she stood up. Ashley stared at the bruises she had gotten from a spar with Ann, then turned her head away to cry some more.

Denise felt like shit for deceiving her friend, but there was no way she could tell her the truth. Denise would be putting lives on the line that she had no right to risk. So, she went to her closet and dressed to make them both feel comfortable.

Trying to distract her, Denise said, "So, how has work been going?" Denise always watched her friend's 6:00pm news slot. So, even though she asked, she knew Ashley's career was doing great.

"You know, work is work. I hate that I can't go out and find stories myself, because sometimes the material I present is so lame." That topic seemed to cheer Ashley up as they bantered back and forth about how hard it was to find good news.

"Everything is so negative and doom-and-gloomish. I just wish for one day out of the week, I can do a whole show with nothing but positive material."

Denise snorted. "Well, good luck with that. Your ratings would fall and the network would fire your ass. No one wants to hear good, positive information."

Denise looked at her phone, which was sitting on the nightstand where one of Daniel's people had to have placed it, and glanced up at Ashley in alarm. "Oh Shit! It's almost 6:00. You're gonna be late for the broadcast."

Ashley smiled. "You thought I was gonna leave you?" she asked shaking her head. "I called out this morning as soon as I saw that you'd been found. I'm by your side until I'm convinced, you're really okay."

Both of their eyes teared up, but Ashley shook her head and said, "Enough of this emotional stuff. I'm hungry as hell. Please tell me there's food in this house."

"Nothing but canned goods and snacks," Denise said sadly.

"Well baby girl, let me see what I can put together," said Ashley. "Why don't you lay down until it's done and I'll come get you. You look exhausted, sweetie."

"Sounds like a plan. After a quick nap, I'll be good as new." The women embraced once more and then Denise crawled under the covers. She knew that she had slept off and on because she kept having dreams about the young girl, Asiah Winecoff.

She woke up this last time and glanced out the window to find it dark outside. She almost rolled over and went back to sleep, but her grumbling stomach wouldn't let her. So, she got up, took care of her hygiene, and used the bathroom before making her way to the kitchen.

Frowning, she saw that no food had been prepared and Ashley was nowhere in sight. This wake up was similar to her nightmare, but this time there was no doubt she was awake. She even pinched herself to be sure.

She walked to the guest bedroom and looked in, but it didn't look disturbed at all. Denise was on her way over to the living room when she heard two car doors close outside. Walking over to the window, she spied Ashley talking to her protection officer.

Smiling, she went and opened the door, about to yell at Ashley not to let the food in the Chic-Fil-A bags get cold. Before she could make a sound, she saw three people advancing from across the street where an SUV sat with its doors open. Too late, she saw that all of them had guns.

"Get down!" she yelled, trying to warn the two women of the coming danger. *Bock! Bock! Bock! Pop! Pop!* was all she heard as she ducked down to avoid the bullets spraying the front of the house.

She realized that she was no help to either woman without a weapon, so she ran back to her room to grab her phone. Denise was already crying and dialing as she raced back to the front, just in time to see the vehicle pulling away.

When the operator picked up, she yelled, "My friend and a cop have just been gunned down in front of my home! Send two ambulances, now!"

Denise was only half listening as she sprinted over to find the cop dead, but Ashley was still hanging on. "Ashley! It's gonna be okay. I'm so sorry. Just hold on, help is coming."

The man on the phone was asking questions, but Denise could already hear the sirens getting close. So, she just ignored him.

"Ashley, just hold on sweetie. This is all my fault. No! Keep your eyes open!" she screamed when Ashley started to lose consciousness.

Denise was staring into her friend's eyes when the ambulance rounded the corner to her block. At the same time, Ashley took one last strangled breath and went still as Denise cried and begged for her forgiveness.

. . . .

"Alisha, you see any heat signatures?" Daniel and Walt were standing inside the tree line, staring at Reggie as he stood beside the lake.

"Nothing other than our assets," Alisha replied from the War Room. "As far as I can see, he kept his word and came alone."

The meeting spot picked by Daniel was a park that the family used to go fishing at near the Concord-Charlotte border. There was only one stand of trees in the more than 50-acre park, and Daniel and Walt were standing in it. The rest of the area was either lakes for fishing, or courts and fields for sports.

"Run through the spectrum just to make sure we won't have any surprises," he ordered her.

After a silent 30 seconds, Alisha said, "Nothing. Everything is clear."

"Ann? Are you ready to go?" Daniel asked.

"On target and awaiting orders," she replied.

"I know I don't have to say this but, if something goes wrong, our lives might depend on how fast you react. So, don't hesitate."

Ann said, "Daniel, trust me. I got you."

Daniel glanced over at Walt and nodded. They both stepped out of the woods in total darkness, dressed in black body armor that would stop any bullet known to man.

Reggie spotted them instantly and tuned to await their arrival. Daniel said, "Alisha, scan for frequencies so we can see who he's in contact with."

Daniel and Walt stopped about six feet from him and noticed he was also wearing body armor. Reggie shrugged and said, "Last time I saw you, you did shoot me."

Daniel chuckled as Alisha said, "Nothing. No frequencies in use other than ours."

"What? You thought I was gonna let you close enough to attack me?" Daniel asked Reggie. "Plus, it was only a knockout bullet."

Reggie nodded and turned to Walt. "Mr. Rogers. Where is your better half? And I don't mean Denise, I know where she is."

Walt shrugged and said, "She's around."

Reggie flashed brilliant teeth and then turned back to Daniel with a serious expression. "What the hell is really going on at the WRA? Why are you so intent on destroying our legacy?"

"Nothing would make me happier than to see the WRA restored back to its glory days. Unfortunately, the corruption has spread too far and too high."

"You see, that's the part I don't understand," confessed Reggie. "Where is this so-called corruption? We're doing the same things now that were done from the beginning."

Daniel shook his head. "How are we redeeming the world by being bigger drug dealers than the cartels? What kind of legacy is it to give up legitimate government contracts just to become hired hitmen? And please explain to me how an Agency being paid on a case by case basis amasses $600 Billion?"

"Listen Daniel, before this war with you started, we were expanding so fast that we needed money to keep pace. The jobs were getting bigger and farther away. We weren't just training soldiers anymore, we were asked to provide protection for whole governing bodies. A lot of these places couldn't afford us long term, but if we pulled out, mass slaughters would have taken place. We needed fast money to pay for this, so we did what we had to do."

"I understand that Reg," he conceded. "But the systematic destruction of our own people to protect foreign land is unforgivable. But that's not the main problem of the WRA."

"That's why I'm here. The mystery caller from earlier hinted at Mom being some kind of evil behind the scenes mastermind. I'm involved in every operation the WRA participates in. Whoever he is, he couldn't be farther from the truth."

Daniel barked a laugh. "So, you know about the oil theft ring in the Middle East? And the professional hit squad operating in China? Oh, I know. You're the link in the WRA that's providing guns to the Cartels and helping them ship their drugs into the U.S."

"But that's what I'm telling you, Daniel. None of that is going on. If it was, I'd know about it."

"All of that is going on and more," he told his brother with sadness. "And worse, much worse that I don't have time to talk about. But coming from me, you won't believe. So, I'll leave that information for someone else to tell you."

"What you're saying doesn't even make sense. If we had all that going on, we would have money to pay our assets. Right now, we are paying out of our own pockets."

"Follow that train of thought and you might find the truth. You ever stop to think why you seem to be the only one panicking about the lost money. You're a Burke, it's time you start acting like one and stop taking things at face value. You need...."

"Oh shit! Daniel, Denise is being hit right now." Alisha's voice clearly revealed how bad the situation was.

Daniel pulled his gun and pointed it right at Reggie's face. "Everyone, go. Just remember, none of you can be seen. Alisha, get one of the assets moving who can get there faster."

Daniel's gun hand was rock steady as Walt took off running towards the woods. He said, "Brilliant strategy, but I bet they weren't supposed to hit while you were still here."

Reggie's hands had spread away from his body as soon as Daniel pulled the gun. "I have no idea what you're talking about. I'm here on my own. I'm not running any ops right now."

"Well, whoever knew you were coming used the opportunity to hit Denise. Either way, it's gonna fall on you."

"Daniel, I swear it's not us. Denise can't hurt us. They were talking about a truce with you before I left. And nobody knew I was coming to meet you."

"Alisha? Status."

"It's too dark Daniel, I can't see much. I backed up the video feed and it looks like three guys with guns got out of a vehicle and opened fire on the cop and Ashley. Denise was at the front door when the shots were fired. It looks like she's okay because she's still moving around right now. Hold on, I'll patch her 911 call to you."

He listened to the call, but he was already doubting the WRA had anything to do with this. It was too sloppy and the men left before finishing the job. Not the WRA way.

"Alright, where's the asset?"

"Already on scene, but staying out of sight. Asset says the area is clear and Denise is now inside talking to police."

"Okay. I'll be on my way in a few. If anything changes let me know." He switched frequency's and said, "Hold him. If he moves in the next ten minutes, light him up."

A red dot appeared on Reggie's hand and tracked up his body so he knew the dot was now on his head. "As long as you were not involved, you can leave in ten minutes. If I find out you were the diversion for this attack, I'll make sure I'm the last face you see before you die."

Daniel backed away before he put his gun away and then turned and sprinted for the woods. Mentally, he kicked himself because he knew the deaths from tonight were on his head. A sequence of events always leads to a consequence. Many times, we don't control whether that consequence is good or bad.

Chapter 9

While Denise had been having a nightmare about dying, and Daniel had been sleeping contently beside his fiancé, another woman had been having the time of her life.

"Oh yes baby! Just like that! Oh God! Pull my hair Daddy!" It was the middle of the day and the house was full of people, but this woman only cared about getting hers.

"Shit baby, you feel so good!" the man moaned in her ear. "Tell daddy what to do."

"Make me cum baby! Make me cum!" she demanded. The man pushed her flat on her stomach, pulled her long jet-black hair until she was looking at the ceiling, and then started jackhammering into her.

"Oh God! Oh shit! I'm comingggg baby!" the woman screamed. The pleasure was so intense, she ripped the sheets off the bed and continued to scream as the man went on pounding into her through her orgasm. Her eyes rolled back as he went harder and faster than before. Finally, she convulsed, causing the man to give a hoarse cry before emptying himself inside her.

Naked, sweaty, and satisfied for the time being, they laid as they were until they caught their breath. Finally, the woman said, "Terrell, I need some water."

He said, "Bring me a Coke when you come back." He rolled off of her and reached for his phone.

She sucked her teeth. "You not gonna get it for me?"

"Girl, you better get your thirsty ass up and get your own water." She stood up and slipped into a t-shirt and boy shorts before starting towards the door. "And don't forget my Coke!"

She waved him off and then opened the door to the living room. A few months ago, after the verbal display she just put on, she would have stayed in the room for the rest of the day out of embarrassment. Now, she stepped out into the room with eight men and three women, still sweaty, with Terrell's come leaking down her legs.

As usual, Javon was sitting on the couch to the left where she'd have to pass him to get to the kitchen. "Damn Candace, you sexy as hell. Why I couldn't have been so lucky to find you first?"

"Boy please! What I look like being with a worker?" He was cute but she didn't do the hired help, at least not when it didn't benefit her. "When you become a boss and get your money up, then come holla at me."

She strutted through the men and women that made up Terrell's crew with her head held high. She absorbed the lustful looks from the men and ignored the envious looks of the women. She knew the thin T-shirt mixed with her sweat made it plain and clear that her D cup breast were not hindered by a bra. And the bikini cut boy shorts made her 42 inch, perfectly shaped ass dance to whatever beat was in their heads. Yes, she was a bad bitch and she knew it.

The former Lieutenant, Candace Shada Price, was once again at the top of her game. She entered the kitchen and grabbed a bottle of water and a Coke and made her way back to the bedroom.

After taking a plea deal and serving one year in prison for being a prison prostitute, she had gotten out and moved to Raleigh where she'd been incarcerated. She'd used some of the money the PGK left her to have all her corrective surgeries and now she was better than ever.

The whole time she was on the inside, she'd worked out and listened to the other ladies on who was who and what was what in the Raleigh area. All she kept hearing about was this big time shot caller named Terrell 'Big Zoe' Rilley.

A couple of her friends had gotten cell phones and, whenever she got a chance to use one, she would research the man and the area, which lead to here formulating a plan.

He was always photographed in this one club in Durham. So, after she was healed up, she got a job working there and the rest was history. She played the role she knew he would respond to, now she had him wrapped around her little finger.

"Damn girl, just let me touch it one time to see if it's as soft as it looks." Javon was damn near drooling looking at her long toned legs and phat ass.

She looked at him and knew he very well might be the boss one day. She turned away from him but stood in between his out-stretched legs. Eyeing the other people in the room, she said, "Go ahead and get a feel with ya thirsty ass!"

He ran his hands up the back of her legs starting at her calves and ending with two handfuls of soft, but firm, ass cheeks. She allowed him to mold and play for a few seconds as he moaned, before she pushed his hands away and walked back into the bedroom.

"Damn! Did you have to go to the well for the water? I'm thirsty as hell." With his dark skin tone, and long dreads, Big Zoe thought he was God's gift to women. As long as he was who he was, and did for her whatever she wanted, she would stay glued to his side.

She tossed him his Coke and said, "I'm going to take a shower. Somebody made a mess in me."

"Hell yeah I did! And mine better be the only mess getting made inside you."

"Boy bye! All them hoes you got. I know if you ever burn me, Imma kill your ass."

"Candy, you better go head with that bullshit. I told you I aint with no hoes." He was fussing, but his eyes never left his phone. She flipped him off and went to take her shower.

Ever since she was a little girl, she'd been told how beautiful she was. Because of that, she couldn't pass a mirror without stopping to inspect herself. While in prison, she avoided them at all cost so she wouldn't have to see what the Prison Guard Killer had done to her. Now that she was fixed, she loved to admire the view.

She turned the water on and stripped naked but stayed in front of her reflection. At 36 years old, she was still curvy and firm where it mattered. Her 6-foot, light skinned body was well proportioned with her 42-inch hips, and her 30-inch waist. Her natural green eyes, and pink lips, coupled with her high cheekbones and long lashes, made her the baddest chick in any room she entered.

At 18 she'd joined the Army and made it out with an honorable discharge after four years. After growing up poor in Wilmington N.C., the Military gave her purpose. When she got out, she went back home, but was lost without the structure she was used to. When she saw the ads for correctional officers, she thought she had found the answer to her problems.

But the system was so corrupt and rifted with illegal activities, it soon swept her up in it as well. She became a prison prostitute and amassed over $2 Million during her ten-year career.

Then, the murdering bastard had come and destroyed her life. Well, fuck him. Big Zoe was worth 10's of millions and she was slowly gathering her wealth again.

She jumped in the shower and rinsed the residue of sex off her body. It wouldn't be long he'd have her yelling on the bed again if he stayed home, but most nights he would take a ride to one of his clubs or restaurants to make sure everything was good.

That's what made him so attractive to her. He was the biggest drug dealer in North Carolina, but he never touched drugs. By the time the money touched his hands, it had been washed more times than a prostitute's panties. The FED's could kick in the door right now and all they'd find was a little bit of weed. Terrell was a real boss and she was good being a boss's bitch.

She dried off, lotioned up, and walked back into the bedroom naked. Terrell eyed her from the bed as she threw on a pair of yoga pants and a sports bra. He liked to rip clothes off of her, so she never wore expensive clothes around the house.

"Baby, I think I'm staying in tonight." He told her. "Why don't you fry up some chicken and maybe some mac and cheese?"

"Alright, Zoe. Is everybody staying or are they going over to the big house?" For some reason, Zoe loved staying in this small 3-bedroom home in Durham. He had a 20-room mansion in Raleigh where, most nights, his crew stayed.

"They'll be here until late tonight, so go ahead and cook for everybody. Anything they don't eat tonight, they'll kill it by tomorrow anyway."

She turned to go and he barked, "Hey!" She turned back around and he said, "Can I at least get a kiss?" She smiled and jumped on the bed where they spent the next few minutes making out. Finally, he slapped her ass making it jiggle before saying, "Alright babe, now feed your King."

She jumped up and walked out the door where she saw a picture on the big screen that stopped her cold. The sound was muted, but she yelled, "Turn that up, now!" Someone found the remote and unmuted the TV.

"…. has been found after being held captive for the last 14 months right here in Raleigh. We don't yet know why Garvin Johnson did this horrendous thing, but in a bizarre twist, the governor and the witness have both died while in police custody. We're still gathering information, but Denise McCarthy was release earlier today and is now resting and recovering with loved ones."

"ZOE! Get in here, now!" Candace screamed. They were showing the earlier footage of Denise leaving the Police Station when Zoe ran into the living room, in boxers, waving his gun around.

"What happened? What's going on?" he asked, looking for the threat.

Candace pointed at the TV and said, "That's her! That's the bitch that embarrassed me and got me locked up on national television."

Zoe glanced from her to the TV and back again. "That's what you up in here yelling about? What the fuck is wrong with you? I could have killed a motherfucker and you yelling over the TV?"

"This aint about no fucking TV, Zoe. I owe that bitch and I want her dead!"

Zoe looked around at all his people who were quietly watching them. He started laughing which caused the domino effect of everyone laughing. She looked at everyone and Javon was the only one not laughing.

Finally, Zoe asked, "And you think I'm putting my crew on the line for some petty beef? You crazy as hell." Still laughing, he walked back into the bedroom.

Fuming now, she followed him in and slammed the door behind them. "So that's what I am to you? A fucking joke? That woman ruined my life! And you aint gonna do shit about it?"

"Denise McCarthy is a reporter!" Zoe roared, showing some anger. "She was doing her fucking job. You want me to risk an empire, a fucking kingdom over some bullshit from the past? You need to woman up and let that shit go!"

"How can you... ?"

"This discussion is over! Leave the bitch in the past where she belongs. I'm not risking everything I worked for over no petty ass revenge of yours." Like a king who had given a decree, he said, "And what the fuck happened to my chicken? I'm hungry as shit, and you stressing me about some bullshit!" He laid back on the bed and picked up his phone, effectively dismissing her.

Candace was so mad, tears started leaking from her eyes. Head down to hide her face, she calmly left the bedroom and ignored the amused looks as she made her way to the kitchen. She'd been cooking for about ten minutes when she became aware of a presence at the door.

"You're too beautiful to be up in here crying and shit. If you were mine, your wish would be my command," Javon said.

"Look, Javon...." she started, about to curse him out before she thought about it. With tears on her face, she looked up with her most vulnerable expression. "That woman took my life from me. She made me the laughing stock of the whole world. For him to not do anything about it, I just don't understand. I thought he loved me," she said, allowing her voice to break.

He rushed over and wrapped her in his arms. "It's okay, Candy. Maybe he'll come to his senses and do what any other man in his position is supposed to do."

She felt him becoming aroused from holding her soft body against his muscular one. Breathing into his neck, she said, "And what is he supposed to do?"

Lightly, he trembled and feathered his hands over her ass. "Any damn thing you want him to."

Softly, she said, "Javon? Will you do it for me?" He kept his hands moving over her curves, but didn't answer her. She reached between their bodies and gripped his manhood through his pants. "I can make it worth your while. And Zoe never has to know what you did for me." She kissed his neck and whispered, "Or what I do for you."

She unzipped his pants and freed his manhood right there in the kitchen. He moaned softly as she firmly stroked him. When he started to shutter, she grabbed a towel and finished him off while he convulsed and squeezed her ass tighter.

She cleaned him up and tucked him back in while brushing light kisses on his neck and jaw. When he regained his breath and his senses, at least part of them, he only asked one question: "You know where she lives?"

Chapter 10

Denise felt horrible that so many lives had changed just because she'd resurfaced into the world. She'd been told that Ashley was in surgery and it looked like she was gonna pull through. Ashley had been hit four times, but the only serious one had been to her chest and it had collapsed one of her lungs.

Even if Ashley did make a full recovery, the governor, Asiah Winecoff, and Officer Brittney Clark would never get the chance. And all of their families were now suffering also. No matter how she looked at it, her return had cause nothing but pain and turmoil.

"Ms. McCarthy? Did you hear my question?"

She snapped back to the present and the three detectives sitting across from her in her living room. She told the older white man, "No sir, I'm sorry. Can you repeat the question?"

The detective who'd been asking the questions was bracketed by a young black woman wearing a no-nonsense black pants suit to his right, and a young white man wearing khakis and a sweater to his left. Neither of the younger detectives had spoken since the initial introductions, but they were writing down every word she said.

"I asked if you had gotten a good look at any of the shooters?" This was probably the third time he'd asked the same question just in different ways.

"Listen," said Denise, showing some of her agitation. "I told you I didn't see any of them. It was too far away and it was too dark. If they hadn't left the dome light on in the SUV, I wouldn't have seen the vehicle either."

"But you're sure it was a dark colored SUV?"

"As I've stated three times before, yes I'm sure it was a dark colored SUV. With the interior light on, I made out three people coming towards my house with guns in their hands. Another person was still in the vehicle sitting in the driver's seat."

"Black, white? Men, women? Color of clothes? Height, weight? Nothing else?" asked the detective.

Denise dropped her head into her hands. She looked up again and said, "It was dark. Now I've been patient and I've given you everything I can remember. I need to get to the hospital so I can be with my friend. Can we wrap this up?"

"Just a few more…." The detective paused as the front door opened and a man wearing jeans and a windbreaker stepped inside. He eyed everyone sitting on the leather couches before his eyes zeroed in on Denise.

Still staring at her, he said, "You three can leave. I'll expect detailed reports at my office in the morning containing everything you've learned. Other than that, you won't be needed. The SBI is taking over this case."

All three stood up without another word and exited, leaving Denise alone with a visibly angry Cpt. William Graham.

"Do you remember who I am, Ms. McCarthy?" he asked, making his way over to the couch the detectives had just vacated.

"Yes," she answered. "You're Walt's friend."

"Ha!" he barked. "I think friend is a stretch. Boss is more like it. Anyway, you want to tell me what's going on here?"

"Well, like I told your colleagues, I didn't see much…."

"No Denise," he interrupted. "I'm not asking for any of the bullshit you've been spreading among the common folk. I'm talking about the truth of what's going on."

"I'm not sure I understand. I'm telling you what hap…."

"Denise, stop! Just stop!" he said standing up. "Maybe I should fill you in on a few things so you'll understand I'm more in the loop than you think." He paused and sat back down before continuing.

"14 months ago, I got a call from Walt telling me that him, you, and Ann, were together and doing something with the PGK. I've been getting updates at least once a month on all of your statuses. So, I know the story with the governor is bullshit. Then the governor and Ms. Winecoff are killed while at the station, but you make it out."

"Mr. Graham, I…"

"No, no, no Denise. Let me finish. Then some people show up and kill another officer and shoots your friend and once again you sit here unharmed. So, now you're gonna tell me what the fuck is going on or I'm taking your ass to jail!" he yelled. Someone started to open the front door, but he yelled, "Close that fucking door!" and the door softly eased shut.

Denise stared the man in his eyes and laughed. A full on, leg slapping, short of breath, laugh. When she could finally speak, she said, "When you first met me, that little display would have scared the shit out of me. I probably would have cried and bared my soul to you." With a sneer, she said, "But Captain, that scared little girl is gone. I've been exposed to real killers. People who myths are made about. So, if you think you can intimidate me, look at my face. Do I look intimidated?"

They stared at each other for a minute before he whispered, "What did he do to you?"

He was talking to himself, but Denise decided to answer anyway. "He let me see the potential inside of me. And he trained me on how to use it to the best of my abilities. So, if you think taking me to jail is the answer, you're welcome to try."

Will's hand moved closer to his gun. Denise said, "You're in a no-win situation here, Will. If you pull that gun, you're gonna have to use it. Seeing as you made a point to get me alone, and this after a cop has just killed the governor, you'll have an uphill battle trying to prove you didn't murder me in cold blood. Not to mention, who'll be coming after you...."

He jerked the gun from his holster and took a huge side step to get out of her range. "Did you forget, there are 20 cops on the other side of that door?" He pulled his cellphone out and said, "All I have to do is call anyone of them and off to jail you go."

Using one finger, he pulled out a pair of cuffs. "Now put these on and start walking towards the front door before I take my chances and blow your fucking head off."

Will made a move to toss her the handcuffs and she missed what actually happened. When she noticed the cuffs weren't sailing through the air, she glanced back over and saw Daniel standing over a disarmed Will, pointed a huge gun at his head.

"You want to try acting tough with me? You don't ever threaten any of my people or I'll blow your fucking head off. Now, get your soft ass up and sit on the couch." Denise could tell Daniel wanted to kill the man. His muscles were actually flexing with the need for violence.

Will stood up patting his head, and Denise got up and walked to the front window. There were still cops everywhere and she wondered how Daniel had even gotten into the house.

Daniel took the Captain's cellphone, keys, and another gun off his ankle before pushing him roughly onto the couch.

It was only then it registered to her that he wasn't wearing a mask.

He sat opposite Will and said, "Whatever you were gonna ask her, you can ask me."

Will cocked his head and asked, "Where are my two agents?"

Daniel shocked them both by saying, "Close by."

"Why are you showing me your face?" Will asked him.

He smiled and asked, "Why wouldn't I? I'm a law-abiding citizen with no record or warrants, and no way for anyone to say I've committed a crime."

"So, you're saying you're not the Prison Guard Killer?"

"The what?" Daniel replied with a smile. "I have alibis from some of the most important people on the planet for the times of any of this person's crimes."

"Well, why haven't you just killed me and made your escape? Why are we sitting here?" Will asked.

"Contrary to popular belief, I don't kill people for no reason. Sometimes I have to teach a lesson, or thin the herd so to speak, but it's never for no reason. There's a lot you don't know, and a lot you don't understand. But, to be totally honest, I'm trying to save your life."

"You're trying to save my life?" asked Will. "I know for a fact that you're responsible for dozens of deaths."

"You're wrong, Will. Not dozens. Thousands," clarified Daniel. "But I don't want to add you to that list. You're sticking your nose into something too big for you. Just go home and let us handle it. When it's done, you won't have to worry about me anymore."

"I don't know who you're used to dealing with, but I can't do that. I can't go home and just let you keep killing innocent people. I watched you take out two SWAT teams just for doing their jobs."

"With that being said, what do you think I'll do to you for doing yours?" asked Daniel.

"I'll die doing my duty and that's fine with me."

"Okay," said Daniel. He gestured for Denise to pick up the Captain's gun. "Denise, I'm gonna need you to play another role. Can you act like old Will here tried to kill you, but you got the gun from him and defended yourself?"

Denise picked up the gun and said, "I sure can. I just hate that it's gonna keep me away from going to Ashley for a little longer." She sat down next to Daniel and aimed the gun at Will's head. She looked at Daniel and said, "When I pull this trigger, cops will come from everywhere. Do you want to get out of here first?"

"No. I want to watch Cpt. Graham take his last breath. I'll use the chaos to get away. And plus, I got a few surprises for all those innocent cops out there."

"Well, alright," said Denise. She turned back to Will and asked, "Any last words?"

"What the hell is going on here?" demanded Walt, stepping from the back of the house. "Denise, put that fucking gun down and stop playing around with my boss!"

. . . .

While Walt and Ann reconnected with their boss, Denise led Daniel back towards her bedroom. Daniel had at first ordered Ann and Walt to stay out of sight, but they convinced him that now was the time to try and bring the captain over to their side. Daniel didn't think it was possible, and he warned them what it would lead to if they failed.

He'd let his mind wander a fraction of a second too long and now he had to take the blow coming towards his head. Of course, he could block it, but if he did it at this late a stage, he would have to shatter her forearm. Not wanting to hurt her, he rolled as much as he could and took the punch on his cheek so she wouldn't break her hand.

The hit was loud and it left no doubt that the sound was a fist hitting flesh. Daniel took a step back just as Walt rushed into the room with his gun raised. He took in the scene and barked out a laugh while putting his gun away. He said, "Guess the training is working," and walked away.

Daniel asked, "Are you done?" She grudgingly nodded, so he went on. "There was no way I could have predicted Ashley would be waiting for you, and I'm sorry she was hurt. So, I deserve the hit, but don't make a habit of it."

Denise said, "I thought you said the WRA wouldn't retaliate this fast?"

"They didn't. It wasn't them." He pulled out his phone and pulled up a video of the attack. "The police found all my cameras on the inside of your house, but they didn't think to look at the neighboring property where I had views of the whole area."

He pressed play and they stood together watching the video. Now that she wasn't upset, he was sure she saw the same things he had. "How do you know the WRA didn't outsource it to these bozos?" she asked.

"Dome light on, no automatic weapons, no positive ID, leaving before the target is eliminated. Absolutely not the WRA," said Daniel. "When they outsource a hit, the contract always goes to a professional who wouldn't make any of these mistakes, let alone all of them."

The video stopped after the SUV pulled off and she looked at him with squinted eyes. "So, why do you still look so guilty? I thought you would be please that it wasn't your fault."

"Because it wasn't really from the WRA, but it was still my fault. Watch this," he said, pulling up another video.

Alisha, being smart and intuitive, had sent the drone after the SUV when it pulled away. Once she locked the target into the drone, it stayed on the vehicle until it pulled into a private hanger at the airport.

"Wait!" said Denise. "That's the same…"

"Hold on," he interrupted. "There's more. Let it play out."

In less than a minute a car pulled out and Alisha switched the target to the new vehicle. Using a street camera, she was able to get the license plate number off the new vehicle and use it to get all the info on the owner.

When the information flashed on the screen, Denise turned on him again. "But you just said…."

"Be patient, Denise," he interrupted again. "Let the damn thing finish!"

They both focused back on the screen and the car only traveled for about 10 more minutes before it pulled up in front of a small home in a fairly nice neighborhood. Four people exited the car and proceeded up the walkway into the house.

"Alisha is becoming very good at her role in all of this. She knew we would need more, so she punched in the address and found a Ring doorbell camera registered to the location. This is what she got for the time when the car pulled up to the house."

Daniel pulled up another video and this one showed each person as they passed the camera. The four files popped up to match the person to facial recognition software that gave a rundown of each of them. The three men and one woman were all WRA agents.

Denise said, "I don't understand. How can you say the WRA didn't have anything to do with it, but their agents did the shooting?"

"Every now and then a situation presents itself that goes against everything it shows to be true," explained Daniel. "Sometimes it's the person being blind to the facts, but occasionally we run into a word that the intelligence community as a whole hates. That word is coincidence."

"I mean, I understand what you're saying, but it looks pretty straight forward to me," said Denise. "Where does the coincidence come into it?"

"Like I said, Alisha is getting good at knowing what we'll need to figure things out. So, you see the other two cars in the driveway? That's the reason the target car had to park on the street. Alisha hacked into the archived videos to see who those cars belong to. So, I have one more video."

Daniel pressed play on this one and a couple was seen making out while they walked towards the front door. When they separated and looked at the door, Denise gasped as she saw the female's face.

Once again, Alisha had run facial recognition on both of them and the man came back as another WRA agent. The woman's info just confirmed what both Denise and Daniel already knew. It was Candace Shada Price, fixed up and looking like her old self.

Daniel said, "I should have killed her stupid ass when I had the chance, but I thought prison would open her eyes."

"But what is her connection to the WRA?" asked Denise.

"I don't think she has one. I haven't gotten to do a deep dive yet, but once I get back to the compound, I will and I'll let you know, ASAP."

"So, what are you gonna do about this?" she asked him.

"Until we get all the facts, nothing. But don't worry about it, I've put some assets around their house and your house so you'll be safe now."

"Fuck being safe, Daniel! That's not what I meant," Denise said with heat. "You take care of yours, well I take care of mine. I'm not letting that bitch get away with hurting one of mine!"

Chapter 11

By the time they all made it back to the compound, it was after 1:00am. Since they all made the journey in different cars, Daniel waited until now to ask Walt about Will. "So, what's the status with your boss?"

Walt sighed and said, "He's impatient and thinks you've corrupted all of us. He agreed to leave Denise alone, but he said he wouldn't stop trying to find evidence on the PGK."

Daniel shook his head. "Walt, that's not good. He's gonna stumble onto…"

"I know and I told him that," Walt cut in. "But he's so damn stubborn, he won't listen to reason."

"There's really nothing more that could have been said," interjected Ann. "He thinks we're turning against him and he doesn't trust us either. We pretty much had to guarantee to deliver the PGK to him before he was satisfied."

Daniel's head jerked up. "That's mighty bold of a guarantee from the position you're both in."

Ann shrugged. "One way or another he'll get what he wants. Or he'll die trying. Either way, it's on him now."

"Anyway," said Daniel, looking at his phone. "Sleep. We'll meet in the War Room to go over the situation with Denise at 10:00. I know it hasn't been exactly quiet, but expect things to crank up until we get to the end."

Daniel left the underground garage and made one stop before he went to his bedroom. As soon as they had pulled into the gate, Alisha sent him a text that said she was going to sleep. She also threatened his manhood if he woke her up. But there was always one person he could wake up at anytime and be greeted with a smile.

But tonight, it seemed he wouldn't have to wake her. When he peeked around the door jamb, she was sitting on her bed in her pajamas watching the news.

Without turning, she patted the queen size bed beside her and said, "I've been waiting up for you. I have to ask you some important questions." Normally he would say something to lighten the mood, but he could tell she was serious about whatever it was.

The news people were blaming the recent tragedies on him. From the death of the governor, to the death of Denise's protection officer, Brittany Clark. They were also rehashing some of his earlier kills, including Gabby's family. He assumed that's what the conversation would be about.

Finally, she grabbed the remote and turned the TV off, plunging the room into darkness. He started to get up and turn the light on, but reconsidered, thinking maybe Gabby wanted the dark for some reason.

She sighed and said, "I want you to be truthful no matter how you think I'll feel, okay?"

"Baby girl, I'll always be truthful with you. All you have to do is ask your questions."

Acting as if she was almost scared to ask, she whispered, "Why me?"

Damn. He had hoped to shower her with so much love that she never had to ask that question. But obviously, she'd been asking it of herself and couldn't come up with a viable answer.

"I mean, I'm happy you took me in, but I wonder why not Matthew and Robert? They were innocent kids, but you chose to kill them. I know some of your family history, so I know it's not because they were white. So, why kill them and not me?"

He did get up then and turned the light on low because he wanted to see her face and have her be able to see his. He laid down on the bed and extended his arms, inviting her to snuggle up with him. She laid her head on his chest as he stroked her hair, preparing both of them for his story.

"Angel, I've never told anyone this story and I need it to stay between me and you. If it gets out, it could cause some pain for your Uncle Walt."

"I've always kept your secrets, Dad. My lips are sealed," she assured him.

He took a deep breath and then told her the story of why Marshall Oakland's family had to die. "Before I met any one of you formally, I was warring with my family. Most of them knew my history with Walt and they knew I'd do pretty much anything to protect him.

"I'd already started my assault on their prison contraband network and they were scrambling, trying to find a way to stop me. Well, one of the things my family does well is a strategy that dates back to the Napoleonic Coalitions."

"Oh, you mean the strategy of indirect attacks on people close to you instead of going against a force they know they couldn't win against?" asked his brilliant daughter.

"That's exactly right," he said, kissing her head. "And my family used this technique by sending an assassin after Walt."

She gasped and looked up at his face. "That's cowardly. Uncle Walt didn't even know he was part of the game yet!"

"You're right, but him not knowing was my fault and not theirs. Anyway, an assassin the WRA uses named The Author sent me a video of him standing over Walt while he was asleep. The threat was clear and he told me I could buy Walt's life, but I had to do something for the WRA.

"It seemed that my family had a huge network running at the prison Marshall Oakland worked. The officer had seen a deal go down and wouldn't accept part of the take to stay quiet. They tried a couple other scare tactics, but the man wouldn't back down. So, they needed him out of the picture."

"So, why didn't they just send this assassin to handle it?"

"Well, they saw it as a way to accomplish two things at once," he answered. "On the one hand, they would get rid of the officer. On the other, they would find out exactly how much Walt meant to me."

"Why didn't you go and take this guy, The Author, out?" she asked.

"Sweetheart, there are people in the world who are better than me. I have a better strategic attack than just about anyone, but when it comes to brute force, the only competition for The Author is my oldest brother, Reggie."

She laid her head back down on his chest, so he continued the story. "They told me to kill the officer's whole family but keep the officer alive. They did want me to injure him in a way that he couldn't come back to work. More importantly, since all the officers I went after were dirty, it made any accusations he could lay on anyone else noneffective. So, not only did I take his family, I destroyed his reputation."

She digested all of this and said, "But I know it would have been better to just kill me and be done with it. At least in the long run, with me here, it just gives you another weakness they can exploit."

Daniel did grow up in a loving family, but they didn't always express that love openly. When he was a child, he was made to be tough and prepared for this type of life. He was never held and told how much he was loved. If anything, it was looked at as a weakness to need such a thing. But he knew that wasn't the right atmosphere to raise a child in. Gabby was asking him why she deserved his love when he was the one who needed to be asking her that.

"Gabby, I love you…"

"I know you do, now," she interrupted. "But you didn't know me in the beginning. Twice you could have killed me instead of trusting me. But you then took it a step further and made me your family. I am truly grateful, but tell me why?"

A sinking feeling settled in Daniel's stomach. "Okay, I will. But first, tell me why you need to know so bad."

She stayed still and silent for a while. She did a good job of hiding her tears except for the fact that he could feel them soaking into his shirt. Finally, she said, "Because I want to trust that you won't change your mind one day because I'm too much trouble. Or you feel like I'm not good enough to be your daughter."

"Oh no, Gabby!" he said, wrapping her in his arms and rocking her gently. Now, she was beyond trying to hide her tears. She was issuing big racking sobs that caused tears of his own to slide down his face. For a while they cried together. A daughter crying out for a love that she thought was fleeting, and a father crying because he felt like he was failing his child.

With his tears filling his ears, and her tears soaking his shirt, he said, "I really don't know how to put this into words but I fell in love with your soul the first time I laid eyes on you. You were so brave and so strong that I ached to take your pain away. When you looked at me with those big brown eyes, you captured a piece of my heart that you still have today, and you'll still have it until the day I die.

"I love you, Gabriella Burke, and that love is unconditional. If I did anything to make you think otherwise, then I beg your forgiveness. I'm not just your father now.

I'm you protector, your friend, your provider, your pillow, and anything else you ever need me to be. And I'm truly sorry that I don't have all the beautiful words to express this better."

Crying softly now, she said, "I know you love me Dad, and you're not doing anything wrong. I just get worried sometimes that I'll do something wrong and you'll decide I'm not worth the hassle."

"Baby girl, look at me." He waited until she turned her beautiful face towards his. "I would give up everything I own for you. Family means everything to me. I'm not talking about blood, I'm talking about the family bond that develops between people who love and care for each other.

"Words can't describe how I feel about you. Only heaven knows how much I do. Girl, I'll put my own life on the line. I'll cherish and protect you with my life…"

She smacked his stomach and looked at him with accusation in her eyes. "Dad! You just quoted a Dru Hill song to me!"

"What? No, I didn't. You just didn't hear me right."

She smacked him again. "You should be ashamed of yourself boy!" She was smiling and playfully slapping at him, so he had succeeded with his ploy. But he got misty again, which he did every time she tried to emulate Alisha.

They sobered up and he pulled her back to his chest. He rubbed her head until he heard her breathing start to become deeper. He whispered, "I love you, sweetheart."

She whispered back, "I love you too, daddy," before drifting off to sleep.

He held her for a while before waking her so he could tuck her in. He gave her one last kiss before he made his way to his bedroom. Alisha was a sleeping mound on her side of the bed, so he stripped and took a quick shower before sliding under the covers beside her.

Taking a risk that not many men would be willing to take, he shook Alisha until she looked at him with murder in her eyes. "Boy, if you woke me up for sex, Imma...." Focusing on his face, she sat up and asked, "What's wrong? Did something happen?"

He couldn't stop the tears from falling from his eyes. She wrapped her naked body around his and just comforted him, murmuring lovingly in his ear.

After a while, he told her about the conversation he'd had with Gabby, leaving out the part about Walt. He finished by saying, "I'm failing our little girl. She really thinks I'd kill her or kick her out."

"No she doesn't, baby. She's just scared," Alisha explained. "She's just so self-reliant we sometimes forget she is a child with childish fears. And after everything she's been through, you can't blame her for having doubts. Tomorrow she'll be embarrassed and awkward for a bit, then she'll be back to being our beautiful, funny, amazing, daughter."

Daniel smiled and said, "You know, I really am a genius."

"I'm the one who just gave you the wisdom. How are you the genius?"

Smiling wider, he said, "Because I'm the one who got you into his bed." She laughed and smacked his chest, something else their daughter got from her. "And speaking of getting you into bed," he cupped her amazing ass and pulled her over on top of him, kissing her deeply. He broke the kiss long enough to say, "Since you're up now, there is something else I need from you."

The only coherent words spoken after that were about an hour later when they said their I love you's, before rolling over and going to sleep.

Chapter 12

By 11:00 the next morning, the computer screens in the War Room were full of all the information needed to draw a pretty good conclusion on Denise's situation. It's a coincidence that the WRA was gonna be pissed when they found out what led to their discovery. Daniel even contemplated just going after Candace and leaving the WRA out of it. Because, if he shut this operation down, it would stop all domestic money going into the WRA.

They had hidden it so well, he was sure the whole family was in on it. And because of a petty, vindictive, sore loser, the WRA could now lose it all.

"I still don't understand why they would use legitimate agents to run a scam," said Alisha. "It looks like a huge waste of resources."

"Actually, it's just the opposite," said Daniel. "They now have 50 plus agents that they don't have to pay. The agents get paid from the scam that they're running, so it's almost like free money for the WRA."

"Yeah, I see what you mean," said Ann. "The agents work harder so they make more money. Which benefits the WRA because it makes them more money, also."

"Not to mention, with the assurance of the other WRA assets, such as the governor, and other officials, they can pretty much operate with impunity," added Walt.

"So, why the guise as a drug dealing operation? Why set it up so that the cops would always be on your back?" asked Alisha.

"That's actually the most genius part," said Daniel. "They conduct themselves as drug dealers so the good cops have something to focus on. Let's say one of the agents leaves the house at 2:00 in the morning with a duffle bag. The police are going to assume it's something illegal. So, they follow the agent, but the agent doesn't give them probable cause for a stop.

"You get enough agents to pull this off, the police will start devoting a lot of resources to what they think is a drug network. They have the look, and they live the lifestyle, but the cops can never catch them with anything. It works because, the whole time law enforcement is focused on the young black guy with the jewelry and expensive car, the older white guy in the Kia get's away with $2 Million in his trunk."

"I bet it also gives the dirty cops a reason to be there if the WRA needs them for something," added Ann.

"So, explain how this scheme is actually benefitting the WRA to the extent that this could be a death blow if we shut it down." Alisha was trying her hardest to understand crime on this level, but some of the bigger picture scams just didn't make sense to her.

"Okay, so first off, you have to understand that most of this is hidden behind shell corporations and non-existent partners. Also, you have to see that the WRA uses a lot of people who would have a lot of explaining to do if they popped up with a ton of money. Cops, Judges, correctional officers, company executives, and so on and so forth.

"So, if you tell a cop you'll pay them $100,000 for doing a job, a smart cop would understand that if he tried to spend the money, it could land him in hot water."

Daniel walked over to the big monitor and entered in a series of commands. A line of businesses started to come up in the first column. "These are all the businesses owned and operated by Terrell Rilley and his crew."

The list included restaurants, clubs, bars, barber shops, internet cafes, arcades, bowling alleys, skating rinks. In all, it came up to 82 businesses spread out along the East Coast.

"Now, look at this list," he told them. A new list popped up next to the other one. This list was identical to the first except for the fact that all the owners on the second list were different. "And there you have it. You see it now?" he asked, turning to the other three occupants of the room. He was greeted with three blank faces.

"Okay, so now I'm completely lost," said Ann.

"Uh, yeah, so am I," said Walt. "So, are they running some type of real estate scam?"

"Hell, I thought they were running an underground drug network but putting the WRA agents on front street to take the heat off the hidden dealers," admitted Ann.

Daniel dropped his head in disappointment. He threw his hands toward the monitor and said, "Look at the information. It's plain as day. I could bring Gabby in here and she'd see it in five seconds!" He looked back at them in exasperation.

"Wait!" said Alisha. "I think I got it." After a pause, she said, "They're laundering money!"

Walt and Ann glanced at her and then back at Daniel. Ann asked, "How in the hell do you get that out of what's on the screen?"

"Don't ask me," said a pleased Daniel. "Ask my beautiful fiancé."

Daniel could tell that Alisha felt good about figuring something out that the two seasoned investigators couldn't. He didn't want to steal her thunder, so he let her explain it.

"Well, if you look at the second list, the owners aren't claiming the actual building as part of ownership. They're claiming assets inside the building. By the names of the secondary businesses, it looks like they are some kind of legal gambling centers."

"They call them game rooms. Pretty much they just play video games that pay out real money instead of a high score," interjected Daniel.

"Alright, but if it's legal gambling, how is it money laundering?" asked Walt.

"Actually, it's quite simple," said Alisha. "When you conclude that they're not actually laundering their own money. The WRA is providing a way for others to launder their own money, and the WRA charges them a fee."

"But how?" asked Ann.

"Okay, let's say this drug dealer has had a good month and he wants to buy a $300,000 car. If he goes out and buys it with cash, BAM! The FEDs pick him up," explained Alisha. "But, if you go to a gaming room and win a $400,000 jackpot, or split the winnings over a couple weeks, then you have an explanation on how you came up with the money.

"Let's assume the WRA takes a percentage. You have dirty cops, and judges, and assets that can't spend the money they're making by working with the WRA. Except now they can. They pay a cop $100,000 a month in protection money. That's $1.2 Million a year. If the WRA charges 30%, they essentially get $360,000 of their money back, and the cop is happy with $840,000 he can actually spend openly."

"And that's just the tip of the iceberg," Daniel picked up the tale. "Drug dealers, arms dealers, dirty politicians, crooked CEOs and executives. For a fee, anyone can get their money cleaned. And with the right programming, you can set it up so your dirty cop wins the jackpot right in front of the Chief of Police."

"How does Terrell Rilley fit into all that? Are they really selling drugs or not?" asked Ann.

"No drugs at all," Daniel explained with a look of admiration. "It's actually a genius setup. The gaming rooms that do the most business are connected to the places Terrell hangs out the most. So, any investigations will look for the non-existent drug trade. As far as I can tell, he never goes into any of the gaming areas. Since they are owned by different people, the cops have no reason to suspect they're not totally above board."

"How does Terrell and the other agent make their money?" asked Ann.

"That's the best part," said Daniel. "All of these businesses are legit. Terrell and the rest of the agents are getting rich by just running the businesses like regular owners. They give a percentage to the WRA and are on standby if the Agency needs them for anything."

"Like trying to kill Denise?" Walt asked with a sneer.

"Actually, I don't think so," said Daniel. "This is where the coincidence comes into play." He turned back to the monitor and pulled up everything on Candace and everything on an agent named Javon Murphy.

"About an hour ago, they took Ashley Kirt in for another surgery. Denise went home to change and wash up. Let me see if I can get her in on this part." He dialed her number and, when she picked up, he projected her image on the top right corner of the screen. Seeing everyone, she smiled sadly and waved.

After the questions about how she and Ashley were doing, Daniel brought the conversation back to Candace and Javon. "Let me start with the info I dug up on Candace while she was in prison. As we all know, she was sentenced to one year and was sent to the Maximum-Security Prison for women in Raleigh. She did all of her time there, but she connected with some pretty well-off women.

"Three different women she hung out with got caught with cell phones while housed in the same block as her. Whenever a cellphone is found in the possession of an inmate, it is sent to the capital police for an information extraction. I hacked into their files and found that all three phones had been used to track the movements of Terrell Rilley.

"When Candace was released, she spent a month getting surgeries to fix her face and body. When she healed, she immediately got a job at one of the clubs where Terrell was known to hang out. Within a week, they were hanging together. A couple weeks after that, they were officially an item."

"She probably enhanced his cover as a drug dealer as she looks like she fits into that lifestyle," said Ann bitterly.

"That's exactly right, but I want all of you to watch these clips from inside the club." All of the first clips showed Javon Murphy trying his best to get close to an obviously not interested Candace Price. All the rest showed him in the background of the videos watching Candace and Terrell having a good time. Whether at a club or restaurant, the man's eyes never left the form of Candace Price.

"Now, a little background," said Daniel. "Javon and Terrell really hate each other. They hold the same rank inside the WRA even though Javon has been there longer. Terrell is an excellent undercover agent and most of those guys go farther, faster. But, it's almost like they were born polar opposites. Javon went to Princeton, Terrell went to Harvard. Javon plays football, Terrell plays basketball. Javon grew up rich, Terrell had to work like hell to get every penny he had. But what really irks Javon is that the WRA always puts him as Terrell's second on these undercover jobs."

"So, you think Candace is playing one against the other?" asked Denise.

"Sort of," Daniel answered. "You see, Terrell would have been who she went to first. But he would have already received some order on how to react to you surfacing. Reggie's comment when I brought your name up was that you weren't a threat to them. If he said that, that would have been the message sent out to all the heads of ongoing operations."

"Oh, I see where you're going," Denise said nodding. "So, after Terrell figured out some way to turn her down, she went to Javon and used his lust for her to get him to do it."

"That would be my guess. You remember the three other agents with him? Well, all of them are under Javon's leadership, not Terrell's."

"So, what's the plan on taking this scam down?" asked Walt.

"I'm not sure that's a good idea," answered Daniel, drawing shocked responses from them all.

"My friend is in the hospital and could still die!" shouted Denise. "And you want to let them get away with that!"

Daniel walked over and took his place at the head of the conference table. "Everybody needs to calm down." He turned to his left and stared at Denise up on the screen. "Candace, Javon, and anyone else who participated in the attack will be punished. I've already set some things up for that. And yes, you will get your personal revenge. What I'm not sure about is shutting down the operation." After a second, he said, "At least not yet. Let me explain."

When he finished, they all looked at him in awe of his plan. Ann said, "That's genius. And you came up with that this morning?"

Daniel smiled and said, "Hey, we're good at what we're good at."

Denise said, "All that is well and good, but when do I settle up with this bitch?"

He thought about it and said, "Let me make a couple calls. I'll come get you when everything is ready. Just go about like normal and I'll let you know."

Denise said, "The sooner the better. Now, I have to get back to Ashley. I'll see everyone later," and she clicked off.

Walt glanced at him with worry on his face. "Being a good actress is one thing. Do you think she's ready for something like this?"

Daniel wanted to be completely honest with them. He said, "Hell yeah, I think Denise is ready. And she's family now. So, even if she's not, I'll be right by her side to make sure she's okay."

Chapter 13

"Yeah Homie, we bout to leave now," Face G told his captain, Big Keith, who he had placed in charge of the Kannapolis rebuild. "It'll take us a couple hours to get there, just make sure everyone is there when I arrive. You know I hate waiting."

"I got you, Big Homie," said Big Keith. "I'll have everyone at the pool hall in an hour." Big Keith came by his name honestly. He was a dark-skinned black man who stood 6-foot 4-inches and weighed 450 pounds. Normally he was stationed in Concord, but after the Big Rollin Crip compound in Kannapolis had been wiped out, along with most of its members, Face G had moved the giant to a new position.

"That's what up, G. See you then." Face G disconnected and looked at the four men who flanked him outside of his Durham estate.

First up was his personal driver and head body guard, Debo. At 6-foot, 275 pounds, the former UNC Chapel Hill football player could easily have made it to the NFL. But, when Face G offered him the promotion in the gang, Debo quit football all together and came home to support his OG. With his dark brown, tatted up body, and his deeply flowing waves, he was an instant hit with the ladies. But, when that smile disappeared, he was the most feared soldier in the set.

Next up was Debo's twin brother, Quette. At only 5-foot 8-inches and 190 pounds, he wasn't exactly a carbon copy of his twin. But, after you got pass the size, it was clear that they shared the same DNA. Not exactly built for sports, Quette took up street fighting. Over the years, he'd earned his reputation as having the fastest hands in the hood.

Everyone who had ever raised hands to him regretted it, after they regained consciousness.

Then there were the brothers, Kenji and Wayne. Both were stone cold killers who couldn't wait for their next target. Other than that, they couldn't be more different.

Kenji was 5-foot 9-inches, light skinned with long dreads. He had a medium build and possessed a quiet intensity that most people thought made him a psycho. He only talked to greet his Homies and then he would fade into the background, eyes constantly moving, looking for his next target.

Wayne was 6-foot 3-inches, dark skinned, with long dreads, but he had a slimmer build than his brother. At 30 years old, two years younger than Kenji, Wayne had the loudest mouth in the whole gang. He lived to talk shit but he never wolfed. If it came out of his mouth, you better believe he was willing to do it.

Face said, "We have to turn it up a little bit on this trip. Even if we have to kill some mothafuckas, we not leaving until we find out something. No way some gang gonna take out a whole line and nobody know nothing. Let's load up and hit the road. Today we learn who's really responsible for the death of our brothers."

Everyone dapped up and headed to their respective vehicles. As his personal driver, Debo opened the door to the all black, bulletproof Lincoln MKS Diplomatic Limousine, and made his way to the driver's seat after Face was locked in. They both settled into the heated leather seats as the 30-inch monitor folded down from the ceiling in front of Face. He would watch how his money was doing in the markets as they made their way from Durham to Kannapolis.

Always tucked in tight behind the Limo was Quette driving an armor-platted Bentley, making sure no one could sneak up on the OG. And behind him was Kenji and Wayne in a blacked-out Hummer H2 with an arsenal of weapons, just in case someone foolishly tried to get to their leader. Face made all of them take defensive and offensive driving lessons, so the whole crew knew what to do in any situation.

The numbers on the screen couldn't keep Face G's mind from wandering. Over a year now, he'd been searching for the bastards who'd murdered his brother, Mickey Brown, and his crew. The two men had met at a basketball tournament in Raleigh when they were both 11 years old. An older boy had talked both of them into being jumped into the Crip set, but Face had made the trip to California a few years later to become stamped. So, even though they had the same amount of time in, Face had become the OG.

The two boys came from two different worlds, with Mickey growing up with money and Face growing up poor. Mickey had also been smart, but Face had possessed only average intelligence. None of their differences seemed to matter when they were on the court or banging in the streets.

It had all started with those two kids almost 30 years ago. Now, the Big Rollin Crips pretty much ran North Carolina. Face G looked at his reflection in the TV screen, but couldn't meet his own eyes. He would only be able to do that once he had avenged his brother.

He leaned his head back for what seemed like a minute but was jerked awake two hours later by Debo. "Face, we almost there. Any last instructions?"

Face thought about it and said, "Just make sure everyone has one in the head because we might have to kill all these niggas today." He checked his own twin Glocks and made sure he was ready for anything. No matter who he was and what rank he had, these were still Big Rollin Crips he was dealing with.

Right as Debo parked in front of the pool hall and got out, Face's cell phone buzzed. He pulled it out and studied the display, but hit ignore because he didn't recognize the number. Debo opened the door and Face G exited the Limo with his gang face on.

Bernie Alston, AKA Face G, got his nickname because people used to say he always wore a serious face. At 5-foot 9-inches, and 175 pounds, he wouldn't intimidate most gangsters with his size. But the dark-skinned, cornrowed, slim, OG Crip legend didn't try to scare people with his size. He did it with his voice, his look, his persona. And all that started when you got a glimpse of his face.

All the Kannapolis Big Rollin set was at the huge bulletproof windows of the pool hall. Face had on a pair of white Air Forces, a pair of blue jeans, and a dark blue pullover to fight off the chill. After him and his crew met at the Limo, with Debo in the lead, they approached the front door.

When they entered, they walked straight up to Big Keith and greeted him first as was Crip custom to recognize his authority. Afterwards, with Debo and Quette by his side, he greeted every other gangster in the room. Kenji and Wayne took up positions so they could hose down the whole room without crossfire if the need arose.

Finally, Face told Big Keith to come into the backroom with him. Debo, Face, and Big Keith went in and Quette stood on the outside of the door with an earpiece in so he could hear if there was any trouble in the room. In fact, Face made his whole crew wear earpieces anytime they were away from home base.

Before anyone could speak, Face's phone buzzed again. He pulled it out and hit ignore after he saw the same number from a few minutes ago. Face put the phone away and then focused on Big Keith.

In his soft, gravelly voice, Face asked him, "You learn anything new?" There was no need to specify, Big Keith knew exactly what he was asking about. When Big Keith responded in the negative, Face said, "Tell me what you've done to try and find out."

"Man, I've talked to everyone in a two-mile radius. Crips, civilians, I've even asked some of our rivals if they heard anything."

"So, basically you aint did shit but talk to a bunch of mothafuckas," Face G said softly. "You fat, lazy, no good piece of shit. That's the same thing you said you did last month and the previous five months. You think I'm playing with you, nigga? What the fuck good are you?"

"Now hold up mothafuckas, you aint bout to, Umph!" he groaned as Debo's fist sunk deep into his belly. As soon as he hit the floor, Debo and Face stripped him of all his weapons and told him not to move.

Face stomped on his chest before asking, "Did you forget who I am? I'm the one who gave you the rank, fat boy. I gave you this opportunity to show me you're ready to move up. But I guess I made a mistake." Face's voice never raised or modulated at all. But Big Keith would be a fool not to recognize the anger boiling below the surface.

"Come on man!" shouted Big Keith. "Don't nobody know shit. I've tried everything to…. Ahgh!" he yelled when Debo kicked him in the balls.

"Shut the fuck up! He didn't ask you no question, nigga!" Debo's tatts started to glisten with sweat as he worked the fat man over.

Face heard Quette say, "Everybody just stay calm. Everything will be what it be." Wayne was telling people only move if they wanted to die, so Face knew the situation was getting out of control.

"Debo! That's enough." When Debo stepped back, Face said, "Come on G, get up. Take a seat, Homie." Slowly, the big man climbed to his feet and fell heavily into his chair.

Everything was quiet as they waited for Big Keith to regain his composure.

"I didn't see the little bitch who gave us the information on that guy. Why isn't she here?" Face asked him.

"She not one of us. You know that. I only rounded up our people." After every word, he glanced at Debo, hoping it wasn't the wrong thing to say.

"You're right Cuz, I did say only our people. But I want you to call her and tell her to get over here, now."

Big Keith pulled his phone out and dialed a number. He had to make several more calls, sweating the whole time, before he found someone who could reach her. He hung up with a sigh and said, "She'll be here in ten minutes."

"Alright," said Face. "Let's go have a talk with some of the soldiers before she gets here."

Quette opened the door and Debo and Face let Big Keith exit first. By the time Face came out, a lot of comments were being made about how he had treated Big Keith.

"Shut the fuck up," Face said in a soft voice. He might as well have had a bullhorn because all talk died instantly. "Everybody in this room is a Big Rollin Crip, so I know it's real gangstas in here. But, if anybody wants to test mine, you're more than welcome to try."

He told Debo to step back and he spread his hands out wide, inviting anyone to step up. He turned to his right and saw a Terry Crews looking nigga grilling him like he wanted some smoke. Face turned towards him and said, "How about you, Cuz? You want to test my gangsta?"

"Naw, Big Homie. You got it," the giant said.

"Well, now I want to test yours since you look so tough," stated Face. When he got close to the man, he saw that the top of his head only reached the man's chest.

Looking the soldier in his eyes, Face said, "Tell me you a bitch made ass nigga and I'll leave you alone."

The man was flexing his arms and chest as his breathing quickened. Face just stood there unimpressed as the man made up his mind. After a minute, the giant seemed to deflate and he mumbled something under his breath.

"Speak up mothafucka! Your heart beating so loud trying to pump all that Kool-Aid, I couldn't hear you."

"Imma bitch made ass nigga," the man said with shame.

Face looked to his left and said, "Kenji." Without another word, Face turned away as the silenced round was fired from Kenji's automatic straight into the temple of the coward.

Nobody else moved or said a word as Face spun in a circle with his arms wide. "I'm not leaving here today without something. The man who formed your line, my brother, was murdered. You guys run this city and you can't find out who killed your leader. You!" he said pointing to a light-skinned guy about his size. "What have you done to find out who killed Mickey?"

"OG, I be on the block all day. I mean, I ask around, but the Homies got to eat. I don't have time…."

"You right nigga," Face cut him off. Looking at his watch, he said, "You don't have time because you got 30 seconds to tell me something or you joining Terry Crews over there in hell."

"You know what Cuz? Fuck you!" the man yelled, showing heart. "You aint did shit yourself but come around here harassing us. I'm not a bitch ass nigga, so it's gonna take more than some guns and a soft voice to scare me, Cuz!"

Face asked him, "What's your name, my G?"

"They call me Ill Will," the man said with pride.

Face nodded and said, "Wayne." Another silenced bullet flew across the room and ended the life of Ill Will.

He had turned away to start another speech, when in walked the young woman he'd been waiting on. He saw on her face when the two dead bodies registered and she saw the beat-up face of Big Keith. But, she squared her shoulders and came over anyway.

Face turned to her and said, "I know we've talked before, but remind me what your name is again." This was a beautiful woman, and she knew how to showcase her looks. She resembled a young Rhianna with her light brown skin and curly dark hair. She stood about 5-foot 9-inches and the black and blue skirt set she was wearing showed off a pair of smooth, toned legs.

She smiled and gave a slight bow before saying, "Hi Face G. My name is Tyiesha."

"Hi Tyiesha. I don't have a lot of time, so sorry for being abrupt. I need you to tell me what you told me the last time we talked."

She glanced around at the gathered men and women before licking her already glossed up lips nervously. Once again, she looked at the dead men before saying, "Oh, you mean about Alisha?"

Face smiled patiently and walked around behind her. He put his hands on her bare, cold shoulders, and said, "Don't play games with me bitch! I told you I don't have time." His phone once again buzzed, but this time he ignored it. He wrapped his hands around her neck lightly and waited for her to talk.

"Like I told you before, I don't even know if this is important. About a year before everyone was killed, we had gone to the club and Alisha met this guy. He said his name was Manuel Adams, or something like that."

He squeezed her neck a little and asked, "Was it Manuel Adams, or something like that?"

She kicked back with her heeled boots and wrenched herself from his grasp. Quette made a move, but Face stopped him with a look. She said, "You aint got to hurt me, I want to help. But I'm not one of your little soldiers. I'm not gonna be manhandled just so you can feel like a man!"

Face nodded and said, "I'm sorry," before punching her right in the nose. Blood exploded everywhere and she instantly hit the floor and started kicking in his direction. He said, "Get your stupid ass up and stop showing the whole room you're not wearing panties. Just tell me what you know and then I won't have to hurt you again."

Still on the ground, she wiped her face with tissue she retrieved from her dropped purse, pinched her nose closed, and lumbered to her feet. The room was deathly quiet as everyone waited to see if she would become the next body.

In a nasally voice, she said, "In the VIP booth at Motions, he said his name was Manuel Adams. About 6-foot, 200 pounds, very handsome, with brown skin, and a bald head. Seemed to be very rich and Alisha left with him.

"They hung together for a while behind Mickey's back, but then she broke it off. That was months before the massacre, so I don't know if the guy had anything to do with it or not."

Face considered her for a minute. He said, "Unlock your phone and give it to me." She reached in her purse and pulled the phone out. She held it up to her face and unlocked it, then handed it to him.

He quickly went through all her text and incoming and outgoing calls. Nothing in the last 30 days showed anything suspicious. He checked her contacts and found a listing for Alisha. He called it and got a recording telling him the number was no longer in service. He handed the phone back and said, "Call her."

"I've tried over and over, but all I get is the recording. That's the only number I have for her," she said.

Face looked over to Quette and gave him a nod. Quette pulled out a pair of all black Craftsmen work gloves and put them over his hands. Tyiesha said, "Can I at least take my boots off so I can fight back? Or does your man need me to be bloody and off balance to win?"

Face laughed, which caused his four soldiers to laugh. His phone buzzed again. He told her, "Go ahead sweetie, if you think it will help," as he pulled the phone out. Same number as last time, so he hit ignore and watched as the young beauty squared up with Quette without a shred of fear. Quette stepped up blowing kisses at her and caught an impressive jab to the mouth for his taunt.

Face laughed again as Quette stepped back and dabbed at his now bleeding lip. His phone buzzed once again. Angry now, he looked at the screen and saw the number had called him eight times since this morning. Quette started to circle his prey as Face finally decided to answer the call.

"Who the fuck is this, and why do you keep calling me?" he asked in his normal, quiet tone.

"Damn OG, this is Lil D over here in Charlotte. Why the fuck you not answering my calls, Cuz?" Lil D ran the Charlotte line of the Big Rollin Crips. He was another one who had been with him and Mickey pretty much from the start.

"What's up, Gang? I'm in the middle of something right now. Let me get at you in a few hours." Quette had landed a nice two piece, but Tyiesha responded with a kick to his balls. Most of the Kannapolis Crips were now cheering Tyiesha on.

Lil D said, "That's cool Big Homie, but I thought you'd like to know I found your girl."

Face hit the mute button and said, "Quette, back up, and everybody else be quiet right now." Once again, everyone did what he said without question.

He unmuted the phone and said, "Lil D, what girl are you talking about?"

"Aint you still looking for that bitch used to be with Mickey? Alisha or something like that?"

"Ah, yeah. I'm actually over in Kannapolis looking for her right now."

"Well, my G, I think I found her. I don't know her all that good, and she dressing a little different, got a new hair style, but I'm sending you a picture of the woman I seen right now."

Face had only actually seen Alisha a couple of times himself. So, he asked Tyiesha to come take a look at the photo when it came in.

The picture showed a dark-skinned woman in designer blue jeans and a white pullover. Beside her was a little girl in the same outfit who looked so much like her, it could be her little sister or daughter. Tyiesha gasped and said, "That's her! That's Alisha!"

"How sure are you?" asked Face.

"She's my best friend and I've known her my whole life. I'm 100% positive it's her."

"Lil D, where and when was this picture taken?"

"I took it myself a few hours ago at Concord Mills mall."

"Shit, Lil D. How the fuck is this going to help me? She could be anywhere by now."

Lil D laughed and said, "Lucky for you, to get promoted in your set, you have to be smart. When I couldn't reach you, I followed her. I watched her and the little girl go into this huge compound in Charlotte about two hours ago. I figured you'd want to know where she went if it turned out to be her."

Face said, "Stay on the phone for a minute." Then to his crew, he said, "Mount up, we need to ride, now!" He turned to Big Keith and said, "Sorry for causing a mess in your home. I'll be back after all this is over and we'll settle up." With that, his crew made their way to the front door.

Tyiesha said, "Can I go with you? She might respond better to a friendly face."

Face G shook his head. "You're one of a kind Tyiesha, and I won't forget the heart you showed here today. But this is a Big Rollin Crip problem, and Alisha needs to answer some very important questions. I'll be back to see you later."

With his four soldiers flanking him, just like at the Durham estate, he was led to the Limo. Once safely inside, he went back to his phone call. "Okay, tell me exactly where it is."

"Well, that's the thing, Face G. We need to meet somewhere else first. This aint your ordinary compound. There's no way to get in, we just have to wait until she comes out again."

Face said, "Give me a meeting place close to the compound. I do trust you, but after we meet, I want to see this place for myself." They agreed on where to meet and Face G's convoy made its way to the Charlotte area.

In his mind, he was thinking that he was finally going to get the answers he'd been searching for. But, if inside those walls was the group that took out Mickey and his crew, he'd need a lot more information before he could make a move. The saying went: If you fail to have a plan, then you planned to fail. Face G was going to succeed in his mission for vengeance, or he would die trying. That sounded like a good plan to him.

Chapter 14

Tonya and Nyaira Burke were out in the field doing what they do best; gathering intelligence. As the daughters of Kashonda Wilson, the oldest of the Burke siblings, and Head of Intelligence for the WRA, they were born and bred to be the best field agents the WRA had.

Both young women had been blessed with their mother's intelligence, as well as her stunning looks. With their nut-brown skin tone, hazel eyes, and short, light brown hair with reddish highlights, eyes of both men and women followed them with interest. Since they also liked to pack their slim, curvy bodies into form fitting clothes, a lot of the eyes never made it up to their faces to appreciate the beauty they possessed. Right now, for the first time, they were conflicted on how to handle a situation.

Tonya was sitting in the parking lot of a Wal-Mart about a mile from her Uncle Daniel's Charlotte compound, with her eyes locked on the unsanctioned target. Her all white BMW 328xi blended in perfectly with all the other ritzy cars in this part of the city. But her target's metallic blue 1969 Chevelle SS 454 stood out like a sore thumb.

Tonya, who was 26 years old, told her sister, who was three years younger, to stay on their original target and let her know if anything changed. Their Uncle Delmas would be pissed to know Tonya was deviating from his directive, but she felt like it was something she had to do.

Earpiece in place, Tonya asked her sister, "So, what do you think?"

Equipment so state of the art, it was like she was sitting right next to her, Nyaira replied, "It's obvious that this guy is waiting for somebody else to make the call. And he's really not a threat now that they're inside the wall."

"I get that Ny, but what do you think we should do? You think I should call Uncle Delmas and let him know what we saw?"

"I don't think we have a choice, Tonya. If we intervene, it might not be what he wants. On the other hand, if we do nothing, and something bad happens, he might be pissed about that."

Tonya was silent for a beat before saying. "This is above our pay grade. I'm calling him." Ny stayed silent as Tonya dialed their uncle, and mission boss, inside the WRA.

As always, Delmas was all business when he answered the call. "What's going on, Agent? Everything go smoothly?" he asked.

That morning Tonya had phoned and informed him that Alisha and Gabby had left the compound and the sisters were following them. He'd told her to let him know where they went and when they returned home. Since it happened three times a week now, this trip was nothing special. But, on this trip, something had indeed happened.

"They made it back to the compound okay, but we had something happen that might be important while they were at the mall."

After a few seconds of silence, he said, "Well, are you going to tell me, or do you want me to guess?"

She gritted her teeth with the need to curse her uncle out. Ultimately, she kept her cool and explained the situation. "While Alisha and Gabby shopped, Nyaira noticed a man studying them in an abnormal way. This happens a lot because she's an attractive woman, but this guy kept trying to get a picture of her face.

"I came on the scene and took a picture of him and ran it through facial recognition. It came back as Damian 'Lil D' Spruce, a captain in the Crip set Alisha was a member of. He made some calls, but didn't seem like he could get in touch with whoever he was trying to reach. He followed her back to the compound, but after seeing where she lived, he broke off and drove to a local Wal-Mart.

"Right now, Ny is at the compound keeping a watch on things there, and I'm at the Wal-Mart keeping an eye on our follower. So, what do you want me to do about him?"

"How long ago did you all leave the mall?" he asked, zeroing in on what Tonya knew he would.

"It's been a few hours," she answered honestly.

And then the explosion. "And you just now saw fit to call your boss and inform him of the situation! What the hell were you waiting for? You don't know enough about what's going on to make the decision to wait a few hours!"

"Nothing happened!" she yelled right back. "You do remember I'm a senior field agent. You think I can't assess a situation and tell whether someone is about to make a move on a target?"

"That's not the point, Tonya! What would you have done if this guy did make a move?"

He had her there but dammit, that's why she was calling now. "I don't know boss. That's why I'm calling now."

"Yeah, a few hours too late, when the disaster could have already happened," he said, unnecessarily.

"Stop being an asshole and just tell me what you want me to do!" She'd had enough of the lecture and now she was starting to regret calling him at all. She should have called Uncle Reggie and been done with it.

He gave her a 30 second silent reprimand for her insubordination before he continued. "Don't interfere in any way, shape, or form. I want updates on the second of all movements and let me decide what your next move should be. You need ears on him as well. We need to know what he's planning, but also who he's planning it with. Any info you collect comes to me and only me. Is that clear?"

She wasn't gonna take any more of his condescending tone. "I know how to do my job. I'll keep you informed," she said and hung up. "God! I hate working for him," Tonya yelled to her sister.

"Yeah, me too. But it seems like he's taking every op that involves Uncle Daniel for his own." Since Delmas outranked their mother, even though she was Head of Intelligence, he could take over any mission he wanted to. Then he could make them keep everything they learn away from the rest of the family. Something wasn't right, but right now, they weren't in a position to do anything about it.

Tonya said, "Stay on the house, but I have a plan to get ears on his phone. Listen carefully because, if I get into trouble, I might need your help. You never know with these fucking gangbangers."

"I got you, Sis. Take it easy on the guy though. He's never been the target of a Burke woman."

Tonya was dressed in a black Prada Tracksuit that conformed to the contours of her lush body. She switched from a pair of all white Jordan 11's to a pair of Red Bottoms with a 4-inch heel. The heels would make her 5-foot 5-inch body look long and sensual. She put on a pair of Gucci shades and a white fur coat and drove her vehicle so it was in a parking spot in plain view of her target.

For her sister's benefit, Tonya said, "If this slimy bastard tries to touch my ass, I'm killing him."

Laughing, Nyaira said, "Can you blame him if he tries? I mean, he's probably never seen a real quarter in person."

"Whatever," was all Tonya could say. "I'm going in. Let's just pray this boy's momma taught him some manners."

• •

Damian 'Lil D' Spruce was not having a good day. Trying to garner a little favor with his OG had led to the Crip Capo becoming a fucking babysitter. He wanted so bad to call one of his soldiers to take over the task, but he knew if anything went wrong, Face G would have his ass.

So, the Big Rollin Crip, leader of the Charlotte branch, sat in the Wal-Mart parking lot waiting on the arrival of his right-hand man, as well as the gang's east coast leader.

Lil D, at 37 years old, was not new to the gang life. He'd been brought into the fold only three years after Face G and Mickey. The 5-foot 8-inch, 210-pound, muscular man used his ghetto looks to build a pretty good reputation for himself. With his midnight-black skin, his face concealing dreads, and his gold teeth, he'd made grown men piss themselves without ever laying a finger on them.

Yeah, he was a scary mothafucka, but he also backed it up with what some thought were unprovoked bouts of violence. He just saw them as a way to keep his people on their toes. He was about to pull his phone out to call his soldier, D-Nice, when a certified dime stepped out of a white BMW.

At first sight, he lost his train of thought and stared dumbly at the magnificent woman. She was covered from neck to toe, but the tight, black tracksuit hinted that it would be a life changing event just to undress such a beautiful creature.

He couldn't make out much of her face because of the shades and fur coat, but he was willing to bet it matched her body perfectly. Not that he would ever find out. A woman like that had to have a rich, debonair husband. He would probably start stuttering the second she turned her attention on him anyway. As the woman walked in front of his car, all he could do was shake his head in admiration. But then the miracle opening happened.

His eyes were glued to her bouncing ass when she stumbled and dropped her purse and phone. Even through the closed door he could hear the impact her phone made with the ground. Seeing his chance, he shot out the car like he was running the 40-yard dash at the NFL combine.

Ms. Beautiful was already squatting down, picking up her belongings, when he went down next to her saying, "Let me help you with that." The first thing he noticed was how amazing she smelled. It was as if she'd taken a peach and rubbed it all over her body. He wasn't sure if it was her lotion or shampoo, but he knew he could be happy smelling it for the rest of his life.

The second thing he noticed as she stood up was that she didn't have a ring on. Any man who was lucky enough to snatch her up would have a diamond ring welded to her finger as soon as he could. The fact that it was absent let him know that he still had a slight chance.

"Thank you! Aren't you a gentleman," she said in a voice that was all money and class. His heart sank just from hearing her voice. With his poor upbringing, and his current status as a gang leader, he concluded this woman was totally out of his league.

He stood up and handed her the purse and phone before saying, "Here you go. Sorry about your phone."

She took off her shades and said, "It's not your fault, sweetie. It's my own clumsy self trying to walk in these heels."

"Son of a bitch," he muttered to himself.

Her hands flew to her waist. "Excuse me! What did you say?"

He stepped back with his hands up and his eyes wide in alarm. He couldn't believe he'd said that out loud. "I'm sorry, I…. I mean…. You…" He paused, opening and closing his eyes, trying to gather his composure.

"When I saw you, I thought you were a dime. Now that I can see your face, and those stunning hazel eyes, I can honestly say you're the most beautiful woman I've ever seen."

She held her frown for a few more seconds and then smiled, showing brilliant, white teeth. "Well, thank you sir. But I can't take credit for that. I guess you should thank my Mom, Dad, and God."

"That sealed the deal for me. That smile, my God, you're probably the baddest woman ever created!"

She laughed, playfully slapped his arm, and said, "You are just too much. You have a name, sweetie?"

Her heels put them eye to eye, something he found extremely sexy. And her short reddish hair made his fingers itch to run them through it. He couldn't even remember the question she'd just asked he was so mesmerized.

She started waving her hands in front of his face and saying, "Hellooo! Is anyone in there?"

He snapped back to reality and said, "What did you ask me?"

She gave another laugh and playful slap before repeating, "I asked if you have a name?"

"Oh, sorry. Yeah, my name is Damian. What's yours?" No way was he introducing himself as little anything to this goddess.

Smiling and extending her hand, she said, "I'm Tonya, and it's so nice to meet you, Damian."

He shook her hand but then pulled back. "Believe me, the pleasure is all mine. Now, I'll let you get on your way before I make an even bigger fool of myself."

Lil D turned to go when she said, "Oh no, Damian! I'm not letting you get away that easy. You got a phone?"

He turned back to face her. "Look, you're a very beautiful woman, and I know yours broke on the ground, but I can't give you my phone. I'm waiting…"

She burst out laughing, causing him to stop talking. Tonya said, "You think I'm asking you to give me your phone? You are just too cute. No honey, I want to give you my number so you can call me."

Mouth agape, he hurriedly collected himself and gave her his phone. He said, "I've never seen you around the Charlotte area. Are you just moving here?"

"No, I'm actually from the Raleigh\Durham area. I'm just down here visiting a friend." She handed him the phone back and said, "I need to get going. Call me when you have time. The number is to my back up phone in the car. Maybe we can get together for a meal real soon." She gave him a little wave, smiled, brushed his arm with her soft hand, and strutted off in the direction of the store.

She never glanced back, he knew because he watched her until she was inside the store. He shook himself and turned just in time to see the 1970 cream colored Nova SS 350 that belonged to his right-hand man, D-Nice. He made his way to the vehicle wondering if this situation would be cleared up in time for him to call the alluring Tonya tonight.

Chapter 15

"Man, I had that bitch howling at the moon on the first night. Acting like she classy. Cuz, she a straight up freak!"

"Cuz, I'm like Scarface around this mothafucka. I done put more coke on the streets than Escobar himself!"

Delmas could only shake his head as he listened to various, so called gangsters, brag about all their money and women. It was almost like they were competing with each other to tell the biggest lie. And no one wanted to call anyone else on a lie because it would only draw attention to their own.

He sat in his office in the underground headquarters of the World Redemption Agency and could do nothing except give props to the WRA women.

The conversations he could now record was made possible by three extraordinary women who excelled at their work. Phung Lei, the flawless, Asian, Head of IT at the WRA, had written the code. LaCora Clay, one of his cousins, but also Head of Research and Development, had built the device. And, of course, his niece Tonya had delivered the program to the target.

For all the work that went into it, the program was very simple. LaCora had made a ring that could deliver a virus to a device on contact. Phung had written the code so that it activated the mic and camera as long as the phone had power. And once the phone was infected with the virus, it used the phone's Wi-Fi to spread to any phone that had contact with it.

The only problem was how much information this actually generated. He had three technicians going over all the info to get rid of the bystanders who just happened to get close to their guy and it still took him hours to analyze all the data. The good news was that, over the past three days, he'd learned all he needed to know.

Using the cameras, he was able to match voices to faces and faces to profiles. So, within hours of the phone hack, he heard this conversation and knew that the threat was real.

Lil D: "What's hood, Big Homie? This is my number one right here, D-Nice."

Face G: "What's poppin? Look Cuz, it's been a long day. What you got for me?"

Lil D: "Well, like I said earlier, I followed her to this big ass compound about a mile from here. Security is off the chain."

Face: "What they got, armed guards or something?"

Lil D: "Naw, not that I could see. But the wall is like 20 feet high and it's got cameras everywhere. And the gate looks like it could stop a tank."

Face: "Alright. Ya'll wait here. Give my man the location and we'll swing through. We don't want them seeing a convoy, so we'll peep it and come back."

Face G and his driver, a muscle-bound guy named Debo, drove over to Daniel's compound and came to the same conclusion any smart person would. They made their way back to the Wal-Mart where Lil D and D-Nice got back in his Limo, then picked back up the conversation.

Face: "You right Cuz, no way can we storm the place. It might be a whole gang of niggas in there."

Lil D: "So, what you want to do, Big Homie?"

Face: "I say we put a couple of soldiers on the house and whenever the next time she comes out, ya'll contact me and we organize a way to snatch this bitch."

They all agreed to the plan and Face told them he'd be staying at a hotel nearby so they could act on the call at a moment's notice.

Delmas was conflicted though. If he let something happen to Alisha, nothing would ever convince Daniel the WRA wasn't behind it. Then he would never stop fucking up their money. But, if he warned Daniel, he would lose a perfect opportunity to catch him with his guard down. While Daniel was focused on eliminating the threat to his woman, Delmas could attack his unguarded flank and be done with him forever.

He was deep in thought, weighing the pros and cons, when Reggie entered his office with frustration all over his face. Delmas sighed, knowing his big brother was there to deliver some doom and gloom message. "What's going on, Reggie? What did I do to besmirch the Burke name?"

"I talked to Daniel again last night and he was asking me about the attack on Denise."

Delmas threw his hands up. "I told you I didn't have anything to do with that. She's a fucking reporter. There's no telling how many people have been waiting to shoot her ass."

Reggie pulled out his phone and said, "I'm sending you a video. I want you to watch it and tell me what you think."

The video popped up on his phone and Delmas turned around and sent it to the monitor on his wall. The HD video started and Delmas watched it with mounting fury. His mother had pretty much banned contact with the huge ongoing operation so no link could be established between it and the WRA. He had handpicked Terrell and Javon to run the op because they were both talented and loyal to the Agency. Now, they were out doing hits for prostitutes that could put the whole operation in jeopardy.

The last scene showed all 50 WRA agents tasked with running the fake drug scheme. He slammed both his fists into the desk and screamed, "Fuck!"

Reggie said, "At least I know now, you really had nothing to do with this."

"Those fucking idiots! Without this op, we're done. Over some big booty whore, they just killed our whole legacy." After a pause, Delmas said, "This is too big. We need to get the family together to make a decision on this."

Delmas picked up his phone to make the call but Reggie reached over and took it out of his hand. "What the hell, Reg? We need to get on this, ASAP. Start saving what we can."

"He's not gonna shut it down," Reggie said calmly.

"What?" asked Delmas. "Fuck that. If that's what he said, he's just buying time to do the most damage." Delmas frowned at his brother. "Or it's you who's stalling to try and help him?"

Reggie's face darkened and he stood up causing Delmas to slide back with hands raised. "Alright man. Just like you needed to see my reaction, I wanted to see yours." After a few seconds, Reggie calmed and sat back down.

"Daniel said he wouldn't shut it down, but only under two conditions." Delmas motioned for him to explain as he rolled his chair back towards the desk. "Number one: The four agents are to be dealt with and the punishment recorded for proof. Candace Price is to be delivered up for Daniel to deal with however he sees fit."

Delmas nodded and said, "I'm cool with that. And what's number two?"

"Absolutely no more aggressive actions from the WRA or any of its assets towards him or any of his people."

Delmas leaned back and shook his head. "I don't know about that one, Reg. We're at war…"

"And he agreed," Reggie talked over him, "to unlock our system and give us $500 Billion of our money back. He also swore that, if we upheld our part, he would never strike at us again."

Delmas exhaled loudly. "Damn! That's a good deal. But, do you think it's a serious offer?"

"I believe so. Daniel just wants to be left alone with his people. I know we'd have to present this to everyone, but I think this is where our family starts to heal."

Delmas said, "Let's take care of the first part before we bring in the family. I can have something…"

"No!" Reggie said forcefully. "Part of the deal is that I handle all this personally to make sure everything goes right. Give me a couple days and after the first part is done, we'll present the second part to everyone."

"That's cool with me. Just let me know if you need anything." Reggie said he would and then got up and left his office.

Immediately, Delmas ran a scan on his office and phone to make sure no bugs had been planted by his big brother. Something was off with his brother, so Delmas just wanted to be extra careful.

When the scan finished with no objects detected, he dialed his mother to see how she felt about this new proposal. She answered immediately. "What's going on, D? I'm in the middle of a conference call with Colombia." Colombia referred to the cartel family that supplied all their drugs for the prison contraband network. They wouldn't be happy to hear the operation was now on hold with the loss of the governor.

"Alright, Mom. I have something important to discuss with you. Just get back to me as soon as you can." He hung up and thought more on the truce being offered by Daniel.

It would benefit both sides, but Daniel would still hold all the power in the compact. There was no way to lock him out the system, not to mention what he could have done to it while he's controlled it for the last year and change. The WRA would be under constant threat that one day Daniel would change his mind and take them over again.

He was lost in thought, going over plans and scenarios, when his phone rang. It jerked him back to reality and he was shocked to see an hour had passed. He saw that the call was from his mother, so he answered it with, "How did Colombia take it?"

The matriarch of the Burke family, and WRA leader said, "Not good, but what can they do? If they try anything foolish, I'll wipe their whole country off the map." To most, that might have been just a saying. But to Lucille Drake, a few phone calls could make it a reality.

"Well, we have a couple things closer to home we need to worry about. I just had a visit from Reg and…" He went on to explain the hit on Denise and the discovery of their lucrative money laundering gig. He also gave her a rundown on Daniel's truce proposal and the pros and cons he'd come up with.

After listening, she said, "I think we have some of the same worries. If something happens to his people that we have no control over, he could take us over again. I don't like that threat always being over our heads."

"Which leads me to something else I've just uncovered." He told her about Tonya and Nyaira stumbling into a plot to kidnap Daniel's fiancé, Alisha. "The part that might come back to us is if he traces the attack back to when

Tonya met this guy. She had to do it how it was done, but now her face is all over the video from Wal-Mart."

"But?" she asked, knowing her son had a plan.

"First off, remember this all has to stay between me and you. I promised to give Reggie a couple days before we told anyone else about this."

"Boy, I taught you the meaning of the word secret. Just tell me what's on your mind."

"Well, that plan we were working on before, nix that. I came up with a plan to get rid of the threat forever. The only problem is, we have to do it before Reggie is ready to approach the family."

Impatiently, his mother said, "Well, don't keep me in suspense!" Then he told her. She was quiet for a while, and then she laughed. "I like it. Let's just hope we get the opportunity to try it out."

· ·

"Got a job for you if you're up to punishing a few rouge agents," Reggie said into the phone.

He wasn't gonna waste any time accomplishing his part in making the truce work. He hadn't even made it back to his office before starting the series of calls needed to reach the WRA problem solver.

The man said, "What kind of punishment and how many agents?"

"The permanent kind and four," answered Reggie.

"Do you want it messy to make an example, or quiet so no one really knows what happened?"

"No, not quiet," said Reggie. "I need the rest of the agents on the op to understand who is really in charge."

"My price is $1 Million, paid up front and in full. The deed will be done within 24 hours of payment."

Reggie typed a few commands into his computer and said, "Money is already there. I'll send you all the details within the hour. The job is in Durham if you want to head that way."

"I will." The man paused and said, "You know, one day me and you have to find out who's better."

"I don't do play fighting. And don't think this desk has made me soft. Twenty years ago, I kicked your ass. It won't be any different today."

"I wouldn't be too sure Reg, but that's for another time. I'll get this done, ASAP. Just send me the details."

They hung up and Reggie shook his head. The man was obsessed with being the best. The only reason he never went after the Ghost was because the Ghost never fought face to face. Eventually someone would have to put the overconfident man in his place. Whoever stepped up to do it had better understand that the only safe place to put The Author was in the grave.

Chapter 16

Still breathing heavy and dripping with sweat, Terrell 'Big Zoe' Rilley turned to look at the beauty laying naked beside him. He really didn't have a complaint with his station in life. Money, power, respect, and all the sex he could handle. But how his life had turned out was drastically different from the goals he'd set early on.

He'd grown up dirt poor in Baltimore, Maryland. Father dead and mother working three jobs just to make ends meet had made it imperative that he be successful at whatever he did. So, when a lot of his friends turned to the streets, he turned to the books.

His father might have been a no good, drug dealing, gangbanger, but he'd been smart and he passed that brain down to his only child. Zoe didn't use his intelligence for crime though. He used it to earn a full scholarship to Harvard University.

He could still remember what his Mom told him when she dropped him off for his first semester: "Temptation will be everywhere for you to waste this blessing God has given you. But I can promise you this; the devil won't have anything on me if you fuck this up." His mother scared him way more than the devil did, so he graduated with a perfect 4.0 GPA.

Zoe had majored in Political Science, but had minored in Theatre. He managed to get a few bit parts in movies and was doing good for himself. Then he was approached by an older white man named Paul Stevens.

He'd just wrapped on a movie where he'd played the role of the head drug dealer of a local gang. Having rated a private trailer, he was surprised when the man came in and made himself comfortable on his couch.

"Terrell Rilley, you're a very good actor, but how much are you making on this movie?"

The man looked prosperous and Zoe could smell an opportunity, so he answered the question. "I made a little over $20,000 for a month's work."

"What if I told you I had a role for you where you could make ten times more than that in a day?"

Zoe shook his head. "I'd say it's something illegal and I don't want any parts of it."

The man nodded and said, "It's not illegal, but the job would be making it appear as though it is."

Frowning, Zoe said, "That doesn't even make sense. Why would you want something that is legal to look illegal?"

The man stood up and said, "The job comes with a million-dollar signing bonus, a mansion, and a car of your choice. We'd have you do a couple of test jobs before you'd be given the main role. My card is on the table. When you've made up your mind, give me a call." He'd walked out without another word.

Terrell had taken one more small role, where the producers cheated him out of half his money, before he'd called the number on the card. Paul had come, blindfolded him, and took him to an underground facility where he'd been inducted into the WRA. Even though he was now well aware they had their fingers in some illegal pies, Zoe himself never participated in anything except the legal part. Eight years later and that was still a fact.

"Hello! Zoe? Why you staring at me like that?" Candy's voice snapped him back into the present and he leaned over and gave her a kiss on her soft lips.

"Everything is cool, baby. I was just thinking how good my life is. I mean, I got money, cars, jewels, clothes." He grabbed a handful of her big, delicious, brown ass and said, "And I definitely got the baddest bitch in the game."

She smiled and grabbed a handful of his lower region, causing him to groan. "Well, if you got me, you better make sure you keep doing everything to keep me."

They kissed and played around for a few minutes before he told her, "Go take a shower. We need to be seen at a few places tonight." She got up, not bashful in the least, as she strutted into the bathroom with his cum leaking down her legs.

As soon as he heard the shower cut on, he threw on a pair of shorts and shot to the bedroom door. Snatching it open, the first face he saw was Javon's. Sick bastard. Every time he had sex with Candy, Javon would move to the seat next to the door. Motherfucker probably got off on being just a few feet away as Candy screamed in ecstasy.

As usual, Javon's crew was on the left with him, and Terrell's crew was on the right. Addressing them all, he said, "In about an hour, we gonna hit a few of our spots so we can be seen tonight. Just want to remind everybody that we're out here."

Javon laughed and said, "You sure you got the energy? Sounds like you enjoying the staying at home part a little too much."

"And, if you wasn't such a fuck up, and a pussy, you would go find your own girl instead of stalking mine."

Javon hopped to his feet, which caused everyone else in the living room to jump to theirs. "Just because you top dog on this mission don't mean I won't stomp your ass. You letting this gangster role go to you head."

Stepping up in his face, Terrell said, "Role? Nigga you grew up in Beverly Hills. I'm from the streets. If I'm playing a role, it's to appear more civilized than I really am. You think it's fake, test it then pussy."

The two men stood face to face with their respective teams eying each other uneasily. Then a throat cleared behind Zoe.

He turned to see Candace standing at the bottom of the bed with a towel wrapped around her body. "Is everything okay?" she asked him.

Zoe turned back to the bigger man standing inches from his body. "Take your bitch ass and get everything ready. And I promise the next time you wolf me, Imma make it your last. Got me, nigga?"

Javon clenched his jaw as he looked at Candy over Zoe's shoulder. The words were meant to make the man lose face in front of her, and Zoe knew Javon would backdown. Javon lowered his eyes and gave a slight nod before Zoe turned around and slammed the door in his face.

"What was that all about?" Candace asked, dropping the towel and walking naked over to the closet. He followed her and hugged her from behind, rubbing his sudden erection all over her thick, entrancing ass. She moaned as one of his hands went to her chest and the other between her legs.

"Just a jealous ass nigga who mad at what I got, but not man enough to take it." She turned her head and started tongue kissing him, still grinding her ass on his manhood. As soon as he felt her wetness coating his fingers, he bent her over and entered her right there in the closet.

Wanting her to be as loud as possible for the punk ass nigga at the door, he latched onto her waist and delivered stroke after punishing stroke, deep into her core. After a few seconds, she was screaming like he was trying to kill her.

She braced her hands on the wall and then turned her head, capturing his gaze with her shocked, green eyes. "Oh my God, baby! That feels so good!" He didn't want her talking, he wanted her yelling out her pleasure. So, he grabbed her swinging breast and started twisting her nipples savagely.

The high-pitched wail, as well as the clamping of her internal muscles caused both of them to spiral out of control. He grinded inside her until she allowed him to pull out and then he carried her weakened body back to the shower.

Thirty minutes later, he was fully dressed, ready to go, and Candy was putting on the final touches of her makeup. "So, was that for me, or was it for him?"

He started to ignore her question, but decided to give her a somewhat truthful answer. "Candy, you are hands down the sexiest woman I've ever been with. I can't look at your body and not want to fuck you right then and there. So, most of it was just seeing you causally walking nude five feet from me. But the other part was for you too, just not in the same way."

Zoe paused and locked eyes with her in the vanity mirror. "It was to show you who the real boss is. I want you to understand that he will always be a second fiddle, and if he tells you any different, he's lying his ass off. I know you wouldn't be with me unless I was rich and powerful, so I'm showing you that Imma get all I can get out of the deal before you decide to move on."

She put down her lip gloss and stood up to face him in her black leather stretch pants and white Chanel shirt. "Look babe, I'm not gonna lie to you. When I first met you, that's all I was looking for. But, do you think I'd be letting you inside me with no condom if I didn't have feelings for you. I've never been in love with anyone, and I'm not really sure what it is. I just know I've never felt like this with anyone else. I don't know what the future will hold, but as far as I can see, I'm not going anywhere."

He shook his head and said, "Okay, let's get ready to go. We'll pick this up at another time."

Her eyes sparked and her hands flew to her hips. "What? You don't believe me?"

"Look Candace, everyone saw you on TV. Everyone knows what you were doing when you were a correctional officer."

"So, that's it, huh?" she asked with her body filling with tension. "I'm just a whore out for another payday? If that's what you think, why are you with me?"

He was saved from answering by the knock on the door. "Yo. Boss," Javon yelled snidely. "Everything is ready. We just waiting on ya'll."

Terrell walked over to Candace and put his arms around her ridged form. He kissed her forehead, then her unresponsive lips before saying, "I don't think of you as a whore, but I know you have your own agenda. Maybe one day we can be honest with each other and we can form something real." Her angry stare caused him to drop his arms from her waist, shake his head, and walk away.

For the rest of the night, Big Zoe went from club to club and from bar to restaurant. Candace stayed by his side, but wouldn't talk to him or acknowledge him in any way. It really pissed him off, but he knew to wait until they had privacy before he gave her a little dose of reality.

His small convoy of vehicles was nearing his home when his cell buzzed with a message. Since Candy was driving, he pulled it out, expecting to see some message from Javon or one of his crew. The message he received caused confusion to enter his mind. He was preparing to call Javon for his opinion when the display lit up showing his name.

Without preamble, Javon said, "I just got a message from Reggie Burke. Did you report me you son of a bitch?"

"Hell no! You know me better than that. My question is why did the message come from him? I've never had any contact with him."

"I've only had one," said Javon. "And I can guarantee that's it's not good. He's like our boss, but 100 times more serious."

Glancing at Candace, Zoe said, "You think they pulling us?"

After a small pause, Javon said, "It's possible, but I don't think they would with us doing so good."

"Well, we bout to find out when we get…. Hold up! Whose car is that in front of the house?" For no apparent reason, Zoe's heart started thumping. The silver Mercedes-Benz AMG GT R Coupe was not in the least bit intimidating. But, it represented an unknown that caused worry to course through his body.

Javon's Bentley pulled into the drive way first with his crew. Terrell and Candy followed in his Rolls-Royce. Then Terrell's crew in a BMW Alpine B7. Javon said, "Whoever it is, they're already in the house. All the lights are on."

Candy, finally picking up on the fact that something was wrong, said, "Is everything okay? Why do you sound so tense?"

Terrell ignored her as both crews poured out of the vehicles and met in front of the house. He and Candy joined them and Terrell asked Javon to show him the text he'd received. Just as he suspected, they had received two different messages.

"Alright everyone," he said, bringing the attention to him. "It seems like one of the bosses want to meet with us. Everyone, take your weapons back to the vehicles because, if you step foot in that house armed, you'll be killed on sight." After everyone reconvened, Zoe said, "I have no idea what this is about, but everybody keep your mouths shut and do whatever is asked. Now, let's go in and get this over with."

Candace was clutching his arm now, so he turned to her and said, "I got you. Just sit next to me and don't speak unless you're spoken to."

When the door was opened, two men stood at the threshold searching everyone as they came in. One of them said, "Sit in this room. Don't go anywhere else for any reason. You'll have a visitor in a few minutes." The two men left by the front door, leaving them alone looking at each other.

After five minutes of silence, Javon said, "Just tell me the truth, Terrell. You got us kicked off the op, didn't you?"

Keeping his cool, he said, "I told you I didn't. I'm not a rat. If I had a problem with you, I'd settle it myself."

"And how would you do that, tough guy?"

Terrell took a deep breath. "Now isn't the time. If someone shows up and we're in here arguing, they might really pull us off the op."

"Fuck this op and fuck you!" yelled Javon, jumping to his feet. "You been tryna get rid of me for years. Soft ass wanna act so tough. Let's settle this before anybody comes."

Big Zoe stood up slowly and walked over until he was right in Javon's face. "Sit. The. Fuck. Down. Nigga." Terrell was grinding his teeth in an effort to keep himself calm. They were face to face with both crews ready to intervene, when Candy let out a yelp.

He turned to see her looking at the bedroom door with a look of pure terror on her face. His gaze followed her's and the image at the door almost made him piss his pants. It was clear when everyone else noticed the presence, because all the life seemed to drain out of the room.

In a calm and soothing voice, the dark-skinned man said, "Please return to your seats and don't talk unless I ask you a question." Everyone did what the man said as he coolly assessed the room.

About seven years ago, Zoe had finally felt financially secure enough to splurge on a car. He'd used the first $1 Million to set his Mom up in a nice house with a nice car and a fat bank account so she could live a life of leisure.

The Dodge SRT Demon was a fire engine red monster that he just had to have. On the day of the delivery, he'd jumped in the driver's seat and raced around his neighborhood like a bat out of hell. Out of the back seat, a nightmare apparition had appeared. He'd gotten the car under control, but the knife at his neck had kept his heart galloping away.

The man introduced himself and said, "Your money is yours. The Agency money belongs to the Agency. If a single nickel is ever missing, well, I promise to give you enough time to write a will if you don't have one. Get rich and stay honest, because if you ever see me again, someone is going to die."

He made Terrell get out and walk home, but when he woke up the next morning, his keys were on the dresser and the car was in the driveway. The message had been received and Terrell never took a penny.

Now, sitting here looking at The Author, as he studied each of them one by one, his bowels liquified. This wasn't about the WRA reassigning anyone. This was about a fuck up. And whoever was responsible for the fuck up would be paying for it with their lives. Seeing as he was the one in charge, he sat and prepared himself for his inevitable death.

Chapter 17

Denise didn't even bother going home anymore. Once the hospital found out who Ashley was, they moved her to a private two-bed room. Denise packed a few things and moved in with her.

It seemed like weeks instead of days since her friend had been shot, but Ashley's recovery was nothing short of miraculous. The doctors were saying that by next week, she'd be ready to start getting out of bed. Secretly Denise was already helping her to the bathroom. After the first night, Ashley had venomously refused to use the bed pan. So, Denise used her new, built up strength to carefully half carry, half walk her best friend to the toilet.

They talked and they joked and they watched TV, but Ashley wouldn't allow Denise to even mention the shooting. Every time she tried to apologize, Ashley would say, "Did you shoot me? Because if you didn't, let it go. God sent me there for a reason and we're both here now, so just let it go."

Men was another topic off limits for the pair. Ashley thought Denise had just spent the past year being sexually assaulted and Denise had to keep up the pretense. So, mostly they talked about news and shows and stayed away from anything too serious.

Ashley had just had her last scheduled surgery that afternoon, so Denise had slept on and off, but checked on Ashley every hour. She was standing next to Ashley's bed, facing the door, when she became aware she was no longer alone.

"You have to work on that, Denise. I've been in here for 15 minutes and the second you felt my presence, you stiffen, which gives me all the time I need to attack." She turned to find Daniel sitting on her bed, dressed in all black.

"How the hell did you even get in here? We're on the fourth floor, and I've been facing the door for the past 30 minutes. What did you do, climb through the vent?"

He smiled and said, "You're not ready to learn the stealth arts yet. Let's clear up some of the bullshit and then I'll put you in a few classes."

"Asshole," she mumbled, making him laugh quietly. She rubbed her friend's hand and then made her way to the back of the room. "So, what brings you out this late at night?" she asked him.

He tossed her a backpack and said, "Get dressed. Everything is set and you have a date with a bitch named Candace."

A nasty smile split her face as she grabbed the bag. "Took you long enough. What are the rules of engagement?"

"None. She's yours to do with as you please. By the way, you want to fill me in on what you have planned?"

The smile on her face stretched wider. "Clean up on aisle three!"

. . . .

Javon knew he was dead the second he turned and saw The Author. The first time they met, he'd been stupid enough to try and fight the stone-cold killer. When he'd regained consciousness in the weight-room of the YMCA, he'd been laid on a bench with his hands secured to a barbell with 600 pounds attached to it.

As soon as he started moving, The Author had appeared over his head and broke the weight from the weight rest. Calmly, he'd set the heavy barbell down on Javon's chest.

The air had been sucked right out of him as he tried in vain to lift the immovable bar. The Author had leaned over him and said, "This is the only warning you'll ever get. You fuck with the WRA and you'll end up getting fucked. Do you understand what I'm telling you?"

On the brink of suffocation, Javon had nodded weakly with tears streaming down his face. The man waited until Javon was sure he would die, then snatched the weight back up like it weighed next to nothing.

When Javon's senses returned to him, his hands were free and only 135 pounds had been on the bar. He would have thought he imagined it all except for the bruise across his chest that testified to the truth of how close he'd come to death. Now, he eyed the man warily as they all sat quietly waiting to see what the psycho would do.

As usual, Javon's team had moved to the left, closest to the kitchen. Terrell's crew was on the right side closest to the front door. Everyone recruited into the Agency got an initial visit from The Author, so when he pointed at Terrell's team and told them they were free to go, they damn near left smoke trails in their rush to escape.

Then he looked at Terrell and said, "You and Candace have a meeting in a little bit. Go wait out in the car and you'll receive a text on where to go. Don't try to run, Terrell, you're safe. Just do what the text says and everything will be okay." Terrell got up and left with a scared and confused looking Candy, which left Javon and his team alone with the killer.

Javon glanced to his left to survey how his team was holding up. The two young men were sweating profusely despite the air conditioner doing its job cooling the house. The young female agent was mumbling a prayer with her eyes shut tightly. When Javon's eyes swung back to the WRA assassin, the man's indifferent stare sent a chill down his spine.

After what felt like hours of silence, but was really only a couple minutes, The Author reached into his jacket pocket.

Javon and his crew inhaled sharply, but the only thing pulled out was a phone. He glanced at each of them and smiled, seemingly enjoying their discomfort. After a series of buttons pushed on the display, the television turned on and a video started to play.

Up until the contents of the video became apparent, Javon still thought this was about Terrell ratting him out to the bosses. But the longer the video played, he had to face the fact his own lust was responsible for him and his crew being in this predicament. And all he'd ended up getting was one lousy hand job out of the deal.

When he and his team had returned from the hit, he had been sure everything had gone as planned. As they'd arrived at the target house, he'd watched the red Supra back out of the driveway. Meka had quickly turned the WRA Range Rover around and followed the car.

They had discussed it and agreed that they would follow the car and make the hit when the woman returned home. None of them except Javon knew who the target was or why the woman needed to die. He'd just told them the hit had come through on his phone from headquarters and, like the good soldiers they were, they did everything he told them to do.

With no research done before the hit, he'd thought the SUV in the driveway was just a second car. He and the two male agents had already been out of the car with guns raised by the time they saw the other woman getting out of the vehicle.

All three guns had been emptied at the target and then they'd gotten the hell out of there. Arriving back at the house, they found Candy sitting on the couch watching a movie. After a few minutes, he dismissed his crew who went to the mansion in Raleigh to rest up, leaving him alone with the super sexy woman. As soon as the others left, she turned the TV to the news as he left his seat to move closer to her.

Softly, he said, "You see what your new man is willing to do for you?" Taking a few more steps closer, he said, "Now, what do you got for your man?" Then her face was revealed and he'd known something was wrong.

"You shot the wrong women you idiot!" she whispered urgently. "I should have known better than to ask a second-rate gangster to do some real man shit."

Getting mad, he said, "I went to the spot you told me. It was only two women there. We hit them both."

"We? Who the fuck is we? Please don't tell me you took the peanut butter league with you!"

"Hey, fuck you Candy! My soldiers do what I tell them to do."

"Well, make sure your soldiers know to keep their mouths shut. If Terrell finds out about this, he might kill us all."

Javon sat down next to her and ran his hand up her smooth inner thigh. The thong and tank-top she had on molded to her curves, inflaming his lust. She smacked his face hard and said, "You loser ass nigga, I know you don't think you getting any of this. If you had done the job right, I'd be riding your dick right now. Instead, I think Imma go wake up my man and ride his." After she walked off, he listened to Zoe and Candy have loud and hard sex for almost an hour before he left to join his crew at the mansion.

Jerking out of his reprieve, he watched as on the screen, he and his crew reentered the house after the failed hit. The video and screen turned off and they once again sat in silence, waiting to see what The Author was gonna do.

He stood up and walked over to the TV, wiped off some of the dust, and placed his phone on the mantle with a clear view of the whole room. He walked back over to the couch and sat down with a sigh. "Anybody want to say something before your punishment is carried out?"

The young, nervous agent, Eric, raised his hand. The Author gestured for him to talk, so he asked, "What are we being punished for? We did exactly what we were told to do."

The Author smiled and pulled a gun from behind his back, causing everyone in the room to groan. After screwing the suppressor into the barrel, he turned to Javon and said, "Be a man and tell your crew why they are being punished."

Javon knew the only punishment dealt out by The Author was death, and he refused to die begging like a bitch, so he remained quiet. Until the bullet blew apart his knee, causing him to clutch his leg and scream in pain.

The Author didn't give him a break. "Tell them what you did or I swear this is gonna get a lot worse." After another ten seconds of moaning, another bullet was sent into his opposite shin.

Rolling around on the floor, Javon knew his time was short. The assassin was renowned for his impatience, so he figured if he could hold on a few more minutes, The Author would go ahead and shoot him in the head. One thing was for certain, he was not going to look those young agents in their eyes and tell them they were going to die because of his lust.

"Huh," said The Author standing up. He put the gun down on the couch and pulled out a knife that looked like something Rambo would use. He started advancing on Javon. "Well, I guess we do this the hard way."

Javon's stomach plummeted and urine streamed inside his pants. "Okay! Okay!" he yelled, all his resolve fading away. "I'll tell them everything!"

And he did. The three young agents looked at him with horror as they realized he'd led them on an unsanctioned hit, which meant all of them would die. Charles, the other male agent, said, "But we didn't know! We thought we were following orders. What else were we supposed to do?"

The Author shook his head sadly and said, "Yeah man, tough spot," and flipped the knife at Charles, embedding it in his throat. After the initial shocked screams, everyone went quiet and watched as Charles tried in vain to stop the blood from flowing out around the knife. It was bloody and painful to watch, but it was over in a matter of minutes.

Eric and Meka were both pleading quietly as The Author picked the gun back up and sat heavily on the couch. "A lot of people think I enjoy this, and to a certain extent, I do. But, when it's like this, where innocent people have to die because of a scumbag motherfucker like him," he said gesturing at Javon, "It really brings me no joy." He turned to Eric. "You have anything else to say?" Eric shook his head, so The Author said, "Good man," and shot him once in the head.

By now, Javon had made it back to his seat and he had a request of his own. "Since I'm going to die anyway, why don't you tell me who it is that's really killing me. I mean, who the fuck is The Author?"

Javon didn't expect an answer, but the man actually seemed surprised by the question. Nodding, The Author said, "All the years I've been killing people, no one has ever asked me that before." He paused and shook his head. "I don't think it's as glamorous a story as you'd expect, but I'll tell you none the less."

Meka didn't seem to care one bit who the man was because she kept up her soft prayers and ignored the two of them. "So, as a young man I read a lot of fiction, and for me, it was the bloodier the better. But I hated how fake everything was. I mean, can you really have a killer murdering people day in and day out but still go about his normal life?"

He seemed to be passionate about the topic, so Javon stayed silent and listened. "So, I decided to conduct a little experiment. I traveled all over the country, killing people in different ways and then writing about my experiences. I wanted other people to know what it felt like to do the things they only read about or saw in movies, so I started sending the stories to newspapers.

"I was young and dumb back then, so eventually I was caught in Texas. I was convicted of four murders and sentenced to death. But one day, I got a letter in the mail telling me to confess to all my killings and I would be set free. I thought it was a spiritual message, you know, some religious bullshitter trying to save my lost soul, but I decided to give it a try.

"My confessions started a chain of events that led to other states wanting me to stand trial for my crimes. So, I was shuttled from state to state and hearing after hearing, and on one of those trips, there was a major accident.

"When I came to, I was in a conference room inside WRA headquarters watching a reporter talk about the death of a serial killer named Wilford Sealy. That didn't make sense because that was my name and I was very much alive.

"After that, I went into hiding for a few years. Did a lot of training. Some plastic surgery and, Voilà! The Author was born."

Javon didn't think the man had any reason to lie but the story did sound like a book he'd read. It didn't matter anyway, that dead look was creeping back into The Author's eyes.

"So, I have two more punishments to administer and then I can go home" He turned to Meka. "You have anything you want to say?" She ignored him and sped up her request for God to keep her safe. "Alright then," he said, raising and firing the gun once more.

. . . .

The Author looked at the last agent and said, "I was only to kill three of you, but I do have to punish you in some way."

Meka was looking at the three bodies slumped on the various couches in stunned silence. "Hello!" he said, clapping his hands. "Earth to Meka."

She glanced at him and said, "You're really not going to kill me?"

"Like I said, I was told to kill those three and then send you back to headquarters so you can train the next assigned crew." She slumped in relief, but he said, "I still have to punish you."

She nodded and he asker her, "Which hand do you write with?" She indicated the right, so with little fanfare, he shot her in the left shoulder.

She yelped and fell back on the sofa, breathing heavily, but stayed silent through the pain. He said, "Get the keys to Javon's Bentley. It's now yours. Drive to headquarters and they'll give you medical attention and brief you on your next assignment."

He watched her go to Javon and retrieve the keys to his car, then she stumbled out the door like she'd just been released from hell. He picked up his phone and sent the text out to Terrell to get him on the move. Then he sent the video to Reggie to complete all but the last of his mission.

The knife would have to stay, even though it was one of his favorites, as well as the gun. He pulled out a second gun and placed one in Eric's hand and one in Javon's. A couple of shots later, both of their hands had gunshot residue to complete the scene of an argument that ended in tragedy.

147

After he was sure Terrell, Candace, and Meka were gone, he called the two WRA Agents to come and finish setting the scene. He wanted to be far away when the cops showed up to the house. Plus, he wasn't really required at the next part of the operation, but he knew death wasn't finished with this night. It might be the serial killer in him, but a jolt of pleasure sent him hurrying on his way so he could secretly watch the next murder.

Chapter 18

Candace always tried to present a brave front. She did it as a Corrections Officer, and she did it as an inmate. But, when she heard the muffled pops that could only be suppressed gunshots, followed by the screams, her insides started to quiver.

"Baby, what's going on?" she asked Big Zoe. "Why can't we just get away from here?"

"Because if we run, we both die." He looked at her like she was dumb for asking. "That man in there is a representative of my organizations leadership. If he says to stay here, then we stay here."

"Is he going to kill us? What the hell happened?"

"I don't know, Candace. Now, sit back and shut the fuck up. He said we're safe, so we're safe. He has no reason to lie."

She sat sulking for a little bit because of the way he talked to her. It helped for her to be angry; it made the fear recede a little bit. Candace didn't have a clue what was going on, but she had a bad feeling it involved the hit on Denise. She wanted so bad to ask Terrell but knew he would flip out over her going behind his back.

They heard one more suppressed pop and then Meka stumbled out of the house holding a bloody shoulder. Candace expected the man to come out after her, but she made it to the car, started it up, and drove away.

"She must have killed him!" she said excitedly. "Now is our chance to get away from here."

He shook his head. "She didn't kill him, he just spared her. The bosses probably wanted one of them alive to brief the new team." Just then, his phone vibrated with a message. He started the Rolls up and pulled away from the house.

"Where are we going?" she asked with trepidation.

"A warehouse not too far from here. All it said was for both of us to go in and wait for some visitors."

"Oh, hell no! They gonna kill us, Zoe! Let me out of this car right now." She scrambled for the handle, but Terrell grabbed her arm to stop her.

"Calm the fuck down, Candace! These people have no reason to want us dead. They probably just want to introduce me to the new team."

"Well, why do they keep saying both of us?" she asked nervously. "I'm just the girlfriend. Let me out and you can pick me up after you're done with the meeting."

"Candy," he said in exasperation. "These people don't ask. They tell you to do something and you do it or you die. They probably have a drone following us, and if we try to run, it will just shoot both of us to shreds."

She started looking up in the sky, trying to spot the drone. "Why are you so nervous anyway. You've been acting strange for a few days now. You have something you want to tell me?" Terrell asked.

Candace shook her head no and sat back in the seat, trying to calm her overexcited brain. In less than twenty minutes, Terrell pulled over in a huge warehouse parking lot and made his way to the open roll up door. He drove into the cavernous space and the door slammed close behind them.

Terrell motioned for her to get out and they met up at the front of the car with only the headlights for illumination. Then, from the right, a bag came sailing from the darkness and landed at their feet. Both of them recoiled from the bag and looked in the direction it came from, trying to see who had thrown it.

A masked man dressed all in black stepped out of the shadows and Candace felt a cold sweat break out all over her body. The shape was the same one that fueled so many of her nightmares. The movements were identical to the ones that caused her to have sleepless nights. But it couldn't be who she thought it was. It didn't even make sense for him to be here.

"Hello, Candace. So, we meet again. I guess you didn't learn your lesson the first time around." The voice made her whimper and grab onto Terrell as she squeezed her eyes closed childishly, hoping the nightmare would fade away.

"And who the fuck is you?" asked Terrell. "You don't know my lady, so talk to me from now on." Candace could not hear any footsteps but she knew without looking the killer was closer to her.

"Obviously, you don't know your lady. She's the reason your crew was cut in half tonight."

"Man, you need to back the fuck up. I don't know you, but you definitely don't know me. State your business so we can all get out of here." Zoe sounded like he was in control, but she could hear his heart hammering in his chest.

The masked man said, "Look at me, Candace." She shook her head no and he roared, "Look at me, you fucking coward!"

Terrell said, "I told you to back the fuck...." Then he gasped and sagged onto the hood of the car. She let him go so he didn't drag her to the ground with him where he landed on his knees, coughing and moaning.

"Look at me, Candace, or I kill this man right here right now."

She jerked around to face him. "What do you want from me? Haven't you taken enough? Why can't you just leave me alone?" Tears were streaming down her face as she yelled at the masked man.

All he said was, "Terrell, get up." Breathing heavily and holding his side, Terrell got to his feet and faced the man with Candace by his side. The man removed his mask and a confused look came over Terrell's face.

"Boss? What the hell is going on? Why all of this?"

"Look closer. You're a field agent, Terrell. I'm not your boss."

"If you're not…. Then you must be…." Terrell was stammering for an explanation. "Daniel?" he asked the man.

The handsome, brown-skinned, bald head man smiled and said, "Very good. I know we've never formally met, but I'm sure the WRA has shown you plenty of videos of me."

Candace was awestruck. This fine-looking man couldn't be her tormentor. He looked like a Wall Street banker or a lawyer. With a smile like that, no way could he have splashed acid on her without hesitation. She watched as he shook hands with Zoe, his charming brown eyes glowed with welcome.

"Anyway," the man said to Terrell, "It's nice to meet you and we'll have a conversation at a later date. But, if you know who I am, you know I didn't set up this meeting to talk." Then the killer returned to his eyes, causing them to go black. "I came here to exact some revenge."

Terrell asked nervously, "Revenge for what, if you don't mind me asking?" He glanced at Candace. "Did she do something?"

The killer's eyes locked onto her face as he ignored the question from Terrell. He kicked the bag at her feet and said, "Change into these clothes. I want to give you at least a fighting chance to survive."

She stood there glancing back and forth between the man and the gym bag at her feet. She grabbed hold of

Terrell's arm and said, "You said we were safe! That the other guy said we were safe! This guy is gonna kill us."

The man smiled. "Actually, I think the man told Terrell he was safe. He never said anything about you. And, for your information, I'm not here to kill anybody. But, whether you live or die is entirely up to you. It might help you live longer if you do what I said and change your clothes."

Getting a little angry at his mocking tone, she snatched up the bag and asked, "Where do I change?"

"Right here. It's not like everyone present hasn't seen it all before. Make up your mind quickly, you only have two minutes to change."

Knowing how serious the man was, she dumped the contents of the bag on the hood of the car. She saw a pair of Nikes, a spandex top and bottom, a thick hair tie, and a pair of socks. As both men looked on, she stripped out of her designer evening wear and replaced it with the all black ensemble that fit her like a glove.

After moving around a little bit and making herself presentable, she looked the killer right in his eyes. "Now what? You gonna beat up on a girl?"

"No," he said shaking his head. He nodded over to his left, her right, and said, "She is." It was only then that Candace could see another figure had stepped out of the shadows. It appeared to be a small woman. The figure took the last few steps so the light could reach her face and a slow smile spread across Candace's face.

Hell, she thought, this wasn't a punishment at all. Recognizing the face of Denise McCarthy, she laughed and said, "Ms. Bad Ass Reporter! I've dreamed of this day for over a year. I figure I owe you a little payback myself. I guess you set all this up to avenge your little friend, but I guarantee you, when I get done with you, you'll wish those bullets had found you instead of her."

. . . .

Denise wasn't here to talk, so she ignored the threats and taunts from the other woman. Instead of responding, she nodded at Daniel who pulled out his phone and activated the lights in the warehouse. Revealed in its center was an official sized MMA cage with an additional steel mesh section welded over the top. Once a person went in and the door was locked, there was no getting out unless someone let them out.

Daniel pulled out a gun and pointed it at Candace. "Get in the cage." With a smirk on her face, she started the trek after one more taunting look at Denise. Daniel looked at Denise and asked softly, "Are you sure?" She nodded and walked behind the suddenly confident, bigger woman.

Denise was only 5-foot 5-inches compared to the other woman's nearly 6-feet. And although she had put on an impressive 10 pounds of muscle, making her 130 pounds, she was still outweighed by at least 40 pounds. She also knew the woman had served in the military and had kept up her training while working as a prison guard. Denise filed all the information away, but knew she had to do this for Ashley.

Terrell walked up to them as Candace was stepping into the cage. "Can you guys please explain to me what this is about?"

Denise was in the zone, preparing her mind for the death match, but Daniel took the time to run down how Candace had used Javon to put a hit on Denise. He explained how the unexperienced crew had fucked up and killed a cop and wounded Denise's friend.

She heard Terrell curse and say, "I told her to leave that whole thing alone. I should have kept a tighter leash on all of them."

Daniel assured him that it wasn't his fault and the people responsible had paid. Then Denise stepped into the cage and nothing else mattered to her.

Daniel locked the door and said, "Only one of you will be coming out. There is no quitting or giving up. The only way to win is to kill your opponent. Whoever wins, you have my word, you will be free to go. There are no rules and you can start whenever you want."

Denise and Candace listened, but their eyes were locked on one another. Both felt like they owed the other some form of payback. And to a certain extent, they were both right.

Even though Daniel had ultimately forced Denise to comply with some of his early wishes, Denise had wanted the ratings and fame that came along with the big stories. So, she had gone along with the plan to humiliate Candace on live TV in front of the world. As a reporter, it had been her job, but the callous way she went about it set the stage for Ashley and Officer Clark to pay the price.

Shaking her head to clear her thoughts, she focused on the woman who had every intention of killing her. Daniel had told her, once she was inside the cage, she was on her own. There were cameras set up so Walt, Ann, and Alisha could watch the fight from inside the War Room at the compound. She had to win this fight and, like with most fights, most of the battle was in the mind.

Candace clearly knew this too as she started taunting her while stalking around the cage. "So, the little girl wants to put her big girl pants on. Maybe to start off, I should put you over my knee and spank your little ass." With that, Candace charged at her with arms outstretched.

At the last possible moment, Denise side stepped to the left, threw a right elbow into the woman's kidney, and then executed a perfect spinning knee to her lower back. Candace screamed as she went down, but had the presence of mind to roll out of the way as Denise tried to stomp on her ankle.

Candace lunged to her feet and massaged her sore back. Element of surprise now gone, Denise knew the woman would now be more careful with her attacks. But her mouth was another story all together. "I guess you gave up some of that tight ass for your killer boyfriend to teach you a few moves. See, we're not so different. We both trade what we have to get what we want."

Denise tried not to respond, but her pride got the better of her. "I'm nothing like you!" she said through clinched teeth. "You've been a prostitute your whole life. You're nothing but a low rent whore, something you probably learned from your mother."

Candace screamed in fury and charged again. This time Denise grabbed the woman's right arm and, with a mid-air flip, took her down to the mat, face first.

Blood gushed out of the woman's nose and mouth as Denise bent her arm up behind her back. Candace tried to spin her body to relieve some of the pressure, but Denise had the hold locked in pretty good. Leaning down onto Candace's back, Denise wrapped her left arm around the woman's neck and changed the hold to a rear-naked choke.

Flipping onto her back, Denise locked her legs around Candace and waited for the lack of oxygen to take its toll. But Candace was strong, and she also had fury burning through her veins. She rolled them back over and crawled to her knees.

Denise's arms were burning with exhaustion, still she upped the pressure a little bit more. But, no matter how tight she squeezed, she couldn't stop Candace from making it to her feet. Once there, she staggered a little and then jumped, using their combined weight to drive Denise into the mat.

The back of her head struck the mat and dazed her just enough that Candace was able to get free. But she didn't retreat. Candace spun around and launched a massive elbow at her face. Denise was able to spin her face to the side, but the elbow connected with her left eye, causing it to instantly swell shut.

Dazed and trying to block all the blows raining down on her, she heard Daniel yelling for her to move. Candace was too heavy, so Denise couldn't dislodge her no matter how hard she tried. And she was too tall, making it impossible for Denise to get her into a clutch.

She felt herself fading fast. Too many blows were slipping through her guard and finding its target. It might have been her mind playing tricks on her, but it felt like the punches were starting to lose their steam. Then, with sweat and exhaustion lacing her body, Candace sagged and rolled off of her.

Candace was bigger and stronger, but she hadn't been training like Denise had. If the woman had been in better shape, Denise was very much aware that her life would have been over. Blood was now flowing from several cuts on her face, but she labored to her feet knowing that to lay there and let the other woman catch her breath would be suicide.

She looked over and saw Candace had made it to her hands and knees. Now that she wasn't on her back getting pummeled, Denise could feel her energy returning. She kicked Candace in her head causing her to crash back down to the mat, flat on her back.

Denise knew she wasn't fully there because Daniel's shouts of, "Finish her! Finish it, Denise!" sounded like it was coming from a long tunnel. She also knew she was leaning and staggering to her left whenever she tried to go straight. Her body felt like it was recharging, but her brain felt like she'd just been in a car wreck.

But her vision was mostly clear out of her right eye when she glanced at Daniel, who was jumping up and down and pointing at Candace laid out on the mat. Denise spun around and focused once again on the target of her mission.

It took some doing, but Denise stumbled over until she was standing next to the bloody woman. As best she could, she lined her knee up with Candace's throat, performed a small jump, and brought all of her 130 pounds down on the other woman's windpipe.

The pain of the blow registered first as Candace rolled around in their combined blood, holding her injured neck. Then her eyes went wide as she realized that inhaling through a crushed windpipe was not possible.

Denise watched with little satisfaction as Candace raked at her neck, unable to make a sound as she slowly suffocated. Understanding that she was dying, Candace looked pleadingly at Denise. She thought this moment would feel good. Would somehow bring her peace. But all Denise felt was sadness.

In training, Daniel had told them it wouldn't be like a movie. The person wouldn't just roll over dead after ten seconds. He'd warned them that it could take up to 30 minutes if the person's body was trained in the lack of oxygen and the crush wasn't complete. After five minutes of watching Candace struggle, Denise couldn't take it anymore.

With tears now mixing with the blood on her face, Denise sat next to Candace and pulled her upper body onto her lap. She grabbed her chin and the back of her head and gave a vicious twist, granting Candace a little mercy by breaking her neck.

Her head was still swimming and she faded in and out of consciousness as Daniel came in and scooped her up. She was aware of Daniel talking to Agent Terrell, but couldn't make sense of the words. Then she passed out.

When she came to, Ann and Alisha were standing over her and she was hooked up to a bunch of machines in a hospital room. Knowing that she was back with her family, safe and protected, she allowed a small, relieved smile to slip through as the darkness once again swam up to claim her.

Chapter 19

"So, we've finished the first part, in my opinion the hardest part, and now we just need to agree to this truce and we can move on from here." Reggie and the rest of the WRA leadership were meeting in the glass enclosure overlooking the underground command center inside their headquarters. He had picked this site for the vote so the family could see all the computer screens that read 'Offline' and realize how beneficial this truce could be.

He also wanted to return them to the place they'd last tried to outsmart Daniel and remind them of the catastrophic consequences. While trying to run an op to take over one of Daniel's underground prisons, the master strategist had turned the tables with a counter-op that stole all of the money and assets legally connected to the WRA. Then he'd locked them out of all their networks which resulted in the loss of all their government contracts. A major blow to the integrity and reputation of the WRA that needed to be corrected.

"Daniel has agreed to return $500 Billion of the taken money and restore our systems. All we have to do is agree to leave him and his people alone. Seems like a no-brainer to me," Reggie stated.

"Well, hold on now!" exclaimed Lucille Drake from her customary seat at the head of the table. "This situation isn't as cut and dry as he's making it out to be." She was looking down the table, addressing the other five people besides Reggie and herself. The seven family members made up the ruling counsel of the World Redemption Agency. All major decisions were decided by them with a majority vote. Everyone would get their say and, whichever side got the vote, the decision would be final.

Reggie rolled his eyes to the ceiling and said, "By all means Mother, tell us why it's so complicated."

Ignoring his sarcasm, she said, "Well, for starters, we have no way of keeping Daniel out of our systems after he gives us access again. And we have no way of knowing what he's done to the system since he's had control of it. He could have infected the whole system with traps and snares that could make it useless to us. We would never be able to just go on as normal because we would always have the threat of Daniel hanging over our heads."

"We are a global Agency," Reggie said, causing all heads to turn his way. "We are always under some threat, whether it be physical or cyber. Our IT department is top of the line, and to suggest that our people are anything but the best is an insult."

"Oh, I know our IT department is the best. All the way up until we run into Daniel. It's impossible to get ahead of him on a normal day. So, imagine how far we're behind now that he's had our system to play with for over a year!" Lucille was all but shouting in her enthusiasm, but Reggie was calm and under control.

"So, are you suggesting we turn down the deal, let him keep us out of our system, and let him shut down the last profitable operation we have going?"

All heads turned to Lucille as she struggled to come up with an answer. When she remained silent, Reggie said, "And if any of you think we are taking a risk, think about the gigantic risk Daniel is taking."

"What risk?" asked Delmas. "From where I'm sitting, he holds all the power in the deal."

"You think so?" asked Reggie.

"Yeah, I do," he replied.

Reggie looked at each person sitting at the table. Every one of them was his family. He would kill or die for any one of them. He leaned back in his chair and said, "How many of you have been attacked by Daniel physically without provocation?" After a silent pause, he asked, "How many of you feel Daniel is a threat to your life?" Again, everyone stayed silent. "The point is, if Daniel doesn't uphold his part of the deal, we lose money and face. If we don't uphold our part of the deal, Daniel could lose his life or the life of a loved one. So, you tell me who's taking the bigger risk with this truce."

After another lengthy silence, Reggie stood up and walked over to the wall of glass overlooking the command center. Behind him, Lucille said, "He might not have come after us personally, but he's killed plenty…"

Reggie spun on her. "Don't give me any of that woe is us bullshit. You don't give a rat's ass about any of the people he's killed. If you did, you wouldn't have sent half our soldiers on a suicide mission to kill him and his people last year at the prison."

After the failed attempt to take over the prison, Lucille made a command decision to kill Daniel, Walt, Ann, and Denise. They all knew Daniel had a pulse weapon that could kill every one of them with no danger to his own people. Lucille had told the soldiers, if they didn't stay and face sure death, agents would be visiting their homes as punishment. Daniel had showed mercy on them and shot them with knockout bullets and dropped them all off at a WRA safehouse.

"As the leader of this organization, I can use our resources any way that I see fit," said Lucille. "I only allowed this vote process…."

"Allow!" roared Reggie. The temperature turned icy as his rage threatened to boil over. "Have you forgotten who you're talking to? Allow? You think I don't know my birthright? I only allow you to sit in that seat out of honor and respect for what you've done for the WRA. But, if you want to start throwing weight around, I think you'll find that I'm the unstoppable force here!"

"Try it!" warned Lucille. "You might be surprised at the loyalties I've acquired over the past 30 plus years."

"Hey!" interrupted Kashonda Wilson. "Why are we in here fighting about this? Let's all calm down, take our seats, let everyone have their say, and then cast the votes. There's no need for all the infighting."

Kashonda was the oldest of the Burke siblings, and the only female. At 48 years old, she was the fourth in command at the WRA as the Head of Intelligence. Standing at 5-foot 1-inch, the brown skinned, hazel eyed beauty had a smile that could light up the drabbest of rooms. With her short, light brown hair, she was always the most fashionable person in sight. She definitely used her attributed to her advantage. Just as she had taught her daughters, Tonya and Nyaira, a pretty face was always underestimated. So, while men were checking her out, she was busy discovering all their secrets.

After a few tense seconds of holding his mother's stare, Reggie went back to his seat at her right hand. Lucille took her seat and said, "There is one more point I want to make before we move on." She looked at Reggie and he shrugged for her to go on. "I'm curious as to the catalyst that started this war in the first place."

"Um, I'm pretty sure it had something to do with us voting to keep him in prison for ten years," said Mary Sue Truesdale.

Mary Sue was Lucille's younger sister and was the property and office manager for the WRA. It was her job to maintain all the property owned by the WRA all around the world. She had gotten her 5-foot 9-inches, as well as her long blond hair and green eyes, from their parents mixed up gene pool. At 56 years old, her body was full and mature and she was still very much an attractive woman.

"No, Mary Sue, I'm talking about before we ever took the vote," explained Lucille. "We know Daniel. He learns every single detail about a target before he ever makes a move. I've never been convinced that he didn't know it was our operation he was infiltrating."

"After all this time, I don't see why it matters," said Mary Sue.

Almost 15 years ago, the old governor of North Carolina, a WRA asset, had grown a conscience and sought help in shutting down the prison contraband network he'd helped set up. Using go-betweens, the job ended up at Military Intelligence where it was offered to Daniel. Without a word to any of the family, he took the job and made a two-year commitment to help the governor. As punishment for going against the WRA, a majority vote led to him doing ten years instead of two.

When Daniel finally got out, he declared war on pretty much everyone. The CIA, FBI, NSA, Homeland Security, and the WRA all felt his wrath. Daniel went through hell those ten years in prison and he made it his mission to unleash hell on them also. The other agencies had been scared to strike at him because of his WRA connections. But Daniel let it be known that the WRA was his main target anyway. Since the other agencies would benefit from the WRA's downfall, they were content to sit back and let the war play out.

Answering her sister's question, Lucille said, "It matters because, if the catalyst is still active, then this isn't a real offer. It's just a move to give him space for another attack."

Delmas nodded. "You know, you have a valid point. He had to have another reason than just wanting to help the governor. No matter what he's turned into now, back then he was extremely loyal to us and the WRA. So, something major had to have happened for him to turn on us."

"But what?" asked Mary Sue.

Hearing her tone, Reggie's head snapped in her direction. He squinted his eyes and studied his aunt from across the table. She knew something. Seeing his scrutiny, she dropped her gaze to her hands on the table. He had no idea what game she was playing, but his normally open book Aunt Mary was hiding something vey important to this topic.

No one else saw the exchange, so they went on with the conversation. Lucille said, "I think the answer to that question, Mary Sue, will lead to the end of this war."

"No!" interjected Reggie. "The end of this war will come with a majority vote for this truce." He glanced around at his family. "All this conspiracy talk is just to confuse the issue. Daniel is offering to leave us alone if we leave him alone. That's the point of us sitting here today. So, let's dispense with the bullshit theories and get on with the business at hand. Anyone has something to add dealing with the truce before we vote?"

"Yeah," said Delmas. "I just want to say that I believe the truce is a legitimate offer, but I don't think it will last. What happens if Walt or Ann goes back to work and gets killed in the line of duty? Do you believe Daniel will think it was anything but a scheme of ours? Or what about if Denise runs with a story that someone doesn't want her to pursue? Whose fault will it be if she gets hurt?"

"Once again," said Reggie, "Give me a solution or alternative to the problem. If you can't, you're telling us to turn down the truce and effectively kill the WRA."

"Or we could go on the offensive and handle the risk before it becomes more of a problem," stated Delmas ruthlessly.

"You mean, kill him and his people while he's trying to offer us a truce?" Delmas shrugged in answer, as if to say, what else could be done. Reggie shook his head at the simple mindedness of his brother, and focused on the rest of the table. "Anyone has anything intelligent to add I should have said." A hand went up and Reggie couldn't help but laugh at his little sister, Phung Lei.

As the fifth in command as the Head of IT, and once fiancé to Daniel, Phung Lei was as striking and smart as a person could be. Standing at 5-foot 2-inches, and weighing 115 pounds, the Asian knockout had the body of a goddess and the face of an angel. With her light brown eyes and extremely long, raven-black hair, she had the power to make men weak in the knees. But it wasn't her beauty that made her so dangerous.

Her intelligence was on par with any of the Burke relatives. And with the computer forensics training she'd received from Daniel, she was easily the second best hacker in the world. But Daniel had broken her heart, and no matter how bright her smile was, she always had a sadness about her.

Reggie nodded for her to talk and she took a deep breath before beginning. "First of all, I want to say that we are no closer to regaining control of our system since the first day Daniel took it over. And I think we forget how much control he actually has. He doesn't just control the money and software, if you recall, the power and hardware is included in all of that. Ever since he took over our system, he could have killed us at any time. But he hasn't."

She looked at each of them in turn before continuing. "As I still very much love him, as all of us should, it sickens me to hear anyone speak about ending his life. No matter what he's done to any of us, he is still our family. I say, if all he wants is to be left alone, that's the least we can give for all the pain we've caused him."

Everyone remained quiet as they thought about their own feelings towards Daniel. Reggie felt it was the perfect time to call for the vote. "Okay, everyone. I am officially calling the vote for whether or not the WRA will enter into a formal enforceable truce with Daniel Burke and his people. I'll start it off with one yea."

He looked at his mother. She said, "Just on the trust factor of the other party, I have to vote nay."

"Okay," said Reggie. "We have one yea and one nay." He turned to look at his brother.

"I too am voting nay on the fact that I don't feel it will last," said Delmas.

"We now have two votes of nay, against one vote of yea." Reggie turned to Phung and nodded for her to cast her vote.

"I vote yea because I truly believe all he wants is to be left alone so he can enjoy life with his new family." Reggie watched a tear track down her face and he knew how much it hurt her to make that statement.

"Votes are tied at two apiece." Next, Reggie looked at Kashonda.

"This situation has destroyed our family and it's gone on long enough. I vote yea so maybe we can start to heal."

"That puts the yeas at three, and the nays at two." He looked to his Aunt Mary Sue with really no clue how she would vote. There was something going on with her and he was determined to find out what it was.

"I fear," Mary Sue began, "that this family is broken beyond repair. So much betrayal and hate and pettiness has torn down the legacy that my father worked so hard to create. This Agency was supposed to be the glue that held us all together, but our own wickedness has pushed us apart.

"Something tells me that it would be a fitting punishment for this Agency to be destroyed by one of its own sons. With that in mind, I vote nay in the hopes that a rejection of his truce will lead Daniel to finally unleash everything he has on this evil organization!"

Everyone sat in stunned silence after the damnation prophesized against the WRA. No matter what the outcome of the vote, Reggie definitely needed to get to the bottom of what his aunt was hiding.

"Well, with only one vote left to cast, we're all knotted up at three for nay and three for yea. While I have everyone's attention, I do want to remind everyone that this is an official WRA vote and the decision will be final. If anyone goes against the majority vote, the consequences will be swift and permanent." With that warning, he turned to the last person in the room, his cousin, Dollis Truesdale.

At 31 years old, Dollis was not just Mary Sue's daughter, she was also the accountant for the entire WRA. She was over all budgets for every operation, as well as the payroll for every agent associated with the WRA. She was a true Burke, a real genius who could recall every number she'd ever written. She was most known for her ability to analyze any situation mathematically.

She had inherited her mother's perfect mixed skin tone, long blond hair, and sparkling green eyes. At almost the exact same height, she represented the slim and curvy image her mother used to possess. Dollis showed very little emotion and never made decisions based on them. There was no way to predict which way she would go as she thought over all the data.

"After analyzing all the data and running all the probabilities, the numbers say there is only a 12% chance this truce would last longer than a year. The chance of it lasting longer than five years in inconsequential. And, if the truce is made and then broken, Daniel and his people will all be dead in under six years."

Reggie's heart sank as he heard those numbers because he heard the ring of truth in her figures. Dollis never went against hard data, so her mind was already made up.

She continued. "I remember when I was a preteen. We would all compete to see who was the smartest." She turned to Reggie. "None of us could ever beat you. Even though you were a lot older than me, I still expected to win, but I never did. Then one day, Daniel won one of the trivia rounds against you. We celebrated by eating a ton of candy even though you still won the game in the end.

"But I learned a valuable lesson from Daniel that day. When I asked him how he had answered a question correctly that he'd never heard before, he said sometimes you just have to go with your gut."

This was probably the longest speech Reggie had heard her make since she'd graduated college at 14 as the Valedictorian. His hope soared with every word out of her mouth.

"I remember also when Daniel decided to go into Military Intelligence instead of the CIA. I was about 13 and everyone was so upset with him. I decided to ask him why he did it. He looked me in my eyes and he said, 'Dollis, even though your last name is Truesdale, you're a Burke. And a Burke always does what a Burke says he or she will do.' And thinking back, Daniel has never deviated from that except to show mercy to those against him.

"This caused me to look closer at the data and I came to a startling realization. The percentages are so low, not because of Daniel, but because of the WRA. Daniel won't be the one to break the truce. The data shows it will be us."

Sadly, the emotion she was showing after all this time was regret. "It's sad but, without some form of truce in place, the time Daniel has is cut even shorter. So, after all the data is filled in, and all the research done, I have to vote yea just because it will result in my cousin living a longer life."

Roars of both disbelief and celebration rose before Reggie made the vote official. "With a vote of four to three, the yea's win on the matter of accepting the proposed truce with Daniel Burke." Looking at his mother and brother, he said, "And I say again, to go against this decision will result in harsh penalties. Think about that before you take any action that could be considered aggressive or oppressive to Daniel or any of his people."

Everyone was talking and moving about as he turned to look down the table. He sprang to his feet when he didn't see everyone he expected to see. He rushed over to the door just in time to see Mary Sue exiting the command center far below.

He stepped out to give chase but stopped at the top of the steps. He needed to contact Daniel and get the ball rolling on this truce. When he turned back around to enter the glass enclosure, he saw Delmas and his mother having a private meeting at the head of the table.

Knowing all of them could read lips, the pair was covering their mouths so no one could ease drop on the conversation. Being pulled in so many directions was nothing new to Reggie. He just pulled out his phone and called Daniel. At least he knew this was one thing he could handle that might bring joy to someone's life.

Chapter 20

Later that night, Delmas made his way to his mother's sleeping quarters where they agreed to meet after the truce outcome was announced. The yeas winning out had come as a total shock as Delmas and Lucille had spent two days dodging Reggie so they could lobby for votes.

As soon as The Author had reported the first objective done, and sent Reggie the proof, he had immediately sent the family a rundown on what was going on. He had also requested everyone send him a time which would be convenient for everyone to meet. While playing as if they were super busy with other stuff, Delmas and Lucille had ventured out in search of votes.

Delmas told his mother that talking to Phung or Kashonda was a waste of time, but she had insisted, so he went. His prediction had been right and the attempt to bring them over to their side had the opposite effect. In fact, it pretty much guaranteed they would vote with Reggie.

Being emotional creatures, Delmas hated relying on women to think logically. They always fought so hard to see the best-case scenario. More than likely, if something was clearly defined right in their face, they'd slip those rose-colored glasses on before making a decision. But while he'd been striking out with his two ladies, Lucille had been winning the gold.

She came back with a guaranteed vote from Aunt Mary Sue and a tentative vote from Dollis, who said she would vote with the statistics. With a majority all but secured, they made themselves readily available for the vote meeting. Only to come up short in the end.

Delmas knocked on the panel door and it slid into the wall to allow him access. The newly installed second door remained closed until the first door slid back into place. This was just a safety feature put in to give the occupant a little warning that someone was coming in, namely Daniel. They had been installed since the last time he'd breached their domain.

The second door opened and revealed his mother, still fully dressed, sitting on the couch waiting for him. The TV was turned to a news station that was showing the picture of the missing, and very dead, Candace Price. Good luck finding her, thought Delmas. One thing he could give Daniel credit for was getting rid of bodies. Alive or dead, if he didn't want you found, you pretty much vanished off the face of the earth.

"What the hell took you so long?" his mother demanded, sitting her drink down.

"I wanted to listen to a few more of the recent recordings to make sure those guys were still in place. Now that we've loss the vote, they're pretty much our last hope."

"And what are they up to?" she asked.

"Getting restless. The leader, Face G, is ready to pack up and head home. He said he would stay a couple more days and, if Alisha didn't come out, Lil D would be put in charge of her capture."

Lucille rolled her eyes and said, "None of these idiots stand a chance against Daniel, but without Face G and his people, I doubt they'll even be able to take on Alisha by herself."

Delmas gave an evil smile, and said, "I think it's time I paid a visit to this Bernie Alston. Now that Daniel has returned our money and unlocked our system, I think I can make the man an offer he can't refuse."

She shook her head. "Reggie was right about one thing: Going against an official family vote is not wise. I'm starting to have second thoughts about even allowing these guys a shot."

"You're forgetting that Tonya and Nyaira have been seen in the vicinity of these guys. Hell, Tonya has been staying close to Lil D since we got wind of all this. Not to mention, Daniel knows one of them is always watching his home. If these guys make a move and don't take him out when he comes to the rescue, then we're fucked anyway. So, we might as well offer our assistance to make sure they at least have a chance."

"You do understand that you can't just coach these guys? We would have to use the opportunity to insert our guys and take them all out, and I do mean all. Face and his people. Daniel and his crew. And we'd have to do it without leaving a trail back to us."

Up until this point, Delmas had been standing beside the couch, ready to leave so he could put action to his plan. But now, he sat on the arm of the leather couch and regarded his mother.

"I'm gonna handle this myself with a very specialized, hand-picked, team. I can't trust anyone else to do a thorough enough job to guarantee our safety. But there's another aspect to our protection that I'm not sure you've thought about."

She laughed at his comment and waved him off. "I can't wait until you're my age and all these young people treat you like an invalid. You think I haven't figured out that at least one more person has to die before we're safe? I've already set that into motion. You handle your part and let me worry about the internal part."

He eyed her critically for another few seconds, then shrugged. It was just as much her ass on the line as his, so he had to trust her to do the job right.

Delmas stood up and said, "I have a few things to handle before I head down to Charlotte. Let's keep each other informed of our progress incase we run into any snags."

"You mean like the old woman not being able to pull her weight?" asked Lucille. Delmas was about to placate her, but she waved him off again. "That's a two-way street. You make sure you let me know what's going on on your end also. It really won't make sense to do mine before yours, but if the opportunity presents itself, I'm gonna move ahead."

"Alright," said Delmas, walking to the door. "Hopefully this will all be over soon and we can finally sit back and enjoy the fruits of our labor." As the inner door opened and he stepped inside, he couldn't shake the horrible feeling that things were about to go to shit. As he headed back to his office for some last-minute preparations, his heart ached. Daniel wouldn't take any of this lying down, and Delmas was sure death would be visiting a few people that neither side anticipated.

· ·

Tonya was exhausted. What had started off as a minor path crossing had turned into a full-fledged operation. She spent most of every night hanging with Lil D and his crew. Then she had to relieve Nyaira at Daniel's house during the day. As things were, she was lucky to get three to four hours of sleep a day. She was trained for it, but she didn't know how long she could keep up this pace.

It was 2:00am and everyone was just now leaving the hotel where Face G was stationed. He'd booked the whole top floor and placed a man at both stairs and another at the elevators. Tonya was somewhat impressed with his security and organization skills. But truth be told, any junior agent at the WRA could infiltrate his set up with ease.

She had met him for the first time only 24 hours ago. His demeanor towards her had been indifferent, gazing upon her as if she was nothing more than warm female flesh. It had been a struggle for her to keep the aggression out of her body, but she'd done it and he hadn't sensed the real threat that she was.

On the flip side, she could sense the danger that the man did little to hide. He seemed to enjoy the fear that he invoked in his own people. In her world, he was nothing but a man with a pistol and a penis, and he didn't care which one he got to shoot off.

She pulled over in the parking lot of the Wal-Mart near Daniel's house so she could change out of her slutty clothes. Baggy sweatpants, sneakers, and T-Shirt in place, she was pulling her BMW onto the street when her phone signaled an incoming text. It was the text she'd been waiting for, and she pumped her fist when she saw the truce proposition had passed.

Smiling, because she loved her Uncle Daniel and didn't want to see him hurt, she drove on and parked about a quarter mile from where Nyaira was still on watch. She exited her car and jogged at a slow pace down the street. As soon as she spotted Ny's red Audi A-5 coupe, she ducked down and sent her sister a text. When she got the all clear, she quickly made her way to the passenger side of the car.

She slipped in and both of them methodically studied their surroundings in silence. After two minutes, they both relaxed, knowing that the two cars Face G had watching the house hadn't seen her movements.

Nyaira started up instantly. "Tonya, you are the most beautiful woman in the world," she said in a deep voice, mocking Lil D. And just like every night, she burst out laughing uncontrollably.

Tonya smartly said, "Ny, find a new joke. We look just alike. If he had seen you, he'd have said the same exact thing." She tried to look sternly at her little sister, but ended up laughing with her. "You are so crazy," Tonya told her, musing her sister's hair.

"Hey! Watch it!" Nyaira exclaimed. "Don't be messing up my hair because yours look like shit." Like the loving sisters they were, they took about five minutes to poke and prod at each other to show that they cared. Then Tonya turned to business.

"Did you get the text from Mom?" asked Tonya. Nyaira said she did so Tonya said, "Thank God this whole thing is over. I'm surprised Uncle Delmas hasn't called with some new orders."

"I wonder if now that we have a truce, they'll want us to take out the threat to him and his family?" speculated Ny.

"I hope so," Tonya said with feeling. "All these dirty bastards just to kidnap one woman. Sometimes I wish they'd go after Daniel so he could wipe them off the face of the earth."

Daniel had always been more of a brother to them than an uncle. No matter what he had going on in his life, he'd always taken time out to be with them. He was more than a decade older than them both, but he would watch animated movies and play games with them whenever he could. And when they were older, he'd turn every situation into a teachable moment. Bottom line, they loved their uncle because he'd never been shy about showing his love towards them.

Tonya's phone ringing stopped the conversation as she showed her sister who was calling. She answered with it on speaker, and said, "Hi, Mr. Burke. You have something new going on?"

"I sure do," he answered cheerily. "I want you and Nyaira to abandon this mission and come to headquarters."

"Alright, but why do you want us at headquarters?" Neither one of them lived in the underground complex. Nor did they spend a lot of time there. They lived in a three-story townhouse in downtown Raleigh.

"Until these clowns do whatever they're gonna do, I want both of you protected. The safest place we have is right here in HQ."

"Wait a minute," said Tonya. "What do you mean whatever they're gonna do? We know what they're gonna do."

"It's not your concern, Tonya. Daniel is on his own now. So, get your sister and get out of there," demanded Delmas.

"My mom said that the truce is now in effect."

After a short pause, Delmas said, "And your point is?"

"My point is, we need to warn him or help him if we're now in a truce."

"As your boss, I'm telling you that you will do no such thing. He is not our ally, okay? He wants us to leave him alone, and that's exactly what he's gonna get."

"So, I'm just supposed to walk away, knowing that these dickheads are gonna kill or kidnap his fiancé?" she asked in disbelief.

"That's what your gonna do because that's what I'm telling you to do. Now, get over here before you get caught in the middle."

"No!" said Tonya. "Hell no! I don't live at HQ and I know you don't want us there to protect us. You want to lock us up so we won't contact Daniel."

"Tonya, don't fuck with me on this. I'm giving you a direct order to…"

"Damn your order. You don't tell me what to do unless it's on one of your missions. I'm not coming to HQ. Now, if you want me to abandon the mission, fine, I'll leave. But, I'm going to my own home and good luck to anyone trying to stop me."

Delmas stayed quiet for a full minute before saying, "Alright. But you and Ny stay at the house and don't contact Daniel. If you go against that directive, niece or not, I'll kill you myself," then he hung up.

The sisters looked at each other with slack jawed amazement. "Can you believe that?" Tonya asked Ny. "All Uncle Daniel ever wanted was to be left alone to live his life. Now, they're so mad he got his wish, they want to sit back and watch his life go up in flames."

"Tonya," said Ny with trepidation. "It's deeper than that now. Daniel knows we've been watching his home. If we disappear right before Alisha is attacked, he'll know that we knew. Then he'll do his research and see you were hanging with these guys."

Connecting the dots, Tonya nodded. "This will connect the gang to the WRA and will be in direct violation with the truce vote." They sat in silence, thinking, when the truth finally hit Tonya. "They're gonna let the gang hit Alisha and use the distraction to go after Daniel."

Nyaira nodded and said, "That's the perfect plan, but it'll still be incomplete. To avoid discovery, Delmas would have to eliminate everyone who could speak the truth against him."

"So, going home isn't an option," said Tonya. "We have to stay so we can warn Uncle Daniel when this goes down. At least I don't have to hang out with those losers anymore. Head back to my car and go get some rest. Delmas won't make a move on us until everything is over. We just have to make sure, when the time is right, we can warn Daniel and get out of dodge before the WRA can link the leak to us."

Tonya hugged her sister and switched places with her in the car. As Nyaira slipped out the passenger side into the shadows, Tonya brushed her fingers down her arm. Nothing would happen to her little sister. Their mother had always taught them that being siblings was the closest bond they'd ever have. Other generations of Burkes might not take that too seriously, but Tonya did.

She sat back in the car, diligently watching out for her uncle's family. The uncle who had once told her that he would die to protect her and her sister. Well, she never told him, but she was gonna show that she felt the same way about him.

Chapter 21

"Man, turn that fucking game off!" yelled Face G. "How in the fuck are ya'll gonna be on point if you stay up all night playing a stupid ass basketball game?"

Face G was in his own room, but Debo and Quette were in the connecting room. They had the volume up so loud that it sounded like they were at a live game. Face was trying to sleep and it was already 4:00am.

"Sorry OG," yelled Debo. "We in the fourth quarter and this the last game."

"Well, turn the sound down so I can fucking sleep." The sound instantly went to a murmur and Face rolled back over to sleep.

The next thing he knew, he was jerked awake by the sound of the game again. He looked at his phone and saw it was 7:30am. "I told ya'll to turn that stupid ass game off. I swear, Imma kick somebody's ass if ya'll don't tighten the fuck up!"

He expected another yelled apology, but all he got was the continuous roar of the game. Jumping up and throwing the covers off his gym shorts clad body, he stormed towards the connecting door. "You motherfuckers think I'm playing?" He snatched his gun off the dresser and kicked the door wide open.

What he saw caused him to shake his head in denial. The person playing the game wasn't Debo or Quette or any of his other men. It was a light-brown skinned, bald head man, wearing a dark grey suit and looking like he was thoroughly enjoying himself.

On top of that, the bodies of Debo and Quette were stretched out on the bed the man was not currently sitting on.

Without hesitation, Face G lined the barrel up with the man's head and pulled the trigger. Nothing happened. He checked the safety was off, cocked the gun, only to see that the gun had no bullets. Cocking back his arm, Face launched the gun at the man's head. Without seeming to try, the man dodged the projectile, paused the game, and finally turned to acknowledge Face.

The man stood with the muscled grace of a born killer, straightened his tie, and then locked eyes with the OG Crip. "In this world, training is everything. Always check your weapon before you engage with a target."

Face G eyed the 6-foot, 200-pound, cocksure man and could tell by his bearings that he was a trained soldier. But he couldn't fathom why the guy had killed his crew and waited for Face to wake up. "Who the fuck are you and what do you want?"

The man smiled as he watched Face looking around for another weapon. "My name is Delmas Burke and what I want is to help you and your men not die as you carry out your mission."

Face looked at his two top soldiers and knew that everyone else had to be in a similar state for the guy to feel so comfortable. Face said, "You're doing a lousy ass job of keeping my people alive."

The man, Delmas, shook his head sadly. "Another training tip: Never assume anything. You can't see your guys breathing? No wonder it was so easy for him to take out your other crew."

Face's eyes locked onto Delmas. "What you say? What the fuck do you know about my other crew?"

"I know that you're looking for Alisha Harden so you can ask her what she knows. I also know that you think it was a crew that did it, but it was really just one guy."

"Bullshit!" exclaimed Face G. "Over 50 guys, 15 of them with military experience. Aint no one guy kill all them people. And then Mickey was the best hand to hand fighter we had. As beat up as he was, I know it was more than one guy."

Delmas shook his head again. "In your world, you would be correct. The level of training and ruthlessness your men possessed made them wolves in a society of sheep. The problem occurred when your man Mickey decided to step into another world that he knew nothing about."

"What's this bullshit you keep talking about different worlds? There's only one world, Homie."

Laughing, Delmas said, "That's what all hunters think. Then that predator stumbles into a Lion and he's dead before he understands that he's not the Alpha anymore. It's the same in the streets. A crew thinks they have enough power to do what they want and they end up stumbling into a real Alpha predator."

"And how do you know so much about this Alpha predator?"

"Because he's my little brother." The announcement was met with absolute silence. Face didn't know if the man was delusional or if he was telling the truth. The fact that he was standing in front of him, having taken out seven of his men in the process, lent some credibility to what he was saying.

"So, why would your little brother take out my crew?" Delmas told him a story about his brother going undercover in a Military Intelligence operation in the NC prison system. Mickey and Daniel, his little brother, had started beefing over one of Daniel's friends killing himself because Mickey had the guy's family killed.

In retaliation, Daniel had killed all the Big Rollin Crips at the prison and beat Mickey up. When they got out, Daniel had finished the job by coming after him in Kannapolis. Through the use of drones and other technology, Daniel had been able to take out Mickey's whole crew.

"Then Daniel took Mickey apart blow by blow to make him suffer as long as possible," Delmas finished up.

Face processed all that, then asked, "So, what role did Alisha play in all this?"

"She was Daniel's inside person. And now they're engaged and living inside that compound you have your men watching."

Face narrowed his eyes. "You know a lot of shit. How do I know you're not the guy who did all this?"

"You don't," Delmas said with a serious face. "But you'll have to trust me when I say our missions run parallel to each other. You want Alisha to pay for her betrayal. Well, I want my brother for the same reason."

Face shrugged. "Well, let's mount up, combine our crews, and go take these motherfuckers out. You know a way into the compound?"

"There is no way inside. Everyone would die before anyone made it close to the house," Delmas explained. "We have to wait until Alisha comes out and we'll use an attack on her to bring my brother to the rescue."

For the first time, Face started feeling good about this early morning visitor. "Since this guy is so good, how many people will we need, and what will we have to do?"

"To tell you the truth, you'll need as many people as you can get. Everyone who can shoot a gun will have a role. Me and my people will take care of Daniel. You just have to have your people keep her alive long enough to call for help."

"Alright," said Face G. "Do we need our crews to meet so we know who not to shoot?"

Delmas shook his head. "No. Just go along like you were going to do. Wait until she comes out and you and your guys attack. She won't call the law, she'll call Daniel. Give her a few minutes to do that and then she's all yours."

"This Daniel guy killed my people. I want in on his death."

"Listen to me. You're thinking about your world again. Any of your men still on scene when he gets there will probably die. I'll handle him and, if you want, I'll send you a video of him dying."

Face G thought it over for a second and then said, "Cool, we have a deal." He extended his hand for the other man to shake. As soon as Delmas moved within range, Face grabbed for his arm and realized he'd made a grave mistake.

The man's arm was like an iron bar. Face was slammed into the wall where Delmas delivered a final message. "I understand you had to try. I don't blame you. But this is another teachable moment for you." Face went airborne and then darkness overtook him.

Face swam back to consciousness, hearing, "Face G? Wake up, Big Homie! Face?" Debo was shaking his arm and loudly trying to bring him around.

When he opened his eyes, Debo, Quette, Kenji, and Wayne were all standing around him looking concerned. "Thank God!" Quette said when he saw Face was awake.

Face G staggered to his feet and asked, "Is everyone good?"

They all looked at each other and Debo said, "Yeah, all of us are good. You're the one had us worried."

Holding his aching head, he asked, "Did ya'll get a report from the three guys in the hallway? Any signs of an intruder?"

"No, OG," said Quette. "They stayed on post after everyone left and we all went to sleep. When we got up, you was on the floor, knocked out. What happened? Did you fall or something?"

Face looked around in confusion. He didn't know if he had dreamed the whole encounter or if his boys were fucking with him. "If something happened in here last night, one of you tell me right now!" demanded Face.

They all looked at him like he was crazy. Even before the answer came, he knew what it would be. Debo said, "Nothing happened, Gang. What's up with you?"

This guy Delmas was the real deal. He hadn't been playing when he said there were different worlds. Clearly Face and his crew weren't the top G's around.

He stumbled back into his room, closing the door on all the bewildered expressions. He stripped and took a long hot shower to clear the cobwebs out of his system. When he stepped out, he almost shit in the middle of the floor. The steam filled room revealed a message on the mirror: "Different Worlds Motherfucker."

Face erased it and then smiled. Now he had a chance. If he had went in blind, all his men would have died. Now, he could get Alisha and revenge for his fallen homies.

He dressed and reentered the room connected to his. Debo looked up from the game and asked, "Are we going home today?"

Face G shook his head. "Hell no, Homie! Call everybody and tell them to get down here. We not going anywhere until we get this bitch."

Debo frowned. "You mean everybody from Charlotte?"

"Charlotte, Concord, Kannapolis. Fuck it, get the whole 704. When this traitor shows her face, she'll die. And anyone with her is gonna join her in hell.

• •

"Mike, I need you to put the whole facility on lockdown. No one in and no one out." Reggie had spent the last 72 hours trying to track down his aunt. The problem was, there were no cameras in the family wing of the compound. And there were so many entrances and exits, it was impossible to pin down her movements.

So, he'd done something that, if anyone found out about, he could be booted from his position as Head of Operations. He'd put up tiny cameras at every crossing so he knew exactly where his aunt was at any given time.

Mike, the head of WRA security, said, "Yes Sir, it's already been taken care of."

"Huh?" asked Reggie. "How did you already do it if I'm just now asking for it?"

"Ms. Drake called about 50 minutes ago and asked for a lockdown."

"Why wasn't I noti…. never mind," said Reggie. He looked in his WRA email account and saw the notice sent out an hour ago warning of a lockdown drill.

Reggie glanced at his watch and saw it was 11:30am. Strange to call a drill in the middle of the day, but what was the point of a drill if it was convenient?

"Alright Mike, I'm changing the drill to a real lockdown. Don't lift it until you've heard from me directly. You got it?"

"Got it, Mr. Burke. Full lockdown until I hear from you," repeated Mike.

"Good man." Reggie hung up and nodded to the three guards who were standing with him. He was careful to not let them see his screen because then they would have to report the presence of cameras where they shouldn't be. So, he took off towards his destination, making sure his body hid the phone from the guys trailing him.

Arriving at the door, he motioned for the men to wait in the hallway and then he pushed into the room. The space was identical to many others spread across the compound. A desk, a computer, and a chair. Pretty much just a sound proofed space to do a little research in a quiet, out of the way, area.

His aunt, Mary Sue, jumped to her feet, and seeing him, her shoulders slumped in defeat. He smiled and closed the door behind him. Leaning his bulky body into it was a way of saying she wasn't going anywhere without his permission.

"You've had me chasing you around this facility for over two days now. Any patience I would have had is long gone. So, I'm gonna give you one chance to tell me what's really going on before this goes any further."

Mary Sue stood there in her comfortable jeans and T-shirt looking like the spitting image of pictures he'd seen of his maternal Great Grandmother. She had been a beautiful, green eyed, white woman who had fallen in love with a black man. The result had been his grandfather, Willie James Burke, and the hate of both the black and white communities. When his grandfather also married a mixed woman, it made every child born into the family a genetic mystery. Some dark, some light. Some tall, some short. No matter what they looked like, every one of them was a Burke at heart.

"I have no idea what you're talking about," she replied haughtily. "I haven't been dodging you, I've just broken my phone. If you wanted to see me, all you had to do was come to my quarters."

Reggie shook his head sadly. "My grandfather and uncles trained you very good. But their training didn't include what you'll be exposed to if you decide to take this route. Just tell me this big secret you're holding in and we can both go our separate ways."

"Reg," she said with a shrug of confusion. "I really have no idea what you're talking about. If there is some big secret out there, I have no idea what it is."

He regarded her for a few seconds, and then nodded. "Okay. You want to be a real agent, I'll show you what happens when you lie to a human lie detector."

He turned and snatched the door open. Walking into the hallway, he said, "Take her." The three agents rushed into the room to bring the woman out.

"What is the meaning of this? Take your hands off of me this instant!" She was still a Burke, so she was trained to defend herself. If she hadn't been in such a small space, she would have taken out all three men. Even with the numbers advantage, it took the agents almost five minutes to get the restraints on her. At the end, one of the men was laying on the floor unconscious, and the other two showed numerous cuts and bruises.

The two remaining agents, who were in their twenties, carried the 56-year-old woman out, and they were still having a hard time with her. Reggie pulled out his gun and pressed it to the side of her head. All the struggles stopped as if she could feel the impatience of her nephew.

"When it comes to the running of the WRA you know how ruthless I can be. You have a secret that I feel is a threat to this Agency. You're gonna tell me what it is. And if you don't, I'm going to kill you. If you struggle or continue to fight, I'll kill you and just go to the source. Now, stop acting like a child and let's go for a walk." Reggie nodded to the two agents and they took off for the special elevator.

The only thing in the direction they were going was the one place no agent wanted to go. When their destination became clear, Mary Sue started whimpering and begging.

"Please Reggie! I'm your family. Don't do this! I really have no idea what you're talking about."

He ignored her and punched in the code for the elevator doors to open. She instantly started to fight and scream for help. Reggie, seeing the agents struggling to contain her restrained body, chopped her on the back of her neck, putting her to sleep. The two men then carried her slumped body into the elevator as Reggie closed the doors behind them.

When the doors opened, even Reggie felt a sense of apprehension flow through his body. There was no lobby or walkway to ease you into the situation you were about to enter. No. The doors opened up right into the dungeon.

Torture devices lined the walls, and table after table filled the dimly lit room. It smelled of blood and feces with a light scent of bleach meant to cover it up. Reggie motioned for them to place her face down on the first table and they switched out the restraints for the ones connected to the table.

Now, her unconscious form had restraining belts holding her body in the letter T. Her arms and legs were so tight to the table, all she could do was arch her back and then straighten out again, or turn her head from side to side. When Reggie placed the smelling salts under her nose, she jerked awake and instantly started testing her bounds and screaming.

Reggie nodded at the agents and they high tailed it back to the elevator like they were scared they'd be strapped to a table next.

Right next to each table was a small rolling shelf that you could wheel over to the wall and place torture devices on for easy transport. As she continued to flex and scream, Reggie wheeled his cart over and surveyed the instruments on the wall.

With Mary Sue watching, he pulled down a blow torch, a pair of scissors, and a striker. When he turned with the devices, she once again started to plead.

Finally, he said, "Shut up and listen to me." He was standing at the side of the table now, and she was craning her neck to see what he was doing. "Aunt Mary Sue, you know I love you. But if you think I'm bluffing, I want you to understand I'm not. One way or another, you'll tell me what I want to know. How much you have to go through in the mean time is up to you."

Whimpering, she said, "But Reggie, I swear I don't know..." He tuned out the rest of her denials, picked up the scissors and proceeded to cut her shirt and bra strap away from her back. While she cried and begged, he walked to a different wall and collected a few more necessary things.

In the CIA they teach you that torture is centered in the mind, not the body. When the body feels pain, it tries to shut itself down. If you trick the mind into believing the pain would kill the body, the survival instinct kicked in and it would force your body to do extraordinary things to stay alive.

All his preparations set up to do the most damage, he started the phycological warfare. "Do you know exactly what fire and heat does to the human body?" While he asked the question, he picked up the torch and striker and stepped out of her view.

Mary Sue was testing her restraints to the max, but the straps were meant to contain men who were several degrees stronger than her. She continued to beg and plead and deny, but it all fell on deaf ears. She had her own training and he knew she would keep denying until she felt it was not a bluff.

"Fire, at the right temperature, actually desensitizes the body. But if you know what you're doing with it, you can cook a person's whole body before they die." Reggie turned on the gas and the hiss caused his aunt to go silent. He flicked the striker out of range a few times before putting it to the gas and causing a loud whoosh.

Now, the real Burke came out of Mary Sue. "You motherfucker! You better not touch me with that flame. All I've done for you, I swear I'll kill you, you ungrateful bastard."

He laughed and continued his monologue. "Of course, I've trained extensively in all torture techniques, so you can rest assured that you'll feel every bit of this." He adjusted the flame to his exact specifications and waved it quickly down her spine.

She screamed as the skin turned a blistering red, but she knew it was only a warning pass. "You rotten son of a bitch!" she screamed with spit flying from her mouth. Her eyes were wide with fright and, except for the red stripe he'd just applied, her skin went pale.

He had her mind, but he decided to push a little bit harder. "I've never been burned myself," he continued over her curses. "But I've heard that after a few seconds of heat, it actually starts to feel like you're freezing. Have you ever heard that?" He did another quick pass from her left to right side, making a cross with the line already on her back.

Mary Sue started to cry. "I can't tell you, Reggie. Please stop this. She'll kill me if I say anything."

"I think you're worried about the wrong threat. If you don't tell me what's going on, I'll kill you. And I guarantee dying down here will be a far worse death than anything she comes up with." He waited to see if she'd talk, then he shrugged and continued his plan.

He put on the white smock that he'd added to his tools, and said, "The worst part about using low heat is that the blood vessels explode from the pressure building up under the skin. Even though I have on black workout clothes, I don't want to ruin them with your blood."

He lined the torch up with her left shoulder blade and started the final steps in breaking her mind. Mary Sue screamed in agony as he lowered the torch, and blood gushed everywhere. She was rolling her head from side to side as her body convulsed in pain. Reggie kept up his slow torture until finally she screamed what he knew she would.

"Alright! Alright! Stop! I'll tell you everything you want to know." He immediately turned off the torch and stepped in front of her with his blood splattered smock. She looked away in disgust, but started to talk, hoping to end the torture.

Reggie had known something was going on, but not in his wildest dreams would he have come up with what she told him. Speechless, he went about cleaning up the mess he'd made of his aunt. Then he released all the straps and threw an extra smock at her to replace her ruined clothes.

When she sat up and saw the blood bags, ice cubes, and torch, her eyes flew to his face in disbelief. Her hands flew to her back and she rushed over to one of the mirrors hanging on the wall. Seeing only the two faint red marks he'd made with the fast passes of the torch, she put her face in her hands and started bawling.

Reggie made his way over to her and wrapped his arms around her body. She fought him and he finally had to fall to the floor, pinning her to the concrete to protect them both. He kept murmuring, "I'm sorry" and "I love you" over and over until she calmed down and hugged him back.

Shaking his head sadly, he understood why she was willing to undergo torture to keep her secret. She had every right to fear her death would be swift if anyone ever found out she had told. Now, her life was in jeopardy because he'd forced her to talk. He was saddened by how tortured Mary

Sue's life had to be by keeping all she knew on the inside. But he was also in awe of how strong she was to continue her day to day as if all was well in the world.

Now that he knew, to protect them both, he'd have to act on the info as soon as possible. He stood both of them up and looked at the dazed face of his beautiful aunt. "I'm so sorry I had to do this to you, but now I need you to pull yourself together and be strong. Do you understand me?"

After a little shake, she said, "Yes, I understand." After taking a deep breath, she asked, "What do you need me to do?"

"Nothing. I want you to go about your day as if nothing has changed. When the time is right, which will be soon, I'll act on this information and then you won't have to worry anymore." He hurried her over to the elevator door and entered the code to bring it back down. Reggie said, "For right now, go back to your quarters and lock yourself in. I'll call when it's safe to…"

As the doors opened, the words froze on Reggie's tongue. Standing in the elevator was The Author, and the gun in his hand meant he wasn't there for idle chitchat. He said, "I'm sorry, but neither one of you are going anywhere."

Reggie placed his body between his aunt and The Author and backed up a few steps. He cursed because now the lockdown his mother issued returned to his mind. If he hadn't been so gun-ho about trying to get to Mary Sue, he would have figured something wasn't right. Because of his foolhardy actions, both of them might die.

The only saving grace was that he and The Author had a history. He could get in his head and hopefully the man's ego still ruled his mind. If not, neither Reggie nor his aunt would be leaving the dungeon alive.

Chapter 22

"We've all been holed up in this house for too long. How about a little shopping expedition?" Ann asked Alisha. They were both sitting in the family kitchen eating a modest, early lunch of grilled chicken salad when Ann posed the question.

Alisha said, "I would love to get out of here, but Daniel doesn't think enough time has passed since the truce." It had only been three days, so Daniel was asking that they at least give it a week so he could monitor some of the WRA movements.

"Well, it's not like he gave one of his famous Commandments. Let's grab Gabby and Walt and hit up Concord Mills."

Alisha was already shaking her head. "Gabby is definitely not leaving this house. Daniel would kill both of us if something happened to his little girl."

"And what do you think he'll do to me if something happens to you?" asked Ann. "My life will be at stake, but I'm willing to take the risk just to breathe a little bit."

"Well, Gabby won't be part of it. We're grown, if we want to risk it, we can. But I'm with Daniel on this one, we can't risk Gabby like that."

Ann nodded and said, "Eventually you both will have to let her be around other kids. You can't expect her to grow up around a bunch of real-life cops and robbers."

Alisha's hand flew to her cocked hip. "And who the hell are the robbers, Ms. Good Cop?"

"You know what I mean," said Ann. "None of us are good role models for children, Ms. Crip Queen." They eyed each other for another few seconds and then burst out laughing. When they first started training together, those were the nicknames they used to get under each other's skin.

"Anyway, Walt is also unavailable, and probably wouldn't want to shop with two women anyway." Alisha shook her head sadly. "He's been taking care of Denise since the Candace fight. Eventually she'll get over it, but right now, she needs him to get by."

Denise hadn't batted an eye over poisoning Asiah Winecoff to cover their tracks with the governor. But, her killing of Candace Price had really taken a toll. The physical wounds she sustained were already fading into history. The emotional and mental wounds of murdering someone with her bare hands were taking a bit more time to deal with.

At first, Daniel was gonna stay by her side, but all Denise kept asking was how Ashley was doing. So, Daniel had asked Walt to stay here in his place while he went to stay with Ashley. Daniel ended up getting her moved to a Charlotte hospital where he could be near his family and keep an eye on Ashley for Denise.

"And what has Daniel been reporting to you?" asked Ann.

"He had Ashley placed in a private wing and she's only a few more days from being released. It's actually one of the hospitals he works at, so he has an office right next door to Ashley and you have to go through his office to get to her. He's pretty much just been monitoring things from there instead of the War Room."

Ann eyed her critically for a few moments, then said, "Let's go," and took off for the stairs.

"What the hell's gotten into you?" Alisha asked her, abandoning her salad. "Where are we going?"

Ann took a right at the top of the sweeping staircase and headed for the main family wing. She steamed pass Gabby's room and said, "Come help me and your momma for a second."

"Ann, slow down! What are you doing?" Alisha watched as Ann entered her and Daniel's bedroom and kept going towards the left.

Gabby stepped out of her room and asked, "What's going on Mom? Is Auntie Ann Okay?"

"Come on baby girl," Alisha said hugging her daughter. "I think your aunt has lost her mind."

They entered the bedroom to find Ann breezing through the clothes in Alisha's closet. Then she spun around with accusation in her eyes. "Where are the rest of your clothes?" she demanded.

Alisha shrugged and said, "T-shirts, workout gear, and sweatpants are in the dresser over there with my underclothes." Motioning to the closet, she said, "The rest is in there."

Ann's mouth dropped in disbelief. "What do you wear when Daniel takes you out on the town?"

"We really don't go out to any fancy restaurants. We order in a lot. But, when we do go out, I wear one of the sundresses at the end there." She pointed to the far-right corner of the closet and Ann walked over and started flipping through the hanging dresses.

She turned with disgust on her face. "You have a Billionaire fiancé and you're walking around in this crap?"

"Hey!" shouted Alisha. "I like that crap." Getting offended now, Alisha said, "He's tried to buy me expensive clothes, but it's not for me. I like to wear comfortable things that are soft against my skin."

Ann looked at Gabby with a look that said, "Can you believe this BS." Gabby folded her slender arms across her chest and walked to the closet herself. After leafing through a few pants and blouses, she said, "Mom, Auntie Ann has a point. I would have to be threatened with death to wear most of this stuff."

Now it was Alisha's mouth that was hanging open in surprise. "Gabby!" she exclaimed. "How can you say that?"

"What?" Gabby said with raised eyebrows. "Dad would never buy this stuff for me. I only wear Gucci and Prada and Chanel, and I never get to leave the house. I mean, have you not seen his closet?"

Ann jumped on that. "Where is it Gabby?" She led Ann over to a closed door next to the bathroom, and pushed it open. Ann gaped as she took in the splendid setup of suits and shoes and assorted designer clothes. Her hand went to her heart when she saw the display cases full of jewelry.

"Don't touch anything!" demanded Alisha. "I think he has the place alarmed."

Ann pointed to a suit hanging on a mannequin. "I just saw this same suit in GQ Magazine. This one suit cost 10 times as much as your whole wardrobe." She twirled around looking in wonder at the closet that was twice the size of the master bedroom. Ann turned to look at Alisha. "Wait, where are your shoes?"

Gabby laughed out loud, but quickly cut it off with the look Alisha gave her. Alisha rotated and pointed to four pair of shoes under her side of the bed. "These are the ones I wear on a daily basis. The ones I wear when I dress up are in those boxes on the floor of my closet."

Ann's hand flew to her mouth as she repeated, "Boxes on the floor of the closet. Lord have mercy!" she murmured when she saw the multi-colored shoe boxes stacked in the closet. She opened a few of them and exclaimed, "God, no!"

Gabby couldn't contain herself any longer. She launched herself on the bed and rolled around in laughter. Ann turned around looking like she was about to cry, but ended up laughing along with Gabby. Alisha tried to hold on to her serious face but, seeing the obvious enjoyment of her daughter, she joined in with a laugh of her own.

After they were calm enough to talk, Ann said, "Put on one of the sundresses and let's go. I'll go get changed and meet you in the kitchen in 15 minutes." Seeing Alisha about to object, Ann held her hand up for silence. "I don't want to hear it. We're going and I bet Daniel will be happy with the outcome." On her way out, she shouted "15 minutes, Alisha!" and was gone.

Gabby looked at Alisha with sadness. "I know it's for my own protection, but I wish I could come with you guys."

Alisha sprawled out on the bed and pulled Gabby to her chest. "Daniel is working on something that will give us all the freedom we want." Kissing her head, Alisha said, "Just be patient with him. He's terrified that you'll get hurt, and his love for you demands he protects you any and every way he can."

"I know," said Gabby. With a huge smile, she said, "It feels really good to have real parents that love me." She then squeezed Alisha into a tight embrace causing Alisha to blink tears out of her eyes.

They stayed that way until they heard Ann yell, "Five minutes, Alisha! I'm not playing with you!" They both laughed, jumped up, and proceeded to pick out an outfit that didn't look too shabby. Alisha knew Daniel loved her no matter what she wore, but she was determined to find something that would wow him. Gabby playfully wished her luck as she descended the steps five minutes late for her meeting with Ann.

Ann was standing in the kitchen wearing a pair of white Velour pants with a teal colored zip up hoodie of the same material. The colors made her brown eyes and long dark braid look luminous. Her pink lips looked smooth and wet like she'd just spent the last 15 minutes kissing her lover. She completed the ensemble with an acre of cleavage and a pair of teal Jordan 11's.

Alisha said, "Wow! Looks like I don't need to go shopping, I just need to pay your closet a visit." She felt completely outmatched in her canary yellow and white sundress and her Paraboot Pacific sandals. She knew the colors matched, but she couldn't stand up to the elegance and beauty of the other woman.

Ann smiled. "Alisha, listen to me. You are probably the most beautiful woman I've ever seen in my life. But the clothes that bring out my assets wouldn't look right on you. We're gonna go to this little boutique about ten minutes from here where the owners will put outfit after outfit in front of you that will make Daniel fall at your feet."

Ann grabbed her hand and started for the front of the house. Alisha pulled up short and said, "Wait, I can't take any of the cars out there." Rolling her eyes, she said, "Daniel made me swear I'd take one of the protection cars if I decided to go anywhere. Just wait at the front door and I'll pull up around front."

Alisha dashed back through the house and entered the horizontal elevator that only Daniel and herself could access. It led to a barely below ground garage that housed all of his plated and protected cars. Almost all of them were multimillion-dollar cars and SUVs, but there were a few that he'd made to fit her more modest taste.

She chose the all black Volvo XC60 T8 SUV, figuring they'd need the extra room for the purchases, and activated the ramp to take her back above ground.

Just looking at the vehicle, you couldn't tell it was anything special, but driving it was like trying to steer a super-fast tank. She'd had plenty of practice on the underground driving course, so she glided to the front of the house with no problem. She blew the horn and Ann stepped out of the house and made her way to the passenger side.

Pulling the door open, Ann said, "My God! This door weighs a ton."

Smiling, Alisha said, "Not quite. But with the bulletproof glass and the armored plates, I'd say it's close."

Ann whistled as she took her first look at the plush interior. The huge panoramic moonroof. The black leather stretching over every surface. The touchscreens that controlled all the vehicles amenities. Daniel hadn't batted an eye at the $80,000 price tag. Instead, he'd been happy she hadn't asked for some cheap ass domestic vehicle. Then he went and ruined it by adding $200,000 in protection upgrades.

The super smart detective figured out the navigation system in seconds, and had the address punched in by the time they made it to the gate. Alisha turned the heavy SUV to the left and they made idle chitchat as she followed the directions to a strip mall in downtown Charlotte.

Alisha frowned as she pulled to a stop facing the storefront. "How in the world did you hear about this place?" she asked Ann. Without conscious thought, she turned the SUV around so she was facing out, just incase they needed to make a fast exit.

Opening her door, Ann said, "Where you hear about anything these days, Social Media. I've been here a few times, and they'll definitely treat you right."

There were no markings on the building what so ever. The only signs that a business was in this location were the clothes in the window and the light coming from the interior. Ann slammed her door and waved for Alisha to follow her. Reluctantly, Alisha stepped out of the vehicle and they made their way inside.

As soon as they stepped inside, Alisha gasped in wonder, recognizing that this was no ordinary store. The interior design exuded pure sophistication. Recessed lighting provided a glow that cast a magical light onto every surface. With her senses stuck on overload, Alisha followed Ann deeper into the structure.

Being in Daniel's world of masculine luxury did nothing to prepare her for this purely feminine space. Plush, oversized chairs and couches made cozy enclaves with semi-private atmospheres. Classical music played through hidden speakers created an ambiance or pure opulence. To top it all off was the heavenly smell of some expensive perfume mixed with a hint of vanilla.

When they'd entered, a bell had pinged to announce the arrival of visitors. They were almost to the center of the space before two black women stepped through a door behind the counter. The older of the two flashed a bright smile, and said, "Oh my God! Long time no see, Detective Grace." She hustled over to Ann and gave her a big hug.

The younger woman embraced her next, saying, "We thought you'd decided to take your business elsewhere."

Ann took a step back and said, "Just been busy with a major case, but I'm back now and I brought some company to make up for my absence." Gesturing towards her, Ann said, "This is my sister and friend, Alisha Harden."

As both women eyed her critically, Alisha had the opportunity to do the same thing to them. The older woman was dark skinned, very attractive, and was probably in her early 50's. She was dressed in a white Chanel pant suit that fit her mature curves to the T. The woman extended her hand and said, "Hello, Ms. Harden. My name is Bridgett Hart and this is my lovely daughter, Chasity."

Chasity was a few shades lighter than her mother, and they both possessed very beautiful smiles. Chasity was also gorgeous, and her thigh-length Chanel Skirt showcased her model-like body to perfection. She looked to be in her late 20's or early 30's. She was a tad shorter than her mother, although the short skirt she was wearing made her legs look a mile long.

Both women gave Alisha warm welcomes and she returned the sentiment, happy they both seemed so down to earth. She probably would have turned and left if she'd been required to deal with some stuck up, judgmental owners looking down on her.

Bridgett and Chasity told them to look around and explore for a bit and to call them if they needed anything. The tap-tap of their open-toed heels echoed around the shop as they made their way back through the door behind the counter.

Everywhere Alisha looked added to her amazement. "This place is wonderful. The owners have thought of everything," she said to Ann.

At the back of the store was a glassed-in section with partitions to make each space separate. In one of them were two pool tables with two big screen TVs showing sports. In the next one was a golf simulator with a huge roll down screen, presumably for the waiting men. Then, in the last one was an area for children with what looked like every toy ever invented. The owners had set up a family service shop that took care of every woman's needs.

Ann led her over to a set of deep-cushioned chairs and said, "Have a seat and take your shoes off." Alisha followed her lead and settled into the comfortable chair and removed her sandals.

"Ahh!" Alisha exclaimed as she settled her bare feet on the heated cheery wood floor. Just then, Chasity bustled back in with a tray sporting a bottle of chilled Rose Wine, and a decanter filled with some dark colored scotch.

After she poured the wine for her two customers, she said, "Take your time and we'll be out in a bit to set you up."

Alisha glanced at Ann as Chasity retreated, and asked, "What did she mean by that?"

Ann smiled broadly and said, "Before I changed my clothes I called them and said I was bringing the fiancé of a billionaire who needed a whole new wardrobe. They shut down business for the rest of the day so they could focus on just you." Alisha wished Ann wouldn't have told them who she was because now she felt like they would act nice only because of the money.

She said as much to Ann who immediately frowned and said, "Alisha, I make $80,000 a year and they greet me like you just saw every time I come in here. These two women love to help women look their best. They are genuine, and even if you don't buy anything, they'll treat you with love and respect." Feeling chastised, Alisha just nodded and stood up to continue her tour.

From the outside, the store didn't look that big. Maybe 40 feet wide, but the length had to be almost five times that size. And in each section, a clothing brand dominated it's given space.

Fendi, Gucci, Louis Vuitton, Chanel, Christian Dior, Alexander McQueen. They all had sections that showcased their evening gowns all the way to their underwear. Each brand was like a store in and of itself. Michael Kors, Valentino, Versace, Burberry, Balenciaga, Givenchy, all had sections of their own. Those were just the ones she was familiar with.

So many other sections were full of beautiful and expensive designer clothes that she could spend the rest of the day just looking at them. And to top it all off, there was an upstairs section that features nothing but shoes, accessories, and make-up. Truly a sight to behold for any woman wishing to up her fashion game.

She had just noticed the huge screens over each brand that showed the displayed clothing being modeled on runways and other environments, when the two owners returned. They both eyed Alisha like a specimen in a laboratory they were about to dissect. Then Bridgett rubbed her hands together, smiled, and said, "This is gonna be so much fun," before sweeping Alisha up in her whirlwind.

The next few hours were a blur of activity. Alisha shopped and drank and had the time of her life. A few of the prices sobered her up at the beginning, but Ann reminded her how many times Daniel had told her money wasn't ever gonna be a problem. So, she stopped looking at the prices and just picked out what she liked.

From one of a kind gowns from Bubu Ogisi, to super-sexy, colorful dresses by Alexander McQueen for nights on the town. Mini dresses by Ali Karoui to pant suits by LaQuan Smith. All the designers she'd seen on all the biggest stars became hers for the taking.

Shoes from Chanel, Monolo Blahnik, and Christian Louboutin, as well as Gucci, Prada, and Dolce & Gabbana were stacked higher than she was tall. Jeans and causal wear from Burberry, Versace, Bottega Veneta and Dior were snatched off the racks fast enough to make her head spin. Some of the lingerie and underwear made her blush until Ann reminded her how much fun Daniel would have peeling it off of her.

After all the clothes, shoes, and various accessories were added up, Bridgett calmly walked over and handed Alisha a folded piece of paper. She was taking a sip of the Rose Wine when she unfolded it, and the wine was sprayed everywhere. Almost jogging in her attempt to get away, Bridgett said, "I'll be over at the register if you need me."

Alisha scowled at Ann and handed her the slip of paper. "Are you trying to get me killed. Daniel sees I've spent this much on clothes…"

"He'll see you in one of these outfits and come buy out the rest of the store," interrupted Ann. Taking Alisha's hand in her own, Ann said, "You have to stop selling Daniel short. If he could give the world to you and Gabby, he would. Take him at his word and live a little."

"I think he would be okay with a few items here and there, but I don't think he meant $1.2 Million when he said spend what I want," whispered Alisha.

"Sweetie, Daniel doesn't misspeak. He says what he means and he means what he says. Ultimately, it's up to you. Did we just spend all this time fucking up this shop, or did we spend it getting you a wardrobe?"

Alisha stared at her for a bit and, smiling the smile you can only get when you're a little drunk, got up and walked to the counter with her Black AmEx card in hand.

Chasity and Bridgett, all smiles now, started wrapping all the purchases for transport. They told Alisha that they would load everything into their box truck and have it delivered later that day. Alisha decided to wear a causal Gucci jeans and T-shirt combo out of the store after Ann recommended finding something to eat before going home. After hugs and farewells, they finally exited Innerwishes, and headed for the SUV.

Alisha had just pushed the keyless entry button when Ann snatched the keys from her. "Um, Alisha, I think you've had one too many glasses of the wine. I'll be driving until we get back home."

She shrugged and said, "Drives like a tank. Take it slow until you get the hang of it." With a dopey smile on her face, Alisha walked around and got in on the passenger side.

Ann turned and told her to buckle up when all of a sudden, a high-pitched noise had both of them covering their ears, wincing in pain. All at once, the windows ruptured and rained glass all over them.

Alisha didn't have time to register much else before Ann screamed and lunged in her direction. Her world tilted as she was simultaneously snatched to her left, and the bullet struck her upper chest, pinning her to the seat. Darkness descended upon her as chaos erupted all around.

Chapter 23

"I'm getting sick and tired of you defying me because you're my niece. This is your last chance, Tonya. Get your sister and both of you get to headquarters immediately," Delmas barked at her.

"Since when do we need to come in for a drill? And if it's already been called, we can't get in anyway," explained Tonya.

In a deadly tone, one she'd only heard him use when ready to kill, he said, "Either you're on our side or his. I have a drone over your car right now as you sit at the Exxon. This should be an easy decision for you; either head to base now or I kill you, and your sister, who is parked at the Walgreens, will be next. You have five seconds to decide."

Starting the car, Tonya said, "Fine, you no good son of a bitch. And don't think this is over. I warned you about threatening me or my sister." She hung up and said in her earpiece, "Come on, Nyaira. He's won this battle, but I promise he'll lose the war."

Tonya watched as Nyaira pulled out behind her and they followed the road to the interstate that would take them to WRA headquarters. Ny said, "You know Ann and Alisha are gonna get hit at some point. Are we just gonna let that happen?"

Earlier that day, they had trailed the pair from Daniel's compound over to a strip mall that appeared to not be in use. After some research they discovered that the store they entered was a high-end clothes retailer that catered to a select customer base. About an hour into their stakeout they started noticing the arrival of a lot of cars parking in strategic places for an attack.

"What can we do, Ny? You know that psycho wasn't bluffing. He'll probably have the drone follow us all the way to home base." They both knew Delmas could be a jackass, but they also knew he possessed the Burke intelligence just like they all did.

The one thing that made them positive of a pending hit was the presence of Lil D at the clothing store. Even though Tonya had not been hanging with him lately, she'd still talked to him on the phone. Nyaira had begged her to call him and see if she could learn anything.

"Hey, Sweetie," she'd said when he picked up the phone. "I'm back in town and I missed you. Did you miss me?"

Softly, Lil D said, "Hey, Beautiful! You know I missed you, but I'm kind of in the middle of something. Can I call you later?"

Tonya could see Lil D in the driver's seat of his blue Chevelle through the lenses of the binoculars. He was motioning his crew into silence as they mocked his words. Seeing as she had only pecked his cheek a few times and let him give her a few massages, she knew what to say to test how important this was to him.

"Um, to tell you the truth, Damian, I came all the way from Raleigh because I really need to see you, if you catch my drift."

"Aw shit Tonya. I really want to see you too, but I'm really tied up right now. Give me a couple hours and I'll meet you anywhere you want me to."

"Lil D!" she exclaimed. "You been tryna get this since day one. Now, I'm ready to throw it at you, and you telling me you're too busy! What in the world could possibly be more important than me?"

"Fuck!" he growled in anger. "My boss got me out here about to do an important mission. If I could leave, baby I would. But, if I leave, he'll smoke my ass. Please give me a little time. I promise I'll make it up to you."

"You know what? Fuck you Lil D. I leave for a few days and you probably with some other chick. Come to me right now or lose my number," she demanded.

After a pause where she saw him leaning his head on the steering wheel, he said, "I'm sorry, Tonya." That's as far as he got before she hung up the phone.

Her and Nyaira listened to his phone's mic as he cursed and exploded with anger. Finally, he said, "I just lost the baddest piece of ass on the east coast. Fuck everything, I'm killing both of these bitches."

That had been a couple hours ago now, and Tonya and Nyaira felt helpless to stop those two women from being hit.

They were about 15 minutes from the underground headquarters when Tonya got the idea. Knowing that their phones and communication devices could be compromised, she said, "Damn Ny, I'm almost out of gas. Let's pull in up here and I'll fill up before we go into headquarters."

She pulled into the gas station and took her earpiece out and put it in the cup holder. She stopped at the pump and got out the car motioning for Ny to stay in hers. Tonya saw Nyaira trying to talk to her and she motioned to let her know she was going quiet.

After pumping the gas, Tonya asked loudly, "Ny, you need anything from inside? I'm gonna use the bathroom real quick."

Nyaira said, "Just bring me a Coke or something. And make sure you wash your hands before you get it."

Tonya sucked her teeth and said, "Shut up, you little brat," before walking off to the store part of the gas station.

As soon as she was inside the small gas station, that she knew only had cameras at the outside pumps, she started moving faster. "Do you have a cell phone?" she asked the young man behind the counter. "Well, do you!" she demanded when he sat there looking stupid.

He nodded and fumbled it a few times before picking it up off the counter and handing it to her. Frantically, she dialed her Uncle Daniel and cursed when he didn't answer. She dialed again and again and again until, finally, he answered the call.

"Whoever this is, you have the wrong…"

"Uncle Daniel, it's me, Tonya. Where are you right now?"

He must have heard the urgency in her voice because he answered immediately. "I'm at the hospital with Ashley Kirt. Why? What's wrong?"

"I'm so sorry Uncle D. I tried everything I could to stop it, but Uncle Delmas recalled me and Ny back to base."

"Stop what, Tonya?" he asked confused. "What are you talking about?"

"They are about to hit Ann and Alisha if they haven't already. They're at a strip mall about ten minutes from…. Hello? Uncle Daniel?" But he was already gone. Confident that he would protect the two women, she returned the phone to the shocked clerk.

She used the bathroom, paid for the gas along with the two Cokes, and returned to the car where her cell phone and earpiece waited. Nyaira knew not to mention any of what she surely saw through the store's front windows. So they continued to curse Delmas as they headed towards the underground facility.

· ·

Daniel knew that all the misfortune befallen the people around him was ultimately his fault. Denise wouldn't be laid up almost comatose with grief, and her friend Ashley wouldn't be in a hospital bed recovering from her last surgery. He hated to be away from his new family, but realistically, he was the only one who could safely be with Ashley right now.

Walt and Ann had to stay off the radar of any law enforcement until the big reveal. There was no way in hell he was letting Alisha pull protection duties. And trusting the cops to protect her would have been negligent on all their parts.

So, he got her moved to a Charlotte hospital and placed her under his immediate care. The set up was simple. His office was in the basement, so he didn't have any windows to worry about. And, anyone trying to get to her private room, had to go through his office to get there.

Motion censors and pressure plates littered the whole area, and there wasn't an inch not covered by at least two cameras. Without all that, he himself was a formidable obstacle to get through. So, he felt the only thing that could possibly do Ashley in was the sheer boredom of being remanded to a hospital bed.

He used his free time to study every move that the WRA was making. Daniel was nobody's fool and, knowing the truce had passed with a four to three vote, he knew the losing side wouldn't just accept defeat.

"Dr. Handsome, I know you not just gonna leave me in here to rot on my own?" called Ashley.

Daniel smiled and said, "Coming my beautiful patient." He stood up, checked the monitors one more time, and made his way in to see how Ashley Kirt was doing.

The Channel 3 co-anchor was sitting up in her bed with a weak smile on her face. She was out of the woods as far as her losing her life, and now they were just waiting for her body to build back up it's strength. The plastic surgeon he'd hired made sure there would be no scars, so in a couple of weeks, she'd be back to her gorgeous self.

"I'm beginning to think you don't have a life at all," she commented when he stepped into the room. "Your fiancé must have a heart of gold."

They'd had a few conversations about each other's lives. The topics ranged from, why she was at this hospital, to his relationship with Denise, to how he was able to spend damn near 24 hours a day with her. She had been distrustful and guarded at first, but once she Facetimed with Denise and Daniel got her endorsement, she'd opened right up. After Daniel Facetimed with Alisha right in front of her, Ashley had pretty much joined the family.

Of course, she had no idea about the other life they were all living and, with the success of the truce, he hoped it would never come up.

"Well, considering I'm a spy, an assassin, a doctor, and a world class hacker, I'd say I live a pretty full life," he answered in a joking manner. "And Alisha knows how important you are to all of us. If I left and something happened to you, she'd be the first one to go upside my head."

Ashley giggled then winced in pain before settling back down again. "I still don't understand why something else would happen to me. Everyone said that the people thought I was Denise. And the guys who shot me are dead now anyway. So, why so much protection?"

Daniel patted her hand and said, "Denise just wants you safe. After what she just returned from herself, I say let's indulge her until you're better. Okay?" She smiled sadly and nodded, just as he knew she would.

When the bodies of Javon, Eric, and Charles were found, Walt called Cpt. William Graham and let him know who the guys were. The guns that were used to kill Officer Brittney Clark and shoot Ashley had been found in the house, along with a sizeable amount of money and drugs. Will didn't even ask how Walt knew the guys, he just ran with it and helped the local PD close the case.

To put Will's mind at ease, Walt did email him the video of the hit and the trail that led back to the house. With a warning to leave the woman out of it, the SBI solved the case and moved on to bigger and messier murders.

Daniel started checking all her bandages and wraps when his cell phone rang. He glanced at the number and didn't recognize it, so he deemed the call unimportant.

"Who is that? If it's your mistress, I swear I will dime you out to that lovely girl of yours," remarked Ashley.

The phone started ringing again when he said, "It's probably a wrong number. I've gotten more calls in the last week then in the previous 15 years. I'm sure it's nothing."

"Uh huh, tell me anything. I bet you got some big booty cutie stashed in the cut somewhere."

He smiled and said, "I sure do. I keep her in a hospital bed behind my office." He laughed as she gasped and took a weak swipe at his head. Seeing that the caller wasn't going to give up, he finally answered the call. "Whoever this is, you have the wrong..." He was interrupted by his niece, Tonya.

Their back and forth confused him because he had no idea what she was talking about. Then he heard her say, "They are about to hit Ann and Alisha..." and he hung up and raced back to his office.

None of his people went anywhere without some form of backup protection, but somehow someone had gotten the jump on him. He dialed Ann and Alisha, receiving no response as he pulled up the video from their follow drone. The image caused him to groan as he watched several gunmen advance on the Volvo. His heart sank when he realized that the windows had somehow been shattered.

"Fuck! Fuck! Fuck!" he shouted as he put the drone into auto attack mode. This would make anyone moving a target unless they had a chip in their arm like Ann and Alisha did.

"Are you okay, Daniel?" yelled Ashley. "Hey! Talk to me!"

He didn't want to but, after sending two more drones to help out, he turned his attention back to Ashley. He pulled a gun from behind his back and ran back into her room.

Seeing the gun, her arms came up in defense, and she yelled, "No, Daniel! Please don't shoot me!"

He flipped the gun around so the handle was facing her, and said, "Here. I have to go. Alisha is under attack right now. This gun has no safety, so be careful, but I'm going to have to lock you in. If anyone comes through that door, they'll have to break it down and you'll have plenty of warning." He pulled out another gun and said, "Keep shooting until you're sure you're safe. I'll be back as soon as I can."

He pushed the guns at her and then turned around in a full sprint. She shouted, "Wait! What the hell are you talking about? Come back!" He ignored her as he closed the inner door and glanced once again at the computer screen. All of the men were now scrambling to find any cover available as the three drones protected his two women.

Daniel took off like a rocket as he slammed the outer door to his office, effectively sealing Ashley off from the world. If he died, someone would come for her, but he would bet his life only his guys could get through that door.

Phone in hand, watching the video feeds, he saw bodies all over the parking lot, but still no movement inside the

SUV. He dialed both of their phones again, and once more got no answer. "Shit!" he cursed as he climbed into his modified Porsche Taycan Turbo. They were actually not that far from him as he burnt rubber getting out of the hospital parking lot.

And just like God had reached his hand down from heaven, he watched as the Volvo started up and shot like a rocket out of the parking spot. Another furious round of shooting started, but most of it was the drones keeping the hitmen at bay.

One thing became abundantly clear as he swerved around another driver, he couldn't watch the screen and drive at the same time. Another thing was, when the Volvo took off at a high rate of speed, it was going in a direction taking it farther away from him.

When the three vehicles fell in behind the Volvo, he slammed on his brakes and pulled over. He had to reprogram the drones or they'd just continue to sit over the parking lot killing people. He sent two of them chasing after two of the vehicles behind the Volvo. One, he left to keep the guys in the parking lot pinned down, but only for a few more minutes.

He then hacked into the Volvo's navigation system and sent it coordinates that he prayed the driver received. When it seemed like the Volvo was taking the path he'd sent, he called Walt as he took off to meet up with the convoy.

Walt answered with, "What's going on, Daniel? Is Ashley okay?"

Daniel quickly brought him up to speed on what was going on, and ended with, "Get over to those coordinates as fast as you can. We'll beat you there, but if my guess is right, I know exactly who's in the SUV directly behind them." Walt didn't ask questions, he just hung up after assuring Daniel he was on his way.

Death would come swift if either one of his girls were hurt. If one of them died…. He couldn't even think like that. They had to be okay. But, whoever was behind this wouldn't be. He vowed to make this the beginning of the last chapter in this book. He was tired of all the pain and suffering he was causing the ones he loved.

He dialed one more number and simply said, "It's time. We start tonight, but first I need you to meet me at the coordinates I just sent you." He listened to the confirmation before hanging up and letting a deadly calm settle over him. Driving on, he knew the time for games was done, it was time to put in some serious work.

Chapter 24

Ann's heart almost stopped when she saw the red dot appear in the center of Alisha's chest. She lunged and pulled her down and to the left, but she still felt the bullet strike Alisha's body before she was able to pull her out of harm's way.

They were essentially sitting ducks now that all the glass was gone from the vehicle. Bullets pinged all over the shell of the SUV, but all it would take was one person to walk up and spray inside the vehicle and that would be the end for both of them.

Ann tried her best to examine Alisha, and from what she could tell, the bullet had entered her chest high and to the right, directly below the collarbone. Her pulse was strong and her breathing was good, but she was losing a lot of blood.

She grabbed the sundress that Alisha had changed out of and ripped a long strip out of it. Ann made a pad to cover the entrance wound and the exit wound on her back. Then she used the strip to tie it into place. Alisha was still unconscious, but Ann thought it was from shock and not some internal injury she couldn't see.

The gunfire had slowed, but small burst occurred every now and then, probably to see if either of them would move or respond. Ann was between a rock and a hard place. If she stayed still, someone would eventually walk up to them and finish them off. But, if she returned fire, they would realize someone was still alive and they'd intensify the attack again.

Ann reached under the seat and pulled the handgun that was standard in every car Daniel owned, and prepared to buy them a little time. She was just about to fire off some shots when her phone rang. Probably from some hand signal, all the gunfire stopped as her assassins listened to see if anyone would answer the call.

She glanced at the display and saw it was Daniel, but to answer it would be suicide. She let it go to voicemail and immediately Alisha's phone started to ring. Ann gritted her teeth in frustration and prayed Daniel figured out what was going on.

When Alisha's phone stopped ringing, everything went silent. This wasn't the most populated part of Charlotte, but Ann was amazed that she didn't hear a single police siren coming their way. Just that alone gave her a hint as to who was trying to kill them. Who else but the WRA could shatter unbreakable glass and keep the cops away from a virtual war zone.

Then she heard an unmistakable sound that caused her heart to calm and her spirits to lift. It was a sound that she'd grown used to over the last year. It was the sound of one of Daniel's drones switching to attack mode.

She smiled as the four miniguns opened up and the hitmen screamed in agony as the bullets tore through their bodies. The drone sounded like a transformer morphing as each gun zeroed in on different targets while the main body swung back and forth to cover the whole area. The only prayer she sent up now was that no bystanders would choose this time to investigate the noise. If they did, the drone, thinking it was defending her and Alisha, would rip them to shreds.

No bullets had been fired in the direction of the Volvo in some time, so Ann chanced a quick glance to see what was going on. The first thing she saw was the three drones presiding over the parking lot, daring anything to move. She then focused on the grounds and saw multiple bodies littering the concrete. Most were still alive but had learned quickly that any movement would cause a deadly reaction.

Some bodies were clearly dead as blood pooled around them, but not as many as she would have thought.

Out of pure anger, she wanted to jump out and start shooting the downed assassins, but she was very aware that the person who shot Alisha could still have the gun trained on them. With that in mind, she inserted the key into the ignition, hit the start button, and, staying as low as possible, took off towards the far side of the parking lot.

Once again, the drones spewed their deadly venom over their attackers and, when she felt she was out of sight of the sniper, she sat up and tried her best to steer the heavily fortified vehicle.

Ann glanced at her phone and saw that Daniel had tried to call her again, but with the noise of the drones, she'd been unable to hear the phone. She'd been steering without thought of a destination, but one glance confirmed that she was going away from civilization. She focused back on the phone, about to call Daniel, when a huge black SUV slammed into the back of the Volvo, causing her to fumble the phone onto the floor.

"Give me a fucking break!" she screamed as the SUV rammed her again. She heard a sharp inhale come from her right and she glanced over to find Alisha staring at her, wide eyed. "Oh! Thank God!" exclaimed Ann.

"Somebody shot me and ruined my new shirt," Alisha said over the roar of wind entering the vehicle. She looked around wildly and then said, "Take the next right."

Ann laughed and said, "Glad to see you're back amongst the living, but why take a right? We need to get back to the house somehow."

Pointing, Alisha said, "Look at the navigation screen. No one except Daniel could hack his system. He's leading us somewhere and I bet he has a plan to get these clowns off our ass."

Ann jerked the wheel to the right and the heavy Volvo briefly went onto two wheels before settling back down and taking off in the new direction.

Watching the rearview mirror, Ann saw that there were two muscle cars following in the wake of the black SUV. Just as the last car made the turn, one of the drones caught up and shot a projectile at the back of the vehicle. The explosion was legendary as the yellow and black car flipped end over end before crashing back down to earth in a ball of fire.

Ann glanced at Alisha and they both sent up a cheer and high fived before the SUV rammed into the back of them again almost causing Ann to lose control. She noticed that it was the exact style of Range Rover that the WRA liked to use and wondered if it was Delmas driving the vehicle. Then she dismissed the notion as ludicrous, thinking there was no way that he'd try to kill her in this manner.

She followed the navigation directions as the Range Rover tried its best to drive her off the road. As a cop, she'd had extensive training in defensive and offensive driving, so it was gonna take more than a few bumps to knock her off her path. But while she was driving, she thought that one thing about the whole attack continued to confuse her. She couldn't figure out if they wanted to kill them or kidnap them.

On the surface, it seemed like they were trying to kill them. The best evidence being that they used a sniper to shoot Alisha from the start. But, the more she thought about it, why didn't they storm the clothing store or shoot them as soon as they came out. Waiting until they were in the vehicle, blowing the windows, and then sniping them made no sense at all. Unless...

She turned and found Alisha looking at her with a grim expression on her face. "They're after me," she said, reading Ann's thoughts. "Someone, and I bet we both know who it is, extended his protection over you and that's why they waited and shot me from a distance. They knew you would fight back and he didn't want to risk you getting hurt. I think the only reason they're after us now is because the sniper couldn't confirm the kill."

Ann looked at her unfocused eyes and cursed. "Shit Alisha! We have to get you to a hospital." The sundress was so filled with blood, it was leaking down into Alisha's lap. She leaned back in the seat and smiled just as another explosion rent the air behind them.

They both looked back to see the blue muscle car had careened off into the ditch and the drone was circling it, filling the inside of the vehicle with round after round. Knowing the drone would stay over the crash site and kill anything that moved, Ann was sure it was just them and the black SUV now. She glanced over to celebrate with Alisha and found she'd passed out once again.

"Alisha? Alisha!" she called as she shook her uninjured arm. No response, but Ann noted she was still breathing so she left her alone and concentrated on keeping them going in the right direction.

The Range Rover all of a sudden starting honking its horn and an arm extended out of the driver's side. The windows were blacked out, so she couldn't see much, but it looked as if the person was motioning for her to pull the Volvo over to the side of the road. Ann ignored the command as she saw the final destination was coming up on the screen.

Abruptly the SUV swung into the oncoming traffic lane and barely made it back into its lane as a truck went screaming pass with horn blasting. Then Ann heard a sound that didn't make sense to her at first, but it soon registered as the ringing of a phone.

She looked on the floor of the vehicle wildly for the phone, but didn't see it anywhere. While she looked around, the ringing all of a sudden got louder and louder. It took her a second to realize that her phone had connected to the stereo system and she was hearing the ringing through the speakers now.

Her last turn was about a mile away according to the navigation voice, but now on the screen was an icon that asked her if she wanted to accept the call. Frantically she stabbed at the icon and almost screamed in relief when Daniel's voice filled the cabin.

"Hello? Hello? Alisha, Ann, somebody talk to me," he demanded.

"Oh my God, Daniel! Alisha's been shot! I fixed her up as best as I could, and she was conscious for a while, but she's losing so much blood. We have to get her to the hospital."

Daniel was silent for a few seconds, and then in a voice that betrayed his anger, said, "When you make this next turn, swing into the other lane and go pass me."

"Daniel, I think it's Delmas in the SUV behind us." When she didn't get a response, she said, "Did you hear me? Hello?" But Daniel had already hung up.

She swung her arm across Alisha's chest to hold her in the seat as she took the last turn with hardly any brakes. "What the fuck!" she shouted as she abruptly shifted to the other lane. She'd come within feet of running Daniel over as he stood in the street holding a weapon that looked like it was designed to blow up planets.

After she zoomed pass, everything seemed to move in slow motion. The Range Rover swung around the corner behind her, but separated by about 50 feet. Daniel raised the weapon and she screamed because she wanted to warn him that his brother was probably in the SUV. She slammed on her brakes and swung the Volvo around just in time to see the devastation delivered by the futuristic weapon.

The Range Rover was supped up for speed and power and had to have been going about 60 mph. Whatever the device was that Daniel used, it hit the SUV like a runaway train. The front of the vehicle crumpled and it did about 20 end over end flips backwards before it hit a tree on the opposite side of the road they'd just left.

She jumped out of the Volvo just as Daniel walked over to his Porsche and stowed the weapon in the backseat. He pulled out a wicked looking assault rifle as another muscle car careened around the corner. Her heart leaped into her throat until she realized that this one was familiar. The car that Daniel simply referred to as The Beast slammed on its brakes and Walt jumped out with full body armor on and a carbon copy of the assault rifle Daniel was holding.

They stood there conversating for a bit and she used the time to check on Alisha one more time. When she touched her neck to check her pulse, her eyes fluttered open again. Ann said, "We're safe now, sweetie. Don't try to move or talk, save your energy and I'll get Daniel over here."

She crawled back out and waved for Daniel to come quickly. He said one last thing to Walt and took off at a sprint towards her. As soon as he was close enough to hear her, she said, "She's conscious but we need to get her to the hospital, ASAP."

Daniel gave he a look that chilled her to her bones, but he breezed pass her without a word, and climbed in to see for himself how Alisha was doing.

Walt was still standing by The Beast, looking towards the crumpled Range Rover, so she jogged in his direction. He heard her coming and, without turning from his post, he lifted her up and wrapped her in his arms.

He said, "I was so scared that one or both of you were dead. The last I heard, Daniel said ya'll had been attacked and were being chased by a group of cars."

"Oh my God, Walt! I was scared to death. They came out of nowhere, but I don't think they were trying to kill me. They were only trying to kill Alisha." She went on to explain the observations that led her to that conclusion and Walt agreed with her.

"Yeah, I think you're right. If that is Delmas in the SUV, I bet he wanted to kill Alisha and kidnap you. How is Alisha doing, by the way? Daniel said she'd been shot."

Ann opened her mouth to respond but movement to her left froze the words in her throat. She and Walt both glanced up as the silver Jeep Wagoneer with blacked-out windows turned onto the road. Walt raised the rifle and shouted, "Go back! This road is closed." The vehicle stopped but didn't reverse onto the other road.

Walt moved them both so The Beast would provide them cover, but then they heard Daniel shouting behind them. He had Alisha in his arms and was yelling for them to let the vehicle pass. Walt lowered the rifle and the Jeep took off towards the waiting pair.

"Who the hell is that?" asked Ann as Daniel opened the door to the Jeep and deposited Alisha in the passenger seat.

"I have no idea, but I've seen that same Jeep around some of our missions." They shared a confused look as Daniel closed the door and the Jeep took off with Alisha as its new passenger.

Ann and Walt watched as Daniel climbed back into the shot-up Volvo and removed a bag from the back, and a few things from the floor. He then moved the vehicle to the side of the road and got out, jogging in their direction.

Her heart leaped again as she feared what he might do to her. She feared for Walt also because she knew that he would try to defend her if Daniel tried to harm her. No matter how much training they had, Daniel could still kill the both of them without breaking a sweat. And the huge assault rifle he was clutching would just make it that much easier.

He stopped about ten feet from them and said, "She's gonna be okay. It was a through and through that didn't hit any organs or bones. But, she will be hurting for a couple months." He took a few steps closer, forcing her to meet his eyes. "She told me that the guys were after her and you saved her life. That, if it wasn't for your fast reflexes, the bullet would have hit her heart."

In a shocking move, Daniel tossed his rifle to Walt and scooped her up in a bear hug. "Thank you for saving her," he said with deep emotion. "I owe you my life and everything I have. Thank you so much!"

She cried as she heard the raw emotion in his voice. She hugged him back and she saw Walt turn back to man his post of watching the SUV. After a few seconds, Walt said, "Uh, Daniel. Take a look at this."

Reluctantly, he set her down and kissed her cheek before turning to what Walt wanted him to see. He laughed and said, "Well I'll be damned. I knew these motherfuckers were full of shit. This time I think I'll have to do more than just teach a lesson."

Ann moved beside them so she could see what they were looking at. Climbing out of the ruined Range Rover was Delmas, and he appeared to only have minor injuries. He looked in their direction, then turned and stumbled deeper into the woods he'd just crashed into.

Daniel pressed a button on his phone and the Volvo parked down the road burst into flames. His eyes settled on Ann as he took his rifle back from Walt. He said, "Go wait in the Porsche. I have some people directing traffic away from here, so don't worry about anyone coming."

She had to ask. "Are you going to kill him?"

The mask slipped back over his face and he went from the appreciative fiancé, to the Prison Guard Killer in a flash. He said, "Wait in the Porsche," and walked away with Walt trailing him.

She watched them make their way over to the trees before she climbed into the Porsche. No matter how thankful he was, this wasn't the time to test Daniel's patience. She really didn't even know why she had the urge to.

Every time a situation presented itself where Delmas could show his love for her, he did the complete opposite. He caused everyone in her circle nothing but heartache and pain. And here she was feeling like she needed to go against her own people in order to keep him safe.

Fuck that! He thought he was keeping her safe by having a team full of assassins shoot at her? Fuck him! He'd get exactly what he deserved.

15 minutes later she'd talked herself into hating his guts. When she heard the distinct sound of two rounds being fired deep inside the woods to her right, she told herself she was glad it was finally over. He couldn't hurt any more of her family.

Angrily, she swiped at her eyes as the stubborn tears continued to fall down her face. She told herself people didn't cry like this when they were happy. A minute later she was blubbering like a baby, curled up in the passenger seat of Daniel's Porsche. No matter how many times she cursed herself for being a damn fool, she couldn't stifle the sobs that racked through her body when she was forced to face the death of her ex-lover.

Chapter 25

"Your beef has always been with me. Why don't you let her go and then we can settle this like the warriors we both claim to be?"

The Author waved the gun to signal Reggie to take a few steps back. The assassin wasn't taking any chances as he moved off the elevator but made sure to stay out of Reggie's reach.

Shaking his head, The Author said, "Can't do that. I have my mission and this is by far the biggest payday I'll ever get."

"I should have known it would come down to money with you." Moving Mary Sue so he stayed between her and the gunman, he said, "So, how much are we worth?"

With a brilliant smile, he said, "$50 million in a numbered account of my choosing. I mean, what kind of hitman would I be if I turned that down?"

Reggie quietly studied the man. He was a broadly built man, not really muscular, but built to showcase his power. Reggie knew the man was a couple years older than him, but a little gray at his temples was the only sign of his age. The dark-skinned killer was one of the best in the game, a legend by anyone's standard. But he had weaknesses, and Reggie was gonna poke and prod at them and see what happened.

"You know whenever you take a job with us, you have to play by our rules. So, I'm ordering you to abandon your mission and debrief on who sent you on this mission in the first place."

Relaxing and enjoying himself, The Author said, "You don't have the authority to give that order this time. You can only do that if the mission came from down the ladder."

"Ah!" replied Reggie, nodding his head. "So, the head of the WRA sent you to kill her sister and her son. I hope you already got paid, and you have a hell of an exit strategy."

The Author frowned. "What's that suppose to mean? I kill both of you and then I get paid. That's the deal I made."

"And sadly, you fell for it." Shaking his head again, Reggie said, "To kill a member of the Board of Directors you have to win a majority vote. And there are strict guidelines that have to be followed during the execution. Since my Mom didn't call for a vote, she can't let the fact that she hired you to kill us get out. So, I'm sorry to tell you, there will be no money. And you'll more than likely get a bullet to the back of your head the second you tell her it's done."

Smiling again, The Author said, "I'm not stupid you know. I do have a plan for getting out of here."

"Yeah, we always have backup plans," said Reggie. "But, I'm willing to bet that your plan will save your life, but will not get you any money." Seeing the shadow pass over the man's face was all the confirmation he needed. Then he threw out the worm. "You know, you always thought you were much smarter than you really are."

"And yet, I'm not the one staring down the business end of a gun," boasted The Author.

"Not right this second," conceded Reggie. "But, all that will change the moment you pull that trigger. You of all people should know what type of monsters the WRA has on its payroll. Even if you make it off the property, I give you three days before one of them tracks you down."

Showing a little anger, The Author said, "Fuck you and your bullshit talk! I'm the best agent the WRA has ever had."

Reggie tried to hold his laughter in, or at least pretended to, before letting it out in a burst of amusement. Mary Sue, having picked up on what was going on, held a hand to her mouth, trying in vain to cover her own giggles. The face of The Author continued to darken with rage.

Finally, Reggie got control of himself and said, "How can you be the best agent when you're not even an agent? You forget yourself, buddy. All you'll ever be is a serial killer who enjoys killing. Real WRA agents don't get caught. Real WRA agents think a job through before they accept it. By you taking this job, you've effectively proven that my mother was right all those years ago."

Reggie paused to let that sink in before he continued. "Yeah Wilford, have you forgotten who set that operation up to save you from Death Row? Do you remember who lobbied to get you into the Agent Training Academy? Better yet, do you remember who the loudest objections came from?"

"So what," said The Author. "You saved me a hundred years ago. Whoopty fucking do. But everyone respects me now. I might not be a certified agent, but I can hold my own against anyone who comes at me."

"You sure about that," questioned Reggie. "The last time you thought that, you challenged me for my spot at the table and got your ass handed to you. Which, if I recall correctly, led to me sparing your life again."

All the Burke men had to stay in top form because they could be challenged for their seat at any time. Coming out of training, The Author felt he was ready to take a leadership role in the WRA. He called out Reggie because beating the oldest male Burke alive meant that he would be only one degree from taking over the WRA.

After Reggie mopped the floor with the agent in training, it was within his rights to kill the man for the insult of the challenge. Because he had lost the challenge, The Author could never be an agent in the WRA. But Reggie had shown mercy to the man and not only let him keep his life, but hired him on as a contracted associate.

"So, what, you think I owe you now?" asked The Author.

"Don't you?" responded Reggie. "From the very beginning, I saw your potential. When everyone else thought you were just a murderous imbecile, I felt you could be an asset to the Agency.

"One of the loudest objections was about your intelligence. No one believed you were smart enough to make decisions on the fly like a real WRA agent. And sadly, as much as it pains me to say it, they were right about you all along."

Shrugging, the gunman said, "None of that matters now, according to you. If I don't pull the trigger, I'm broke and Mrs. Drake will hunt me down. But, if I do, I'll still be broke and on the run."

"That's what should have popped into your head the second the offer was made to you. But, to override the conclusion you might have come to, she offered you enough money that you became blind to the consequences." Reggie knew the man wasn't stupid, but as a mercenary, understandably he took the jobs with the highest pay.

"But, I'll make you a counter offer that will see you safely away and with the pay you deserve."

A lengthy silence ensued after Reggie made his statement. If The Author didn't shoot them both in the next few seconds, then Reggie knew he had him. The man seemed to be frozen, not even breathing, as he thought about what this new deal could entail. Finally, his curiosity got the best of him and he asked, "What's the offer?"

Dispensing with all the bullshit, Reggie said, "If you look me in the eye and tell me we have a deal, I'll send you the $50 Million right now for you to let my Aunt Mary Sue leave unharmed."

Reggie stayed quiet after his offer. He figured only good things would come from making the man feel like he had a choice. Nodding once, The Author said, "I like that part of the deal, but what about the part involving you?"

If he hadn't asked that question, Reggie would have known the man had no intention of taking the deal. He said, "Like I said from the get go, this is between you and me. Once she is safe, we can discuss where me and you go from there."

With a dead serious expression, the serial killer turned hitman said, "I give you my word: You send me the money, and don't try any bullshit, I'll let her go unharmed. If the transaction has any bumps, I'm killing both of you and I'll take my chances with your mother."

The Author kept the gun pointed squarely on Reggie's chest as he slowly pulled out his phone. "I can't send it straight to your regular account, my mother will be watching it for such a transaction. Give me one of your hidden accounts and I'll send it from one of mine."

He gave Reggie the account number and within two minutes, Reggie looked up and said, "Done. Now let my aunt go."

The Author pulled out his own phone and verified the money had been sent. He nodded once again and said, "She's free to go, but don't hold me accountable if Mrs. Drake kills her as soon as she leaves."

Reggie kept his eyes on the other man as he cautiously directed his aunt from behind him. She clutched his hand and whispered, "What about you? I don't want to leave you."

"It's okay, Aunt Mary Sue. Do what I told you to do before we were interrupted. If I don't make it back, call

Daniel and he'll come get you out. Don't trust anyone else. Do you understand?" he asked urgently.

She nodded and he lightly pushed her towards the elevator. Reggie continued to watch The Author as Mary Sue skirted him slowly and made her way to the elevator. It had never left after the man had rode it down, so as soon as she entered her code, the door opened.

Mary Sue stepped in and pressed the button to return her to the surface. She gave Reggie a thankful smile when the doors started to close, but at the last second, one hand shot out to stop the doors progress. Then she pulled out the gun she'd taken from Reggie with the other hand and said, "See, not that smart."

The Author had kept his gun trained on Reggie, but had watched Mary Sue's progress with his peripheral vision. When the doors to the elevator started to close, he'd focused back on Reggie. Mary Sue's statement caused The Author's body to whip around with the gun pointed somewhere in the middle of them, which was why the statement was needed.

As soon as the barrel was no longer lined up with his body, Reggie dove behind the table that, not long ago, Mary Sue had been strapped to. Now, with him out of the line of fire, Mary Sue unleased a barrage of bullets in the direction of The Author.

He fired in her direction also, but she had cover and he didn't. All his shots went wild as he scrambled, finally finding some semblance of cover behind a rack of torture devices. From his count, Reggie knew his aunt only had three more shots, but he had no idea how many The Author had left. For all he knew, the man could have extra clips in his pocket.

"Reg, I got him pinned down! Come on and we can lock him down here!" yelled his aunt.

Reggie hollered back, "No can do, Auntie! I'm going to finish this little beef once and for all. You go ahead and leave and stick with the earlier plan."

After a brief pause, she asked, "Are you sure?"

"Well, I'm sure that we can workout our issues, or one of us will have to die. Either way, I want to face him man to man and see what happens."

The Author stayed silent and still throughout this exchange, probably trying to figure out if it was a trick or not. He had no way of knowing if Reggie had a gun also, so staying in cover was the best hope to survive.

Without a word, Mary Sue slid his gun as if she was bowling for a perfect 300, and Reggie caught it just as the doors closed and she was gone.

Just in case the other man had been counting, Reggie ejected the clip and pretended to insert a fresh one to throw the man off. "It's just you and me now," Reggie shouted. "You want to handle this like men, or like little boys?" He silently crawled deeper into the dungeon so the other man couldn't find him by his voice.

Glancing around another table, Reggie could see that The Author was no longer hiding behind the rack, but he knew he was still in the room because he hadn't heard the elevator. To flush him out, he told him just how deceiving the last few minutes had been. "If you're thinking about skipping out, you might want to check that account balance again."

After a few seconds, a muffled curse came from the opposite side of the room. The man had guessed Reggie would attempt to flank his hiding spot and had skirted the room to get away. Knowing how aggressive the man normally was, Reggie guessed this meant he was out of bullets. Tauntingly, he said, "You might as well check all your accounts while you're at it. You'll find that you're not as good at hiding money as my people are at finding it. And just to show you how thorough I am, I have people on the way to all three of your homes to confiscate any valuables and burn everything else to the ground."

Everything Reggie told him was the absolute truth. While he had been faking like he'd sent the man the money, he'd really sent Phung Lei, the WRA tech guru, a text telling her what he needed done. She'd sent a phantom $50 Million and then cleaned out all his other accounts, as well as contacted the field agents on where to go and what to do at each location.

"FUCKKKK!" roared The Author, having just realized that Reggie hadn't been lying to him. "Fuck you, you son of a bitch. You just signed your own death warrant motherfucker."

Laughing, Reggie said, "That's big talk coming from someone with no more bullets."

The gun sailed over Reggie's head as The Author screamed, "I don't need a gun to kill you. Come out and face me, you coward motherfucker!"

Reggie crawled about five yards away from his previous spot and then popped up with his gun leading the way. The Author stood 30 feet from him with his arms stretched out away from his body. Reggie walked closer and ordered the man, "Take off your shirt and spin around slowly or I'll shoot you right now."

The Author complied and said, "See, no weapons. Now, put your gun down and let's do this."

Reggie sighed as he racked the gun to remove the loaded round and ejected the clip before putting them both in his pocket and laying the gun down. He said, "You're always five steps behind when you think you're a step ahead. Put your shirt back on and we can settle this once and for all."

He put his shirt back on and then they both cautiously side stepped until they were back in the open area in front of the elevator. "Why don't we make this official, Reg? That way, after I kill you, nobody can come after me and I can get all my money back."

Reggie thought about it for a second and then nodded before pulling his phone out. He propped it up on the nearest table, making sure the camera could pick up the whole open area. He said into the lens, "Wilford Sealy has challenged me for my spot at the table. This will be a battle to the death with no weapons whatsoever. If either of us cheats to win, a standing death warrant will be issued and will remain open until the perpetrator is killed. If Wilford Sealy wins, because he can't legally occupy my seat, he will be paid $100 Million to replace the money and property he's lost today. If I win, well, I guess everything will remain as is."

He turned to The Author and asked, "Do you understand and accept these conditions?"

"Why can't I have your seat if I win?" asked Wilford.

"Because you have to be an agent to issue a seat takeover challenge. Since you failed the last time, that's no longer an option for you." The subtle dig had The Author clenching his jaw in anger.

"Yeah, I understand and I accept," said Wilford. "Now, stop with all the bullshit talking, I didn't have lunch today and I'm a little hungry."

It had been over 25 years since the last time Reggie lost a fight. His first Judo competition when he was a teenager had resulted in him losing by submission to a 20-year Judo master. One moment of lost concentration led to him being put in an ankle lock that cost him the match.

Everyone had congratulated him for making it to the championship, but he could feel the disapproval over the fact he'd given up. He vowed to never lose again, and the next year, he set a record by beating the Judo master in 12 seconds.

Most people never saw how deadly of a fighter Reggie really was. With Master level black belts in four different martial arts, it really didn't matter how good his opponent was. All that really mattered was whether or not Reggie wanted to kill or show mercy.

As both men squared off about 20 feet from each other, Reggie closed his eyes for a few seconds and centered himself. He put all the crap with the WRA out of his mind. He pushed his past and his future to the side, just focused on the present. He knew the other man had put in a lot of work over the years, but he also knew The Author had never faced the monster he was about to encounter.

Finally, he opened his eyes on a deep exhale and slowly advanced on his prey. The Author sported a small, cocky smile as he beckoned for Reggie to come closer. Just about in striking range, Reggie broke off his direct advance, and proceeded to circle his opponent.

"He who knows others is clever," said Reggie. Without warning, he executed a perfect leg sweep that had Wilford crashing to the floor. He launched himself back up and sent a neck breaking kick at Reggie's head before another leg sweep put him on his back again.

"He who knows self is enlightened." Reggie let the man get back to his feet as he continued to circle him. The Author went on the attack and, although the moves were powerful and deadly, none of them came close to its target.

In a fit of rage over not being able to hit his target, The Author tore his shirt off, revealing the hundreds of memorialized tattoos dedicated to the people he'd killed. Some were just names, others were small portraits. His dark skin did a good job of hiding most of the details, but Reggie could clearly see the names Javon, Eric, and Charles, the three WRA agents he'd killed recently. Faded, but still readable, were all the people he'd murdered on his serial killing tour around the world.

Running at full speed, the man bellowed, and in a surprising move, checked his headlong charge and slid into Reggie's feet like a runner stealing third base. They both wrestled on the floor for a few seconds before Wilford rolled away with a shout of pain.

They both popped up on their feet with Reggie once again circling the other man. He said, "He who overcomes others is strong." Wilford's eyes were huge as he looked at his dislocated fingers. It had only been a fraction of a second with his hand in the wrong place and all four fingers on his right hand were twisted and broken. He eyed Reggie with hatred as he tried to pop the bones back into their correct alignment.

"But he who overcomes self is mighty." Lightning fast, Reggie grabbed the already hurt hand and jerked the man towards him. The scream of agony was cut off as the vicious elbow plowed into the man's stomach, stealing all of his breath. Launching his body upwards, Reggie delivered an uppercut that lifted Wilford off his feet.

His head hit the floor with a loud crack and he immediately curled up grabbing at the new injury. Sensing the fight was almost over, Reggie grabbed the man's leg and applied a debilitating ankle lock. The Author screamed and kicked out at Reggie, landing a couple of well-placed kicks to Reggie's leg. With deliberate calmness, Reggie gave a powerful twist to the captured ankle that broke bones and ruptured tendons all the way up to Wilford's knee.

Reggie released the ruined leg as The Author rolled around in pain, begging for his life. "Oh God! Oh God! Stop! You win, man. You win."

Reggie stomped on the ankle causing him to gasp and crawl away. Reggie said, "Rules, Wilford. Rules. Remember, this is a fight to the death."

The Author continued to crawl towards the elevator as he pleaded for Reggie to spare him. "I promise I'll never come at you again. Please Reggie, I'll leave the country. I'll disappear forever. Just show a little mercy."

"Ha!" laughed Reggie as he put his foot on Wilford's butt and pushed him back to the ground. "All the mercy I've shown you over the years and we still ended up at this point. No, we end this here and now so I don't have to worry about you ever again."

By now Wilford had made it to the wall about 15 feet to the left of the elevator. Reggie stopped about 10 feet from him and watched as he used the wall to clumsily get to his feet. The Author leaned against the wall, breathing heavily with pain, watching Reggie as blood flowed out of his busted mouth.

He spit and then started to laugh. Reggie smiled and said, "I'm glad you're amused with your impending death."

Ending his laugh with a coughing fit, The Author breathed in enough air to deliver a message of his own. "Fuck you and your smart-ass mouth. You said something earlier about being five steps ahead. This time, you son of a bitch, you should have been six."

Without warning, a door opened up behind his back. The Author took one leap backwards as Reggie lunged to try and pull him out of the tunnel. The door closed with alarming speed, but not before The Author could deliver one more surprise to the reaching Reggie.

Just as his hands slammed into what felt like solid rock, he heard something rolling across the floor behind him. He turned to see a grenade settle to a stop right about the place he'd changed the door from. Knowing he was well within the blast radius, he took off running towards the rack of torture devices which was his only viable cover.

He made it to within five feet of the rack when the grenade exploded. The wave of death lifted him off his feet and bounced him off the wall to his right. Not that he had any clue what the blast had done to him. Darkness had descended over his mind way before his battered body crashed back down to the concrete floor.

Chapter 26

"Why do you always have to be so fucking secretive?" demanded Walt. They were standing at the edge of the woods, about to head in and track down the elusive Delmas Burke.

Daniel cut his eyes to him for a second but continued to focus on scanning the area. "What the hell are you talking about? You better get your head in the game. I can tell you now, there is nothing more dangerous than a hurt and cornered Burke."

"All I'm saying is we are one team. Why are you torturing Ann by making her think we're about to kill Delmas?" asked Walt.

Patiently, Daniel said, "We are one team, but my fiancé wasn't supposed to get hurt. So honestly, I have no idea if I can see him and not kill him. Remember, he doesn't have to be alive for us to carry out our plan."

"But that's what I mean," said Walt. "She's gonna have to play a pivotal role in this plan. Why do you want to keep her in the dark until the last minute?"

"Walt, she loves him," he explained. "That shit will make you do crazy things. The last thing I need is for her to be sitting around thinking and then not being able to act when we need her to. Now, can we go in and track this fucker down, or do you want to let him get to Canada first?"

Rolling his eyes, Walt said, "Track him down? I'm not even that good of a tracker and I can see the path that he took."

"Oh yeah?" asked Daniel. "Well, why don't you lead the way, smart guy?"

Daniel watched Walt swagger down the slight decline and make his way over to a tree with what looked like fresh blood on it. When Walt was about three feet from it, Daniel said, "I wouldn't go that way if I were you."

"Why not?" asked Walt, confused. "This is the way he went when he stumbled out of the SUV, and you can clearly see his bloody hand print."

Daniel eased over next to him and said, "You have to stop thinking that the guys we go against now are like the criminals you use to chase. The people you're dealing with now have had extensive training in fields you don't even know exist. One of them being counter-pursuit measures. Another being sabotage."

Moving Walt out of the way, Daniel pulled out his knife, bent down, and cut the thin tripwire that was connected to a mine buried in some leaves. "Why don't you let me lead on this one, Sherlock? Like I said, a hurt and cornered Burke is very dangerous, but still very, very smart."

Daniel took a path that led them at a 45-degree angle from the false path Delmas had left for them. About a hundred feet in, Daniel sent a quick glance at Walt and saw the confusion written all over his face. He smiled to himself, but wondered how deep they'd have to go before Walt voiced his concern.

Fifty feet later, Walt said, "This doesn't feel right. I understand you guys are in a league of your own, but I haven't seen one thing that would have led me in this direction."

Daniel continued to walk for another 100 or so feet before he stopped and turned to Walt. "Let me walk you through a scenario and I want you to tell me what you think."

Walt nodded, but said, "Don't you think we need to stay quiet and keep moving? I mean, your brother could be anywhere."

Daniel just smiled and went on with what he had to say. "So, you have this guy. He's been fired from his job and he's telling everyone who'll listen that he's gonna kill his boss. After convincing himself to follow through, he goes to his boss's house and confronts him. Well, the guy's boss kicks his ass and then, to protect his family, goes into hiding.

"Now, this guy is pissed. So, achieving this goal takes over his life. He's searching all over for his ex-boss, but now he has a gun because he can't beat this guy. Finally, he decides to head over to his old job and take his revenge. When he gets there, he's running around, waving the gun, and demanding that people tell him where his ex-boss is. Things turn ugly and he ends up shooting a couple people.

"Someone calls the cops and, giving up his search, he flees the scene to avoid getting locked up. Now, my question to you is, if the police were gonna try and find this man, where do you think they should look?"

Walt shrugged and said, "I guess I'd start looking for the man at his home and then visit some of his family and fri…" he broke off when he noticed Daniel shaking his head. "Well, you tell me what I should do, Oh Great One," he said smartly.

"That's the mind state that you have to get out of," said Daniel. He put the rifle up to his shoulder and aimed back towards where they had entered the forest. "While you would have been driving all over, wasting valuable time, the answer to the question is really quite simple. His goal now is to kill his boss. He won't abandon the goal just because the police are on to him. Instead, he'll backtrack to wherever his boss is."

Without warning, Daniel sent two rounds flying through the air before lowering his rifle and turning back to Walt. "If Delmas was trying to get away, he wouldn't have chased after the women. He had a goal and our presence wasn't going to discourage him."

242

They started walking back the way they'd come when Walt finally understood what had just happened. "So, Delmas entered the woods, set up a false trail, ran all this way, and then backtracked? Why didn't he just hide behind a tree and shoot us down?"

"Walt, think. He's hurt. He didn't run anywhere. You ever heard the saying 90% of people looking for things never look up? Well, I fall in the other 10%," explained Daniel. "Delmas set up the false trail and then, because he couldn't run, hid in a tree and waited for us to leave his sight before coming down."

By now, they were standing over the man who looked so much like Daniel. He had fallen face first and hadn't moved a muscle since the rounds had struck his back. Walt looked up at him and asked, "When did you figure all this out?"

"I figured that, when he saw me standing in the road, after the Range Rover turned the corner, he pulled his gun, intent on shooting me. The impact from the wave gun, and the resulting crash would have disarmed him. I didn't think he would take the time to look for the gun because he was hurt and he needed to exit the vehicle fast.

"When the only tracks led to the false trail, I knew he couldn't have gone far. I started scanning the trees and found him within 15 seconds. I figured he'd want to make another run at Ann, so I made him think the coast was clear and then took him down."

With a slow, sarcastic clap, Walt said, "Bravo, genius. Now, do you want the legs or the arms?"

They flipped him over and Daniel grabbed his legs as they carried the limp body back towards the vehicles. When they got close, Daniel said, "Just follow the plan and everything will work out fine. Make sure Ann knows how important it is to play her role and a normal life could be within reach in a few days." They made it back to the Porsche and one glance at the interior had Daniel shaking his head. Dropping Delmas' feet, he said, "Look at this bullshit. And you wonder why I don't tell everyone everything."

Walt lowered Delmas the rest of the way to the ground and walked over to see what Daniel was talking about. Ann was curled up in the seat with her feet tucked under her, crying her heart out. If anyone but them had come along, she would have been helpless to defend herself.

Daniel said, "She's your problem now. Whatever the hell is going on in her head, fix it. We're down to hours now, not days. Get this setup right on your end, and I'll handle mine. Did you get her bag ready?" Walt ran over to The Beast and removed a duffle bag from the passenger seat before jogging back to the Porsche.

With one last look at Ann, Daniel shook his head and made his way over to The Beast. He climbed in and set out to see who all had to die for daring to harm his fiancé.

. . . .

Walt watched as Daniel drove away, then he pounded on the passenger side window of the Porsche to get Ann's attention. Her head jerked up and she wiped her face like she could hide the fact that she'd been crying. She stared at him for a few seconds before she opened the door and stepped out.

He gritted his teeth as he took in the teal and white ensemble she had on. Tossing the bag into her arms, he said, "Go to the front of the car and change your clothes." She opened her mouth to say something, but he walked towards the back of the vehicle before she could get it out.

Ann had been Walt's partner at the SBI for almost ten years now. She was his family and he loved her as such. He couldn't remember a time when he'd been more angry or disappointed in her. As smart as he knew her to be, he couldn't figure out why she was acting so stupid.

He heard her footsteps advancing in his direction and he glanced at her at the exact moment that she looked down and saw Delmas stretched out on the ground.

She gasped as her face crumpled and she turned away to try and hide her reaction from him. He saw that she had changed into the black body armor and black boots that he'd packed for her, and she'd wrapped her hair into a tight bun. She looked young and small and he hated the fact that the word that popped into his head was weak.

With no sympathy at all, he said, "Get your shit together. We need to load up this body and get going." He did nothing to hide the disgust in his voice. Instead, he emphasized it, hoping to piss her off a little.

She took a few fortifying breaths, wiped her face a couple more times, then turned around, but she still wouldn't meet his eyes. Walt was already at the head of the body, so Ann made her way to the feet. Walt said, "Pop the trunk."

Ann, still without saying a word, walked to the driver's side door, opened it, and removed the keys. Leaving the door open, she used the fob to pop the trunk and then rejoined Walt at the rear of the car.

Seeing her hesitation after he had already grabbed the man's arms, his frustration finally boiled over. "For fucks sake Ann! The man isn't dead, he's just unconscious. Now, do what you're fucking told and let's be done with this asshole."

The old Ann came roaring back after that. Finger extended, Ann yelled, "Fuck you Walt! This isn't the SBI. You're not my boss anymore."

"It's a good thing too, because I'd fire your ass right now."

"Oh yeah!" Fast as lightning, Ann whipped out one of the guns he'd packed in her bag, and pointed it right at his head.

New training kicked in and Walt dodged to the side, grabbed her extended arm, and twisted the gun out of her hand. Pulling her off balance, he snatched the second gun out of her holster and then slammed her to the ground with both guns aimed at her face.

Both breathing hard, Walt screamed, "What the fuck Ann? You pull a fucking gun on me!" He expected screams, and curses, and maybe an attempt to get her guns back. What he got was another emotional breakdown that finally told him that this was more than just her being upset over Delmas.

With Ann curled up on the road sobbing, Walt stored the guns inside his body armor and stepped back over to Delmas. Lifting the lid on the trunk, he bent down and scooped the man up, depositing his 200-pound body inside. Closing the lid, he made his way back over to Ann.

He stood over her for a second to try and ascertain if she was gonna attack him again. Throwing caution to the wind because of the time constraint, he bent down and scooped her up, holding her to his chest like an infant. She didn't fight him, she just let her emotionally exhausted body relax against his.

Walt deposited her into the passenger seat of the car and then made his way to the driver's side. Before getting in, he glanced around and saw the Volvo burning in one direction, the Range Rover leaning on a tree in the other, and wondered how in the world Daniel could hide all of this. Hearing sirens in the distance, he got into the car, took the keys from Ann, and pulled off back the way he'd come.

They had about a two-hour journey ahead of them, but Walt would need most of that time to fill Ann in on the plan for their passenger. That conversation would have to take a backseat to a way more important one.

"Ann, what's going on with you?" Grabbing her hand, he said, "You need to talk to me because we have some important stuff to go over."

She pulled her hand out of his and propped herself up with her back to the door facing him. "The Burkes are the ones with all the degrees. When did you take your Psychology classes?" Walt smiled a little at her attempt to show him that his partner was back in control.

"Come on Ann, please, let's just get this over with so we can move on. Now, tell me what's bothering you."

She pulled in a deep breath and let it out slowly as she realized that Walt wasn't gonna let her off the hook this time. "Growing up as an only child can be very lonely, as you know, being an only child yourself. But in my case, with my dad being a cop, and my mother a nurse, I was constantly left to fend for myself."

Walt stayed silent and exercised patience because he knew her whole childhood, and they didn't have time to take trips down memory lane. But she needed to get out everything that was fucking with her head, or she might make a mistake that could cost them in the end.

"When you're young, you don't understand what being left alone all the time can do to you. It's exciting at first. You get to do whatever you want to do, eat what you want to eat. But at some point, you look up and all you feel is abandoned.

"I didn't have many friends because I wasn't white enough for this crowd, or Indian enough for that crowd. And the horror stories my dad told me about what happens to young, friendly girls kept me at arm's length of anyone who would have welcomed me in."

She paused for a bit while she just stared down at her lap, probably reliving her lonely and miserable childhood. When she started back, she cleared her throat, and her voice was a little stronger than it had been.

"Then, when I finally opened up to the man of my dreams in college, he turned out to be a monster. I was only 19, Walt. Just a sophomore, when he decided I had led him on enough and took my virginity by force.

"I laid around my parent's house for two years, pouting, and feeling sorry for myself, when my father forced me to go to the Police Academy. I felt so empowered as I learned all the basics on how to protect myself and others. Now that me and my dad had things in common, we would talk on the phone all night or visit whenever I could get away. But, just like every other good thing in my life, it didn't last long."

Walt glanced at her face and saw the silent tears spilling from her eyes. He asked, "Is this when your father was killed?" He'd known the year and that she'd still been in the Academy, but he hadn't known that they were in the process of fixing a strained relationship.

Ann nodded and took a couple of deep breaths before continuing. "The Commander called me to his office, and the second I opened the door and saw my mother's face, I knew. They told me he'd been chasing a suspect when he lost control of his vehicle and went head on with an oncoming truck." She had to take a few more breaths before she could go on.

"After his death, it was like me and my mom both decided it was a good idea to just concentrate on work and give each other space. Over time, we just drifted apart. Even to this day, we might touch bases only a couple times a year. At one of the most vulnerable times in my life, in stepped another man intent on sweeping me off my feet.

"Delmas was a dream come true. A real-life Prince Charming. He gave me space and was patient with all of my faults and insecurities. He just seemed to know exactly what to do and exactly what to say to make me feel safe and loved. It happened so fast, but before I could wrap my head around it, I was deeply in love with him.

"But, you have to understand, just like everyone is saying Daniel changed for the worse, the man we've been interacting with is not the Delmas I knew. He used to be so sweet and gentle and fun. Believe it or not, we were actually together for two years, and he'd just asked me to marry him before, once again, my life turned to shit."

"Is that when the agents showed up and threatened you?" asked Walt.

"No," she answered on a sigh. "That happened a few months later. First, he just became really preoccupied and busy and never seemed to have time for me anymore. He would disappear for days and wouldn't give me a straight answer when I asked where he'd been.

"On top of that, he became angry and we had some terrible fights." When Walt's head whipped in her direction, she said, "None of them turned physical, at least not on his part. I admit I slapped him on a couple of occasions.

"Anyway, after one of our fights where I demanded he tell me the truth or I'd leave him, he broke down and told me everything."

Walt glanced at the dash and saw they still had plenty of time, so he asked his question. "The first time I heard anything about this Agency shit, I felt like I was in a bad movie. Did you believe him when he told you his story?"

"Well, he started out by telling me the name I'd been calling him for over two years, Raymond Brown, was a fake and his real name was Delmas Burke.

"Then he told me he wasn't an Entertainment lawyer, but an agent in some deep cover organization with the U. S. government. We argued back and forth but ultimately, I did start to believe him. But he told me that the knowledge he'd given me could get us both killed if it ever came out that he'd told anyone.

"So, after the secretes came out, I thought we were on the path to our happily ever after. Wrong! After that day, I never saw him again until you and Daniel brought him to the prison."

"Alright," said Walt. "So, where do the agents and this cabin come into the story?"

"Out the blue, after months of not hearing a word, I get a phone call from Delmas. Scared the shit out of me. I didn't even have to answer the call, his voice just started coming out of the phone's speaker. But he told me to meet him at a location and that I was in danger if I didn't go immediately. I tried to ask questions but he just screamed at me to hurry up and get out while I still could.

"I didn't know it was a cabin until I pulled up in front of it. All I know is it was cold as hell and I was somewhere in Ashville, sitting in this cabin in the middle of nowhere, waiting for him to show up. Hours passed and I was getting angry and scared and I got up to leave when, all of a sudden, I was surrounded with guns pointed in my face.

"One of the men stepped to me and held up a picture of Delmas. He kept asking me if I knew him. Finally, I said yes. Then he asked me what his name was. I remembered what Delmas told me, so I told them Raymond Brown. He stared at me for so long, I just knew I was dead. Then he nodded and told me Raymond was dead, and if I ever tried to look into his death in any way, I'd join him.

"Because of that, I put in my transfer to the SBI and I did the hardest thing I've ever had to do: I let him go and went on with my life."

After a few minutes of them riding in silence, Walt said, "Okay, I understand that part. Now, get the rest out."

Ann turned so that her body was now facing the front, and her face was in the passenger window. "That's it, Walt. There's nothing else to tell." She sounded emotionally drained, but Walt wanted to get it all out in the open.

"Look Ann...." he started.

"Don't Walt," she interrupted. "Just let it go. Where are we going anyway?"

Walt wasn't having any of it, but he knew he had to navigate this conversation carefully. "I remember the first time I saw you while you were doing a walkthrough at the SBI headquarters." Her head whipped in his direction, but he went on while steadfastly staring out the windshield.

"You were in your mid-20's and you had on your full CMPD uniform, except you didn't have on the hat, and your hair was flowing freely down your back. I remember thinking that I hope you didn't get in because you looked like a woman I'd like to get to know.

"I went over your admissions application and I knew that my hope would not come to fruition. You were a perfect candidate to fast track into the homicide department I was part of.

"When you got hired on, I asked Will to put you in the homicide labor pool to go along with your training. Every time you were called up to help on one of our cases, it was because I personally requested you."

From the corner of his eye, he saw the confused expression on her face. After a few seconds of silence, she said, "I don't understand. You never said a word to me on any of those occasions. Hell, I tried to put myself in your path and you ignored me whenever you could."

"I told myself that I was grooming you to be a good agent. I convinced myself that the attraction I felt for you was not because you were so beautiful, but because you were so smart. You were excellent at your job and I knew, with the right training, you would become an irreplaceable asset to the Bureau.

"I watched you for two years before I requested to make you my partner. I hated myself for being so selfish, but I needed to have you around me." He glanced at her bewildered face, and said, "Those first couple of years were hell because I had to fight tooth and nail to keep my hands off of you."

"Why would you have done that?" she asked angrily. "I knew what I was feeling from you wasn't my imagination, but you made me feel so stupid every time I said something."

He knew that she was mad, but he needed her to be. This way they could both air out all of their feelings. "Ann, no matter how much I wanted to be with you, I couldn't put my own needs ahead of the needs of the SBI."

"What the hell are you talking about? You had my head fucked up for years because I knew you felt something for me, but you kept pushing me away."

Her shouts led to him raising his voice. "Your value to the SBI was too great for me to fuck it up by becoming intimate with you. Can't you see that? If any of the brass thought for a second that we were involved, both of our careers would have been over. And how many people would have paid the price for us to be together."

"You fucking idiot!" she yelled at Walt. "I could have quit and had the life I always wanted. Don't you understand? I joined the SBI because I needed to get away from my old life. But the only reason I stayed was to be near you!"

Trying to ease the tension, softly Walt said, "I know that Ann, and that was something I struggled with every day. But you are so good at your job. You're better than I could ever hope to be. Your potential makes you so important to the SBI, and that is bigger that either one of us."

Turning her face to watch the passing scenery, she said, "That wasn't your choice to make. We could have had a grownup discussion about this. Instead, you chose to make life decisions for the both of us. And that, Walter, was not right."

Sighing heavily, Walt said, "The past is the past, but if I had to do it all over again, I wouldn't change a thing. I love you Ann, and you'll always be my family. I just hope one day you'll understand that I take duty very seriously. When I commit to something, if it's at all possible, I follow through. I apologize if you feel like I stepped over the line, but look at how many people we've helped over the years. How many lives we've saved because we worked as a team to solve cases no one else could. Look at the bigger picture and tell me I made the wrong decision."

She faced him again and all her anger was gone. With a sad smile, she said, "We'll have to agree to disagree." Grabbing his hand, she said, "But thank you for explaining, and I love you too. Now, fill me in on what we're about to do."

It took him almost 30 minutes of explaining before she could truly understand what they were planning. It was bold and it was devious, but this was a big step in them returning to a normal life. Ann asked a lot of questions, some of which Walt didn't know the answers to. But, by the end, she sat staring at him speechless.

Then she started to laugh. Walt thought for a second that she had lost her mind, but then she looked at him with mirth in her eyes. "Daniel is a genius, but he's also merciless. I thought sparing his brother's life was a good thing. But, when Delmas wakes up, I'm not sure he'd agree."

This time when she laughed, Walt joined her. He thought she was wrong about one thing though, Daniel was very merciful. To the people he cared about, he could be a true angel. But, to the people he called his enemy, absolutely nothing was too harsh.

As they neared their destination, reality set in. They both sobered up as they thought about this chapter of their lives finally coming to an end. A lot still had to be done but, after all the cards fell, Walt wasn't sure he'd be able to walk away from all the excitement he'd found in this strange new underground world.

Chapter 27

"Fourteen dead in what authorities are saying looks like a kidnapping gone bad. Witnesses say that armed men attempted to abduct two women when chaos erupted.

"In an area not really known for violent attacks, six bodies were found in a shopping center's parking lot in West Charlotte. Witnesses say that dozens of others appeared to be injured, but all who could, fled the scene before police flooded the area."

The camera panned to show bodies with sheets over them with rivers of blood flowing to low spots in the parking lot. "Apparently," the white man continued, "the women had some kind of protection detail who engaged with the assassins."

New shots of multiple vehicles on the side of the road flashed across the screen. "Not deterred by the protection detail, the gunmen gave chase to the women which led to three addition crime scenes where a total of eight more bodies were discovered in cars riddled with bullet holes.

"Amazingly, no civilians were caught in the crossfire as this brazen, daylight attack spilled over into the Lake Norman area. Also, we need to point out that no arrests have been made and police seem to be at a loss coming up with clues. They are asking that if anyone has information about what happened today, please call the number listed on the bottom of your screen.

"They also have no idea what happened to the two women, or who they actually were. This is a developing story and we will bring you updates as we learn more."

Face G looked around at the three other men in the room with him after he turned off the TV. Debo, Quette, and Big

Keith all stared back with dazed looks on their faces. "Have any of you heard anything from Kenji or Wayne?" asked Face G.

The three men shook their heads but Debo voiced his answer. "The last I saw them, they both jumped in the cars that took off chasing Alisha. If the reporter is right, Lil D, D-Nice, both their crews, as well as Kenji and Wayne make up the eight bodies that were found. You saw the cars. Nothing could have survived that."

Everything was still and silent for a minute as everyone thought on the situation. Then the explosion. "FUCK!" roared Face G as he swiped all the empty takeout containers off the table. He walked over to the wall and unleashed a barrage of blows until a hole the size of a basketball emerged. No one said a word or tried to stop him because they all pretty much felt the same way.

Before the attack, Face had received a call from the mysterious Delmas Burke. Face hadn't said anything to his men about the early morning visitor, so he had stepped outside the Limo to continue the call once he realized it was him on the phone.

Delmas didn't waste any time before delivering his demands and threats. "Alisha is with another woman who is not to be touched. If anything happens to her, I will personally wipe your whole gang off the face of the earth."

Laughing, Face said, "You don't have to threaten me my man. All you have to do is ask me nicely." He paused to see if the man would ask, but the line stayed silent. "You not gonna ask me?"

"Listen, you low life motherfucker, I'm not playing with you. I have a sniper in place who will kill her when she gets in the vehicle. Tell your men to stand down and let me handle this."

"No, you listen to me motherfucker. It wasn't your family that bitch betrayed. It wasn't your brother who she set up to die. I'm not sitting back while some uppity nig…" He stopped talking when the red dot appeared before him on the ground and tracked up his body to stop on his chest.

"Do we understand each other now?" Delmas asked him. Figuring he could be seen, Face just nodded. "Good, but I want you to know this; I can kill you anytime I want. That bullshit bulletproof Limo can't protect you from what I shoot. Keep that in mind because the actions of your people will reflect on you."

Face listened to a few more instructions before he heard the click on the line at the same time the red dot disappeared. When he climbed back in the Limo, he said, "When the women come out of the store, let everyone know to hold their fire. Once they are in the vehicle, the glass will break and a sniper will take Alisha out."

He paused and weighed his options for a few seconds. Nodding to himself, he finally said, "And after the sniper shoots his round, fill the inside of the vehicle with bullets. No one in that SUV is to leave here alive."

Within minutes, the attack was underway, and then everything turned to shit. Those drones came out of nowhere and sprayed death at anything that moved. It was a miracle only six of his guys died at the initial attack, but almost all his soldiers were wounded by the war machines.

Standing in the living room of the South Carolina home they had fled to after the attack, Face G yelled, "Drones! Fucking killer drones!" He walked back over and retook his seat. "Who the fuck are these people?"

Debo leaned back in his seat and glanced around before focusing back on Face G. "OG, you know I have nothing but love and respect for you, but my niggas are dead. Kenji and

Wayne are dead! So, stop bullshitting us and tell us what the fuck is really going on."

Face looked at the only person on the East Coast who could get away with talking to him like that, and decided to give him what he asked for. "You want to know the whole truth? Fine. But I'm telling you now, this shit will be hard to believe."

He told them everything that had happened from the time he'd walked into the hotel room and came face to face with Delmas Burke, up until they had fled the strip mall parking lot. Everyone sat in silence, flabbergasted by the information, until Debo expressed his doubts.

"OK Cuz, I have to say this because I know I'm not the only one thinking it. You were either dreaming, drunk, or high, because aint no nigga took out all three sentries, Kenji, Wayne, me, and Quette, and none of us remember shit. Sometime during the night, you got up to do something, fell, and hit your head. You imagined all the rest of that shit."

Face G smiled, but he was steaming on the inside. "So, I'm some Daffy Duck motherfucker who walks around seeing shit? Just imagining shit? Did I imagine the phone call in the Limo? Did I imagine the fucking glass shattering on the Volvo and the sniper? Did I fucking imagine the killer drones that just killed 14 of our brothers?"

Debo leaned back and said, "All I'm saying is...."

"You aint saying shit, motherfucker!" yelled Face G, jumping to his feet. "I know you aint saying shit because you don't know shit. None of us do!" he screamed, waving his arms around wildly. This outburst was so out of character for Face, the other men just sat in silence waiting to see what he'd do next.

"Shit," he said on an extended exhale. He flopped back into his chair and looked at each of them in turn. "Homies, I apologize. I'm on some other shit right now."

Debo said, "Nah Cuz, we all mad as hell right now, but we just need to figure this shit out. We so used to being Godzilla on the block, it's crazy to think we not the Alphas out here."

"This nigga, Delmas, kept saying something about different worlds and shit. To keep it real, I thought he was just talking. But, this the third time our people done went up against his so called brother, and every time, we got our asses kicked."

Quette finally decided to join in the conversation. "You were right about one thing though, Big Homie: We don't know shit. The main thing we need to do is figure out how to get some intel on these guys."

Face turned to Big Keith. "I know this aint your hood, but this is still your area. Have you heard anything about these motherfuckers?"

"Hell nah," he replied with confidence. "All the 704 sets share info with each other, and then we send it to you. If we had heard even a whisper of a group being out there that posed a threat to us, we would have been moved on them."

Quette snapped his fingers and said, "You know who we need to talk to? That motherfucker Joseph."

"The white boy Joseph? Diesel, goofy ass looking motherfucker?" asked Debo.

"Come on Cuz, don't do the kid like that. He got swag and he into all that hacker shit. I bet he know something about something. Or at least he can point us in the right direction. Every time he does a job for us we got to listen to all that conspiracy shit."

Joseph Tarlton was a world class hacker from Southern Pines, a rich suburb of Raleigh. At 6-foot 1-inch, and 210 pounds of solid muscle, most people look at him and think football star. In reality, he would probably wow you more on the golf course or tennis court because a football player he was not.

One thing about Joe was that he was truly too smart for his own good. He'd graduated high school at 15 and hightailed it to MIT on a full scholarship to escape his small-town existence. His dad, being an investment banker, and his mom a teacher, he never had to worry about money. So, when he was expelled for stealing and selling people's banking info on the Dark Web, it had more to do with the challenge than any financial gain.

About three years ago, Face wanted to venture into the world of credit card fraud. One of his little homies knew Joe from a couple parties they'd both attended. Introductions had been made with the then 18-year-old Joseph Tarlton, and ever since, at least once a month they get together to handle some business.

"Hell," said Face, "Call his ass up, but make sure you Facetime him. I don't need him talking about this in front of all his stupid ass friends."

Quette whipped out his phone and placed the video call. The first call went unanswered, but the immediate callback yielded results. "What's up, Cuz? I'm kind of in the middle of something. Can I hit you back in a couple hours?"

Quette laughed and tossed the phone to Face G. He looked at the screen to see that Joseph was indeed in the middle of a party, but not one of those ragers white boys are known for. Nope! Joe was laid up in a king-sized bed with three beautiful, healthy, and very naked, white girls.

Face could barely see the man as it looked like his whole upper body was covered in titties. Impatiently, Face G said, "No you can't call us back, I need to talk to you about something important." After Joe swam out of the sea of breast, Face said, "Alone."

Joseph must have noticed that Face wasn't in the mood for any of his bullshit, so he began shooing the young ladies out of the room. "You heard the Big Homie. Ya'll sluts got to go." The women flashed all their ample assets at Face as they sulked and pouted, but Joe stood firm. "Get all your shit and go wait outside. I know ya'll nosy bitches be ease dropping on my calls."

It took about two minutes for the ladies to vacate the house and then Joe laid back on the bed and asked Face what was going on. "Put some fucking clothes on Joe," demanded Face. "I swear, if you flash me, I'll have one of the little homies castrate your ass."

"My bad, OG," he said, laying the phone down and getting dressed. In a minute he was back and he said, "I just got rid of some prime tail. Now, what's so important it couldn't wait?"

"First off, I've told you about talking to me like you Gang. You not Crip, Joe. You gone catch me on a bad day, like today, and that shit gone get you killed.

"Second, don't question me motherfucker. If all I wanted to say was hi, then that's important enough. Now, do we talk, or do I call the homies?"

"Okay! Okay! Just tell me what you need."

Face studied him for a second, and then went on with his question. "So, we're down here in Charlotte and we ran into some people that's got us worried. Some government types that have attack drones and snipers and can put people to sleep without them remembering what happened to them. Have you heard of some shit like this?"

"Aw fuck man!" Joe exclaimed. "You're on their radar. No, we're on their radar. They're gonna fucking kill us all."

"Who is 'they' Joe?"

261

"'They' is the fucking WRA, and once you're on their radar, you're as good as dead."

Face G had the phone sitting in the middle of the table so everyone could hear. Debo asked, "What the hell is the WRA?"

"The WRA is like the CIA on steroids," said Joe. "They're based somewhere in North Carolina, but they are a global problem-solving Agency for the United States of America." Joe was already up throwing clothes, cash, documents, and weapons into a duffle bag. "I don't know where you guys are, but I suggest you get out of the country as fast as possible and pray that they don't consider you a threat."

"Joe," said Face G with a smile. "You're forgetting who you're talking to. I have thousands of Crips I can call upon. I'm not worried about these fools."

Joe spun around to face the phone. "Listen to me man. These guys eat gangs for breakfast. They have weapons and gadgets that you've never even heard of. They could send a group of three and probably rid America of every gangbanger on its streets. I'm trying to help you guys. Just fuckin' run."

"How do you know these people, anyway?" asked Face. Joe resumed packing and didn't respond to the OG. "Joe! Sit the fuck down for a second and explain to me how you know these guys. A couple of minutes won't hurt."

Joseph took a deep breath and snatched the phone off the bed. With the most serious look Face had ever seen on him, he explained how he knew about the WRA. "A little over a year ago, I was at this party at N.C. State. Everyone dancing, drinking, just having a good time. Out of the blue this fine ass Asian chick comes up and starts flirting with me. She was about 5-foot 2-inches tall, 120 pounds, with long black hair all the way down to her tight, bubble butt..."

"Joe, come on man," said Quette. "We get it. Now go on with the story."

"My bad, but this chick was out of this world beautiful. Anyway, I got a little buzz going and, after a while, she asks if I got somewhere private where we can talk. I tell her we can go get a room and we take off.

"We vibing, everything going good, when this bald head, black guy walks in the room. I jump up to confront him and I wake up some time later tied to the bed."

Face interrupted. "This guy? Was he about 6-foot, 200 pounds? Did he tell you his name?"

"Size is about right," answered Joe. "Said his name was Delmas Burke."

Face looked around at his crew and noticed the unease flowing through them. Joe had just confirmed that Face wasn't tripping about the story he had told them earlier.

Joe said, "That's a bad motherfucker right there. All I can tell you, if he's the one after you then you're already dead."

"Finish the story, Joe," said Debo. "You've told us we're dead a hundred times."

"Sorry man. Anyway, the Asian chick tells me her handle and I'm shocked because she's one of the most famous hackers in the world. The guy, Delmas, introduces himself and explains that they need my help trying to regain control of their computer system. I pretty much explain to them that, if the Asian woman couldn't do it, then I definitely couldn't handle it.

"Delmas left and came back with a laptop, untied my hands, and told me I had one hour to fix it or he'd kill me. The bastard sat down and started playing games on his phone while I'm over there shitting bricks trying to hack into an unhackable system."

Shaking his head, Joe said, "I'm good, really good, but I couldn't get pass the first level of security. They were both disappointed, but they didn't harm me at all. Phung, the Asian chick, grabbed the laptop, gave me a sad smile, and then walked out the door.

"Delmas finished his game and then looked up at me like he'd forgotten I was there. He told me that they'd been locked out of their system by the best hacker in the world, a guy called Turtleboy. They had been going around to all the other hackers trying to find someone to help them. No one could get through the first level.

"After a few warnings not to talk about them with anyone, he walked out and I've never heard from them again. But the encounter made me curious. I started discretely asking about them on the dark web and it's hard to separate myth from reality. The one commonality is that they are the best of the best, and if they come after you, run and keep running.

"Now gentlemen, it's time for me to go. I've told you all I know, and they'll probably come and kill me for helping you guys. Don't contact me again and I'll leave you with this advice: Pack up and run and never come back or go to a familiar place." Joe disconnected the call and Face sat speechless.

No one ever accused Face of being stupid, at least not and lived to talk about it. But it didn't take a genius to figure out that he had led his crew into a hornet's nest. He had sensed it when he'd come face to face with Delmas, but he'd let his pride take over his actions. All he could do now was try to salvage the situation as best as he could.

"By now, the police have identified enough of the bodies to point them squarely in our direction. With Lil' D and D-Nice dead, and Big Keith with us, no one is left to lead the 704 branches of our gang. We all know that eventually the police will find a weak link and that person will talk."

Face G paused to allow anyone to refute his claim. With the silence, he continued. "With the combination of the cops and the WRA on our ass, I think we need to hit the homeland for a while. Unless any of you have a better idea."

The twins looked at each other, but it was Debo who voiced his thought. "I don't like this running shit. We leave our territory and go out west, them niggas gonna look at us like we weak as hell. I say we stay here for a few days, let the heat die down, and then bomb on any niggas that dare to challenge us on our home turf."

Face looked at him in stunned disbelief. "Did you not just listen to what Joe had to say? This isn't some bullshit ass neighborhood beef. You're forgetting that one of these motherfuckers, just one, wiped out the whole Kannapolis branch by himself. I'm tired of burying my family, Debo. We don't know enough about these people to fight them. We need to get the hell out of here, regroup, collect some intel, and live to fight another day."

Debo nodded slowly, but still looked unconvinced. "Everything in our world is based off perception. If niggas see us as weak, we'll be fighting every day because people will see us as a target. You're right Face, we don't know enough about these guys. But we damn sure won't learn anything new all the way in Cali. All I'm saying is, right now, nobody knows where we are. Let's do our regrouping right here, and in a few days, if things are too hot, then we leave. Bottom line, you're our OG. If you say go, we go. I just feel like the situation is not as urgent as you think."

Face looked at his homies and the same message was reflected on all their faces: They didn't want to run away in defeat. But he was conflicted. People who didn't know their culture thought OGs were just there to point out targets. They didn't understand that they were also there to protect the people under them. If he made the decision to leave, everyone would live, but their reputations would be destroyed. If he decided to stay, and more of his people died, their blood would be squarely on his hands.

Knowing that a bad reputation was a death sentence in their world, he said, "Alright, we'll stay for a couple days."

All three faces around him showed relief. Like real gangstas in their world, they were willing and ready to die for their flag. But while they were relieved, Face G was troubled. The only thing that kept flashing in his mind was the message Delmas Burke left for him on that hotel mirror: Different Worlds Motherfucker.

After leading his crew on their first foray into that world, 14 of his homies had paid with their lives. He could only pray that those 14 bodies were enough to satisfy the hunger of the beast he now knew as the WRA.

Chapter 28

Daniel sat in his hospital office staring at his computer screen. He'd just run across the last piece of evidence that assured him the WRA was really behind the attack on Ann and Alisha.

All he could do was shake his head as he added up all the people who could have possibly been in on this conspiracy. A lot of people would die over the next 24 hours. Some, it was a foregone conclusion. Others, he would interrogate, their own answers deciding whether they lived or died.

After leaving Delmas in the care of Walt and Ann, he'd made the trek to the hospital where his partner had admitted Alisha. He had a short discussion with her surgeon, who assured him everything would be okay, then made his way to his basement office.

As soon as he opened the outer door, he saw Ashley propped up in her bed with both guns pointed at the door. He waved and smiled, but she kept the hardware pointed his way. He unlocked the inner door, pushed it part ways open, to see what her reaction would be.

Looking through the glass he could see that both guns were level and still as she stared back at him with anger on her face. He said, "Um, Ashley, you can lower the guns. Everything is good now."

"Let me be the judge of that," was her reply. "You can come in. I won't shoot you until I give you time to explain yourself."

He wasn't really reassured by her comment, but he stepped in anyway, closing the door behind him. With raised hands, he asked, "Did I do something wrong?"

"Maybe, maybe not. But one thing's for certain, you're not just a doctor that's a friend of Denise. Not when you're running around with multiple guns on you. So, you want to fill me in on who you really are?"

Stopping about four feet from the end of the hospital bed, he said, "I am exactly who I told you I am. Now, is that the sum total of me? No. But I swear to you that I mean you no harm and all I want to do is keep you, Denise, and every other person I care about safe."

She didn't take much convincing. He'd shown her over their time together that he really did care about her. She lowered the guns and said, "I'm gonna hold on to these for a while longer." After settling into a more comfortable position, she asked "So, did Denise hire you to be my bodyguard? Is something going on where I would need a bodyguard?"

Lowering himself to the edge of the bed, he said, "Denise didn't have to hire me, I volunteered for the position. As far as what's going on, you have your phone over there on the table. You'll have to ask Denise because it's not my place to tell you."

He checked all her vitals, made sure her bandages were still clean and in place, then said, "I really have to check on a few things. If you need me for anything, holler." Then he left her to start his research into the attack.

It took him hours to figure out what had really happened, but in the end, he had a list of people who he would be paying visits to very shortly. Most of them probably thought themselves safe because their parts were so small. Others would be trying their best to hide from what they knew was coming. But in today's world, it was impossible to hide from technology. All of the players were under some form of surveillance by the time he stood up to leave.

He thought about telling Ashley what had happened to Ann and Alisha, but decided against it because he didn't want to add any stress. He'd mentioned it before he left her the first time, and the fact that she didn't bring it up when he returned, to him meant she couldn't handle anything else right now.

When he entered into her hospital room this time, she was sleeping peacefully, but still clutched one of the guns. Smiling to himself, he left her a note saying he would be back tomorrow. She was already able to get food from the refrigerator by herself, so he didn't worry about her starving.

Daniel wished he had time to take a shower, but he settled for a quick wash up in his private bathroom. He took off his dingy, battle stained clothes and replaced them with a Kevlar infused bodysuit covered by a black sweat suit. The armor was so light and flexible, you couldn't tell he had it on. But it was strong enough to stop damn near any handheld weapon in existence.

He closed everything up behind him and made his way back to the ER to check on Alisha. When he walked into her recovery room, he locked in on her sleeping form laying on the hospital bed. He was aware of his partner emerging from the shadows, but he chose to ignore him and focus on his fiancé.

After 15 minutes of studying her breathtaking face, he turned to the old man who stood to the side and slightly behind him. The old man said quietly, "Let's not disturb her. Step in the hallway for a minute. I made sure the room is secure from all threats." After one last glance at Alisha, Daniel led the way into the hall.

Soon as the door closed, the man asked, "Was it her?"

Daniel said, "Not directly. It seems that Alisha's old gang wanted to strike at her, and people at the WRA lended a hand to give them a better chance." Daniel turned so he was eye to eye with the other man. "One of the gadgets they used...." He didn't finish the sentence, just shook his head sadly.

"No way!" the man said shaking his head. "Don't even go there. You know just as well as I do that she is firmly on our side."

"It doesn't matter what we think, I still have to go see her."

"No!" shouted the old man, drawing several concerned looks. Leaning in closer, he said, "No. You will do no such thing. I won't allow you to..."

"Allow?" asked Daniel. "It's been a long time since anyone allowed me to do anything." Daniel felt his rage boiling to the surface, so he took a few deep breaths to calm himself down. "My woman could have died today. I won't leave any stones unturned to find out who all participated. I only plan to question her, but if she's guilty, she will be punished along with the rest of them."

They stood eye to eye, locked in a silent battle the people around them were unaware of. Finally, the old man dropped his gaze and his body sagged. "You're right. At this stage, everyone's loyalty needs to be tested. But Daniel, don't be too hasty in casting blame. Some people won't let the insult stand."

Smiling at his mentor, Daniel said, "I'll be careful, but this has to be settled fast. Everything is in motion. If some feelings have to be hurt for us to achieve our goal, then they'll have to get over it." Patting the man's shoulder, Daniel said, "As soon as it's safe, get her out of here and then make your way north. Everything we've been working for is at our fingertips. Let's take these last few steps and live the rest of our lives in peace."

After a brief pause, the two men embraced and Daniel walked away with grim determination spread across his face.

The old man was right. Some of the alliances they had were very flimsy, and one wrong move could turn them into enemies. Fuck them, is what he thought. If anyone wavered, they would be treated like any other enemy of his.

He was almost to the Emergency Room exit when he heard his name being called behind him. He turned and saw four nurses eyeing him from the reception desk. With a genuine smile on his face, he walked over to speak to the nicest nurses he'd ever encountered.

Amber and Britney were twin sisters who shared their love of helping others with the world. Their bouncy, blonde ponytails and sparkling green eyes seemed to convey to the world their love for life. Their playful banter never failed to make Daniel laugh.

Chanel and Shawanda were best friends and loved life just as much as the twins. Both were light skinned black women who tried to put forth a stern outer appearance. But, once you scratched the surface of their ridged shells, two loving personalities emerged.

All four women had gone to UNC Charlotte and became fast friends their freshman year. After college, they all moved to the same housing development and applied for jobs at the same hospital. Since being hired, they always tried to work the same shift so they could be close to each other.

"Hello ladies! How's everyone doing tonight?"

Chanel, always the spokeswoman for the group, said, "Oh, we're doing fine. We're wondering how you're doing?"

Before Alisha came into the picture, Daniel and the four women would lightly flirt and banter playfully about each other's sex lives. Nothing serious on either end as all four of the women were married. But to an outsider, some of the comments could have sounded like open invitations.

271

The first time Alisha had visited him while the women worked, they had welcomed her into their group with open arms. Alisha loved spending time with them whenever she came to the hospital, but for obvious reasons, she never accepted any of their request to go out. Daniel thought both sides were sad about this at first, but Alisha and the group became content with the time they could share with each other.

"Thanks for asking, but I'm good now. Not going to lie, I was scared to death at first. But, when her doctors told me she would be okay, a huge weight lifted off my chest."

"Where's Gabby?" asked Amber. "If you need us to watch her for a while, you know we're more than happy to."

"I know you are," replied Daniel. "She doesn't even know anything has happened. I have someone with her at the house, but I didn't want to worry her for nothing. Alisha will be released later tonight and she'll let Gabby know she's alright."

Britney asked, "Do you know what happened?"

"The good Samaritan who brought her in thinks she was hit by a stray bullet from that incident earlier. He said her vehicle was parked not too far from where the action took place. All I can do is thank God the bullet hit her where it did. She would have bled out..." He fell silent as he thought about what he'd just said.

He was silent long enough that all four women came around and hugged him. He looked around at the four misty eyed women and hoped every human being, at some point in their life, would be surrounded by this much love.

Just then, a group came in with a screaming toddler and the women had to break off and help the new arrival. Shawanda said, "We left some gifts for Alisha and Gabby at the nurse's desk on her floor. Let us know if you need anything else." She then joined her friends and coworkers in making the world a better place.

Daniel was thinking that he would have to do something extra special for the women when all this bullshit was over. He exited the building through the automatic sliding glass doors still thinking about what he could do. His mind was occupied, but his body was very much still on point.

He dove to the right and rolled behind one of the stout columns as the door behind him shattered into a million pieces. Only after he was safe did his mind register the flash from the rifle shot that propelled his body into action. Years and years of training had once again saved his life.

As bullet after bullet continued to pepper the ground around him, he thought back to some of his early gun battles. He remembered his heart hammering in his chest. His breath would come and go in huge gusts. All sound would fade other than the blood that rushed to his brain.

Those things were no longer issues for him. He could hear the ricochets of the bullets. He could hear the women and children yelling and crying as more windows exploded. More importantly, he could hear sirens coming from several directions.

Shaking his head at the stupidity of some people, he took out his phone and opened the app he'd developed to control the chips he implanted into his allies, and some of his enemies. He pulled up the right profile, sent a few commands, and the shooting stopped immediately.

He had too much to do to spend hours talking this over with the police, so he sprinted to his car and took off just as they arrived. He followed the flashing icon on his screen until he came to a parking deck almost half a mile away. He activated the 3-D image of the structure and found that his target was on the top level. When he got there, he saw that only one vehicle was parked up there. And also, a man was laying facing the wall, still clutching the gun he'd just used to try and kill him.

He parked right next to the man and got out. He looked down at the Ghost and laughed as his body continued to jerk sporadically. The electric current from the chip, leaving the man conscious, but unable to control his body.

"How could you be so stupid? You don't think I know you missed Alisha's vital organs on purpose? I was actually thinking of letting you live. That's no longer an option," declared Daniel.

He deactivated the chip and went about stripping and securing the elite stealth killer. It would be hours before the police figured out where the bullets had been fired from. When they did, not much would be left of the WRA agent.

After he was naked and hog tied, Daniel leaned on The Beast and talked to the Ghost. "You know Jamar, I always liked you. I respected the fact that you had integrity and morals and you didn't take every job offered to you. But you had to have known I wouldn't let you come at me and just let you walk away."

Daniel was talking about the WRA sending Ghost to kill him and retrieve Delmas at the prison last year. Daniel and his team had loaded up all the unconscious bodies of the defeated WRA soldiers, but had left Ghost laying in the field. While he was still knocked out, Daniel had injected a control chip in his arm. No test or scan could pick it up, so Ghost had been tracked during every step he'd taken since.

He explained all this to Ghost and said, "But I didn't keep a constant watch on you because I thought you had honor."

"If I didn't take the job, they would have found someone else to kill Alisha," the agent explained. He tossed his head so his dreads fell away from his face. "I shot her, but I aimed for the sweet spot. I didn't want her to die."

"I already told you, I understand that. But then, why come after me? I might not have figured it out at first, but you knew I'd see her injuries and come to that conclusion."

"You don't have to kill me Daniel. I just panicked. I didn't know if you would go after my family in retaliation."

"First off, I do have to kill you. I gave you a couple passes that I wouldn't normally give. But Jamar, I won't hurt your family. In fact," Daniel said, retrieving the man's phone, "I'm going to let you talk to them one more time. Something you wasn't going to offer me."

Daniel dialed the man's home number, turned on the speaker and laid the phone next to his head. "This is your last call, my brother. Make it count."

His wife answered with a cheery, "Hey babe! You on your way home?"

Ghost took a deep breath and squeezed his eyes shut. Tears were already rolling down his face. Daniel muted the phone and said, "She deserves the truth. Give it to her so she can pass it on to your daughters when they're old enough." He un-muted the phone and Ghost told his wife who he really was.

When he finished, she laughed. "Jamar, you're a network security advisor. I think I'd know if my husband was a secret agent for a secret government Agency."

"Babe, I'm not joking and I need you to listen to me. I fucked up. I took a job against someone and I got captured. He's giving me this call as an honor because he has morals. I tried to kill him tonight and I forfeit my life for the failure."

She was silent for a minute. "If this is some kind of joke, you need to stop right now. You're scaring me." They could both hear her fear and her tears.

"Donna, this is all my fault," he admitted. "But I need you to be smart and I need you to stay safe. This Agency will kill you and the girls if you make any attempts to find them or expose them. Be mad at me, hell, hate me. But don't do anything to put the girls in danger. Don't alert the authorities, Donna. Just let me go."

"Jamar, no! What are you talking about? What's going ….?"

"We're out of time, baby," he said, cutting her off. "I love you very much and I need you to tell the girls their daddy loves them."

"No, Jamar! Wait! Don't…" He nodded at Daniel who picked up the phone and ended the call, silencing her wails.

Jamar now used his dreads to hide his face as he silently cried.

Daniel pulled a hunting knife from under the tail of his sweatshirt, head shaking at his own stupidity. Jamar was still crying when Daniel rolled him over on his stomach and cut the ropes restraining him. He issued a moan of pain as his numb limbs crashed down on the rocky roof.

"Roll over and face me like a man, Ghost." Taking deep, even breaths, Jamar rolled to his back and stared up at Daniel.

Replacing the knife, but taking out his gun, Daniel leaned against his car, studying the other man. "When I was a little boy, my uncles use to tell me stories about how honorable things use to be." Daniel placed his gun on the hood of The Beast, next to Jamar's phone before he continued.

"My Uncle Kenny always beat into me that a Burke was honorable above all else. I struggle sometimes with the concept because we don't live in those times anymore. And we haven't for a long time.

"I've never been taught that families of targets are off-limits. I've never been told to show my enemies mercy.

Since we've been through most of the same training, it's no wonder we're always at odds. But as I'm getting older, I'm starting to see why my uncles wanted me to learn the old ways."

Jamar's phone continued to buzz as call after call came in from Donna. Daniel picked it up before it could fall and placed it in his pocket. Ghost was still laying on the ground, naked, but his breathing had normalized. Always the warrior, he looked around for a weapon every few seconds.

"Now, I gave you a promise at the arcade, what I would do to you and your family if my family was hurt. Even though you had good intentions, you hurt my fiancé." Reaching over and picking up the gun, he said, "I'm sorry, but you have to pay for that."

Bang! Jamar's hand flew to the same area Alisha had been shot in. "Ahhh shit! You motherfucker!" Ghost cursed at him. "I didn't hit her fucking collar bone."

"Stop bitching. I could have shot you in your face." Daniel waited as Jamar rolled around clutching his upper chest and cursing. When he had calmed down enough for Daniel to continue his message, he picked back up the conversation.

"I think we're one step closer to being even." Daniel pulled the man's phone from his pocket and called his wife one more time. She was hysterical when she answered it.

"Oh my God! Jamar? Jamar? Please tell me you're okay!"

Daniel said, "Donna, this isn't Jamar, but he's right here…"

"You motherfucker! You better not have hurt my baby. I don't care if you're with some secret Agency. I'll hunt you down motherfucker."

He muted the call as she continued to issue threats against Daniel and his forebearers. "Jamar, ger her to shut up or I just might change my mind about killing you."

Daniel un-muted the call and Jamar yelled, "Donna! I'm right here. I need you to shut up and listen to him before you get us all killed."

"Oh Jamar! Thank God! Are you okay?" she asked him

"I'm bleeding, but I'm alive. If you want me to stay that way, listen to this guy."

When she was quiet, except for an occasional sniffle, Daniel explained the situation. "Jamar and I pretty much work for the same Agency. Not too long ago, we started having a kind of civil war. Jamar chose one side and that side sent him after my fiancé earlier today."

"Ughhh" she gasped. "Oh my God! Was she hurt?"

"Yes, but as Jamar was hurting her, he was also saving her life. So, I retaliated in kind. He is hurt right now, but if he gets to a hospital fast, he'll be alright."

"Are you going to let him go?" she asked, voice full of hope.

"Well, that's really up to you," he answered.

"Do I need to come get him or something? What do you want me to do?" she asked desperately.

"No, I have a bigger job for you. I need you to make sure your family stays alive and well. Can you do that for me?"

"Yes. Yes. Whatever you want. Just let my husband go," she pleaded.

"What I want you to do is stay on top of your husband. He is now on my side of this conflict. I need you to stress the importance of him being honest and loyal from this moment on. If you think you can handle this important task, then he's free to go."

"Yes, I can handle that. He won't leave this house without me being attached to his hip. Thank you so much for your mercy. Now Jamar, get your ass to the hospital so they can save your life. Nobody's going to kill you except me for putting me through this shit!"

Daniel told her where he would be, then terminated the call. He tossed Jamar his clothes and laid his phone on the ground. "You're out of this now," Daniel told him. "Heal up and wait for my call. This is your last pass. Come at me or any of my people again, and your whole family dies. Do you understand?"

Ghost was gingerly putting his clothes back on, wincing and moaning through the process. "Yeah, I understand."

"No, Jamar. Look at me." When Ghost looked him in his eyes, Daniel said, "No more chances. I appreciate what you did for Alisha and me, but we're even on that. Keep your head down and stay away from the WRA. I'll be in touch," he said as he climbed into The Beast.

He started it up and rolled his window down. "Hey Jamar!" The man looked up after he was fully dressed. "Word of advice. Don't try to remove the chip. If you do, at least wait until you're alone. That way, you'll be the only one to die." He rolled the window back up on the pissed off look of his new ally.

Close call after close call, and the night was still young. Daniel roared off as he watched Jamar hobble over to his vehicle. One down, too many to go. Everyone wouldn't be as lucky as Ghost had been. Matter of fact, death would come swift at his next stop.

Traitors will die. Enemies will suffer. Empires will fall. Kings will be crowned. But first, friends will be tested. As Daniel continued his journey for retribution, he hoped that others were pushing to achieve their goals also. One way or another, in less than 24 hours, the WRA will have a new look. Or a couple of big notches under its belt.

Chapter 29

"Jessica, what the hell is that smell?" Phung Lei asked, fanning her nose as the ungodly aroma filled the living room. "Turn on the exhaust or open a window. Smells like you're cooking dog in there."

"I told you I was gonna make this tofu dish I saw on YouTube. They warned about the smell, but they said it taste amazing."

"Nothing that smells like that could taste good. I think I'll pass on this one, Sis." Phung loved Jessica and always tried to support her in everything she did. But she was sick and tired of being her culinary guinea pig.

Jessica peeped around the corner and laughed at Phung's attempts to avoid the horrid smell. "Where's your sense of adventure, Sis? And stop being racist. My people are from the Philippines, not Korea. You of all people should know that not all Asians eat dog."

Jessica Singpalm was the oldest friend Phung had, except for Daniel. They had met in high school and Phung and Daniel had welcomed the half White, half Filipino into their circle.

Just like Phung, Jessica was short, dark haired, and very good-looking. Her brown eyes always danced with mirth and kindness. She was smart and loyal and was Phung's second in command in the I.T. Department.

Phung waved her friend away and focused on the news she'd been watching for most of the day. The stupid reporters kept promising updates but came back with the same information every time. All she could do was pray that the WRA didn't have anything to do with the intriguing situation.

When she'd seen the location of the attack earlier that afternoon, she had phoned Kashonda to find out what she knew. She hadn't known much, but she did know that the two women were Ann and Alisha. Phung didn't know either of them personally, but knowing they were important to Daniel was enough for her to root for them.

Jessica came in with two plates and sat one on the table in front of Phung before tucking into the other. The dish did look good, but the smell caused Phung's stomach to roll. Sitting on the other end of the couch, Jessica said, "Oh my God! You have to try this. It's delicious."

Phung shook her head and flipped the channel, trying to see if another station had any up to date info. Even if the food was to her liking, she couldn't eat because she was stressing too much. She needed to know that those two women were okay.

Then, pay dirt. A local Charlotte station was showing a fuzzy, cell phone video that had captured the scene moments before the gunfire erupted.

The reporter said, "As you can see, the camera is focused on the passenger of the car as they waited for the light to change. We can see the SUV sitting in the parking lot, but it's kind of blurry. You can see a young woman walk pass the SUV and we can only thank God that she didn't do so a couple of minutes later.

"The video doesn't show the shooting, but while the car was stopped at the next light, you can hear a vicious gun battle erupt. The woman taking the video didn't stick around, but as she fled the area, you can hear what sounds like hundreds of rounds being fired.

"At this moment, 14 bodies have been connected to what authorities are calling a failed abduction attempt. We still know nothing about the two women witnesses say were the target of this attempt. We have put this video on our site

282

and we're asking anyone else who was near the area during the attack to contact us.

"We'll have updates as more information comes to us. All we can do now is rely on the police to find the remaining culprits behind this brutal attack."

Phung tuned out the rest of the man's diatribe as she raced over to her laptop. The media might not have the capabilities to clear up blurry videos, but Phung sure did. She went straight to the site and pulled up the video before downloading it into a software program she'd written years earlier.

"Phung, why are you stressing so much over this thing? We're on vacation. We've been busting our asses for years non-stop. Can you please just come eat some food with me and leave that computer alone?"

"Just give me two seconds, Jessica. I want to see if I can clean up that video so I can run facial recognition on the woman. I'm willing to bet she was either involved or she saw some of these guys. Either way, I'd like to find her," said Phung.

"God dammit Phung! Why do you always have to be little miss perfect employee? Why can't anything be easy with you?" asked Jessica.

Phung heard her words but the computer was already done converting the video. She wondered why Jessica was so mad, but pushed the thought out of her mind when the crystal-clear video started to play.

For the next five minutes, Phung was locked in. Progressing in some parts frame by frame to verify what she thought she was seeing. At one point, the woman's hand shot out and seemed to brush against the passenger side window. Any vehicle owned by Daniel would surely be everything proof, so why would the woman touch the glass?

She couldn't come up with a logical answer, so she moved on to trying to get a good look at the woman's face. The woman proved to be a pro as she hid her face expertly with the help of glasses and a ball cap. But Phung wasn't called a computer wizard for nothing.

Piece by piece, Phung mapped out the parts of the woman's face as they appeared. Soon, she had everything but the eyes and forehead. The mouth and the nose, as well as the general coloring, should give her enough info to start the search. She added basic height, weight, and age range and let the program do its thing.

While the facial recog ran its course, Phung went back and watched the video several times. Her head cocked and her eyes narrowed as she focused in on the movements of the woman. Something was twitching in the back of her mind. She lost her train of thought as the software signaled that the results had come in. Surprisingly, it only contained ten matches.

The first three subjects she dismissed as impossible. The fourth woman was possible, but after digging a little, Phung found the woman was out of state with her family during the allotted time. The fifth woman had the right look, but she didn't feel right to Phung. The sixth and seventh she also dismissed for one reason or another. Then came the eighth.

The dark-haired woman seemed to stare out of the screen at Phung in defiance. The familiar, delicate face caused Phung's world to tilt on its axis. "Jessica, please tell me..." she started as she spun around in the chair. She inhaled sharply when she saw the gun pointed at her face.

Jessica said, "You are so fucking hard-headed. All you had to do was eat the food and you would have just drifted off to sleep. Now, I have to do this the messy way."

Phung could only shake her head in denial as she watched her best friend in the world stand up with the gun trained on her face. "Why, Jess? Why?" was all she could force herself to say.

Jessica cocked her head like Phung had just asked the dumbest question in the world. "Maybe because I'm tired of being your fucking sidekick," she growled. "Maybe because everyone sees you as perfect miss sunshine and I'm always the one left out in the rain. I'm sick of being the afterthought to Queen Phung."

"Jess, you're my sister. I love you. You've been my best friend since I laid eyes on you 20 years ago." Phung was completely caught off guard. This was coming out of nowhere.

"Jess, you're my sister. I love you," mocked Jessica in a childish voice. Switching back to her regular, she said, "Fuck you, Phung! Yeah, you've loved me alright. Like I was your pet dog."

"How could you...?"

"Shut the fuck up, Phung!" interrupted Jessica. She was now about six feet away from Phung with the gun pointed directly between her eyes. "Look at how my life has been. While you are cuddled and loved, I'm excluded and overlooked. Everyone loves you, and everyone tolerates me because I'm your little pet project."

No one ever really saw Phung get mad, except for Daniel, but Jessica was pushing all the right buttons. "I've never treated you like that! All I've ever done was include you because I was the one being excluded until Daniel did what he did. You honestly think the Burkes love me? If you do, you're a fucking moron."

Jessica drew in an angry breath and took a step closer. "You're on the Board. They listen to you. They give you money. They gave you this fucking mansion. Don't try to act like..."

"They gave me all that because they needed what Daniel put in my head!" yelled Phung. "You think I'm so blind that I can't see they're using me. You stupid bitch, I kept you close because you're the only one I thought I could trust. But I guess I really was blind, huh?"

"Don't try to turn this around on me," said Jessica.

"It is on you. Aren't you the one with the gun pointed at me? You think this is my fault? Look at my actions, Jess. Look at all the things they've given me. What have I done with it?" She gave her a few seconds to think it over. "I'll tell you! I've turned around and given it to you!"

Phung stood up slowly when she saw the lost look enter Jessica's eyes. "The money, who do I spend it with? The house, who lives in it with me? The Board seat, who do I discuss every topic with before I vote? You, Jess. You. My best friend in the whole world. You're not my sidekick, Sis, you're my partner. I couldn't do any of this without you."

She let a few of her tears escape as she saw Jessica's mouth start to tremble. Phung took a small step towards her friend, and Jessica's back went straight and her other hand came up to solidify her stance. Phung ignored this and took another step.

"Stop, Phung!" she said. "All this changes nothing. You still have to die."

"Says who?" Phung asked her. "The same people who you're saying cares nothing about you? Your gonna let them manipulate you into taking out the only person who really cares? And then what? You'll be the only evidence left that could lead back to them. You think they'll let you live?"

Steady tears falling now, Jessica said, "They promised me your spot."

With a sad shake of her head, Phung said, "Honey, it doesn't work like that. In order to take someone's seat, you have to call them out in battle. Any other way is null and void. They're using you to keep their own hands clean. Then they'll use retribution laws to kill you for killing me. Jess you know our rules."

Phung was now within arm's reach of the gun. Although Jessica was sobbing now, the gun had only slipped down to point at her center mass. In a soothing voice, Phung said, "Let me help you. We can get through this together. Just like old times, me and you against the world."

Very slowly Phung reached up and put her hand over the gun. They stared at each other for what seemed like hours, but was really only a few seconds. With one loud cry, Jessica released the gun and Phung wrapper her in her arms.

They cried together as they both apologized to each other, over and over again. But the two of them were crying and apologizing for two different reasons. One was thinking about past mistakes, while the other was thinking about the near future.

One of the laws of being a WRA agent is you have to be armed at all times. Even in the shower, there was a cubby hole to place your weapon. Didn't matter if you were home on vacation with your best friend, WRA agents had to be armed.

So, when Phung spun and executed a perfect hip toss on her best friend, Jessica shouldn't have looked so surprised to see her standing there pointing the 9mm down at her. This is Phung when she is mad. The cursing and yelling were just props. This is what her ex-fiancé had taught her. When someone makes you angry, don't show them your true intent until you're in a position to carry it out.

"You ungrateful bitch! You want my spot? You want my seat at the table? Well, if you get another life, and there is a next time, don't hesitate. Just look your target in the eyes, and pull the trigger."

Her finger had just started to flex on the trigger when she was pushed from behind and the gun was yanked from her hand. She rolled and snatched up the gun Jessica had dropped. Before she could lock onto a target, the gun was kicked from her hand, breaking her wrist in the process.

She screamed from the sudden pain, but froze when she looked up and saw the hateful glare of the man who'd just assaulted her.

• •

"I'm telling you now, Mike, if you don't open that fucking door, your job will be the least of your worries!"

The fat, old, Head of Security at the WRA headquarters looked around like he expected a savior to appear. He swallowed audibly before he returned his attention to the two hellions in front of him. "Tonya, you know I can't let you out. I can't let anyone out, not even myself. Reggie pulled rank and turned this into a full lockdown. I can't lift it until I hear from him."

Nyaira said, "But you let us in. If it's a full lockdown, nobody should be able to come in or go out."

Mike just shook his head. "You're both Burkes. The law states that during lockdowns, family can always take refuge inside the compound. Even a Burke in exile can always come in. But during a lockdown initiated by the first or second in command, no one can leave." Glancing at them, he said, "You both know this. Why are you busting my balls?"

"We were ordered to come here, but we don't live here," said Tonya. "The WRA doesn't have the authority to hold us against our will."

"But that's what I'm trying to tell you!" exclaimed Mike. "Once you're inside, they do have that authority. I'm sorry ladies, but I can't help you. Mrs. Drake has a private exit, go ask her if you can use it. But, until I hear from Mr. Burke, this exit is shut down."

Tonya wanted to kick the shit out of the old man, but she knew he was just doing his job. Since before she was born, Mike had been protecting her family. No matter what she threatened him with, he would never go against a WRA protocol.

The problem was, no one could find her Uncle Reggie. His phone went straight to voice mail. He wasn't in his office. And, if he was in his sleeping quarters, he wasn't answering the bell. From what she could tell, no one even knew if he was in the compound.

Tonya gave Mike one last menacing glare, grabbed her sister's hand, and stormed back to the car. She drove back to the lift and re-entered the underground portion of the compound. Several agents were still milling about the parking area when they exited the car. Tonya and Nyaira ignored them as they hightailed it to the family wing.

Almost four hours ago, they had gone to their grandmother's suite for permission to leave. Normally, when they were off mission, they could sweettalk her into anything. But this time had been different.

Tonya had rung her bell, but the buzz of the opening door never came. Instead, Lucille had come over the intercom with a stoic, "What do you want?"

The two girls had traded a look before Tonya launched into her plea. "Grandma Drake, Uncle Reggie turned your drill into a full lockdown. Now, no one can find him to lift it. Can me and Nyaira use your exit so we can go home? We're tired and we've been here all day."

After a lengthy pause, Lucile said, "No, the lockdown is for a reason. If you're tired, use your old rooms. Now, I'm busy trying to run a global Agency. Entertain yourselves somewhere else." Then the intercom went silent.

The conversation with their mother had been just as frosty, but at least it had been face to face. She had buzzed them in and then basically ignored them while she focused on the news. After they asked her to talk to Lucille for them, she'd said, "You're adults now. Sometimes adults have to put up with stuff they don't want to. You've both been through lockdowns before. Just rest up and hit the ground running when it's lifted." Then she'd ushered them out of her suite.

Now, Tonya led her sister back into her old suite, and they both flopped down in front of the TV to see if anything new had surfaced. Nyaira said, "I hate not knowing if Uncle Daniel got to them in time. With all the bullets, it's hard to imagine they got away with no injuries."

"Uncle Daniel wouldn't have let them go out unless they were driving a tank. The fact that the gang had to chase them all over Charlotte means they survived the initial attack." Tonya grabbed her phone and dialed both her Uncle Reggie and Uncle Daniel, but both calls went to voice mail.

She slammed the phone onto the couch just as Nyaira said, "Hey! Look at this. They got new video of some woman." Nyaira handed Tonya her phone and they both watched the news clip a few times.

As top Intelligence Agents, they were trained to study people. They never forgot even the smallest nuance of a person's gait or mannerisms. They both knew who it was after the first viewing. The other two times were just to make sure.

Tonya looked at her younger sister and then picked her phone back up to make a call. It was answered on the first ring. "What's going on, sweetie? I'm...."

"Mom!" Tonya cut her off. "Have you seen the new video of the woman walking next to Alisha's SUV?"

"Yeah, and I've been trying to reach Phung for the last ten minutes." She paused as if struggling with what to say. "With this attack, and with Reggie going missing, I want you two to stay in that room. I don't know what the hell is going on, but I think someone's making a play for us."

"Mom, we're in the compound, in the family wing. No one can get down here," said Tonya.

"What if it's family doing the hunting?" Tonya had nothing to say to that. "I'm serious, Tonya. You and your sister stay put. I'll make some calls and get back to you." They hung up and Tonya just stared at her sister.

Nyaira, looking worried, said, "We're loose ends. If Uncle Delmas is killing everyone connected with this hit, then he has to take us out too."

Tonya looked skeptical. "I can see him trying to keep us locked down here. Obviously, if he made a play for us, he'd have to kill his own sister. He's a dick, but I don't think he'd go that far."

Nyaira gave her an incredulous look. "Come on, Sis. He's batshit crazy. He's been trying to kill Uncle Daniel for years. Uncle Reggie's missing. Jessica just helped him in some way and she's probably done something to Phung. We're all locked down here and he's the one who ordered us to come in. You're too intelligent to not connect the dots!"

"Well, if that's the case, we need to get the hell out of here. We're sitting ducks in this room."

"But Tonya, Mom said…"

"I know what Mom said, Ny," Tonya interrupted, "but this room was never switched to an adult room setting. That means anyone from the Board can just enter their code and come in."

"So, what do you want to do?" questioned Ny.

After some thought, Tonya focused on her phone and said, "There's one more person we can call. Let me see if she answers." The phone rang four times, and she was about to hang up, before the call was answered.

"Uh, hey Tonya. What's going on?"

"Hey, Auntie! I'm so glad you picked up." She put her phone on speaker so Ny could join in. "Me and Ny might need some help. Where are you right now?"

"Um," Mary Sue hesitated. "I'm, uh, in the compound. Where are you guys?"

"Hey Aunt Mary Sue," said Nyaira. "We're stuck down here too. Right now, we're in Tonya's old suite."

"Yeah, and we were wondering if we can come stay with you?" Tonya asked, picking up the conversation. "Some weird stuff is going on and we need to be in a more secure setting."

Her aunt was quiet for so long, Tonya checked the phone to see if the connection had dropped. Finally, Mary Sue said, "I don't think coming here is the right solution. Who's with you? Where is your mom?"

Tonya and Nyaira traded knowing looks as the nervousness of their aunt got worse. Tonya ignored her questions, and asked one of her own. "Have you seen Uncle Reggie?"

More silence. Then, "Um, Uncle Reggie? Uh no, I haven't seen him for a while. Why are you asking about him? Who's looking for Reggie?"

The sisters stood up and prepared to leave the suite. Tonya said, "I don't know what the hell is going on with you Auntie, but we're coming over. We need answers and you seem…"

"Oh my God! Tonya, hurry up and turn the TV to Channel 5," Mary Sue said, interrupting her.

Nyaira grabbed the remote and punched in the channel. Instantly, they both fell back on the couch in shock. The reporter was saying, "…Don't have many details other than authorities are positive they have their man. Sources say that the inside of the Apex home where the PGK was captured contains evidence that links him to several of the murders. Here is a short clip of two undercover SBI agents bringing him out."

Tonya and Nyaira gasped as they watched Walt and Ann perp walk their uncle out of the home. It was dark and the clip was only seconds long, but it was light enough and long enough for them to understand that the shit had just hit the fan.

Daniel had once again been playing a game where the pieces didn't even know they were involved. The long game always goes to the prepared. No one was ever more prepared than Uncle Daniel.

Tonya told her aunt, "Never mind. I think we're good," then hung up. She turned to her sister who sported a huge smile on her lovely face. They laughed and fell into each other's arms as tears of joy fell from both their eyes.

When they tuned back into the television, the reporter was saying, "No idea yet as to who the man really is, but we're told he fits the profile perfectly and the evidence is overwhelming. Remember folks, everyone is presumed innocent until proven guilty in a court of law. Even with that being said, I know a lot of people will sleep easier tonight knowing that the Prison Guard Killer is behind bars."

Chapter 30

"If I had any doubt as to how negatively influential my family is, this solidifies it. Look at you two. What happened to the sweet young ladies with the hearts of gold?" Daniel was standing over Phung and Jessica as they laid on the floor with their arms spread wide.

After he had disarmed Phung, he'd injected both of them with a small dose of the paralysis drug. He'd stripped them down to their underwear, removed their hidden weapons, and arranged their bodies how they were now. Within minutes, he had a splint and ice on Phung's injured wrist, and had moved all the furniture away from the pair.

When they regained their movement, he'd simply said, "If you move, you die." Although Phung was whimpering in pain, neither woman had moved an inch.

Daniel sighed as he sat on the couch staring down at the motionless women who were once dear to his heart. Emotions boiled to the surface as he thought about all the childish dreams they use to have. How they promised nothing would ever tear them apart.

He swiped at the tear trailing down his face before he started to talk. "I get no joy out of this. I never in a million years saw myself hurting either one of you. But we're not children anymore. And when we do grown up things, they have grown up consequences. Jessica," he said focusing on her, "please give me a reason not to kill you."

After a brief pause, she gave a muffled reply. "I was following orders. I didn't have a choice."

Daniel was confused. "So, unless things have drastically changed since I've been gone, the only orders you have to follow are from your department head. Are you saying Phung gave you the order to kill my people?"

She gave a simple, "No."

"So, who gave you the order and why did you follow it?" asked Daniel.

"You know who gave me the order, and I did it because I was promised Phung's seat at the table," said Jessica.

"Oh, so you're a real badass now. Just killing my people wouldn't have gotten you the seat. You were planning on killing Phung, your best friend, for a seat at a fucking table." The silent gun didn't make a sound, but Jessica screamed as the bullet struck her left elbow.

Phung jumped when Jessica screamed, but all she did was close her eyes and turn her head in the other direction. "Jessica, stretch your arm back out," Daniel demanded.

Jessica curled up in the fetal position trying to protect her injured arm. "Fuck you Daniel!" she shouted. "You're gonna kill me anyway. Just get it over with"

Daniel sighed again and sent three more bullets in her direction. One struck her left shoulder, one entered her hip, and the last one went into her left knee. "Who gave you the order, Jessica? I need to hear you say it."

In an anguish filled voice, she said, "Delmas gave it."

"Tell me exactly what he told you to do. And, you're right, Jessica. I am going to kill you. But whether it's fast or filled with pain is up to you." Phung continued to look the other way, but her breathing kicked up a notch.

Taking deep breaths, Jessica said, "He called me early this morning and told me to go pick up a device from LaCora and come to Charlotte. I met him at a hotel and tried to give it to him, but he said he needed me to deliver it to the target. At first, all he said was an SUV. When I pushed for more, he told me about Alisha and Ann.

"He said all I had to do was stick it to one of the front windows and I could leave. He never told me they were gonna kill them, I thought it was a tracker."

After she went silent, Daniel said, "Finish the story. Tell your friend, your sister, what you did."

"I told him I wanted a promotion. A position with responsibility and a voice. He told me I could always kill Phung and take her seat. I told him that the laws were specific about those kinds of promotions. He said that he and Mrs. Drake were gonna make new laws, and if I wanted to move up, I needed to open up the I.T. position."

She was starting to fade from the blood loss, so he said, "Turn over and look at me, Jessica." She turned over and tried her best to focus her eyes on his. "You did good. You proved you have the heart of a real WRA agent. I still love you, friend, and I'm proud of you. Do you have something you want to say before you leave us?"

Tears falling down her face, her hand shot out to touch Phung's arm. Phung shook her head and let out a deep sob, but wouldn't turn around. Jessica said, "I'm sorry, sister. I'm so sorry." She was weak and suffering, so Daniel shot her once in the head to put an end to her misery. Her body went slack and the house went eerily silent.

Daniel gave him and Phung both a couple minutes to mourn their friend, then it was time to get back to business. "Phung, sit up and look at me." When she shook her head and continued to cry, Daniel said, "Don't make me do this. Just listen to me so we can get this over with."

Slowly, she rolled over on her back and sat up with her arms self-consciously covering her chest. Her eyes, light brown and luminous, took him back to those nights when they use to talk about their future. When they would talk about how wonderful their children would be, and then make slow love for hours. Daniel didn't think he would ever stop loving this woman, but he had to deal with the fact that he hated her also.

He didn't try to hide his hurt and pain as he asked her the only question he needed the answer to. "Why?"

Her eyes rolled up to stare at the ceiling as the tears continued to fall. She said, "Can I at least get dressed before we do this?"

He shook his head and said, "I'll dress your body after we're done."

Fury crossed her face as she rolled to her feet. "You're not gonna kill me, Daniel. You know I'm not a threat to you, and I'm not doing this half naked."

He sat back as she dressed and then sat in her computer chair to continue the conversation. She swiped at her tears angrily and said, "You could have asked me this question years ago. You've moved on now, so why do you need to know?"

"You don't think I deserve to know why my best friend, my fiancé, my everything, decided to betray me? I opened my life, my world, to you, and when I needed you the most, you locked me out of yours. You don't think I deserve an explanation?"

"Quite frankly, no," she said calmly. "Don't try to play the victim here. I was sitting in our suite wondering where you were when I got the call from your mom. You don't forget anything, so I know you remember who abandoned who. I just reacted to what you did to me."

Daniel nodded his head and stared at Phung. "We were both WRA agents, and you knew I could take a mission at any time. What was the difference?"

"The difference was you went against all of us and we had no idea what you were doing. You committed to something that would take you away from me for years and you didn't tell me anything. And what the hell is so funny?" she screamed.

After her first sentence, Daniel burst out laughing. "You still believe everything my family tells you?" Sobering up, he said, "I sent a message to you through Paul. He stupidly gave it to my mother and she sent a reply back pretending to be you. The message to me said that you felt we needed a break anyway and this would be a good time for you to explore your options."

Phung gasped. "How could you think I'd say that to you? I was devastated when you left."

"Well, I never thought I was good enough for you anyway, so I took the job like your note said. It was only when I was released that I found out my mother had orchestrated the whole thing to teach me a lesson." He stood up and smiled sadly at his ex-fiancé. "But, like you said, none of this matters now. I've moved on to better things and you've turned into the person my family always wanted. A pawn who stands for nothing, and falls for everything. Anything you want to say before we finish this?"

Phung smirked smugly. "Daniel, you might have moved on, but you still love me. You'll never be able to pull that trigger."

Daniel shrugged, lifted the gun, and fired two shots into her chest. Her body jerked back into the chair as she struggled, trying to take deep breaths, and stared pleadingly at him. Her body slumped and tears flowed down her stunned face. He said, "You're right, I do still love you. But you won't be the only person I love who will feel my wrath tonight."

He walked over and covered Jessica's body with a blanket and then moved Phung's over to the couch. He planted a small kiss on her forehead before he also covered her body. He was preparing to leave when he looked up and saw the headline on the screen.

Chuckling, he said, "Good job you two. Just a little bit longer and we'll all be free." He exited the house and drove the short distance to the WRA HQ. He made sure he had plenty of ammunition before he got out. He reminded himself that no one was innocent as the picture of his next two victims flashed in his mind.

Dashing into the pitch-black wooded area, he navigated his way to one of his underground tunnels. Taking one last deep breath of the night air, he entered. Tonight, he would either die, or achieve his objective. The delightful faces of Gabby and Alisha floated into his mind and he knew the first option wasn't an option at all.

Making his way down the dark slope, he thought about the quote he once used to teach Denise a lesson: Sometimes your objective isn't to win yourself, but to make sure the other guy doesn't win. He smiled as he continued towards his destiny, knowing the other guy didn't stand a chance in hell.

. . . .

As the news reporters were in a frenzy over the capture of the Prison Guard Killer, one man was sitting silently in the dark taking it all in. The day he'd been waiting for had finally arrived.

After his recovery, he worked tirelessly to transform his body and his mind.

At first, it was difficult to come to grips with what he knew he had to do. Now, all he did was take a few hours a day out of his training to watch the news. He took a deep breath and glanced around at his surroundings.

His savings had run out months ago, so he had sold his house and all his belongings. He bought a small cabin out in the boondocks, put in a small bed and a few necessities, then went to work.

Since he was alone, his days were filled with running, working out, and target shooting. He had no idea the form he would use to deliver his payback, so he made sure his body and mind were ready for anything.

The biggest obstacle he faced was whether he could kill someone in cold blood. He'd never broken the law in his life, so jumping straight into murder wasn't an easy task. After a couple of failed attempts, six months ago, he killed his first victim.

Afterwards, he hid out in his cabin for a full month, knowing the authorities were closing in on him. The reporters said the police had no leads, but he'd convinced himself the message was so he would drop his guard. As time passed, and no more reports came out, he began to feel safe. He continued his training by racking up four more bodies before he felt numb to the crimes.

As he sat in his recliner listening to the reporter give all the salacious details about the capture of the PGK, he committed every word to memory. He needed to know every detail so he didn't make a wrong move. When one channel started to repeat itself, he flipped to another one to hear what they had to say. He didn't move for several hours.

Around four in the morning is when he heard the one tidbit he'd been waiting for. Not wanting to be idle, he started doing push-ups and sit-ups while he listened in. He had just switched to jumping jacks when the reporter gave an update on the killer's status.

The woman said, "Since the Prison Guard Killer has committed crimes in numerous jurisdictions in North Carolina, the SBI has decided to hold him in Wake County

Jail. Right now, he is being detained at the Justice Building where I'm sure he's being interrogated by top SBI Agents. So far, we haven't been given a time table, but we know that, following the questioning, he'll be transferred to the county jail. Because of the seriousness of his crimes, you can rest assured that he will be under heavy guard to prevent any chance of escape. We will have updates for our viewers as they are presented to us. For now, let's give our thanks to the SBI and all the other police agencies that helped in the capture of the serial killer known as the Prison Guard Killer."

As he knew they would, the news started listing some of the crimes being attributed to the PGK. He stood still until they came to one that caused silent tears to run down his face. Then, he turned the TV off and started to get dressed. He put the few items he would need in a duffle bag and slung it over his shoulder. He took a quick glance around the room and then walked out of the front door.

He loaded his bag into the full sized, black van, and then took out the two 3-gallon gas jugs. The man walked around the cabin, soaking the walls in the foul-smelling liquid. One strike of the lighter was all it took to set the structure ablaze. It had served its purpose, now it was time for him to serve his.

With nothing left in this world to hold him except for this one mission, he pointed the front of the vehicle west. He was going to extract his pound of flesh. He had no illusions about coming out of this alive, and he was content with that. He would die with a smile on his face as long as he sent the Prison Guard Killer to hell first.

Chapter 31

The crime scene technicians were still hard at work processing the area when Walt and Ann returned from the SBI lock-up. They had left Delmas Burke sitting in a cage that not even the WRA's might could penetrate. Walt had been all set to interrogate him, when his boss ordered him back to Apex.

Walt glanced over at Ann with a questioning look. She exhaled audibly and said, "I'm good, Walt. Cpt. Graham is gonna try and shake us up, but I can handle him. Let's get this over with so our part will be done."

Before she could exit the vehicle, Walt grabbed her hand and held on tight. He said, "I'm so proud of you. I know we are going down a path that neither of us envisioned, but I do feel we're going in the right direction. I know your loyalty to me is what drove you to accept this mission. And I want you to know that I love you and I'll always be here for you, no matter what."

Eyes glistening, she said, "We're a team. A family. I love you too and I know you'll always have my back." She leaned over and lightly kissed him on his cheek. "Now, let's put the nail in the coffin of these WRA assholes."

They exited the Porsche and followed the path marked by the yellow tape. As they walked, Walt pictured Delmas' face when he first came to in the small house. At first, he had been baffled, then he'd been amused.

Walt had pointed his gun at the WRA agent and said, "Daniel told us we don't particularly need to keep you alive. A dead PGK is just as sellable as a live one. So, if you do anything I don't like, you will die." Delmas had laughed out loud and remained silent through the whole ordeal.

Ann walked ahead of Walt and entered the house first. Cameras flashed. Hushed conversations filled the air. Serious and solemn detectives took notes of everything they saw. The public probably thought the police were celebrating the apprehension. There was nothing to be happy about in this house of horrors.

Captain Will Graham must have had someone watching for them. He marched in from a back room and said, "Everyone but you two, out right now." Everyone who was senior enough to be in the house knew Cpt. Graham. So, they knew when he told you to do something, you did it.

After everyone exited to wait in the yard, Will asked, "How did this come about? You both were just buddy-buddy with this guy, now you're turning him in! Tell me what the deal is."

Walt said, "I told you from the start that I would bring you the PGK. It took a while to lock down some real evidence against him. I had, no, we had to play his game until he led me to this house. The fucker thought we were really on his side, so he brought us here to show off all of his conquests."

Will, still far from convinced, said, "You must have done some serious shit for him to think you both were on his team." He turned to Ann. "And what do you have to say about this?"

A year ago, Ann would have deferred to Walt, or tried to be as agreeable as possible. That Ann Grace was gone now. She said, "What do I have to say? I say, we got the shit done when nobody else could. I say, we just got you the next director's spot. I say, instead of interrogating us on what we had to do to catch him, how about a thank you and a good fucking job!"

"Ann!" screamed Walt. "Calm the fuck down. This is our senior officer and he can ask us whatever he wants!"

Turning back to Will, he said, "We did what we had to do. Look around you. Do you feel like we didn't do enough?"

The house was lit up like a Christmas tree. Not only were all the lights aglow, but flood lights had been brought in to eliminate all the shadows. Almost every available surface contained some form of evidence against the PGK.

Pictures of victims and crime scenes. Files on each victim. Detailed plans about how each target would be hit. Articles that were later published on each crime. Then there were the trophies.

Pieces of hair taken from the dead bodies. Articles of clothing with blood stain splatters. Small trinkets taken from numerous scenes. Replicas of the cameras and tools found at some of the scenes. Not to mention, all the evidence collected from the various scenes would match perfectly to Delmas Burke.

Will walked around the main area of the house and just smiled. "You know, I could demand that you both take lie detector tests. The problem with that is, I would have to give a reason to the Brass. I've seen this guy with you two before, so I know it's him. It seems, the only thing I would be doing by making such a demand, would be tarnishing all your hard work."

He walked over to Ann and Walt and stuck his hand out. "Good job you two. I will, as you know, need full reports of your time undercover and what happened here today. For now, I don't need you here. If you want, you can go try to get a confession and a guilty plea out of our killer. With all this evidence, he has to know it's over for him."

They both shook his hand and walked out of the house. As they got in the Porsche, Will stepped out and waved all the police back to work. Walt drove away with the image of a speculative looking Cpt. Graham in his rearview mirror.

The drive back to the Justice Building was quiet as they focused on their own thoughts. Walt had no idea what was going through Ann's head. All he could think about was the interview they were about to conduct. He was worried what would come out of the agent's mouth. Daniel assured them he would only make veiled comments to get in their heads. But what would they do if he employed another tactic?

They couldn't kill the man while in police custody. Of course, they could make it look like a failed escape attempt. But, with the amount of security around him, someone else was bound to end up dead. No, the window for killing Delmas Burke had closed. Walt would just have to make sure the agent thought he was still in control.

The first rays of sunlight were peaking over the horizon as they pulled into the underground garage. They shared a brief look before they exited the vehicle and made their way to the elevator. They rode it down two more levels until they arrived at the bottom floor.

The SBI lock-up didn't look like a jail at all. To Walt, it looked more like a hospital. All white floors and walls, only interrupted by wood-grain paneled, steel doors. Other than the occasional bathroom door, all the other ones had small observation windows about five feet off the floor. Even that small opening was triple-paned and had a wire mesh running through it.

Even though the lock-up did have cells for offenders slotted for longer stays, the cells they were bypassing were for short interrogations. Walt and Ann were headed for the most secure area hidden deeper in the maze. To get there, they had to go through several manned checkpoints, as well as electronic obstacles. It was a 15-minute process that pretty much made escape impossible.

Finally arriving at the secure wing, they went through an additional 5-minute security check to access the single-cell area where the WRA agent was the only occupant. Ann nodded at Walt, and then went off to commandeer the control booth to get rid of any potential WRA spies. After the two SBI agents vacated the area, Ann opened the outer door so Walt could conduct his interrogation.

Seeing as the PGK was attributed with killing so many cops, no one really cared about his comfort. Delmas was still in full restraints and was fastened securely to the iron rings welded to the table and floor. For his part, Delmas didn't seem uncomfortable at all. He just sat silently, watching Walt with the same amused smile he'd sported since waking up in the set-up house.

Walt pulled out the chair opposite the man, and sat down with an amused smile of his own. "You do know that you're fucked now, right?" Walt leaned back and crossed his arms over his chest. "I played around in your world for a while and now I'd like to welcome you to mine."

Delmas smiled and glanced at the two-way glass. Walt said, "Oh, don't worry about that. For right now, it's just me, you, and Ann."

Immediately, Delmas changed his whole demeanor. "In that case, I want you both to know that you, and your families will be dead in the next week. And after your bodies are found, mutilated beyond recognition, I'll walk right out the front doors of this building." No more smiles. Now Walt was seeing the real killer that Delmas barely had control of.

Walt looked around in mock worry and shuddered. "Ooooh, I'm sooo scared." He laughed out loud, causing Delmas to scowl with hatred. "For any of that to happen, you better pray your family is prepared for Daniel. Right about now, he's going through eliminating everyone who could help you. After he's done, you'll be executed as the PGK, and all of us can live out normal lives." Laughing again, Walt said, "Man, you got to love Daniel and all his planning."

"None of that will work," Delmas said. "We have assets all over the world…"

"Who are loyal to the WRA leadership," Walt interrupted. "Oh, did I forget to mention that the leadership will be under construction. Once all the bad apples are removed, new members will be put in place. You will be officially exiled from any and all WRA help and labeled as a traitor. Which leads this conversation full circle. You Are Fucked!"

Knowing that without WRA help, he would indeed be up shits creek, he tried a different tactic. Delmas turned to the observation window and said, "Ann, you gonna sit back and let me be executed for crimes I didn't commit? I saved your life once upon a time. You don't have the love or loyalty for me to return the favor. There is no way you can look me in my eyes and tell me you don't still love me."

Walt's phone began to ring. He took it out and glanced at the screen. He accepted the call but didn't say anything. Ann said, "Put me on speaker so you both can hear this." Walt did what she asked and sat the phone down in front of him on the table.

Ann said, "Delmas, once, in my naïve youth, I loved you. But those days are long gone. You were willing to take me to your family when you knew they would kill me. So, looking to me for love or loyalty, sorry to tell you, you won't find any in regards to you. And as far as being innocent, I watched you execute Officer Green for no reason. So, when you get the needle, you'll be getting exactly what you deserve." With that, she disconnected the call.

Walt put the phone back in his pocket and looked up at the hate filled eyes staring at him. "The only thing left for you to do is confess, plead guilty, and serve out the rest of your life behind bars. I know it's a tough pill to swallow, but, if you go to trial, you'll be found guilty and sentenced to death. I'll leave you to make up your mind…" Walt said, standing up.

"No need for that," Delmas said with a grim look. "You show me in writing that I'll get life instead of death and I'll confess right now."

Walt sat back down. "You think you'll have a chance to escape somewhere down the line?"

The agent shrugged, and said, "If I'm dead, a worry is removed. As long as I'm still breathing, none of you can rest easy. Even if I never make it out, I'm content to fuck up all your perfect plans for a normal life."

Walt turned to the control booth, and said, "Okay Ann, turn the…"

"No, wait!" interrupted Delmas. "I have one more message for you before we do this." Walt nodded for the man to continue. "Daniel will never let you go. This mythical normal life you keep talking about, will never happen. You think he'll allow you and Denise to run off and have babies?" Turning, he said, "Ann, you think he'll let you find love and settle down as an SBI agent? You're dreaming. He'll continue to use all of you to carry out his personal mission. And once he's done, he has no need to keep any of you alive."

Walt remained silent as Delmas turned his head back and forth from him to the observation window. "You're both cops!" he shouted. "You want your legacies tied to the biggest mass murderer since Hitler? I might not be an angel, but come on man. A year and a half ago, you both had integrity. Look at what you've become. And what the hell is so funny?"

Walt had been choking back his laugh as Delmas made his pitch. The guy was unbelievable. "What's funny is you thought this bullshit speech would work. We're way beyond switching sides. This conversation is just to offer you a chance to save your life. Now, do we proceed with your confession, or do I call the D.A. and tell him to prepare for a Capital Murder trial?"

Delmas stared at Walt until he made like he would get up and leave. Finally, he said, "Alright, you piece of shit. Start the recording and let's get this over with." Walt nodded to Ann and Walt saw the red light connected to the camera illuminate.

"This is Sgt. Det. Walter Rogers of the SBI and I'm in the secure wing of the Justice Building in Raleigh. Det. Ann Grace is in the control booth observing. I am conducting an interview with the man accused of being the Prison Guard Killer. Can you state your name for the record?"

Delmas said, "My name is Tremayne Michaels."

"Have you been informed of your rights Mr. Michaels?" This was the first time Walt was hearing the name, but he knew Delmas would have an alias.

"Yes, I have. And I waive those rights and am ready to give a statement."

Walt motioned for him to continue, so the newly appointed Mr. Michaels did. "I've been told that, if I confess to my crimes, the death penalty will be taken off the table."

"That is correct," interjected Walt.

"In that case, I am the man the media has dubbed the Prison Guard Killer. My first victim was Officer Trevor Jones, about four years ago. He was an officer at Foothills Correctional Institution in Morganton N.C. I killed him because he got away with starving inmates in Restrictive Housing."

"Were you one of his victims?" asked Walt.

"No, I wasn't. I never met the guy, but the stories I heard from other inmates made him a good place to start."

"So, you were incarcerated at some point?"

"Yes," replied Delmas. Looking at Walt with a smoldering hate, he said, "I was locked up under another one of my aliases."

"Can you state, for the record, what that name was?"

"Manuel Adams."

Walt said, "Okay, you can continue."

"My second victim was an inmate named David Prig…" and on and on he went. Walt asked hm several times if he needed a break. He said, no, he wanted to get it over with. It took about 2 hours of continuous talk for him to name all the victims. The fact that he knew them all showed how close the surveillance had been on Daniel.

By the end, there were several more agents in the booth with Ann, including Cpt. Graham. Walt was getting text updates from Ann every couple of minutes on what was being said. The mood was celebratory as the SBI agents saw a closing of one of the deadliest times in North Carolina history.

Walt thanked Delmas for being truthful and forthright and left the interrogation cell. When he entered the control booth, everyone patted him on the back to celebrate the victory. Through it all, he looked grim. He watched as four agents went into the cell to move Delmas into the sleeping quarters attached. Even with the restraints, Walt had no doubt Delmas could kill all four of them, but for now, he was playing the defeated role. He allowed them to lock him in before they removed his chains.

As the walls were glass, they observed as he relieved himself, washed his hands, and laid on the concrete slab. Walt glanced at Ann and motioned that it was time to go. All the other agents were celebrating their win, but for Ann and Walt, the battle was still raging on.

Chapter 32

Making it to one of the central hubs of his hidden tunnel network, Daniel activated the low wattage lights. A stain on the wall had him immediately pulling out one of his weapons, and dropping down to one knee. He did a quick visual scan down each tunnel and saw no eminent threat, so he pulled out his phone, did a thorough check of his network and found that he was alone in the tunnels.

Holstering his weapon, he took a closer look at the stain. Just as he predicted, it was blood. He knew it hadn't been there the last time he'd visited. Putting his back to the wall, he used his phone to back track the camera footage until he saw movement.

"How in the fuck?" he muttered to himself when he saw The Author stumbling around. He tracked him until he saw Wilford gain access through the torture chamber's hidden door. The son of a bitch even used one of his grenades to aid in his escape. The man was hurt pretty bad, but he managed to make it to one of the exits and disappear.

Switching to a different app, Daniel went back to the torture chamber and watched the events that led up to The Author using his tunnel. He took off running down the hall that led to the access door. When it opened, he immediately turned to his right and locked eyes with his brother as the door closed behind him.

"You just gonna stand there and stare, or are you gonna get this damn thing off of me?" Both of Reggie's legs were trapped under the rack of weapons he'd been attempting to hide behind.

"Are you pinned, or are you hurt?" asked Daniel, making his way over.

"Just pinned. I don't have the leverage to pick it up and slide back at the same time."

Daniel chuckled as he lifted the heavy rack and Reggie slid out of the way. He stood up as Daniel let the rack crash back to the floor. "What's so funny?" asked Reggie.

"This is what happens when you play with your food. You should have killed him over by the tables."

"Fuck you, Turtle Boy. I can't let you have all the fun." Reggie walked to the elevator and said, "Guess I finally get to see your tunnels. The elevator is useless." Turning around and walking to the first table, Reggie picked up his broken and useless phone. Slamming it back down, he added, "And my phone's done for. Plus, I'm hungry as hell."

Daniel said, "Sorry Bro, not yet," as he opened the tunnel door once more. As he stepped inside, he said, "Got a lot of work to do and I don't need you in the way. I'll come back and get you when I'm done."

"No, no, no! Wait Daniel…" That was all he heard before the door closed and Daniel took off to finish his mission.

. . . .

Tonya was sound asleep, dreaming about swimming in some tropical paradise where she could see all the way to the bottom of the ocean. The next thing she knew, she was jerking up from her bed, looking around in confusion. Something had awakened her, but everything was silent now. She was just about to lay back down and try to recapture her dream, when a muffled thump came from the living room.

She grabbed the gun from under her pillow and swung off the far side of the bed. Nyaira was sleeping in the other room, but something didn't feel right. She pointed her gun at the door and waited to see who would come for her. After five minutes she began to feel stupid. Not stupid enough to put the gun down, but she did jump up and make her way to the door.

When she entered, her eyes were drawn to movement in the kitchen area. She frowned when she saw her sister just sitting silently in one of the hardback chairs. "What are you doing, Ny? Are you okay?" Tonya took a couple steps closer, and only then did she notice the ropes tying her sister down, and the tape over her mouth. Before she could react, she felt the cold steel of the gun pressed into her back.

Fast as lightning, her gun was stripped out of her hand, and she was pushed against the wall. A fast, but thorough, search relieved her of the knife she kept taped to her leg. Then, she was marched over to the chair sitting right next to her sister's, and pushed down into it. The lights flipped on, almost blinding her for a second. When her vision cleared, she was staring into the face of the PGK.

Not the fake PGK that had just been arrested, but the real one. Shaking her head, she said, "Uncle Daniel, what's going…"

"Tonya, right now, I'm not your Uncle Daniel," he interrupted. "Right now, I am a pissed off man who is on a mission to kill everyone who contributed to Alisha's pain."

"So, she's alive? Thank God!" Tonya said with feeling. "What about Ann? I tried to stop it…?"

"But you didn't try hard enough." A silent tension filled the air after his comment. "You were hanging with these guys for days before they carried out this hit. What information did you give them?"

Frowning, Tonya said, "None! I tried to stop it from happening!"

Daniel swung the gun up, pointing it at Nyaira's chest. "I'm gonna ask you one more time. What information did you give them on me and my family?"

Crying now, Tonya said, "Please, Uncle Daniel, I didn't tell them anything. We saw them watching your house and we were gonna intercept them. Uncle Delmas ordered us to get intel to see what they were up to. When we figured out it was Alisha's old gang, Delmas pulled us off the mission. Me and Ny both stayed on, against orders, so we could warn you if they made a move."

She implored him with her eyes to believe her. He took a couple steps back, and she saw it on his face before he committed the act. He said, "I don't believe you," and shot Nyaira twice in the chest.

Tonya screamed and attacked like a wild banshee. She was clawing and crying and kicking and screaming. She was half blind from the tears and weak from grief. Not one of her attempts landed. Instead, she found herself looking up at her uncle from the floor. "Why? Why would you do that? We tried to help you," she cried.

With merciless eyes, her Uncle Daniel said, "I can't take the risk. You're a Burke, which makes you an excellent actor and liar." *Bang! Bang!* And her whole body went numb. She fought for breath as she watched him tuck his gun and head towards a solid wall. Just as her world was fading to black, she watched him disappear into thin air. Knowing that wasn't possible, she willed herself to wake up from the nightmare that refused to let her go.

• •

Kashonda Wilson had just stepped out of the shower and was drying her hair, when she felt the atmospheric shift that told her she was no longer alone. A brief moment of hesitation was all it took for the assailant to realize his presence was no longer a secret. The cocking of the gun was all the threat he needed for her to not do anything stupid.

She knew exactly who it was because he was the only person capable of getting into a senior agent's room unannounced. Kashonda said, "If you're here to celebrate, I fear I'm a little underdressed. And don't you think the gun is a little much?"

Daniel revealed himself in the mirror standing behind her and motioned for her to go into the bedroom. She put the blow dryer down, pulled her robe tighter, and marched into her bedroom. Her whole suite was ablaze as she'd still been up, trying to catch the latest on the PGK's capture. She flopped down on the bed and looked at the grim face of her youngest brother.

"Why are you here like this, Daniel? I've done nothing to you. In fact, I'm the only one who has always been on your side."

"Is that why you sent Tonya and Nyaira to help Delmas kill my fiancé? Because you're on my side?"

Her head cocked, she said, "Delmas asked for them to help on a surveillance mission. As he outranks me, I could hardly tell him no. Why do you care about them? They just follow orders."

"Well, I'm not worried about them anymore," he said snidely.

Sitting up straighter, Kashonda said, "Daniel, don't fuck with my girls. Whatever beef you have with this family, you take it up with the grown-ups, not the kids."

"You start putting kids into grown-up business, and the consequences can affect everyone. Anyway, I know you, sister. You won't let those girls go on a mission that you know nothing about. So, tell me the truth, what did you and Delmas cook up against my family?"

Laughing, Kashonda said, "Little brother, I love you. Why you think I'd conspire with Delmas against you is baffling to me. I've lobbied for you from the start of all this mess. Remember, you got two votes to keep you out of that prison, and one was my vote. The other was our Aunt Mary Sue. So, place your anger where it needs to go, and leave me and mine alone."

"Like I said, it's too late for that. I will punish everyone who played a role, and I started with Tonya and Nyaira."

Kashonda jumped to her feet and demanded, "What did you do to my girls, Daniel?"

"The same thing I'm doing to every corrupt member of this family." The shot propelled her back onto the bed. Her hand flew to her chest as fire seemed to consume her whole being. She looked down at her hand to find it soaked in blood.

She reached out for her sibling one last time. "I still love you, Daniel."

"Yeah, I know. I still love you, too." The next shot took the last of her strength and her body went limp. She never got to see Daniel shut off all the lights and disappear into the darkness.

• •

LaCora Clay didn't operate under the same schedule as most people did. She didn't base her actions on the rotation of the earth, or its position in reference to the sun. All her actions were based on whichever project she was currently working on. At the moment, she was trying to replicate Daniel's work with semi-transparent metal. So far, she hadn't been able to get it as clear as glass like he was able to do, and it was driving her crazy.

She had no idea what was going on in the WRA world. She had no idea that Ann and Alisha had been attacked. That the facility was on lockdown. Or even that the PGK had supposedly been captured. All she knew was what was going on inside the lab that she had sequestered herself in. From her latest results, it wasn't much.

But, like all Burke women, LaCora was smart, resilient, and tough. She had no plans to leave this lab until she had solved the problem at hand. If Daniel could figure it out, she'd be damned if she was gonna fail at it. Competition was fierce in their world, because not being able to figure something out could very well result in the loss of life.

Her eyes were glued to the lens of the microscope when she felt a slight breeze on the back of her neck. In a nonchalant motion, her hand reached for the gun holstered inside of her lab coat. The click of a gun behind her told her that the motion hadn't gone unnoticed.

Slowly, she removed her hand and raised both her arms over her head. Since she hadn't been ordered not to, she turned around to face her attacker. When she saw who it was, she smiled and started to lower her arms. "What's going on, Daniel? I was just thinking about you."

"Keep your hands up. This isn't a fucking social call." The harsh words and tone made her head cock to the side. But, confused or not, she knew her little cousin. She dropped the smile and put her arms back up.

"Did I do something wrong, Little Cousin? I thought we were on the same side."

Eyes flashing, he said, "Yeah, so did I." Only a few people on the earth knew that LaCora was the mole Lucille Drake had been searching for. She had been feeding Daniel information and resources for years. Their shared knowledge of the most protected secret in the WRA had led to their partnership. She had no idea what had gone wrong, but it looked like their bond had been severed.

So, like most Burkes did when they were confused, she got angry. "Okay, Daniel," she said, standing up. "I don't have time for this shit. Either tell me why you've got that gun pointed at me, or get the fuck out of my lab. You got a lot of nerve coming at me like this. If my father…."

"Don't bring him into this!" roared Daniel. "This is between me and you." She could see the muscles of his right arm flexing with the need to pull the trigger. But, if she was gonna die, she wasn't gonna go down whimpering and crying.

Lowering her arms, she said, "Well, get it off your chest. What did I do that would make you forget I've risked my life for the last 15 years? I've done everything in my power to help you. Now, you come in here like this?"

Ignoring her outburst, he said, "You gave Jessica a device about 24 hours ago. That device was used to shatter the glass on one of our vehicles so that assassins could kill Ann and Alisha."

Her hand flew to her mouth as she gasped. "Oh my God! Daniel, I had no idea."

"Ann wasn't harmed, but Alisha was shot in her upper chest area. The only reason she survived is because Ghost spared her life." He took a deep, fortifying breath before he continued. "None of this could've happened without you giving her the device."

"I still work here, Daniel," she explained calmly. "What use would I be to our side if the other side didn't trust me?"

"But, why didn't you warn me? Jessica said Delmas ordered the weapon. Why would you turn it over to him without letting me know he had it?"

She pointed to her work station. "I didn't tell you because the device shouldn't have been a threat to you. Why would you allow those women to drive around in a car with glass when you have the ability to protect them with transparent metal?"

A slight flash, but she caught the look of guilt displayed on his face. It was quickly replaced by anger. "Don't try and turn this around on me. Our agreement was, any technology you turn over, I get a heads up. You went back on our deal, so now you'll get the same thing everyone else is getting."

"And what would that be, Daniel?" The two shots took her completely by surprise. She fell back onto her lab chair and stared down at the red staining her lab coat. She glanced back up into the angry eyes of her little cousin before her vision started to blur.

She wanted to ask him how he could do this to her father, but no words would come out. Then she thought about if her father was still alive. She used all her strength to tell her cousin, "Don't hurt him." Before the darkness consumed her, she took solace in the nod of acknowledgement he gave her.

. . . .

When Dollis Truesdale heard the muted footfall in her living room, she wasn't surprised at all. In fact, she had been waiting for it for a couple hours. Not knowing what the tunnel system looked like, or the exact order Daniel would go in, she left a lot of leeway in her predictions. Being the analytical mind that she was, she was also prepared for his arrival.

Daniel entered her bedroom to the sight of her nude body stretched out on her bed. The data told her that, if she wanted to survive this encounter, she needed to appear as non-threatening as possible. Spread-eagle and naked was about as least threatening as one could get.

She was looking at his face as he rolled his eyes and snatched her robe off its hanger. He arranged it neatly around her body, but kept her arms spread and unobstructed. He asked, "How did you know?"

When she was younger, people would always tell her she gave reports like a robot. Her voice took on a monotone quality like she was reading from a screen. In a sense, that's exactly what she did. Her brain would churn out a script for her mouth to follow. With her life on the line, the one thing she could always rely on, her brain, did its thing.

"Earlier today, we went on a total lockdown. With this being so close to the truce vote, the lockdown could only be because we were under attack or we were attacking. When I saw the news and noticed one of your fleet vehicles had been attacked, and two women wore involved, I knew the WRA had broken the truce. On a later video clip, I saw Jessica apply a device to the vehicle. Then, not too long ago, I saw that the PGK had been captured in a house full of evidence against him. When I saw it was Delmas, I knew that you were on your way.

"Since the WRA could have Delmas out in hours, you wouldn't have made that move unless you could prevent the WRA from interfering. The only way that could happen is to remove the leadership. So, I knew you were coming to kill us."

Dollis was not a field agent, but she had been exposed to all the training a Burke was expect to have. She could shoot, fight, gather intel, trick, manipulate, and lie with the best of them. A Burke was supposed to face any obstacle or mission with an air of fearlessness. So, Dollis kicked herself mentally for the tears that escaped from her eyes.

Daniel used his hand to wipe them away before saying, "You were always my favorite cousin. So smart and so much like a Burke is supposed to be." She was very much aware of the gun clutched in his right hand as he stood over her. She was also aware of the speculative look on his face as he stared into her eyes.

With a careless shrug, he tucked the gun back into his side holster. He said, "I'm not gonna hurt you, Dollis. I know you're innocent in this. I'm here because I want to know if you want to keep your job when this is over. Lord knows I could never find a mind to replace yours."

She took a shuttering inhale and deep exhale before she could respond. "I would like to keep my job, Daniel."

He smiled and said, "Stay here and keep your phone close. I'll contact you to come out when everything is set." Tenderly, he brushed her long blond hair off her face. "Sorry to put you through this. I promise, things will be better after today."

She watched him leave, expecting him to change his mind at any moment. One thing she could always rely on was mathematics. As the saying goes, numbers don't lie. The numbers she'd come up with had given her a 5% survival rate if Daniel showed up in her suite. A number small enough to pretty much guarantee her death. This was the first time her analyzed data had been wrong.

Dollis curled up and cried with relief. She had never been so happy that she'd made a mistake in her calculations.

Chapter 33

Daniel left his cousin Dollis with a smile on his face. He was so happy that his family hadn't been able to corrupt her. She was a perfect example of what a Burke woman was supposed to be. He was glad that she'd agreed to accompany him into this new era of the WRA.

Growing up, she had always been a wonderful child. Now, she was an equally delightful woman who had the strength of mind and spirit to earn the respect of anyone who encountered her. He chuckled thinking about a man trying to tame or conquer her. The man would be drawn to her soft spoken and shy demeanor. He'd be in for a rude awakening when she decided to flex her muscles.

He needed to make a quick detour before he continued on with his quest. Stopping at another hub, he pulled out his phone and pulled up the cameras in the main facility. It took him 30 seconds to find the agent he was looking for and to dial his number. Knowing he wouldn't recognize the number, Daniel wasn't surprised when he answered the call, but remained silent.

Daniel said, "Agent Rilley, do you recognize my voice?"

Agent Terrell Rilley, boyfriend of the late Candace Price, said, "Uh, yeah, I know who this is. What can I do for you, Sir?"

"I need you to go and get your new partner, Meka, and both of you need to come to the conference room nearest the family wing. When you get there, sit down and wait for me. Do you understand?"

"Yes sir! I'm on my way now." Daniel tracked his progress through the camera app. He watched as Terrell found Meka in the cafeteria and whispered something in her ear. She hurried to her feet, leaving her tray of food on the table. It was about a 5-minute trek on a normal day, but the agents made it to the assigned meeting spot in under three. Daniel was already at the hidden door to the room, but he watched them for a few minutes before he entered.

The door was silent, and their focus was on the front door. When he spoke, both agents damn near jumped out of their shoes. "I don't have a lot of time, so let's make this quick." He walked around and sat in front of them, but placed his phone where he could watch the camera that covered the entrance.

Daniel eyed both of the chosen agents before he continued. Terrell Rilley, senior field agent, with his dark skin, long dreads, and thin build, fit the stereotypical image of a drug dealing gangster. But his Harvard education and excellent mission evaluations marked him as a smart man and huge asset to the Agency.

Meka Moore, with her nut-brown skin, short hair, and luminous eyes, put him in the mind of the actress, Nia Long. She was still a mid-level agent, but she was already making a name for herself. Genius level IQ, and aptitude test scores off the chart meant she had a vast pool of potential just waiting to be tapped. Even with her arm still in a sling, she looked willing and able to complete her next mission.

Daniel said, "The WRA is about to be under new management. Would either of you have a problem with that?" They glanced at each other, then shook their heads. "Good, because there will be some changes that some people won't like. One of the biggest changes will be the move from anything illegal. Which means the money laundering ring will have to go."

Daniel locked in on his phone as an agent wandered into view. When he kept walking, he turned his focus back to the pair. "Right now, Terrell, you are responsible for the running of 82 WRA owned businesses, correct?"

"Yes Sir."

"So, all I want you to do is keep running them and expand your empire where you can. Meka will be your second in command. The WRA will take it's cut, and you both can live your lives without the bullshit of corruption hanging over your head. Does that sound good to both of you?"

They looked at each other and smiled. They both nodded enthusiastically, and Terrell said, "Absolutely! That's the best news I've had in a long time. But, how will we stop the game rooms from doing what they do? Your brother runs those personally, and his clientele might take exception to any interference."

"You let me worry about that." Standing up, he extended his hand to the two agents. To Meka, he said, "Sorry for being rude. My name is Daniel Burke."

Shaking his hand, she said, "Yeah, I know. I watched all the videos on you." Looking a little worried, she asked, "Are you gonna be the one running things now?"

Laughing, he said, "Hell no! But the guy who will be, he'll make sure you guys are given the same loyalty you've shown the WRA. I have to go but, before we make a move on the game rooms, I'll make sure you get a heads-up to clear out."

With a huge smile on his face, Terrell said, "I really appreciate this, Mr. Burke. We won't let you down." The two agents left the room, talking excitedly back and forth. He allowed himself a few seconds of joy for restoring some of the integrity to his Grandfather's Agency.

Then the grimness returned because he still had work to do. All of the cancer cells had to be dispelled before the healing process could begin. Reentering the tunnel, he made his way back to the family wing. His next target had been guilty for almost 30 years, but today was the day to collect on all those overdue reparations.

. . . .

Daniel sat and watched her pace in the darkness, gun in her hand. He'd only been present about five minutes, but she'd tried to call his brother five times. After the last failed attempt, she put the phone in her pocket and froze in thought.

She had changed out of the clothes she'd worn in the dungeon. Blue jeans and black T-shirt were still her clothes of choice, but this set didn't have fake blood splattered on it. She completed her ready to go at the drop of a dime outfit with black tennis shoes.

Without warning, she tipped her head back and roared at the ceiling. Calming down somewhat, she continued with her pacing. She mumbled, "Never should have opened my mouth. Now he's probably dead and, as soon as I leave this room, I'll be next." Pulling her hair in anger, she said, "This stupid fucking family, with it's stupid fucking secrets."

"My sentiments exactly," he said, finally revealing himself. "And if you haven't dropped that gun by the time I get to three, those secrets will die with you. 1...2..." she dropped the gun. Slowly, she turned to face him, and he switched on the light beside him so she could see his face. He wanted her to know that he was serious.

With hands raised, Mary Sue said, "Listen to me, Daniel. I had nothing to do with your people getting hit. I haven't even left this compound since the truce vote."

"Oh yeah, the truce vote that you said no to."

"I only voted no so you…"

"Would come and unleash hell on the WRA. Yeah, I know. But next time, you might want to think about that wish before you make it. I only have one more room to visit after I finish with you…"

"What?" she asked looking confused. "What do you mean, visit?"

"Just what I said. I've already been to all the family rooms. This one and my mother's are the last two."

"But…Dollis…She didn't…" she stammered.

"You wanted me to unleash, that's what I did. This Agency will be rid of all its cancerous cells by the end of the day. Dollis, let's just say, got exactly what she deserved."

Her face crumpled right before his eyes. Her knees grew weak and her body tumbled to the floor. Heart wrenching sobs filled the air. He gave her a few minutes before he started his questioning. "Were you part of the actions, or the cover up?"

Still crying, she said, "Fuck you Daniel! Leave me alone."

"I'm sorry Auntie, but I can't do that. You need to look me in my eyes and answer me right now."

Mary Sue surged to her feet with a raging fire in her eyes. "Fuck! You! I'm not answering shit. You come in here and tell me you murdered my child, my baby girl, and you think I'll talk to you?" With a faraway look in her eyes, she said, "You have nothing to threaten me with. You've already killed me."

She started looking around on the floor and Daniel said, "Aunt Mary Sue, don't do that. You're gonna force my hand."

"You're gonna kill me anyway." She located the gun and swooped it up. Daniel fired, hitting her in the right shoulder. She screamed and fell back, but kept control of the gun. She switched it to her left hand and Daniel shot her left forearm. The gun dropped to the floor and his aunt paused and then charged him with her teeth bared.

This was the problem when dealing with a warrior family, Daniel thought, as he put three shots in her center mass. Even when they didn't have to, they thought it was their duty to go down fighting. He stood up and made his way over to his gasping aunt. He flipped her over and stared into her frightened eyes. He said, "Dollis is not dead. I told you she got what she deserved. In my opinion, she's the best of us all, so I let her be. You can rest easy knowing she's okay."

Her breathing evened out and her expression calmed. She released a long, shuttering breath, then her body settled to stillness. Daniel walked back over and slumped in the chair. He pulled out his phone and dialed his partner. When the call was answered, he said, "Everything is ready on the inside. How's your side going?"

"It would have been impossible if it wasn't for Alisha. We're all at the rendezvous point, was just waiting for your call."

"I'm on my way to the last target now. Just proceed with the plan and this will all be over soon."

"Roger that," said the old man. "Meet you at the spot." He disconnected and Daniel stood up so he could place the most important piece in the war. Whoever said the pawn was the most important piece was destined to always be a second-rate player. The masters all knew that to debilitate an opponent, you had to take out his Queen. Being the most powerful piece on the board, the Queen sometimes gets complacent. That's when a Master of Minds can step in and deliver a death blow that will reverberate throughout the whole kingdom.

. . . .

There would be no sitting in the dark watching Lucille Drake. Daniel smiled as he surveyed her massive suite through the hidden cameras placed liberally about her rooms. Every light was blazing at full power and his mother sat in the middle of the living room, facing the front door. Backing up the camera footage, he could see his mom had been on point since the attack on Alisha and Ann. Whatever those pills were that she was taking, they were doing an excellent job of keeping her focused.

She was seated facing the door, but her head swiveled around so no one could sneak up on her. He also knew the all black outfit, with the dark shades resting atop her head, was more than a fashion statement. That would be her camouflage if she had to press the button in her left hand.

A simple precaution that was designed to give the operator an extra second of surprise. When a person entered a room blazing with light, their pupils shrunk. The button Lucille held would cause all the lights to cut off. Then, with her night vision shades in place, she could pick the person off from the darkness. He acknowledged it was a good plan, but since it was set up to pick him off, he didn't like it much.

But he could certainly smile at the situation, because he had a few surprises of his own. One of the first things you learn in the military is repetition breeds familiarity. If they wanted to teach you something, they forced you to do it over and over again until it became an instinctive response. Another lesson he learned was, if it aint broke, don't fix it. With these lessons in mind, he would use the tried and true method of showing them what they expected, and use the distraction for the real attack.

Over top of the entrance to her suite was a monitor with a view of the area between her two doors. Since it was against WRA rules to monitor the family wing, this was all the warning she could legally have. Daniel hacked into the WRA intranet and uploaded a video to her screen.

He put the handheld computer back in his pack and focused once again on his phone. Her screen showed the outer door opening and a masked man stepping inside. Lucille stood up quickly and walked behind the chair she'd been stationed in. She bent down and rested her gun, pointed at the door, along the back cushion. The screen showed the outer door closing and the man manipulating his phone at the final obstacle.

Daniel readied himself with his own button and his own gun. The final door and the tunnel door opened at the same time. When the doors were half open, she dropped the shades into place, hit the button, and started firing. Of course, nothing was there for her to hit.

Calmly, Daniel walked up behind her, hit his own button to turn the lights back on, which blinded her, and pushed her over the back of the chair. Before she even knew what was going on, he had disarmed her and used flex cuffs to bind her hands behind her back. It took only a few additional seconds to pat her down and remove two more guns, two knives, a garrote, and an additional phone. When he was sure he had everything, he stood her up again, and put his gun to the back of her head.

"Now, that was cold-blooded," he said to her. "What if I had only come to talk? You were alright with killing your baby boy?"

Through clinched teeth, she said, "Knockout bullets. I would have let you stand trial before I killed you."

"Well, I guess I'll have to do the same for you. Let's go," he said, dragging her towards the door. When the inner door closed behind them, he asked, "Seen anything good on the news lately?"

"Oh sure," she said cheerily. "Attack on two women in Charlotte. Man, I hope they're okay."

"Yeah, I'll bet," he mumbled. "To put your mind at ease, the sniper bullet that hit Alisha didn't do much damage. She's already out of the hospital. And Ann wasn't hurt at all. I also had a little chat with Ghost. He apologized and now he's on my team. Who would have seen that coming?"

She frowned in response, then said, "I saw something else early this morning. Seems Ann and Walt captured the Prison Guard Killer." Smiling, she said, "I have it on good authority he's innocent and will be free in the not too distant future."

"Huh! Innocent? Go free?" Now it was his turn to smile. "I guess we'll just have to see about that one." He led her over to one of the family wing's many research rooms and ushered her inside. More flex cuffs secured her limbs to one of the sturdy wooden chairs before he turned to leave. "I have to make sure all the preparations are in place. I'll be back to get you shortly."

"Daniel, whatever you're up to, it's not going to work. Anyone who says they're loyal to you will turn on you at the drop of a hat. I am the WRA. Have been for a long time now. Being loyal to the WRA is synonymous with being loyal to me." He smiled, nodded, and closed the door on his mother's furious face.

Daniel made his way back to the tunnels to go retrieve his brother. This time, Reggie was not going to let himself be left behind. Daniel checked his phone and saw his oldest brother standing directly in front of the door, waiting to charge in as soon as it opened. Just to mess with him, Daniel opened it about an inch.

While Reggie immediately started wrenching on the door, Daniel said, "Back up, dumbass, I'm here to get you. It's showtime."

Peeking through the crack, Reggie said, "I swear, if you leave me again, the next time we meet, you will die." Daniel laughed and opened the door the rest of the way.

As they made their way back to the upper level, Reggie looked around the tunnels in amazement. "When did you even have time to do all of this?"

"You remember when mother ordered the reinforcement of all the walls, and the sound proofing? Well, I paid the company $10 Million extra to install these tunnels. Unfortunately, I had to kill them all afterwards, but the money went to their families. Anyway, over the years I've come back and upgraded and expanded into what you see now. The only place I can't get to is the main control room because all the walls around it are pure steel."

Reggie looked at him in wonder. "How long have you been planning this?"

Daniel shook his head. "In a little bit, you'll have the answer to that question. Sometimes showing is more impactful than telling."

Standing outside the research room, Daniel said, "I saw what you did to The Author. I have to figure out how he got access to my tunnels. I have a pretty good idea, but the answer doesn't make sense." Shrugging, he said, "Another problem for another day. Anyway, you ready for the spectacle of the century?" At Reggie's nod, Daniel opened the door.

His mother was sitting calmly right where he'd left her. Daniel smiled and said, "Surprise! It seems all your plans went left tonight. As you can see, The Author also failed in his assignment."

Seeing Reggie, all she could do was drop her head. For his part, Reggie didn't gloat or talk trash, he just looked at Daniel to see what was going on. Daniel, still smiling, cut the flex cuffs holding her in the chair and pulled her up. She went willingly and they all marched out of the closet sized room.

Stopping right outside, Daniel said, "Oh damn, I almost forgot." He pulled his phone out and sent instructions to Dollis on what she needed to do. She replied that she was on her way and the silent threesome walked on towards their destination.

After a ten minute journey, they finally made it to the main floor of the underground facility. Daniel led them over to a giant set of double doors, but stopped before they entered. He turned to Reggie. "Everything will be revealed today. Things you thought you knew and things you never dreamed of. I need your word that you won't interfere with anything that happens beyond these doors."

Reggie stared at him for a full minute before saying, "You have my word."

"Good," was all Daniel said before he pushed the doors open and revealed a sight that had his brother and mother gasping in shock.

Chapter 34

The amphitheater style setup was built to put emphasis on whoever was holding court at that time. The 200 plus seats were plush and designed for comfort. The gold and crystal chandeliers hanging from the 50-foot ceiling were meant to dazzle and amaze. The polished and gleaming wood floor was needed to add a bit of warmth and welcome to the otherwise overbearing space. Since Reggie and Lucille had seen the setup hundreds of times at WRA events, that wasn't the sight that held them enthralled.

As Daniel led his mother down the aisle, Reggie said, "I hope you know what you're doing. Just them being here could mean a death sentence for you all." Daniel smiled at his brother and continued on towards the stage.

The throne-like chair was placed in such a way that all eyes were immediately drawn to it. With its gold fixtures and dark wood trim, museums would pay exuberant fees just for the privilege of displaying it. The chair had always been symbolic of the majestic Burke legacy. Today, it would be a backdrop to how far they had fallen.

Daniel sat his mother down in the throne that befitted her station as WRA head, then he used flex cuffs to secure her limbs to its arms and legs. He walked about a quarter of the way back up the aisle and then turned to survey the scene he had created.

To his left, sitting in the front row facing the stage, were Walt, Ann, Denise, Alisha, Gabby, and Dollis. Denise still had some discoloration around her eyes, and Alisha had her arm in a sling, but to him, his family was spectacular. They looked back and forth between Daniel and his mother sitting restrained on the throne. Reggie had glanced at them only once since he'd made it to the stage. His eyes pretty much bounced from Daniel to the showcase on the other side of the stage.

Daniel swung his eyes to the right where he encountered six pair of hate filled eyes staring back at him. Phung, Kashonda, Mary Sue, LaCora, Tonya, and Nyaira, all sat gagged and secured in chairs of their own. He smiled and waved as he turned his back on them and made his way over to his real family.

The first thing he did was pay homage to the real Queen of his world. He tenderly pulled Alisha up and gave her a lingering kiss on her soft, pink lips. Leaning his forehead on hers, he said, "I'm so sorry for your pain. I failed to protect you and only by someone else's mercy are you here right now. I swear to you that nothing will ever hurt you again."

Smiling sadly and shaking her head, she said, "You can't promise me that, Daniel. But everything is okay. I love you and let's just finish this chapter of our lives so we can move on to the next." She kissed him once more and he moved on to his somber daughter.

He scooped her up in a bear hug and kissed her soundly on her forehead. "You alright, Princess?"

She nodded but tears filled her eyes. "I was worried about you and Mom. I didn't know where you were and I thought you were dead and they just didn't want to tell me," she explained. With years of wisdom in her gaze, she said, "Don't scare me like that again."

His own eyes filled as they held each other tightly, trying to use their strength to relay their love. When they let go, he saw everyone around them were just as affected by the emotional display.

Next, he touched his cousin Dollis on her shoulder. She touched his hand and nodded, which he knew was a major sign of love and respect from his normally emotionally repressed cousin.

He hugged Denise and lightly touched her bruised face before moving on to Walt and Ann. He hugged them both and said, "We're at the finish line. I want to thank both of you for your help. I couldn't have done this without you two."

Ann said, "Enough with all this mushy shit, you have some explaining to do." On a whisper, she asked, "What's up with the old guy? Alisha said you'd explain everything when we got here."

"And I will. But first," he said, inviting his brother over to meet his family. "You know Walt and Dollis, but you've never been formally introduced to the rest." After the introductions Reggie nodded over to the side for a private moment with Daniel.

"What's going on, Bro? Is there a problem?" Daniel asked when they were alone.

"Listen Daniel, I know what Mom did. Aunt Mary Sue told me."

"I know, I saw. And let me tell you, that was a genius way to get her to talk."

With a puzzled look, Reggie asked, "How did you see...." Shaking his head, he said, "Never mind. The point is, Mary Sue could clam up and then we have no corroboration. Without proof, Mom can call for all your people to be executed. After you just tied up a majority of the vote, I don't think it's looking good for us."

Daniel smiled. "Us? I think I like the sound of that. It's been a long time since I've been part of an us with my brothers."

"Well, I don't know about Delmas, but I'm with you, Little Bro." They hugged and then made their way over to Daniel's birth family.

With fidgety movements, and flashing eyes, there was little doubt the brothers were being cursed out behind the gags. Daniel let some of the killer enter his eyes before he started his speech. "None of you are here by accident. This stage was set long before the Prison Guard Killer was born, and even before some of us were alive. I never wanted the responsibility of saving the Burke name, but it was my destiny, like it or not. I was chosen because I showed resistance against going with the status quo. Even before I learned how full of betrayal and corruption our history was, I refused to conform to what I knew was wrong."

He looked at each of his family in turn, making sure they understood how serious the situation was. "I won't make you sit through this like you are now, but I need to stress the importance for quiet and respect as we venture down this road. This is a life or death situation and interruptions will not be tolerated. So, I will remove the gags and your restraints, as long as you can remain quiet and respectful. Nod your head if you can do this for me." All of them nodded and Reggie helped in the freeing of their family members.

Daniel said, "If at any time you go back on your word," he patted the gun in his holster. "The bullets in this gun will do more than splatter red paint and knock you out."

Phung's hand shot up, but Daniel already knew what she wanted to ask. "Jessica is dead, Phung. She was, as my mother so aptly put it in reference to me, beyond redemption. Delmas and my mother had been in her ear for years and she really felt like she deserved your position. I'm sorry, but she had to go." Phung lowered her head and cried silently for the demise of her best friend.

Daniel had arranged for 14 chairs to be added to the stage along with the throne. His new family walked up and occupied the six chairs on the left. His old family followed suit and moved to the six on the right. There were also two additional chairs, one on either side of his mother. Reggie took the one closest to the Burkes. Everyone eyed the other chair, but Daniel wasn't here to sit down. It remained vacant.

His mother started off the festivities with a snide comment. "You dare to bring these people into our inner most sanctum? Sitting them on this stage like they belong? This is a disgrace and I call for a vote to execute all of them for the insult."

Daniel whipped his gun out and pointed it at her head. "I've had enough of your bullshit. Now, I'm trying to do this the right way, the WRA way, the Burke way. But, you open your mouth again, we'll have this trial postmortem. Nod if you understand me." She nodded so Daniel put his gun away.

He paced, first looking at his new family, and then eyeing each member of his old. Finally, he turned to face his mother and Reggie. "I'm not gonna drag this out any longer than I have to. I'm going to tell everyone present the truth as I know it. My mother will then tell you all a bunch of lies to make herself seem like a victim. When she is done, there will be no vote. I will give her the same options she gave my father, then we will go from there. Don't interrupt me and this will be over quickly."

Daniel took a deep breath, looked at all the gathered personnel, then launched into his tale. "Lucille Drake is a monster. A greedy, murdering, scumbag, who kills when things don't go her way."

Snorting, she said, "Are we talking about me or you right now?"

He laughed and continued on with his dialogue. "Not only did she kill our father in cold blood, but she murdered each one of our uncles too." The exclaims of shock and disbelief projected loudly from the Burkes until a deadly look silenced the objections. "After our grandfather, Willie James Burke, died, our uncles Calvin and David took over the Agency. They had this great idea to turn the WRA into a kind of charity for war riddled countries that needed help setting up a fair governing body. The WRA would still be a wealthy organization, but nothing like the billions it has in its reserves today.

"Unfortunately for them, they had a younger sister who was as greedy as she was ambitious. She pictured a future that didn't include the powerhouse she wanted the WRA to become, and she just couldn't live with that. So, on one of their trips to meet with Rebels in Africa, a drone attack shot their plane out of the sky. No one survived."

Daniel started pacing again, and he could see that all faces were extremely interested in his story. "The problem was, the hit was done spur of the moment. It had a lot of potential to lead back to the responsible party. For one, drones back then were super expensive. None of the Rebel opposition could afford one. Plus, this was a time when terrorist basked in their kills. Ironically, no one claimed this one. In fact, every group went out of their way to prove they were not involved. So, the WRA was left with a mystery on its hands."

Throughout his speech, his mother tried very hard to hide her feelings. She glanced at Mary Sue a few times, but for the most part, her face showed disbelief and puzzlement. Daniel knew she was trying to figure out how he knew so much.

"So, up steps our Uncle Kenny. Of course, he had went through all the same training as every Burke did at that time, but he was never interested in becoming a professional soldier. All he wanted to do was build cars on his land in South Carolina. But, as oldest male Burke, he had an obligation to, not only run the WRA, but to find out what happened to his older brothers. He bumbled around for a bit, but ultimately, he came to the conclusion he needed help.

"Kenneth reached out to some of his old CIA connections and they filled him in on some details that hinted at an inside attack. Namely, who had access to the drone and where the drone was at that moment. It seemed that whoever operated the drone crashed it into the sea after the attack to destroy any evidence. But, it didn't work. Uncle Kenny sent out a dive and recovery team and they found the drone and returned it to D.C. In its programming, he found all the intel he needed."

He stopped pacing and zeroed in on his mom. "Now, here is where it gets tricky. Witnesses say they saw a small woman with light skin arguing with Uncle Kenny at a park in D.C. moments before two shots were fired. None of the witnesses got a good look at the culprit, and paramedics pronounced Uncle Kenny dead at the scene. Also, within minutes of his death, the lab where the drone was stored, was torched. But, once again the perpetrator didn't understand how to destroy the evidence.

"Fast forward a couple years and Uncle Glendo is running things. As we all remember, he was considered the, well, difficult one out of the bunch. But, he was smart and he was a soldier through and through. By then, he realized that his brothers' deaths didn't add up with any of the conspiracies floating around. Being a man who never took things at face value, he discreetly started digging into the past.

"He enlisted the help of two up and coming agents in the WRA. Not only were they very smart and resourceful, they also happened to be married to his sisters. Raymond Truesdale and Alan Lee Drake. Two very good men who also happens to be men murdered by my mother here."

Mary Sue gave a muffled scream and covered her face with her hands. Daniel motioned to Reggie, who got up to comfort their aunt. As far as Daniel knew, this was the first time she'd heard anything about Lucille killing her husband.

"This is the part of the story where out late friend, Paul Stevens, comes into play," Daniel continued. "Uncle Glendo was a real threat because he didn't fail to see the threat in his sister. A direct attack on him was out of the question. If it failed, she knew her brother would kill her. So, she asked the CIA to borrow one of its promising agents that would then act as a liaison between the two agencies.

"Paul started training with Glendo and they built quite a friendship. When our mother revealed the true purpose for his arranged relationship, he felt he didn't have a choice but to kill his new friend. Paul got Uncle Glen drunk one night, shot him three times, and set it up to look like a robbery gone bad."

Shaking his head, Daniel said, "Paul was never a spy for me or for anyone else. He was loyal to Lucille Drake until the day he died. She setup that whole elaborate scene about him being a traitor so she could finally rid herself of the threat she imagined him to be.

"Now, the story she told about our dad is actually true. With Kashonda and Mary Sue finding all that evidence against him. The only part she forgot to mention was, she's the one who planted all the evidence against him in the first place. You see, Uncle Glen had confided in Dad his suspicions about Lucille. Of course, he defended her, but small things kept needling him. A suspicious look here, a question asked there. His wife had no choice but to kill him to keep him quiet."

He turned to his still crying aunt who had her arms wrapped around Reggie. "Aunt Mary Sue, Ray was a good man. And if it's any consolation, my mother wasn't going to kill him even though she had here suspicions about what he knew. We were just settling down in this new area. Agents were starting to look at Lucille funny because of all the deaths. But, one thing about good men, they will always do what they think is right. In this instance, him doing the right thing got him killed.

"Raymond approached Paul because he thought, as a CIA man, he could get the info to the right people. Paul took the information to Lucille, and the rest you know. He came out to drive into headquarters the next day, and his car exploded. I can't say for certain who planted the bomb, but I think the evidence speaks for itself."

"Evidence? What evidence?" yelled Lucille. "You've told everyone a nice fantasy and you've backed it up with nothing. You weren't even born when some of these situations occurred. If any of what you said was true, I would have been dead long ago. But, since all of it is false, here I sit as the Head of the WRA."

Daniel smiled and pulled out his gun. He walked to a spot ten feet in front of his mother and stopped. "My uncles made the mistake of seeing you as their little sister. With you being a Burke woman, you knew how to capitalize on their weakness. It seems though that Uncle Glendo was sort of a fortune teller." Glancing around to make sure all eyes were on him, he summed up his speech.

"I remember when I was six years old and I had a conversation with Uncle Glen about his father. He said that his father had a famous quote when it came to the Burke legacy. 'If you educate a man, you educate an individual. But, if you educate a woman, you educate a nation.' Uncle Glen said that was his father's way of making sure the Burke women were treated as equals.

"I asked him, 'Well, what do you do if the Burke women turn bad?' Uncle Glendo got this far away look in his eyes and he said two words: 'Kill them.' He went on to tell me to always acknowledge the threat of a woman the same as I would from a man. Because, when it came down to it, the knife, or gun, or drone, would still kill you no matter who controlled it.

"Now, I told you in the beginning, there wouldn't be a vote. But, I will give you the same options you are so fond of giving others. I will put a couple billion dollars in an account. You can take the money, leave the United States, and never return. Or, I can shoot you in the head as punishment for being a traitor to the Burke name. But, you can only get the first option if you admit to all you've done."

All was silent for a full minute as everyone waited to see what Lucille Drake, Head of the WRA, accused traitor, would do. Then, she laughed. It started out in soft, amused chuckles. After another minute, she was issuing full belly laughs. This went on for several minutes until she finally got control of herself.

She said, "Boy, I invented this game. You think I'm gonna breakdown and confess to a bunch of lies because you have a gun? Child please! I'm a real Burke. Tried and true. So, son, if you're going to shoot me, let's get it done. I'm tired of all the theatrics."

Daniel lifted the gun and said, "So be it." He was ready and prepared to kill his mother when he saw movement off to his left. "Where are you going?" he asked Alisha.

His mother chuckled and said, "You always had a thing for weak ass women."

Alisha gave her a withering look before she turned her attention back to Daniel. "I'm getting Gabby out of here. She doesn't need to see this."

Gabby looked up at Alisha and said, "But Mom, I've seen death before. It's no big deal." Daniel was about to agree with Gabby until he looked up into the pleading face of his fiancé.

Alisha said, "She's 11 years old, Daniel. We can't keep piling trauma on top of trauma."

"But Mom…"

"No, Gabby," Daniel said, turning to his family. "Your mother is right. You've already been exposed to too much."

With a nod from Daniel, Alisha led a complaining but resigned Gabby towards the big double doors.

When the doors closed behind them, Daniel's gun came back up, but he was interrupted once again. "Daniel, I know that she deserves it, but a son should never kill his mother," said Reggie.

Daniel glanced over at him and said, "You know the rules. I don't even have to give her the option. I'm well within my rights to blow her fucking head off."

"And then all you've done is ended her misery. If you want to punish her, send her away with no resources, no power." Walking into his view, Reggie said, "But if you do this, you'll have given her power over you for the rest of your life."

Reggie walked back over to the Burkes and left Daniel gritting his teeth, pointing his gun at the smiling face of his mother.

"You might have changed in some regards," taunted Lucille, "but you're still the same on the inside. Still a lost, scared little boy with a big brain, but no balls." She kept up her insults and taunts until she screamed, "Shoot me, you little bastard! Shoot me!"

It's funny, but her tirade had the opposite effect of what she obviously intended. All the anger drained out of Daniel and his gun hand fell by his side. He glanced at Reggie and said, "You're right. A son should never kill his mother. But to be honest, whether she lives or dies is not my decision to make."

"So, the scared little boy is gonna call for a family vote after all," snarled his mother.

"No!" said a booming voice from the entrance behind him. "A family vote won't be necessary. The decision is all mine."

Daniel turned to find Alisha and Gabby smiling as they bracketed the old man. Shouts of surprise and disbelief filled the room as Reggie, Kashonda, Mary Sue, and Lucille got their first look at the trio. Louder than all the rest, Mary Sue yelled, "Glendo!" and took off running towards her brother. Alisha and Gabby moved off to the side as the siblings embraced and cried for all the time they had lost.

Phung, Tonya, and Nyaira had never met him and Dollis had been a newborn when he'd disappeared. But of course, they all had heard his name over the years. Walt, Ann, and Denise stood speechless as the identity of the old man was revealed. Reggie and Kashonda, just as shocked, were frozen in place with their mouths hanging open. LaCora walked over and slung her arm around Daniel's shoulder. In unison, they turned to stare at the dazed Lucille Drake.

LaCora said, "I've been waiting years to see the expression on your face when Daniel exposed you as the traitor." Turning to look at Daniel, she said, "I bet this stupid bitch still thinks she can lie her way out of this." With that, she rushed off the stage to join Mary Sue and her dad.

Daniel walked over and stood beside his mother. "Well, I guess now you know LaCora was my mole the whole time, and my source of information was Uncle Glen himself. You murdered the one person who was unconditionally loyal to you because of your own paranoia. My job here is done, but I'll leave you with a word of advice: Wherever he decides to send you, don't come back. I'll be watching and I'll know if you do." Turning his back on her and looking at his family celebrating, he said, "I don't have to tell you what will happen if I ever see you again." Without looking back, he slowly walked to his new combined family.

Daniel had hope that, without the cancer, they all could heal and work as one to restore the Burke legacy. A lot of work had to be done, but looking around, he was confident they had the people to achieve that goal. When he reached the group, they all started clapping in acknowledgement of his hard work. Daniel took a small bow and exhaled in relief as a plan, almost 20 years in duration, finally bared fruit.

Chapter 35

Daniel wished he could've stayed to celebrate with his family, but he still had work to do. He did stick around for the takeover ceremony where his uncle officially stripped his mother of her title and rank. Then, in a move that shocked them all, he passed control of the WRA to Reggie, and took the role of Head of Operations for himself. He tried to appoint Daniel as Head of Mission Development, but he declined and had a brief sidebar with his uncle. Everyone was happy and excited, and all the festivities were done right in front of his still restrained mother.

He'd also had a brief conversation with Alisha who gave him some additional intel for his next mission. It complicated things a little bit, but he was more than happy to honor any request from his future bride. Plus, he owed her for all he'd put her through recently.

So, here he was, slowly creeping closer to a house near Rockhill, South Carolina, which contained the local leadership of the Big Rollin Crips. He felt that they would be on guard, so he waited until nightfall to make his move. This wasn't gonna be a drone attack, even though he did have one covering the front of the house so no one could run. He wanted to end these motherfuckers one at a time, and in the most vicious ways. He wanted to send a clear message to anyone still left, what would happen if they fucked with his people.

Daniel had used a surveillance drone earlier in the day to get a rundown on the layout of the house and its occupants. The outside of the house was impressive with its saltwater gunite pool, raised garden beds, and cobblestone entry. The Crips probably thought they had bought security with the ten acres surrounding the property. What they actually got was a place to die where no one could hear them scream.

The interior of the house was exquisite, and the five bedrooms were spread over the two stories to provide each room maximum privacy. His scan yielded five people currently inside the house. Inside the master suite was Bernie 'Face G' Alston, and a woman. The other three gangbangers, Debo, Quette, and Keith, were in the three bedrooms farthest from their leader. Poor decision making and poor security. He would save the leader and the woman for last.

Daniel arrived at the sliding glass door off the pool area and entered the residence. The open kitchen and dinning room area were deserted. No sentry or alarm. Face G really thought that the location and hidden connection to his gang was all he needed. Not wanting to waste any more time on these scumbags, he made his way to the first bedroom.

Big Keith, all 6-foot 4-inches and 450-pounds of him, was sleeping in the first room. He was tucked comfortably under the covers, but there was no mistaking who it was. Daniel pulled out two knives as he rushed over to the sleeping man. He slowly pulled the covers back until the man's heaving upper body was revealed. Lining everything up perfectly, Daniel used all his strength to slam down one knife in Keith's throat, and the other in his stomach.

The man's eyes flew open as he started to choke on his own blood. He tried to roll away, but the double-sided blade in his guts just ripped him open more. His mouth opened on a scream, but more blood came pouring out instead of sound.

"You fucked with the wrong women," Daniel said to him. "But you're not the first, and you won't be the last. When you get to hell you can compare notes with the rest of your homies I've sent before you." Savagely twisting the knives, Big Keith shuddered until the light finally left his eyes. Only then did Daniel remove the blades, use the dead man's shirt to clean them off, and stored them for easy access at the next stop.

In the next room, Quette was up playing a game, sitting at the foot of the bed. Daniel, entering at his back, closed and locked the door behind him. They were the only ones left alive on this floor of the house, so Daniel wanted to test the self-proclaimed fighter's skills.

When the lock engaged, Quette dropped the controller and reached for his gun. "Unh Unh! Keep your hands up, motherfucker." Daniel had his own gun pointed at Quette's head. The man smiled and raised his hands. Daniel put him on the wall and removed his gun, a set of brass knuckles, and a knife after a thorough search. After storing the weapons in a drawer, Daniel put his own gun away and turned to face the Crip.

Quette said, "What's hood pussy? Why you put the gun up?"

Daniel shrugged and said, "I heard you consider yourself a fighter. I wondered if you felt that way because you only battle guys who can't fight. Now me, I'm a real fighter. So, let's see what you got."

"And I guess if I win, I go free, right?"

"You'll only win if I'm dead, so I guess all of you will go free. Well, except for Big Keith. But in a sense, he's already free." With a snarl, Quette attacked.

Giving the man a chance didn't mean that Daniel had time to waste. As Quette was throwing his first punch, Daniel was placing a kick to the man's right knee. The crack was audible and Quette crashed to the floor, clutching his ruined leg. Daniel laughed and asked, "Is that it?" Quette couldn't answer as he rolled around moaning in pain.

Another kick to his face left him conscious, but flat on his back. "Make sure you find Big Keith in hell and tell him how I ended you. I at least had to use knives on him." Daniel stomped down on Quette's chest, caving in his chest cavity. Ribs broke, lungs collapsed, heart ruptured, and the Crip died within seconds from the massive trauma.

Behind him, the door knob stated to rattle. "Quette? Why you stop the game? Everybody's waiting on you." Daniel looked at the screen and saw Quette's military Avatar standing idle on the street. He didn't play games all that often, but he recognized this one as *Call of Duty* because sometimes he played with Alisha and Gabby.

Debo shook the whole door when he didn't receive an answer. "Yo Cuz, what the fuck you doing? Why you got the door locked?" When he still didn't get a response, Debo started throwing his muscular body at the door. Daniel pulled out his gun and waited for the man to crash through.

It only took two more hits and the lock gave way under the tremendous force. As soon as he was in sight, Daniel sent two bullets towards his chest. Both found their target, but the gangster was wearing a bulletproof vest. The force made him stumble back, which was good for him because it allowed him to duck around the corner before Daniel could get another shot.

As he ran, Debo shouted, "OG! He's here!" before heading for the stairs. Daniel was steps behind him when he saw Debo pull the gun from behind his back. He unloaded his gun at the fleeing man just as he dived behind the wall separating the stairs from the living room.

For about 30 seconds, everything was quiet. No part of Debo was visible and Daniel had no clue how many times he'd been hit, if at all. Foot steps overhead let him know that Face G and the female were now preparing themselves to take him on. A door upstairs opened and a male voice said, "Debo?" After a pause, the voice said, "I called for backup. If you're in a safe place, answer me." All stayed quiet.

Daniel knew Face G was full of shit. The upgraded black box made sure no cellphones could be used. But, full of shit or not, without the element of surprise, there was no way for Daniel to get to the OG Crip without making himself a target. So, Daniel retreated and pulled out one of his friends to do a little hunting.

Daniel got behind the marble island in the kitchen and sent his bee drone out to finish the job. Using his phone, Daniel steered the drone high up on the ceiling as he sought to see what was behind the living room wall. Focusing the lens down, a shot to shit and very dead Debo lay at the bottom of the steps. Pointing the lens back up, he could see Face G standing at the top of the stairs with nothing but his head and gun visible.

"Quette? Big Keith? Any of you motherfuckers alive?" Face was whispering but Daniel could hear him loud and clear through the drone's mic. "Shit!" he cursed as he realized all his men were dead. "Hey man, whoever the fuck you are, I got a hundred soldiers on the way. If you run now, you might can escape.... Ouch!" Face exclaimed as he smacked at the drone Daniel had just used to end his life.

Face G tried to swipe at it, but Daniel was able to navigate it back down the steps with no damage. It returned to him and he stored it in its case before standing up and heading back to the living room. Daniel wanted to fill Face in on some stuff before he died.

At the bottom of the steps, Daniel yelled, "Face! What's going on my man? You don't have that much longer, so I came to talk."

The OG Crip yelled, "Fuck you!" and fired off three shots into the barrier wall.

"Don't you want to hear about all your minions I've killed?" asked Daniel. "You want to ask me about Mickey Brown?" Four more shots hit the wall causing Daniel to laugh out loud. "At least Mickey was man enough to face me. You don't want to look me in the eyes before you die?"

"You want to face me Cuz, stick your fucking head around the corner."

Daniel laughed at the comment before he explained himself to Face. "All these people dead, all this wasted life, because one man liked to bully others. I've killed damn near a hundred of you fuckers because your man Mickey killed my friend's family. I killed Mickey's whole prison crew with poisoned K-2 before I kicked his ass the first time. You'll find this funny: I killed his second crew with a bunch of drones that looked like bees. All I had to do was sting them once and, within 15 minutes, they were dead." Looking at his watch, Daniel said, "You should be feeling it now. I'd say you have about three minutes to live."

Face G coughed and Daniel heard his gun fall to the floor. He did a quick peek around the barrier and saw Face slumped on the wall near the top. With his gun trained on the Crip leader, Daniel slowly made his way up the steps, very much aware the woman was still walking around freely.

Daniel stopped about four feet from Face and said, "You don't come after my woman and your little crew would still be alive. You let my brother, Delmas, use you and now all your people are dead."

"Not all," Face said, coughing up blood. "The Gang is bigger than me. There'll be more to come."

"And more of you will die. To protect my people, I'll wipe you motherfuckers off the face of the earth." Nothing else was said as Face G fell over on the floor, bleeding and wheezing, until he took his last labored breath and died.

Daniel pulled out his phone and called Alisha. "She's the only one left. You ready for your part?"

"Go ahead and do it," was her reply.

Daniel called another number and the woman's phone could be heard ringing in the bathroom. She didn't answer it and the phone was silenced quickly. Daniel called her twice more before the call was answered. "Who is this?" whispered the woman. "I'm kind of busy right now."

"Too busy to talk to your best friend?" asked Alisha.

The woman inhaled sharply. "Alisha? Oh my God! Is this really you?" asked Tyiesha.

"Yes, it's me, and I sent my man to pick you up. You ready to go?"

"Is that Manny out there killing everybody?" she asked on a whisper. "Alisha, I can't go out there. He's gonna kill me."

"Sweetie, no he's not," Alisha assured her. "He killed them because they tried to kill me yesterday. I sent him to get you because I want you to come and join me in my new life. I'm engaged and everything. But, I need you by my side."

The line was silent for a full minute before Tyiesha said, "Tell your man not to shoot me. I'm coming out."

"He's on the line, Sis, he can hear you. And his name is Daniel, not Manny."

Daniel was standing at the top of the steps with his gun pointed at the bathroom door. Tyiesha came out wearing blue jeans and a blue hoodie with black sneakers on her feet. When she saw him standing there, she paused and frowned. "Uh, Alisha? I'm not sure your man got the message. He has his gun pointed right at me."

"Alisha, hang up," Daniel demanded. "I'll talk to you when I get home."

"Alright. I love you and be careful." She hung up and Daniel lowered his phone.

"Alisha? Alisha?" the woman cried before turning to run back in the bathroom.

"Move another inch and I'll hit you in the stomach so your death is long, slow, and painful." She froze with wide eyes and her hands out from her sides.

She whimpered, "Please! Alisha said you're not supposed to kill me!"

Daniel shrugged. "Shit happens. You panicked and pulled out a gun. I tried to shoot your arm but you twisted at the last moment and I hit your heart instead. I can think of a million different ways to kill you and make Alisha understand."

"But why? I didn't do anything. I only got here this morning because Face G called me." Her comment caused her eyes to shoot over to Face G before quickly moving back to Daniel. "I had nothing to do with their attack on Alisha."

"I know, that's the only reason you're still alive. Anyway, turn around and put your hands on the wall. You can drop the phone, you won't be needing it anymore." She stared at him for a few seconds before dropping the phone and turning. Her deep breaths told him she was struggling to stay calm.

Daniel searched her and removed a small knife from the pocket of her hoodie. He took a few steps back and then ordered her to turn around. Now facing each other in the semi-darkness, he said, "Alisha really loves you, and I really love her. For that reason, I'm going to invite you to come live with my family. You'll be very comfortable and very safe, but you'll be watched closely until I can gauge if you're trustworthy or not."

"What if I don't want to go with you? What if I'd rather go home?"

"Oh, you can go home. The fucking funeral home in a pine box. I'm willing to accommodate my fiancé, but don't push me. You either come with me or you die. The choice is yours."

"So, you're kidnapping me?" asked Tyiesha.

"Fuck this!" Daniel said before raising his gun.

She dropped to the floor and yelled, "Okay! Okay! Don't shoot!"

"Alisha, you better be glad I love you," he said under his breath. To Tyiesha, he said, "Let's go. I don't have all night to be playing with you."

She stood up and he followed her as they made their way out of the house. He gave her directions as he led her through the fields and trees until they were standing next to The Beast. Daniel said, "Thanks for not making me carry you all this way." She turned with a confused look and Daniel shot her once in the chest.

She screamed and fell back against the car before sliding to the ground. Her face showed the feeling of betrayal. Daniel shrugged, and said, "Just makes things easier." She slumped and he opened the back door and tossed her 5-foot 9-inch body in the car.

He sighed as he thought about Alisha slapping him upside his head. But, she'd get over it. The main thing now was to get back to his family. There was still a lot of work to do before everyone could breathe easy.

Chapter 36

It seemed like hundreds of officers were present at the Justice Building in downtown Raleigh. Some would actually be participating in the transfer of the Prison Guard Killer. Most were there just to catch a glimpse of the notorious captured killer. The show of force was quite impressive, but to Walt, it posed an unnecessary risk. Delmas had been in custody long before Lucille had been subdued. She'd had enough time to organize all types of events that could lead to any one of these officers turning dirty.

A total of ten days had passed since the PGK had been in police custody. He'd been poked and prodded by the SBI, FBI, Homeland Security. Even the Secret Service had stopped by for a chat. Every word spoken and every action taken had been recorded and scrutinized to make sure none of the visitors had tried to help the captured villain. As far as Walt could tell, nothing untoward had transpired. Now, the SBI was gearing up to move the prisoner over to the Wake County Jail.

The trip wasn't that far, but it would represent the first time the PGK had a chance to escape. No one at the SBI wanted to send the man anywhere but, no matter what he was accused of, he had to have his day in court. If they kept him at the Justice Building, they would have to do this transport, dog and pony show, at least once a month. Everyone agreed that it would be safer for all involved to only have to do this one time.

Walt, Ann, Cpt. Graham, and the SBI SWAT Commander were making final preparations when Walt asked Ann to step into an unoccupied office. When they entered, Walt gave Ann a small hug and a relaxed smile. "We did it, partner. After today, you can finally return to your normal life."

She cocked her head. "Don't you mean 'we' can return to 'our' normal lives?"

Over the past ten days they only returned to their homes to shower and change clothes. They were either here at the Justice Building, at WRA headquarters, or down in Charlotte with Daniel. Just because things were trending in the right direction didn't mean their training was done. At least that was the sentiment Daniel expressed.

It actually made sense after Daniel explained the situation. Although Glendo Burke was back, and Reggie was now over the WRA, there were hundreds of agents and assets that had yet to be contacted. Until everyone was up to speed, and all opposition eliminated, there was still substantial risk to all parties involved. Daniel didn't want anyone relaxing and being caught off guard.

In response to Ann's 'we' statement, Walt exhaled loudly. "Three days ago, while we were at WRA headquarters training, Glendo pulled me to the side. He explained to me that the Investigative job that Lucille had offered me was a very important position and needed to be filled. He thought I was an excellent choice and he asked if I'd take the job."

Ann was stunned. "What the fuck Walt? We just went through hell to get our lives back. Now you want to commit long-term to this!"

"Ann, without Lucille and Delmas in the picture, I think this Agency can get back to what it used to be. I won't be going out on missions or anything like that. My sole job will be to investigate wrong doings inside of the organization."

"So, what about the SBI? You're just gonna leave us?" Ann gave him a stern look. "I hope this meeting isn't to convince me to come with you. I love you Walt, but I'm done with the WRA and all its bullshit."

Walt smiled. "Actually, I wasn't gonna ask you to come with me." He held his hand up to stop the tirade before it started up again. "I'm taking the job, but I'll need someone here that I can trust and that knows what's going on. With that in mind, after today, there will be an opening at the Sergeant of Detectives position. And I was wondering if you wanted it?"

Again, Ann was stunned. With her mouth hanging open in surprise, she dropped her gear heavy body into one of the office chairs. Finally, she said, "There are at least ten detectives with more seniority than me. Plus, Captain Graham has to...."

"I've already talked to Will and he agreed you are the best candidate for the job." He took her hands and pulled her back to her feet. "I told you in the car that I recruited you from day one. I knew back then you would be the one to take my job if I moved up or retired. The other detectives love and respect you, and no one can question your dedication to the job. All you have to do is say yes and the job is yours."

After a brief hesitation, a huge smile lit her face. "Yes! Hell, yes, I'll take the job!" She threw her arms around Walt and he lifted her off her feet as they both expressed their excitement. In the middle of her squeals, the door opened and Cpt. Graham stepped into the room.

"Well, isn't this sweet," he said, eyeing the smiling pair. "While the rest of us are getting ready to tangle with a psychopath, you two are in here hugging it out."

"Shut the hell up, Will. Ann's agreed to become your new Sergeant."

"Don't tell me to shut up! We have work to do. Don't make me fire your ass on your last day." Will and Walt scowled at each other until Will said, "And stop hogging all the attention. I want to congratulate Ann, too." Walt set her back on her feet as Will extended his hand to her.

With both Will and Ann encased in body armor, she slapped his hand out of the way and hugged her new boss tight. "I won't let you down, Captain," she proclaimed with feeling.

Walt laughed as Will awkwardly tried to figure out where to put his hands. He ended up patting Ann on the back, saying, "I know you won't, Sgt. Det. Grace." Ann released him and got herself together. But, before they exited the room to join the transport team, Will explained why he'd come looking for them.

"First of all, the takedown of the game rooms went exactly according to plan. I still don't know how you managed to discover a money laundering ring while shadowing our killer, but the results speak for themselves. It was a major bust and it might help me elevate to that Director's chair."

Walt used all his restraint to not glance at Ann guiltily, and just smiled, nodded and headed for the door. "One more thing," Will said, stopping his progress. "A Lincoln Limousine and a Bentley Continental linked to those dead bodies in Charlotte, was tracked to a house down in South Carolina. When police went inside, they found the dead bodies of the leaders of that same gang our killer was linked to last year. Now, if our killer has been locked in that cell this whole time, who do you think went after these guys?"

"I told you last year the connection was flimsy. This just proves it wasn't him in the first place." Will eyed him with suspicion for a minute before nodding and leading them out the door to join the others.

Will gathered everyone together and made sure everyone knew what their job would be. When everyone declared themselves ready, Ann and Walt entered the cell area and walked the already fully restrained Delmas to the middle of the group. He looked around at the officers gathered and chuckled unimpressed.

All 15 of the gathered officers put on their most fearsome look, except for Walt and Ann. They were the only ones who knew that no display of force would scare Delmas. He proved it a few seconds later with his comments.

He looked at the young SWAT Commander and said, "You ought to thank me. I'm pretty sure you have your rank because of all the SWAT guys I've killed in the past." The Commander laughed and then launched a sneak attack at Delmas. Even fully restrained, he dodged the sucker punch and used his lightning reflexes to head butt his attacker in the face.

For a minute, chaos erupted. The head butt caused blood to explode from the officer's nose and mouth. Walt and Ann pulled Delmas out of the circle of people as Will and two more SBI agents tried their best to calm the SWAT team down. The yells and threats had no effect on Delmas as he stood with an impassive expression. No guns were drawn, but Walt could tell some of the officers wished they had taken the chance during the melee.

Cpt. Graham yelled and pushed until he had everyone's undivided attention. He said, "The next one of you fuckers to try some shit like that, I'll see to it personally that you're fired and charged. Do I make myself clear?" Everyone nodded and cast looks at the Commander who had his head titled back and his nose pinched. "We have the death penalty fellas. All we have to do is be patient and his day will come."

Will glanced at Walt and Ann, guilt darkening his face because only a select few knew about the deal they made for his confession. The confessor was also told to keep it quiet until court was in session.

Delmas barked out a laugh which caused every head to turn in his direction. With a smile on his face, he said, "I'm not going to Death Row. In fact, I won't make it to prison. I'll sit in jail for a while, recharge my batteries, then I'm going to get out and kill every single one of you. Might not be today. Might not be tomorrow." Looking every officer in the eyes one at a time, he said, "But I'm going to enjoy killing each and every one of you. And for taking me through this, I think I'll kill your families first." Then he did the thing all Burkes seem to be good at. He let the killer enter into his eyes to broadcast that he meant every word.

Walt hated the looks of uncertainty on the faces around him. They didn't know the man's true identity, but they could feel the utter confidence behind his spoken words. Will cleared his throat, and said, "Let's go, people. Let's get this done."

They passed through sally port after sally port and checkpoint after checkpoint until they were in the underground garage, loading Delmas into the reinforced inmate transport vehicle. It was still early, 6:05am, so traffic in downtown should be light. Cops with their hands on their weapons were all over the place. He told Ann to stay on point as they got into the Porsche Taycan Turbo S and moved directly behind the vehicle carrying Delmas.

As they exited the garage, Ann said, "I don't know if this means anything, but Raleigh PD is reporting a missing officer." Looking at her phone, she said, "His vehicle was discovered abandoned last night, but no evidence of foul play was found." They shared a look, but both knew they would be the only two panicking over the news. All they could do is stay on point and move fast if something happened.

Two minutes from the jail, Walt's phone rang. He glanced at the display and answered when he saw Will's name. "What's up, Cap?"

360

"Five minutes ago, the gate for the underground garage at the jail malfunctioned. I called the Brass and they said to just take him in the back way. I want to take him back to the Justice Building, but they said no. Just wanted to let you know why we were changing routes." Cpt. Graham hung up and Walt cursed.

Ann asked, "What's going on now? More bad news?" Walt relayed the Captain's message and Ann cursed right along with him.

They didn't have time to think or plan as the transport vehicle turned to pull up at the service entrance of the jail. Walt shook his head at the nightmare image in front of him. Raleigh and Wake County officers milled about all over the grounds. He knew anyone of them could be here to help or harm Delmas. Walt didn't worry about the harming part, but the helping could result in a massive loss of life.

Walt and Ann exited their vehicle and stood at the back of the transport truck, waiting for everyone to get into position. Walt looked around carefully, but didn't spot any officers who looked out of place. He had no idea if the missing cop would be the one to strike, or if the cop was dead and his uniform taken. After a five-minute delay that Walt used to survey the area, he nodded to the SWAT Commander to open the back door.

Delmas hadn't seen the sun in almost two weeks, so even the early morning glow had him squinting. He slowly made his way down the steps as he too looked around for the help he expected to come. They had taken maybe ten steps toward the jail when Walt caught the unnatural movement out the corner of his right eye.

He wasn't the only one who caught it. Delmas frowned and jerked to a stop which caused all the focus around them to shift onto him. Too fast, the hand pushed out of the crowd, and a voice said, "For my family, motherfucker!" The pistol spit fire as four rounds escaped before the officers around the man grabbed the gun.

The SWAT guys raised their weapons, but had them pointed at Delmas. Will, Walt, Ann, and the other two SBI agents threw their bodies on top of Delmas, but Walt knew they were too late. The bullets had struck and Delmas had already fallen before they could react.

A few more shots sounded before one single shot put a stop to the exchange. Walt and Will exploded up, grabbed the PGK by his arms, and dragged him the rest of the way into the building. About 20 correctional guards were waiting in the receiving room, so Walt ran back out, figuring they could handle the body he'd just delivered to them.

Walt could smell the blood all over his clothes as Ann joined him and walked over to see the assassin. Three SWAT guys moved out of the way to reveal a 40-year-old white male with a single gunshot wound to his head. They both gasped when they saw the man's face.

Daniel had tried to convince them that the WRA was in no position to help Delmas at this time. They hadn't wanted to believe him, but it seemed he had been right. The WRA didn't have anything to do with what had happened two minutes ago.

The man who had killed an officer to get his uniform, and Walt was sure had also caused the gate to malfunction, was only here for pure and simple revenge. Well over a year ago, the PGK had taken this man's family. So, Marshall Oakland had showed up to get some payback.

They gave the SWAT Commander and Will the rundown on who the man was, then made their way back to the jail. A janitor was mopping up the blood left behind by Delmas. Walt an Ann made their way to the official receiving area and was greeted by another shocking sight.

Delmas was sitting in one of the cells with his shackles removed, his shirt off, and a pretty doctor patching up the bullet hole in his shoulder. Walt laughed and looked at Ann. "Un-fucking-believable! Literally just a flesh wound." They walked into the cell and Delmas looked up with a smile. Walt said, "Now, aren't you glad I made you wear the dumbass vest?"

He laughed and said, "I sure am, but in the near future," all humor left Delmas as he said, "I can promise you, you won't be. You should have let him kill me. Remember, when one of us makes a promise, we always keep our word."

The doctor, feeling the tension, glanced at them both and walked out with a nervous last glance. Walt was nervous, too. Once again, events had been set in motion that Walt didn't understand. If it was up to him, Delmas would be dead. How could Daniel expect any of them to live a normal life with this monster still lurking just out of sight?

He touched Ann's arm and they exited the cell as the door closed to seal in the accused killer. Delmas smiled and laid back on the bench like he was really just here for a much-needed vacation. Walt shook his head as he thought about the future. He couldn't shake the feeling that they were still all pawns in someone's master plan.

Chapter 37

Control of the WRA was his. He had his favorite uncle back. His youngest brother was on good terms with the family. Personally, and professionally, things couldn't be better. So, Reggie was having a hard time trying to figure out why he felt so off kilter.

Yes, a guard bent on revenge had tried to kill Delmas earlier that morning. Yes, his mother was scheduled to be shipped off to Europe in a few hours. But the rest of the family seemed to be getting on fine. Reggie just couldn't shake the unease that had been hawking him.

Nine days since his uncle had returned and already the WRA was getting its government contracts back. LaCora was revealing top of the line gadgets that she'd previously developed only for her dad and Daniel. He'd caught Kashonda flirting with a Supervisory Field Agent in the cafeteria. Even his Aunt Mary Sue had a little more bounce in her step. The WRA was an organism recovering from an illness after all the sick cells had been vanquished.

Daniel had unlocked their computer systems and even gave them a few upgrades. He'd uploaded the specs for some additional security measures they really needed to implement. He still wouldn't allow anyone in his tunnels, but even he seemed to enjoy the time he spent in the underground headquarters. And, although he'd turned down the Head of Mission Development job, he was fully on-board with Walt heading up Internal Investigations. But, as the family and Agency continued to heal, Reggie became more and more troubled.

The day after Daniel had made all his revelations, and Uncle Glendo had returned, Reggie pulled his uncle into the family library for a chat. "So, Unc, tell me what happened between you and Paul back in the day."

His uncle had poured them both drinks, sat down, and then launched into his tale. "Reg, there was a mountain of evidence that pointed to Lucille being the murderer of our brothers. But, everything was circumstantial or just loosely tied to her. Nothing that would make you 100% sure, but I had suspicions, and that was enough for me to be extremely cautious.

"So, I had spies watching her every move. One of them reported to me about a meeting she had with a young, but good, CIA agent named Paul Stevens. And what do you know, about a week later, he shows up asking me to train him. I felt it would be better to befriend him than to push him away and some unknown person snipes me from long distance. I needed to find out what exactly they wanted from me.

"Early on, it became apparent that he was digging for information about my brothers' deaths. He wanted to figure out how much I knew. One night, after we had become friends, I decided to give him a little test. I intimated to him that I knew exactly who killed my brothers and I had the proof buried where no one but me would ever find it. I told him I was just waiting for the right time to use it. I had my people watching Lucille and, once again, the two had a clandestine meeting. The next night, he called me to go out on the town.

"I called the bar ahead of time and told the owner to set up a scene for me. I would order drinks, but all my drinks would be alcohol free. Paul drank as little as possible while I pretended to get plastered.

"When we left the bar, Paul had to damn near carry me. I played it up so the man would think I was easy pickings. Back then, whenever Paul drove, he always removed his gun and placed it in the center console. I was acting drunk and I picked his gun up and started fumbling about. I pressed the eject button for his clip and it fell between my feet just like I planned it. I had a similar clip hidden under my seat with rubber bullets and blood packs on the inside. In case you're wondering, that was the prototype to the knockout bullets everyone uses today.

"Anyway, I gave him the gun, now loaded with the dummy rounds, and we continued to my house. When we arrived, I stumbled out of the car and Paul screamed my name. When I turned, he shot me three times, jumped in his car, and left me there.

"I paid some cops and the coroner to claim I was dead. I told them that it was really for my protection, but I didn't want to go into the Witness Protection Program. The coroner made up my body so it appeared I died from the gunshot wounds. He contacted my sister to come ID my body. After she confirmed and left, they acted as if there was a mix up in the paperwork and my body had been cremated.

"I knew then that I really had to disappear. Lucille was too powerful and she was making friends with some very dangerous people. I wasn't gonna come back unless your mother died. But then Daniel started digging into all of our deaths."

"What!" exclaimed Reggie. "I've never heard him mention anything about that."

"That's because, as soon as I found out he was digging, I paid him a visit. This was right before his 18th birthday, and was the reason he went into Military Intelligence instead of the CIA. He told everyone it was because of Walt, which in some part it was. In truth, it was because Lucille had no inroads inside Military Intelligence.

"From the time he entered the Military, until he entered the Prison system, we were working on a plan to take back the WRA. I told him taking the prison job was too dangerous, but he insisted, so I gave him my blessing and in he went. When you guys voted to keep him in, I was heartbroken. I thought he would be forced to serve out the whole 26 years.

"Anyway, you pretty much know the rest. I trained Daniel in the old ways and I've been his silent partner in the war against the WRA."

Reggie had sat and looked at his uncle for a while in silence. He wanted to ask him why he'd stayed hidden even after Daniel was freed. His birthright guaranteed he could take control over the WRA at any time. Something didn't add up, but Reggie didn't want to reveal his suspicions. They had spent a couple more hours shooting the shit before they went their separate ways.

A knock on his office door brought him back to the present. He hadn't felt right taking over his mother's office while she was still in residence, so he'd stayed in his own. He looked at his phone and was shocked to see that hours had passed while his brain had been working. "Come in," he yelled, seeing his aunt on the monitor over the door.

She stuck her head in and said, "Glendo sent me to get you. It's time to bring Lucille up for her flight." She started to close the door when Reggie told her to come back in for a moment.

His aunt looked confused, but stepped in and shut the door behind her. Reggie studied her before he asked his question. "What do you think about all this?"

"What do you mean?" she asked, shaking her head.

"Everything," he responded, stretching his arms out wide. "Uncle Glen coming back. The story about my mom. The deaths of my dad, and your husband. What do you think about it?"

She smiled and walked closer to his desk. "I told you in the dungeon that she admitted to me she killed our brothers.

She made it sound like she had no choice, but Lucille is and has always been full of shit. She's evil and greedy and she's been a cancer to my father's Agency since she was old enough to dream.

"My father just wanted to help people. Wanted to give the underdog a fighting chance. He never cared about the money, power, or position. Lucille, on the other hand, doesn't care about helping anyone but herself. She had this dream she used to tell me when I was little. She would say that the WRA would be the dominate force on this planet, and she was gonna be the driving force behind it.

"So, you want to know what I think? I think exile is too good for her. I think we should take one of those swords in the dungeon, and chop her fucking head off." With her smile still in place, she turned around and left his office.

He sat for another five minutes before he got up and followed his aunt out the door. His destination wasn't far away. The WRA had a small prison on one of its lower levels. Nothing on the scale of what Daniel had access to, but it could hold up to 24 people. It was damp and musty and used more as a threat than to actually hold people. So, due to its deplorable condition, his uncle thought it more humane to place Lucille in a secure room in the hospital wing.

When he arrived, four guards and his Uncle Glen were already waiting outside her room. They were in full body armor and Reggie took a couple minutes to put his own armor in place. The fact that they'd only be out in the open for a couple dozen feet meant nothing. No one was more capable of pulling off the impossible like a Burke backed into a corner.

All geared up and ready to go, Reggie nodded for the guard with the keys to open the door. He unlocked it, pulled the door wide, and then stepped out of the way. Lucille was sitting on the bed, watching TV, and she took her sweet time responding to their presence. After a full minute, she turned the TV off, sighed, and stood up to face them.

She was dressed casually; jeans, sweater, and tennis shoes. She was only carrying a small toiletry bag as most of her personal items had already been stored in the jet. Lucille didn't look happy, but didn't appear too upset either. Maybe a little annoyed with the whole process, but also ready to get it over with. She exited the room without directive or acknowledgement of them, and made her way to the hospital's exit.

Glendo had passed down the decision to grant his sister rights to every continent except for the Americas. He gifted her with a private WRA jet, and the freedom to travel at will. Glen wasn't stupid, so he warned her that all her traveling had to be on the jet and she'd be watched at all times. He made her understand that no warnings would be given if she tried to conduct any forays into the intelligence world. Glen gave her land and money, about $5 Billion, and told her to live a long, but quiet, life.

Now, it seemed she would take his advice to heart. In her late 60's, maybe she would take the time to enjoy the life she'd created through her treachery. All of them knew the life of luxury they had was only because of her ruthlessness and drive to be great. Through grit and force of will, Lucille had turned the $100 million Agency into a $1 Trillion global empire. Reggie just prayed she could put the hectic lifestyle behind her and focus on a life of comfort.

Once in the garage, Glen called everyone to a halt as the two SUVs waited at the rollup doors. He sent the guards ahead to the lead vehicle to give the Burkes a little privacy. Turning to Lucille, he said, "No more contact is to be made with anyone in the Agency or this family. We've said all we have to say to each other. I'm giving you a couple minutes with your son and then you're out of here." He walked off towards the second vehicle and left the two of them alone.

Reggie said, "Mom, I...."

"No time for sentiments, Reggie," she said, cutting him off. "I only have one message for you." Capturing his gaze with her own, she said, "Master manipulators run in our family. Nothing is ever how it seems or appears to be. Us Burkes were born with the ability to sense bullshit when it's around us. In the end, we have to be masters of our own minds. Don't trust anyone and always go with your gut." Kissing his cheek quickly, she said, "I love you, son," and then followed her brother to the second SUV.

Reggie wasn't a monster, so he felt horrible about his mother's dilemma. As Head of the WRA, he technically had the power to stop this whole thing and keep his mother here. On the other hand, Uncle Glendo could then strip Reggie of his power and then exile them both. Having no other choice, Reggie made his way over to the SUV to join his mother and uncle.

Once everyone was safely inside the armored vehicles, the rollup doors opened and the WRA airfield was revealed. The two SUVs took off to make the short drive over to the waiting jet that now belonged to Lucille. Everyone was looking around, expecting some kind of attack, but everything looked peaceful and serene.

The vehicles made it to within 50 feet of the jet before coming to a halt. The guards exited the first SUV and surveyed the area, looking for snipers off in the distance, but also explosives around the immediate area. They gave the all clear after about ten minutes of searching.

Glen glanced at Lucille like he was surprised she wasn't putting up a fight. Ultimately, he shrugged and opened his door to get out. Reggie went to do the same on his side, but his mother gripped his leg. Her eyes blazed into his as she said, "Remember what I said, don't trust anything or anyone." Then, like she hadn't said a word, she faced forward again and let him go.

He got out and joined his uncle on the side of the SUV closest to the jet. Eyes bouncing everywhere, Glen nodded to the guards, who formed a cocoon at the mouth of the door, and demanded Lucille to exit. Without incident, she climbed out and was immediately swallowed up by the bodies around her.

The human convoy made its way in the direction of the plane as everyone remained on point. Reggie had his eyes glued to his mother when they arrived at the bottom of the steps. That's the only reason he knew there was no way of saving her.

When she went to step up on the first landing, it appeared to everyone that she tripped. Reggie didn't see how anyone could mistake what happened because of the huge red cloud that sprayed out of his mother's head. Seeing the way she jerked and the way her body tumbled, Reggie immediately turned in the direction the bullet came from and emptied his sidearm. The closest concealment was a mile away, so the sidearm was ineffective, but you never know when you could find luck on your side.

Realizing he was wasting time, he pulled his phone and called the control room to order a drone over to the area. Within a minute, he was watching on his phone as the drone revealed no signs of human life in that direction. Broadening the search area didn't shine any new light on where the shooter had gone. After ordering a crew to go find the shooter's hide, Reggie hung up the phone and turned back to his mother.

The guards had formed a protective ring around her body, but it was far too late for that. Reggie walked over and stood next to her. The whole top of her head was missing. To hit a moving target from that far away made the suspect list very short. Every one of them had better have a hell of an alibi, or they would be joining his mother in death.

His Uncle Glen was leaning against the SUV with his eyes locked on his dead sister. Reggie settled next to him and asked, "What do we do now?"

Without hesitation, he said, "Find out who did it, track them down, and make them pay."

Reggie looked up to the sky as he thought about the legacy his mother was leaving behind. A lot of people would focus on all the bad, but in her way, she wasn't as selfish as people made her out to be. She'd loved her family and, in her twisted way of thinking, was doing everything in her power to solidify their place in history.

He would do exactly what his uncle had suggested. He would find out all the information, and whoever was involved in his mother's death, he would rid the earth of their whole bloodline. Turning away and pulling out his phone once again, he started dialing numbers. The investigation would have to wait a few more minutes as he had a hard task to perform first. Reggie had to inform the rest of the Burkes that Lucille Drake, the matriarch, mother, grandmother, sister, aunt, and former Head of the WRA had just been murdered.

Chapter 38

"Are you sure you're okay, Sweetie?" asked Alisha. "It's okay to be upset. No one is expected to lose their mother and not be affected."

Daniel was hiding out in an old dilapidated farm shed, but figured he could have a quiet conversation with his fiancé, over the phone. There wasn't much he could do until his target returned, but the questions about his mother were starting to get on his nerves.

In a whisper, he said, "Alisha, it's been a week. I've told you a hundred times, I'm good. Stop acting like I just lost a mother of the year candidate." He hated being abrupt with her, but he needed her to leave it alone.

"Aright Daniel," she said softly. "I'm just making sure. I won't bring it up again, but know I'm here if you need me."

Daniel could hear her banging pots around in the kitchen with Gabby and Tyiesha talking in the background. "How's everyone doing?" He'd been gone for three days, so these brief phone calls were all he had to keep up with his growing family.

"Gabby's fine, and she said to make sure I sent her love." He could hear Gabby yelling her love for him in the background. "And Tyiesha is still mad that you shot her." Now, Tyiesha started yelling that she would get her revenge on him before it was all said and done. "And the rest of the crew are working hard and enjoying their freedom."

Ann had seamlessly taken over Walt's old position as Sergeant of Detectives at the SBI. She loved her new job and her position was mutually beneficial to both Agencies.

Daniel had released Ashley from the hospital and she was now staying with Denise while she continued to recover.

She still had no idea about the world running parallel to her own. He was gonna leave it up to Denise to tell her, if and when she thought Ashley was ready.

Walt, the newly installed Head of Internal Investigations at the WRA, had landed in a hornet's nest. With Lucille getting killed, and the shuffling of the hierarchy, Walt was working nonstop to untangle what was really going on in the Agency. Reggie had revealed the strange message their mother had delivered before her death. It could have been a last-ditch effort to garner sympathy, but it also could have been a dire warning of the future to come.

Daniel sighed and told Alisha, "I should be done tonight. Everything is set, I'm just waiting for the rat to enter the trap. Tell Gabby I love her, and I love you too." Alisha returned the sentiment and he ended the call. He was just getting comfortable, settling into his hidey hole, when he heard the return of his next target.

Although, no one else could access the property, Daniel still peered through the freshly drilled hole to make sure it was the target. Upon seeing the 1957 Ford 100 come to a stop in front of the house, Daniel began packing up all his gear and preparing to finish his mission.

This was it. This was the last person who needed to die to fulfill the reparations owed to him. Daniel would finally be able to rest and relax with his family, knowing none of his enemies would be doing the same. He shouldered his backpack and crept closer to the door, the feeling of death being close at hand forced a smile to split his face.

Daniel watched as the jeans and flannel clad man lumbered out of the red and white two-toned truck. The man glanced around the huge, wide open, farm land before whistling and shouting, "Blue! Here boy! Time to eat!" He whistled a few more times and went silent, waiting for the old Blue Tick hound to come bounding towards him.

He waited a couple more minutes before flapping his hands, shaking his head, and heading towards the house. The man was grumbling about something, but Daniel was too far away to hear what was being said. Soon, the screen door slammed behind him, and Daniel could hear him calling his wife.

Daniel exited the old, beatdown structure and used the truck for cover to make it to the side of the house unseen. His back pressed to the siding of the gleaming white, two story, antebellum style mansion, Daniel could hear the man's progress through the open window. When his wife didn't answer his calls, he mumbled something under his breath, and made his way to the kitchen.

A chair scraped across the tiled floor and Daniel heard the distinct sounds of a hungry man eating a meal. Silverware clanked, lips smacked, and hums of enjoyment issued from the kitchen area. This was the sound of victory that Daniel had been waiting for before he made his presence known.

He boldly walked back around to the front of the house, walked up on the porch, and let the screen door slam behind him after he entered the entry hall. All sound in the kitchen cut off as the man waited to see who had entered. "Rose?" the man asked.

Daniel strolled over to the kitchen's threshold and stopped. "I'm afraid not," he stated. They both eyed the other, Daniel with hate, the other man with fear. "Mind if I take a seat?" Without waiting for an answer, he walked over and took the seat directly across from former governor of North Carolina, Richard Noland.

Richard was 75 years old, but didn't look a day under 90. His life had always been easy and full of leisure, until he'd gotten mixed up with the WRA. His greed ended up making life harder as the worry and stress stared eating him alive. It had been almost five years since the two had sat face to face, but Daniel felt the man knew this day was inevitable.

Silence ruled the conversation until Richard coughed a few times and a grin spread across Daniel's face. "I read an article about you about 16 years ago. Buried deep in one of the paragraphs was a tidbit about you being deathly allergic to almonds." Daniel glanced at the plate the man had removed from the oven and had been eating from. "Just to let you know, your wife didn't prepare that meal."

By now, the former governor's eyes were bulging, red, and leaking tears. He was clutching his throat as the coughing fit was taking his breath away. Richard fumbled in his pocket and pulled out a small injection kit. He removed one of the needles and stabbed it into his arm before depressing the plunger. Daniel laughed at the man, causing him to look up in alarm.

"I switched those out two days ago. You see, I wanted you to suffer, but since the PGK is locked up, I have to make this look like an accident. So, I traded out your medication for an out-of-date batch that is no longer effective." By now, the ex-governor was on the floor looking pleadingly up at Daniel. Fixing his face with a mask of indifference, he watched as Richard slowly started to fade.

Knowing the WRA had totally corrupted a man who had just suffered a moment of weakness, Daniel decided to grant him a small bit of solace on his journey to the grave. "Your wife is upstairs sleeping peacefully, and your dog is taking a nap behind the house. No scandal will mar your family or your reputation. My vengeance will stop with your death."

Richard's face seemed to take on a thankful expression as he stopped fighting so hard to live. He took three short inhales, then one long exhale, and then took on the stillness that only death could accomplish.

Daniel sat looking at the dead man for a moment as he thought about his future. The WRA was no longer a threat to him. He had a beautiful daughter and an amazing fiancé he was prepared to spend the rest of his life with. His evil, vindictive, brother was in prison with no one to get him out. And he couldn't think of anyone that he needed to kill.

Feeling at peace for the first time in many years, he got up from the table and exited the house. Old Blue came trotting around the side of the porch with his tongue hanging and his tail wagging. Daniel petted the dog for a few seconds and then took off at a leisurely pace across the field.

The day was hot. The sun was shining bright. Daniel smiled and walked as a euphoric feeling flowed through his body when he realized he was finally free.

Epilogue

"Michaels! Michaels!" the guard yelled, beating on the door. "Get up and get dressed. You have a visit in five minutes."

Delmas didn't have a watch, but he guessed it to be about 4:00am. He rolled over and threw the covers off because he was excited the day had finally come. He threw on the bright orange jumpsuit, took care of his hygiene, and then told the guard he was ready.

Tremayne Michaels, AKA Delmas Burke, had been in the Wake County Detention Center for a month. He had no money, no way to make a call, and hadn't heard a thing from anyone in the WRA. Facing over a hundred violent felony charges, most people would say his future looked bleak, but Delmas knew his mother wouldn't let him languish away in this hellhole for long.

The officer opened the trap door and Delmas stuck his hands through to start the shackling process he went through every time he left his cell. This process was in response to what he had done to the first officer who had run his mouth to the confessed Prison Guard Killer. Delmas wanted to set the tone early on, so he broke both the man's arms and knocked out most of his teeth. There was no doubt the C.O.'s hated him, but now they thought twice about expressing it openly.

After the four officers made sure he was secured, they escorted him out of the block and down the hall to the visitation room. Delmas, with his legs shackled, had to shuffle quickly to keep up with their pace. He could feel the animosity floating off the men. In his current state, they could kill him with little difficulty. But then what? They would end up being escorted down halls with orange jumpsuits on. So, they remained stern and quiet as he taunted them with smiles of amusement.

Finally, they reached the visit room and they secured his shackles to hooks welded into the floor and table. After checking to make sure he couldn't move, they exited the room, closing the door behind them. His mind started racing with the possibilities. There wasn't a chance in hell he could walk out of jail today, but news of a plan would be very welcome. He sat in the room alone for about ten minutes, letting his mind wander, before the door opened again and his world tilted on its axis.

As the older gentleman strolled in like he owned the place, Delmas had no problem identifying him even after so much time had passed. The man didn't smile, speak, or gesture in any way. All he did was take the seat across from him and stare blankly at his face.

Delmas, still reeling in shock, said, "What the fuck? How are you sitting here right now? Where have you been?"

The man sat in silence for a couple more beats before he leaned forward to address his nephew. "I'm sure you have a ton of questions, but I'm afraid I'm not here for that. I'm here because I needed to tell you in person that Lucille is dead."

Delmas regarded his uncle as he waited for him to tell him the plan that would get him to his mother's fake funeral so he could escape, but his uncle remained solemn and serious. He started to feel a little uneasy, so he said, "Okay, what do you need me to do for the plan to work?"

Frowning, his uncle said, "What plan, Delmas? Lucille is dead."

It slowly dawned on him that his uncle wasn't leading up to anything. He was simply giving Delmas a piece of information. That info was that his mother was dead. He leaned back as far as the chains would allow and clenched his teeth as tears streamed down his face. Delmas grieved for his mother, but also cried in shame because he hadn't been out there to protect her. Getting control over himself, he asked his uncle, "How did it happen?"

With no outward emotion, he said, "I exiled her for the crimes she committed against the WRA and the family. We were in the process of loading her onto an Agency jet, when a sniper took her out. We're investigating, but this killer was good. No traceable evidence left behind."

Delmas nodded and said, "Daniel did this."

His uncle shook his head. "Daniel and all his assets were under surveillance and none of them could have done it. We've heard some rumors that it could have been the CIA in retaliation for Paul. Or the Noriega Cartel out of Columbia for failing to uphold a bargain they struck with her. As you know, your mother hadn't been out of HQ for years. There's really no telling which one of her enemies decided to take a shot."

Delmas knew his uncle was right. Lucille hadn't been out of the underground compound for 15 years. She had so many enemies from all over the world, it would have been suicide for her to show her face. But her recluse status kept the rest of them safe. If there was no way to get to the Queen, no one would dare strike at any of her subjects. At the beginning, a few had tried, and the consequences had been swift and brutal.

"So, what's going on with the WRA now?" Delmas felt like he could talk freely since his uncle had been since he walked in. Something was making the man confident that no one else could hear them, so Delmas followed his lead.

"I appointed Reggie Head of the WRA. I took his position as Head of Operations. Phung, Kashonda, Mary Sue, and Dollis all have their same assignments. Walter Rogers came onboard as the Head of Internal Investigations.

We're still trying to find a new Head of Mission Development since Daniel turned it down."

"Whoa! Whoa! Whoa!" said Delmas. "Why are you hunting for someone to take my position?"

His uncle threw his hands up like the answer was obvious. "You can't exactly fulfill your duties from prison."

"Well, isn't that why you're here? To tell me how you're gonna get me out of this hellhole?"

Looking perplexed, he said, "Why would I do that when it was my plan to put you in here?" The statement left Delmas dumbfounded as he tried to make sense of all he was hearing.

"But Daniel…."

"Daniel did exactly what I told him to do," interrupted his uncle. "Daniel is a good man. Smart as hell and loyal to the Burke name. But his problem is that he thinks he's smarter than everyone else. IQ wise, he might be right. But, when it comes to manipulation, no one compares to my generation of Burkes."

"I don't understand. What the fuck did I ever do to you?" asked Delmas.

His uncle shrugged. "You can't be trusted. You were too loyal to your mother and not enough to the WRA. You and your mother continually broke WRA protocols and now you have to answer for it." Standing up, he said, "Starting today, you'll be well taken care of. All of your needs will be met no matter where you go. But, if you try to contact anyone from the WRA, you will be immediately cut off." Turning his back, he started walking towards the door.

"Hey! Wait! You're just gonna let these fuckers kill me?"

He stopped at the door and faced his nephew once more. "You and your mother conspired to keep Daniel inside for ten years. I think that time will be sufficient for you also. Stay out the way, keep your nose as clean as possible, and I'll try my best to bring you home in ten."

Before he could leave, Delmas said, "Hold on. I want to know where you've been for all this time. Since you were alive, why didn't you join us before now?"

"Your mother thought she had killed all three of her brothers. I realized she was too strong to contend with, so I had to use Daniel to weaken her and the WRA before I made my move."

Delmas shook his head in confusion. "What the hell are you talking about? My mother wasn't the one who killed her brothers. I know it was...."

"And that's another reason you needed to be in here," his uncle said, cutting him off. "You think you know things and you don't mind opening your mouth about them. Maybe after a little time spent in isolation, you'll learn some self-control."

Delmas chewed on his inner cheek so he wouldn't say another word to his departing uncle. After the door shut behind him, Delmas thought about how his family was being played. Mastermind was an understatement when he thought about how good this man was. There was no way he could sit back for ten years and let him destroy what his family had built. When the officers came to escort him back to segregation, he was still deep in thought.

Ten minutes later, he was back in his cell and all the officers were gone. He flopped down on the bed so he could rest, and he heard something crumple under his pillow. He sat back up and moved the pillow to reveal an envelope that had not been there when he left the cell earlier.

Delmas examined it closely, even held it up to the light, but couldn't make out what was inside. There were no markings at all on the outside, but it was sealed with clear tape. Thinking he was being paranoid, he shrugged and ripped into the envelope.

There was nothing dangerous. No powder that exploded out in an attempt to assassinate him. In fact, the only thing inside was a 2X6 inch piece of paper with a single line of typed text. Delmas smiled when he read it because his future didn't look so drab after all. He had no idea who the message came from, but the last guy who received it, things had worked out well for him. He tore the message and the envelope into tiny pieces and flushed the remnants down the toilet.

Delmas banged on the door, yelling, "C.O.! C.O.! I need to talk to someone, now!" It was a good thing he kept up with all the illegal deeds done by the WRA. He would definitely need the information for this to work. The message had been simple: Confess to all of your sins and you shall be set free.

With no time to waste, Delmas began kicking the door. "Guard! Guard! I need to talk to someone, right now!"

EXTRA!

Ashley was sleeping and Denise was relaxing in her room when her phone signaled a text. She read the message, exhaled in frustration, and jumped up to go see what Daniel was up to.

She slipped into a pair of hands-free sketchers, pulled a sweater over her head, and made her way to the front door. Exiting, she saw Alisha sitting in the driver's seat of a black Lamborghini Gallardo LP570-4 Blancpain. Alisha waved at her through the open window as Gabby yelled, "Hey Auntie Denise!" from the passenger side.

They both jumped out and walked up the driveway as her eyes were pulled to the other beautiful vehicle parked on the road. Daniel stepped out of the metallic grey 1968 Ford Mustang Shelby GT500CR with black racing stripes. Denise loved cars and she had drooled over both of them while touring Daniel's underground garages. The chrome almost blinded her as she stepped out farther to greet her family.

Daniel was dressed casually like she was. The only difference being his jeans and sweater were accompanied by designer boots that cost one of her mortgage payments. He completed his outfit with a pair of shades she knew ran about $2,000.

Alisha and Gabby, on the other hand, were dressed to impress. They both wore purple and white sundresses, with Alisha's being predominately white with purple designs, and Gabby's being inverted. Gabby also had on a pair of white leggings under her dress, but Alisha chose to let her world class legs gleam in the sunshine.

After kisses and hugs were exchanged all around, Daniel asked, "How is Ashley doing?"

"She's good. Mostly just rearing to get back to work. She still loses her energy a little too fast, but she works out on the regular and should be ready to go in a few more weeks." Denise glanced at each of them before asking, "What brings you by so early on a Saturday morning?"

Alisha said, "Me and Gabby are gonna drop Daniel off at WRA headquarters and then we're heading into town to shop 'til we drop." Alisha and Gabby beamed at each other before slapping a high five.

Denise frowned, looking around them towards the street. "Why would you have to drop him off if you're both driving?"

Daniel rubbed his bald head before saying, "Well, I don't think it'll look right if you popped up with the same car you had before you disappeared. So, since it's my fault you lost the Benz, I thought I owed you a replacement car."

Denise just looked at them in shock. "Which one is mine?" she finally asked.

"Whichever one you choose," was Alisha's response.

Denise squealed like a little girl, causing Gabby to laugh, before running over and inspecting both vehicles. Both were in pristine condition as Daniel would only have the best. The decision was almost impossible, but she managed to make one in under five minutes.

She climbed into the custom-built Shelby and turned the key just to feel the roar shake her soul. The interior had been redone, so it looked like an airplane cockpit with all its dials and controls. She revved the engine a few times and then climbed out and launched herself at Daniel.

He caught her as she rained kisses on his head and face, saying, "Thank you! Thank you!" over and over again.

Alisha chuckled and said, "If I didn't know any better, I'd say Daniel knew you'd have that reaction and he planned it." They all laughed as Denise dropped to the ground and raced back over to her new car.

They talked and joked around as Daniel transported the contents of the trunk over to the Lambo. Right before they prepared to leave, he pulled Denise over to the side and handed her a Black American Express credit card. He said, "That card is connected to an account in your name with $100 Million in it. Spend it. Enjoy life. But, don't slack on your training. I might have to call on you at any time." He kissed her forehead as tears of gratitude streamed down her face.

As he walked over to his daughter and fiancé, Denise thought this was the real man. With all his anger and hate extinguished, this was the beautiful man that had been trapped inside the monster. She waved them off as they turned their car around and left the area.

Happiness coursed through her veins. She skipped and giggled like a school girl as she headed back inside. She pulled up at the threshold when she saw Ashley standing a few feet inside the house, frowning. "Doctor friend, my ass!" she said, folding her arms across her chest. "A new car? Kisses and hugs? What the hell is going on, Denise? And I swear, if you lie to me, our friendship is over!"

Denise studied her angry, but still glamorous, friend and knew she couldn't continue lying to her. With a sigh of resignation, Denise stepped inside and closed the door behind her as she prepared to bring her best friend into the secret life of her new family.

EXTRA! EXTRA!

The Saint Thomas waterfront estate was hosting a party to end all parties. Music was blaring from hidden speakers. Alcohol was flowing from every direction to lower everyone's inhibitions. The clothing optional beach was packed with nude bodies frolicking in the surf. Even though it was night, the holographic water screens, and the dozens of LED lights provided enough illumination to intrigue the senses.

One thing was for sure, if you were looking for a place to hide out, you definitely couldn't go wrong with the Virgin Islands. With so many tucked away slices of paradise, you could float in luxury for years and never stay in the same place twice. When you were paranoid that the Boogieman could be around every corner, sometimes you just needed a place to lose yourself for a while.

It had been three months since the muscular American had started his journey to get lost in the world. He'd been to remote castles in Ireland, Chateaus in Italy, mountain retreats in Canada, and luxurious penthouses in the Ukraine. All his travels had been under different names in the hope of throwing his pursuers off his tracks.

He knew that trying to hide from these people was like trying to hide from the sun. It was possible, but no one wanted to die, sick and alone, in the dark. So, he settled on taking every precaution he could while trying to enjoy life a little. Plus, he had no idea if the people he was running from were even chasing him.

Slowly coming back to the party raging around him, he became aware of the scrutiny from two goddesses swimming in a clear, overhead pool. He tried to never get close to anyone because no one could be trusted. But, when two bronze-skinned beauties, who looked like twins, beckoned you, sometimes you just had to take the chance.

Not wanting to seem eager, he eased off the lounge chair and slowly made his way up the spiral stairs that circled the well-lit pool. He studied the bikini clad bodies of the two young ladies through the glass and sent up a small prayer of thanks to God. Reaching the top of the stairs, he finally got a clear look at them and thought the hazel-eyed 20-somethings would give any actress in Hollywood a run for their money.

They both eyed him up and down, looking appreciative at what they saw. Their perfect white smiles almost brought him to his knees, so he quickly jumped down into the pool to join them. Trying to be cool, he asked, "What're your names?"

One of them glided up to him and said, "My name is Tonya, and this is my sister, Nyaira. What's your name?"

Some kind of peach fragrance was drifting off of her and it was driving him wild. Senses on overload, he said, "Joseph Tarlton," and could have kicked himself for the blunder. But neither one of the women showed any recognition to his name, so he released a relieved sigh and kept chatting with his new friends.

They talked about their travels and where they were from. Really just idle conversation to fill up the time before everyone had to decide on the sleeping arrangements. Joseph's dream of having them both was dashed when Nyaira kissed her sister's cheek, gave him a small hug, and excused herself for the night. Alone, tucked in their own private heaven, Tonya took the reins of the conversation.

"Me and my sister have separate rooms over at the Estate Bellevue." Moving closer so he could practically feel her words, she said, "Would you like to come over for some fun and games?"

Trying to sound like gorgeous women always asked him to their rooms, he said, "Let's get out of here. You play your cards right, and you'll get to taste one of my world class omelets in the morning."

He jumped out of the pool and extended his hand to help her up. The way the water rolled off of her curves and glistened on her skin made him hope the fun and games didn't include Monopoly or Scrabble. On the walk over, they caught each other checking the other out several times. He just kept wishing that this wasn't a dream and he'd wake up on the lounge chair on the beach sporting a woody.

They made it to the room and she led him into a beautifully appointed space with a huge TV and its own bar. He noticed all the splendor around him, but his focus was laser sharp on the young lady and the huge bed in the middle of the room. She made him a drink and then excused herself to visit the bathroom.

Seeing her hips work from side to side was enough to have him rearing to go. He quickly threw his drink back and made himself comfortable on the bed.

When he came to, the sun was streaming down on his face. He groaned and tried to roll away from the rays, but found that his movement was restricted. His eyes snapped open and he saw his hands tied to the two ends of the headboard. Looking down, he saw his feet were secured to the post on each end. He fought his restraints but neither the ropes nor the solid oak gave at all.

Then the door opened and the two women from last night entered the room being followed by a bald black man that made his cheeks clinch. The women were now dressed in shorts and T-shirts but didn't look any less attractive in the sunlight. The man looked slightly different from the last time, but the casual look of khakis and T-shirt didn't diminish his menacing air.

All three stopped at the foot of the bed and eyed him like a specimen under a microscope. The man said, "My name is Daniel Burke, you probably know me as Turtleboy. A while back, you had the pleasure of meeting my brother Delmas, and he gave you a directive to never talk about the WRA to anyone." He reached behind his back and pulled out a wicked looking blade. The two young ladies stepped back like they didn't want to get blood on them.

Daniel continued. "For some reason, you didn't think it was a directive you had to follow."

Sweating profusely from fear, Joe said, "I'm so sorry man! You don't have to kill me. I'll never...."

Softly, the man interrupted with, "Shut up. Don't talk again unless I ask you a question." He paused to make sure Joe understood him, and then he continued his speech. "Face G, Debo, Quette, Kenji, Wayne, and the rest of their crew's leadership are dead. No one else who you opened your mouth to is alive. So, it seems you're the last loose end that needs to be taken care of."

Joseph trembled with the need to talk, but disobeying a WRA command is what got him here in the first place. So, he cried quietly and awaited the fate that he'd earned.

"You've taken me and my nieces all over the world tracking you down. Because of you, I've missed time with my fiancé and my daughter. My time is way too valuable to spend it chasing your stupid ass all over the earth." Twirling the knife so it caught the sunlight, he said, "So, before we get started, I only have one question for you." After a brief pause, a smile lit his face. "You want a job?"

· ·

Daniel was on the plane back to North Carolina, but Walter wasn't sure he could wait for his friend to arrive.

He'd only been in his new position for a few months, but as a seasoned investigator, it didn't take him long to smell a rat.

After Walt caught up on all the rules, regulations, and laws inside the WRA structure, Reggie assigned him the task of finding Lucille Drake's murderer. There were tons of rumors and theories about who was responsible, but not one speck of evidence supported any of them. So, Walt did what any good investigator would do, he went all the way back to the beginning in an effort to find a clear motive.

On the surface, there were too many motives to name. From the things she was accused of, to things she was really guilty of, the list of people who would want her dead was endless. But, looking through personnel files, which he now had unrestricted access to, he stumbled across something that kicked his instincts into overdrive.

As far as he could tell, no one had tried to fill the massive holes in this story. It concerned him that Daniel was obviously taking the man's words as truth. But, this small hidden fact he'd recently stumbled on threw a wrench the size of Montana into the story about Glendo, Paul, and Lucille. It was something that the only living party would never want to come out.

Walt pulled his phone out and called Daniel. As the phone rang, he belatedly wondered if his office was bugged. He was thinking he might need to wait and place the call from somewhere else when Daniel's voice filled his ear. "What's going on, Walt? How you liking the new job?"

Skipping the pleasantries, Walt said, "I need to talk to you about something very important. I'm not sure it's even safe to say over the phone."

Daniel was quiet for a few beats, then said, "Okay. Your office is now clear. There were four listening devices but I just fried them. The phone you're on is one of mine, so you never have to worry about it. Now, tell me what's on your mind."

So, he did. For twenty minutes he told him all he had found and asked Daniel how everyone else had missed it. Daniel told him to stay in the room and he'd call him back within the hour.

Thirty minutes later, Walt's phone rang. When he answered, Daniel said, "You have reason to be concerned, but we'll have to do more research before your theories can become facts. Keep a low profile, go through the motions, and don't talk to anyone else about this. I'm sending you the access codes and blueprints for my tunnel system. Study it and stay on point. Your knowledge of the access door locations might save your life. I'll see you when I get back." Then Daniel hung up and Walt was left alone with his thoughts.

Leaning back in his chair, Walt smiled at his new station in life. Not once did he regret his decision to join the WRA. He felt like he was uniquely equipped to do the job he'd been hired to do. Focusing back on his work, he now had only two objectives to concentrate on: Finding out the real story behind the man claiming to be Glendo Burke, and why he was methodically murdering the children of Willie James Burke.

Available Now

About The Author

L. A. Burch is a Philly native who now resides in North Carolina. Burch attended Temple University and majored in Criminal Justice.

He can be reached at authorlaburch@gmail.com. You can also learn more about him and keep up with his work on Amazon, Goodreads, Barnes & Noble, and Google Books.

www.ingramcontent.com/pod-product-compliance
Lightning Source LLC
Chambersburg PA
CBHW020507020726
47493CB00001B/226